Recipe for Mr Perfect

Anni Rose

Happy reading, enjoy

Anni x

Choc Lit

Where heroes are like chocolate – irresistible!

Published 2021 by Choc Lit Limited
Penrose House, Crawley Drive, Camberley, Surrey GU15 2AB, UK
www.choc-lit.com

EPUB: 978-1-78189-503-0
PRINT: 978-1-78189-509-2

For Beryl, who taught me not to suffer fools gladly.
And for Elvis, who never did.

Acknowledgements

I am probably going to keep saying this, but I am incredibly grateful to everyone and writing groups who have helped and encouraged me with *Recipe for Mr Perfect* and with my writing in general. Again, you are far too huge a crowd to mention in person, but I do have to give a special mention to team "Rose" – Keith, Jane, Sarah, Xenia, Hilary, Pauline and Mandy, without you I'd never have got this far. Thank you all for your cups of tea, cakes, comments, suggestions and unfailing ability to make me smile and keep going. And of course, my writing companions, Brian and Rocky who listen, usually in silence, to my endless readthroughs of everything.

It really has been the most amazing year. I still have to keep pinching myself to make sure I'm not dreaming and that I am a published author. I'd like to thank the Choc Lit team, and of course the Tasting Panel readers at Choc Lit and Ruby Fiction who passed the original manuscript and made publication possible: Margaret Marshall, Liana Vera Saez, Jenny Mitchell, Ruth Nägele, Bee Master, Jill Leonard, Amy Nordon, Julie Lilly, Lorna Baker, Gillian Hill, Jo Osborne, Gill Leivers and Sharon Walsh. Thank you too to my lovely editor – for everything and for making the whole editing bit so enjoyable.

Thank you to my designer for another amazing cover (I fully intend to match my next nail polish colour to this one too). Thank you to all book bloggers for your lovely reviews and finally all you Choc Lit and Ruby authors for being so kind, supportive and lovely in taking a new author under your wings. You are just the nicest bunch of people a girl could hope to meet, and I hope one day soon, we get the chance to do that in person.

Chapter One

Neil Jackson's first thought when he reached the civic offices was that someone had forgotten to tell him it was fancy dress. *Again!* Okay, this time thankfully he wasn't dressed as a lobster.

He slowed as he turned down the path signposted to the Register Office, but ground to a complete halt when he spotted the group by the front door.

Were they really wearing ammunition belts?

He moved forwards slowly.

He must've had a "What the hell?" sign above his head; a woman in a suit, sporting a registration officer badge, took pity on him.

'Steampunk wedding,' she said. 'Sort of fusion. Think industrial revolution meets Victorian Gothic,' she added, as his left eyebrow joined his right one, somewhere close to the top of his forehead.

'Thanks,' he said.

'You must be here for—' She consulted her black folder '—the Littleton-Drew marriage?'

Neil nodded.

'We'll call you all through shortly, but I'd recommend staying out here until we're ready. The waiting room is full and stuffy this morning.' She signalled for the *armed and dangerous* group to follow her indoors.

Neil didn't doubt it. Only a few people were supposed to have been invited to the Register Office ceremony for Ross and Annette's legal bit, but he and Ross had never been on the same page when it came to sizing anything.

For Neil, a few people equated to a number less than five, but by the numbers crowding round the building, he judged Ross and Annette's definition was at least ten times that.

He recognised three of Ross's groomsmen from the stag do and smiled.

This wasn't even the proper do. More people were expected later at Annette's father's house for the more elaborate ceremony, speeches and meal in the huge marquee they'd hired for the purpose.

Ross had been obsessed with his wedding for the last couple of months. Every time Neil answered the office phone, it would be Annette and yet another message or crisis she needed him to jot down and pass on as soon as Ross got back to his desk. No point wasting his breath and announcing he ran a business consultancy firm not an event planning business; both of them were far too wrapped up in the complexity of table plans to give a stuff that he would be inconvenienced.

'Thanks,' he said again. At least there was a sharp breeze to prevent him from melting, or worse, sweating. Not that he could get far, the walkway behind him was packed now, with people, a few more he recognised, pressing forward.

Thankfully everybody was more soberly dressed than the last wedding. A formal wool, dark grey suit wouldn't have been his choice for a late summer funeral, even without an unseasonable heatwave, let alone a wedding. Annette had been talked out of a black-tie affair. A change of heart that might have had something to do with a chance remark she'd overheard in Neil's office when one of his customers had been talking about his own daughter's wedding and said that it seemed the amount of money people spent on outfits for weddings was inversely proportional to the size of their gifts, a factor which, when you'd lodged a lengthy and extravagant list with a leading department store could, Neil imagined, be a major cause for concern.

He had been grateful for small mercies, until he read the note at the bottom of the gold embossed card he'd received, in what he took to be Annette's writing, that read, "Dark suits only".

The doors to the ceremony room opened and guests from the earlier wedding started to spill out.

'Neil darling.'

Neil froze, only one woman ever called him "darling" and he would really rather she didn't. Ross's aunt – Mrs Ogbourne St. George. He didn't know her well. At all really. She used their visitor's space outside the office whenever she went into town. Always made a point of putting her head round the door and saying, 'Only me, Neil Darling, you don't mind, do you?' Then she'd purse her lips, blow him a kiss and walk away before he had a chance to say, "Yes I mind". He needed to have a word with Ross. He would, as soon as he was back from honeymoon.

She must be somewhere behind him. He'd seen her earlier and managed to avoid her then. If he kept his head down and didn't look up, maybe she'd find someone else to bother. She was dressed head to toe in shocking pink in a frothy ruffles sort of way with an equally frivolous enormous pink hat, covered in feathers.

So, he focussed on the emerging group on the other side of the small wall. A woman, in a top hat with goggles attached, raked up her dress, layers of black net petticoats and what looked like bloomers, to show a thigh to an elderly man in knee-high brown leather boots who was trying to light a cigarette.

'Neil darling.'

The words were clipped this time. Was she sending him a thinly veiled threat that warned him against ignoring her again? Next time, would it be a full bellow? Ear drums would shatter and he'd be to blame. Thankfully the packed walkway meant she couldn't get much closer to him without flattening half a dozen people first. Of course, if she was determined it would be like a battleship in full battle mode, albeit in an unusual colour, and she'd make it without hopefully too much loss of life on the way. He turned and waved, but his eye was taken by an elegant shoe, then a leg in ankle length black trousers edging backwards. The rest of the body followed. A slim woman with a riot of chestnut curls edged slowly along the path. When she got level with him, Neil realised she was looking through the viewfinder of a camera.

Her hair bounced around her shoulders. Judging by the way she fiddled with it, she wasn't entirely comfortable with the style. However hard she pushed those chestnut curls back behind her ear, the moment she looked through her viewfinder, they sprung forwards again. She looked vulnerable and completely out of her depth. Something about her made Neil's heart race and him weak inside. These weren't normal feelings. Nothing he'd felt for a long time.

'Neil darling.' The words were louder this time and seemed to arrive with a gush of warm air on his cheek. His arm was jerked backwards. He spun round to see a bony, wrinkled hand with long shocking pink nails clutching it.

'Got you,' Mrs Ogbourne St George said, cheerfully.

Chapter Two

Rays of late morning sunlight played along the concrete facade and darkened windows of Redford Register Office. Another party were on their way in for their ceremony as Jess Willersey backed down the narrow path to get a better picture of her bride and groom. Darren and Leanne pushed through the revolving doors; Jess signalled for them to keep walking towards her.

One, two, three then she held up a hand to stop them. Four strides – all it took for them to be clear of the doors and defibrillator. Their party crowded onto the steps behind them, hiding the no-entry signs too. The picture looked promising.

The austere greyness of the building made a great backdrop for the bride's deep purple, corseted dress and black veil, and the groom's tartan jumpsuit and chains. If the photograph looked as good when she enlarged it on her computer as it did on the back of her camera, she shouldn't need to spend too much time editing in Photoshop.

'Could we have the bridesmaids in front?' she called.

An army of six girls of varying ages wearing electric blue dresses and Doc Martens pushed forward. Trying to get them all into the picture, she took another step back and in doing so trod on something soft and squidgy. She shuddered, hoping it wasn't something too unpleasant but dared not look. She was squeamish at the best of times. Ever the professional, she clicked the shutter. Another couple of shots to be safe – someone was bound to have closed their eyes or be making inappropriate gestures.

Then a woman screamed.

An agonising, blood-curdling scream. Jess jumped, her pulse quickened and everyone in both wedding parties turned round to see what had happened.

Jess froze, rooted to the spot. Everyone was staring. At her. She pulled her camera into her chest as if it were a shield, although in an ideal world it would have been a machine gun cunningly disguised as a camera. James Bond, why haven't you thought of this? With the lens focussed on the wedding party on the other side of the wall, she could have pressed the shutter and wiped out all those appalled expressions.

In reality, she felt, as she had aged nine, when as the poodle in the school's production of *Pinocchio* and stuck in the middle of the stage, a child in the audience announced there wasn't a poodle in *Pinocchio*. The child's accompanying grown-up, possibly a parent, but at Redford Primary more likely a social worker, replied in an equally loud voice that the school created parts so everyone could take part even if they weren't any good. Jess was riled. From that moment, she wasn't going to be simply good: she was going to be bloody fantastic. She would show them the poodle had life.

In her opinion, she made the part hers that day. Owned it. The script called for her to lie on a rug, then sit up and smile every time someone stroked her head. Count to ten and lie down again. It wasn't a speaking role, but people talked about her portrayal for days afterwards.

The following year, she'd turned down the part of the inn door in the nativity, and school had never suggested another part. Okay, okay, acting hadn't been her thing, but she'd always tried since to be the best she could be, at everything she undertook, be that accountancy or photography. Distinctions across the board meant she had letters after her name in both subjects. This might be her first paid photography job but she was determined Darren and Leanne would be happy with their photos. Except right now, stuck in the middle of the exit path, she felt as she had in that moment twenty-three years ago, only this time there was no chance of humping the carpenter's leg or lifting her leg on a prop.

The small entrance area to the Register Office was badly designed. A three-foot high wall ran down the middle of a narrow path designed to separate those on their way in from those on their way out. Tall buildings either side made it something of a wind tunnel.

On the other side of the wall, a woman dressed head-to-toe in pink hopped up and down. Jess stood mesmerised by the clouds of bingo wings and fuchsia chiffon wafting in every direction.

A man in a charcoal grey suit tried to leap the wall. An ambitious attempt and he didn't make it, but undaunted, he levered himself up onto the top, swung his legs over and jumped down. He came across to where Jess stood on something soft.

'I think it's dead,' he said.

'No.' Jess stared into the stranger's eyes, completely hypnotised.

Amazing eyes – blue, not the clear deep royal blue of the Aegean Sea. More English Channel than Greek Islands. Blue, no, almost grey, perhaps with a fleck of green. They sparkled and when he smiled the creases at the side of his eyes deepened to suggest that smiling was something he did a lot.

He was seriously hot and watching her. Oh God, was she staring? She looked away and fought hard not to look straight back. 'Please don't tell me that,' she mumbled.

Her eyes started to itch as tears formed. Her mouth felt dry. She couldn't stop it opening and closing, but nothing came out. Her pulse raced.

'If you move your foot, I could take it away and dispose of it properly.'

She chanced a look.

'A hat,' she said, with the same sort of emphasis Lady Bracknell used when discussing accessories.

Jess Willersey, specialist subject: the bleeding obvious. She blushed.

'Are you sure? Not roadkill?' The stranger threw his hands up in mock horror. 'That is a relief.'

Jess giggled. She couldn't help herself.

'Neil darling, please hurry.'

She was aware of heat creeping up her neck. Any minute now her cheeks would be glowing.

Of course, someone as gorgeous as "Neil darling" wouldn't be single.

He lifted her camera bag to one side, watching her intently. Jess wished he wouldn't stare like that. It was doing strange things to her stomach, and she still had a reception to photograph.

'I'm sorry,' she said, lifting her foot quickly. 'I think your girlfriend wants her hat back.'

Jess stroked her camera with a tenderness normally reserved just for her cat as she watched the stranger walk down the path and back up the other side to join his party.

Bloody men. She wished she didn't embarrass so easily. At thirty-two she was hardly a lovesick teenager.

Get a grip girl. She adjusted the lens ready to focus on her wedding.

One of Darren and Leanne's guests, a tattooed man in a silver and black brocaded waistcoat was running a book on how long their marriage would last. The outsider Jess had backed in last April's Grand National had shorter odds than he offered for anything longer than a year. She'd be happy if they could stick together long enough to see and pay for the photos. It wasn't looking good. Darren, standing some distance from the rest of the party was talking on the phone.

'Sorry doll, I can't make it tonight. Yeah, more's the pity … Nah, something came up … I'll give you a bell in a day or two … You too …' He listened for another couple of seconds, snapped his phone shut and thrust it back into a trouser pocket so tight that frankly it made him look deformed.

'Here Jessie, over here,' Leanne shouted. She was making absurd movements with her hands which Jess took to mean something was about to happen. Either that or she wanted odds of seven-to-one on her marriage lasting.

Darren glared at Jess. 'What?'

'You're needed for the group shots,' she said calmly as Leanne shouted.

'Oi everyone over here, the photographer wants you.'

Darren grunted and marched over to the recycling bins where his new wife showed off the tattoo she'd had done to mark the happy occasion.

A general shuffling about, a couple of catcalls later and someone – Jess couldn't see who – called out, 'She can have me anytime she likes.'

She hoped it wasn't the man in the braided trousers and knee-length leather boots, with the seriously odd-looking goggles and walking stick. But judging by the sneer on his face, it was. She shivered and busied herself arranging the group.

The next-door wedding party kept on staring. Great. She was nervous enough as it was; she didn't need a blooming audience.

The ivory bridesmaid next door was being photographed fussing around the bride in the back seat of a white Mercedes. A classic shot. The other photographer adjusted their dresses, repositioned their hands, made sure they were smiling. He had time, no one pushing or shoving each other.

Jess wished she could swap places. He had two expensive-looking cameras hanging from his neck and looked every bit the professional. Not for the first time today, she wondered whether wedding photography was a serious career option for a disenchanted accountant.

An older man, presumably the bride's father, came forward and was photographed helping his daughter out of the car.

Jess was under no illusion: she'd only got this job because she was cheap. Leanne hadn't been interested in the letters after her name, her portfolio or references; she wanted to know the cost.

Having explained her various packages and gone through prices with her, Leanne had even refused to pay a deposit.

'I'm not paying nothing 'til I see the photos,' she said, 'just in case, some of them don't come out. I ain't going to pay for no rubbish.'

Jess should have walked away. She didn't and now she had a job to do. She'd only met the groom for the first time an hour ago. While she photographed Darren with his best man, she overheard someone asking how long he'd been out of prison. Darren asked whether it was eleven o'clock. He was told it was.

'Twenty-four hours then,' he said, and laughed.

Everybody joined in. Jess assumed it was a joke, now she wasn't sure.

Taking a deep breath, she turned back to the bridesmaids lined up on the wall. 'Okay, sit very still and look this way,' she said, smiling at them encouragingly. 'And give me your biggest smiles.'

'I don't want to sit next to her.' One of the older girls pointed at a cherub-like thing, all blonde ringlets and green eyes. 'I hate her.'

Jess could sympathise. She wasn't sure she would want to sit next to her either. The bulge "the angel" had in her pocket looked like something had been extracted from the ceremony room. The child, despite her looks, was clearly an ASBO in waiting.

'One minute please.'

They started fidgeting.

Jess straightened up, to see whether what she'd seen through her viewfinder was happening. Yes, two of the younger ones were punching one another. If she wasn't quick, this could go belly up. 'Could you lift your dresses so I can see your boots? Thank you. That looks great. Leanne will love this one.' She pressed the shutter.

'No, she won't.'

No point in arguing. Jess hoped the shutter speed was fast enough to freeze any movement – and they all had their eyes open. There wouldn't be a chance to take another shot. The cherub, already off the wall, had sprinted over to one of the guests and thrust a hand into a woman's handbag. Whatever it was she'd pulled out, she put in her mouth. When she turned round, she stuck out a very red tongue.

Jess was conscious of the next wedding party observing the proceedings with varying degrees of amusement. The hat retrieving stranger in his dark charcoal grey suit seemed to be staring at her. She looked away, then glanced back immediately; she couldn't help it. Her insides twisted themselves into knots. It had been a long time, a very long time since anyone made her feel that way.

'Is this what you mean?'

The red-haired, pasty-faced little bridesmaid, for whom electric blue had not been the kindest choice of colour, was the only one left on the wall.

'That's perfect poppet. You're a natural,' Jess said. The child's face lit up and she posed happily for a few more minutes.

Out of the corner of her eye, she saw the hat retriever run a hand through his dark blond hair, a hint of a smile playing on his lips. The registrar appeared and asked the guests to take their seats. Jess had been about to smile back when a thin, elegant woman approached and kissed him on the cheek. He said something. The woman stopped, looked over her shoulder at Jess, then laughed, slipped her arm through his and turned him away.

Chapter Three

Sarah Maynard had taken the afternoon off work. She needed time to prepare. Fridays were always her favourite night of the week and tonight was going to be special. So special, she'd endured Maggie's moans about being left alone in the office with the temp for a whole afternoon without comment.

In Jess's absence, Sarah had taken her urgent request for a half-day's annual leave due to a personal emergency to the managing director. Thankfully, Frank had agreed without asking any awkward questions. The stomach clutching and throwing of her best "you don't want to know" look might have been unnecessary in the end, but it killed the need to come up with any implausible lies.

'It had better be a huge emergency,' Maggie hissed, when Sarah told her she was off at lunchtime. 'I hope for your sake we're talking life and death trauma here.'

'Seismic,' Sarah said, without expanding, because what was lack of time to get ready for the most important date she'd had in ages, if not a personal emergency?

Maggie stared at her, daggers drawn, all morning, refusing to ask for details, but clearly desperate to know, while the temp wittered on about her latest personal issues.

Sarah blew a kiss on her way out which resulted in Maggie's stress ball being lobbed at the door. 'Have a good weekend,' Sarah said, grinning and stepping around it. If all went to plan, she'd fess up on Monday. She might even bring in cakes by way of an apology.

The house was empty when she opened the door. She was pleased to find it still smelled of lemony disinfectant and the kitchen wasn't covered in plates of half-finished breakfast.

Over the last week, she'd deep cleaned her bedroom. Sarah wasn't an untidy person. She was the one who usually cleaned the kitchen and the loo. But there wasn't an inch of carpet anywhere that hadn't been hoovered. Or an inch of bedroom furniture that hadn't been polished.

Everything put away. Clean sheets on her bed, laundry done and a packet of condoms in the top drawer of her bedside cabinet.

She put the bottle of wine she'd bought on the way home from work in the fridge and wrote a note for her housemates warning an imminent hospital visit would be required for anyone who felt the need to touch it.

She checked she'd followed the "How to make your room and yourself sexy" website to the letter. Everything done. She hadn't repainted the walls in pink, but it wasn't her house and she couldn't imagine the landlord being too pleased. She'd changed the bulbs in the lights for lower wattage ones. The room glowed gently. She'd gone for the romantic ambience the website recommended, but practically the room was now too dark to see anything important. She'd kept the bulbs. She'd change them back in the morning.

Scented candles were supposed to be the final touch, but with fire alarms in every room that wasn't sensible, besides when she removed the plastic wrapping, they smelled more like toilet freshener than the "sensuous subtle love" the marketing bumph promised.

She changed her pictures. A large abstract rose that looked like someone had dropped red paint from a great height hung on the wall, replacing the Paddington Bear sketches her father had framed last Christmas. Those were stored safely out of sight under her bed.

Her watch showed an hour and a half to go: time for her own finishing touches.

Submerged in a bath so deep that her housemates wouldn't have warm water for at least another hour, Sarah wondered about Maggie's afternoon.

The temp had spent most of the week implying she was too good for office work and not listening to any suggestions about how to be more accurate or efficient. She couldn't answer the telephone because no one had given her a script. She couldn't make drinks because she was a vegan and couldn't handle the milk. Maggie was fast losing patience – a pile of snapped ballpoint pens sat on her desk.

It was partly Maggie's fault Sarah needed the afternoon off. Jess and Maggie had made her promise, after several large cocktails when her last relationship failed, that she wouldn't sleep with anyone again until at least the seventh date.

'Next time,' Jess had teased her, 'second date – no questions about marriage and children and third date – no sex.'

'No sex until at least the tenth date,' Maggie had chimed in.

'Tenth?' Sarah had exclaimed.

'Are you looking for a relationship or a quick hook-up?' Jess had asked. 'Maggie is right. Play hard to get, leave them wanting more. Get to know them first.'

It had been all right them saying that. Up until Ryan, sex hadn't been planned. It had just happened. Sarah wasn't promiscuous. She only slept with people she felt an overwhelming physical attraction to. That was down to her passionate nature.

Both women had sat, arms folded, until she caved in and negotiated the number, with the help of a White Russian or two, down to seven. They wouldn't budge below that.'

Seven it was then. She'd stuck to that – almost. If you were being pedantic, tonight's date would be the sixth time they'd met in person, but they had FaceTimed one another. One call had gone on for hours. It should definitely count and that made seven, although Jess and Maggie would probably argue the point when she told them next week.

It would be too late by then. Tonight she planned to have sex with Ryan. They would have a meal. She wouldn't drink much. She'd bring him back to the house. Maybe they'd hold hands on the way. They'd collect the bottle of wine from the fridge and take it to her room, the romantic playlist she'd downloaded playing in the background.

Sarah shut her eyes. She was nervous. It had to be perfect: it was big, massive, like losing her virginity all over again. Not that she'd expect Jess or Maggie to understand. Maggie was single and Jess lived with Martin, not Sarah's idea of a dream date, blind date, or anyone she'd want to bump into in a dark alley, for that matter. He was rude, never bothered to remember her name and dismissive of anybody's ideas except his own. They didn't often meet as he rarely bothered with company events or personal ones by the sound of it. It had been Sarah and Maggie who'd supported Jess at her photography exhibition and presentation evening because he was too busy. Wanker.

Whatever she thought, Martin and Jess had been together for eons. No accounting for taste. Of course, expectations were lower back then: they had to be when you were probably only ever going to meet your partner face to face, at work, or out socially; the world of on-line dating had still to take off. Nowadays, you could meet just about anyone from anywhere.

Sarah couldn't imagine Jess posting a "sex-god wanted for long-term relationship" request, that included the blond, bleached surfer-boy look with no personality, an expanding gut and, lately, a small goatee.

Jess was lovely, kind, quick-witted and intelligent. She made the office a happy place to work. Sarah wished sometimes she'd smile more. Some days, she'd come into work looking like she had the world on her shoulders. She seemed to spend all her weekends alone or entertaining Martin's mother for Sunday lunch. Sarah would never be like that. Any potential partner had to share her love for meals out, movies, walking, travelling and music festivals. Ryan liked all those things. She smiled as she went for a final total submersion under the layer of cooling bubbles.

He was perfect.

She pulled on a black, scooped neck, knee-length cocktail dress. She'd gone for elegance and sophistication. The layered skirts flared from a waist she was extremely proud of. The cut-out back dipped from between her shoulder blades to just above her knicker line. She'd bought new underwear specially. The whole outfit was absurdly extravagant, but if it had the desired effect, it would be worth every penny. She checked for telltale straps and labels before flipping her head upside down and pulling her blonde hair into a loose ponytail she then twisted into a messy bun on the top of her head. To make it even messier she pulled out sections to create an artfully dishevelled, sexy and chic look.

She checked her watch – fifteen minutes; her phone – no new messages. A good thing, right? He hadn't cancelled. She slipped her feet into her four-inch heels, took a deep breath and checked a final time everything was as it should be.

Chapter Four

General Gordon lay flat out in front of the garage door when Jess pulled onto her drive, and clearly was not going to move, however close she got. She bottled first. With at least two feet between car and cat she switched off the ignition. Thankfully, pitiful meows erupted the minute she opened the door.

'Faking death is a pretty low trick even for you,' she said and was answered by a louder meow.

There was no post on the mat as she let them both in, but a pile had been neatly arranged on the kitchen worktop.

Please, not tonight.

She listened for any sound to indicate she wasn't alone. Her heart rate increased. The last thing she needed after the day she'd had was a confrontation with Martin.

Being ignored again, General Gordon started to sound like a child being tortured. Any minute now, Jess would find she'd been surrounded by police and social services, alerted by the neighbours, concerned some sort of paediatric massacre might be happening next door.

'It'll be your fault,' she said, opening a tin of tuna and spooning some into his bowl.

The meows stopped.

'Don't blame me when they take you into care or whatever they do with animals they think are being cruelly treated.'

If cats could look disgusted, General Gordon's expression went way past that. The look of contempt he threw her indicated he considered her the world's worst cat mother.

Crap mother as well as crap photographer. Her day kept getting better.

She stroked his back until he settled down, wrapped his tail round his legs and started to eat. Then she cooked some noodles to bulk up the rest of his tuna for her own supper. When both had eaten their fill, they moved into the front room and curled up together on the sofa in front of the telly. At least Martin hadn't taken that.

General Gordon commenced his nightly washing routine and Jess opened a bottle of wine. She wouldn't normally drink alone, but it was a

Friday night, and had been a tiring day. The post and photographs could wait. She had the whole weekend to sort them out. She took a large gulp and exhaled. She was home, safe and alone. And even if she wasn't ready to admit it to anyone other than her cat, she liked it like that.

It should have hurt, shouldn't it? She should scream and shout about the injustice of life, shouldn't she?

Three days ago he'd packed and left. She'd been in the supermarket when he rang to tell her they weren't working and needed to call it a day.

That was it.

The end.

She'd been confused. She was next in line at the checkout. He hadn't even fed her the "It's not you, it's me" line as she tried to arrange her shopping on the conveyor belt. He hadn't even waited to discuss it. By the time she got home, he'd gone. That was the hardest bit to understand. That was why she hadn't told anyone he'd gone. Someone was bound to ask, and she couldn't tell them why. She honestly didn't know.

When her sister's husband had left, he'd written a seventeen-page letter explaining all her faults.

But Martin had always been a man of few words. He didn't even text in full sentences: *Supper? When? Now?*

As far as he was concerned, life was too short for unnecessary discussions, even dates; he had set them both up with shared, computerised diaries.

That's how he knew she'd be out!

She pulled her mobile out and stopped sharing the "Jess's Life" diary before she realised Martin must have already done the same because only her own entries were now visible.

Tomorrow she'd change the locks. Then he would have to let her know if he planned on calling to collect another little treasure he couldn't live without. Mind you, as he'd already cleared the office, taken the computer, the stereo, the coffee table and most of the clean bed linen and towels, there couldn't be much left he wanted.

She should be angry. She was, not because he'd gone, but because she hadn't had the guts to go first.

They'd been together twelve years and lived together for nine, a decision that boiled down to practical reasons rather than romance. Both had been paying extortionate rents, but following a financial market crash when the bottom fell out of the housing market, they realised they could afford a home in Redford for less a month than they were shelling out in rent, and bought their own place. When Martin's business took a hit too, she helped him turn it around. That meant long, unpaid hours spent chasing work, agreeing contracts, invoicing jobs and collecting payments. And when he needed an injection of cash for his business, it was her idea to increase the mortgage on the house. Her day job gave them financial security during the dark times and cut him some slack when contracts were thin on the ground.

Their relationship had never been about drama and passion, yet it was still a shock to realise how spectacularly it had fallen apart without her noticing or minding. Looking back, the writing had been on the wall for longer than she cared to think. Martin no longer needed her input on business matters.

She'd become invisible. That dawning realisation had been the inspiration she needed. She wanted more from life. So, she'd bought a camera and enrolled on a photography course.

She took another sip of her wine. To be honest, she'd never felt about Martin the way she'd felt about her first camera. She'd known the Canon DSLR was coming home with her as soon as she saw it. She wasn't leaving the shop without it.

Martin hadn't been scathing about the course, but not encouraging either.

'Another course,' he said, dismissively. 'The college must love you. One of their perennial students. You never made much use of the business entertaining one.' That wasn't entirely fair. True, they never entertained. She loved cooking, but Martin's idea of entertaining was to take his mates or colleagues out to ever more expensive restaurants, where they ate ever more expensive meals, topped off with equally expensive bottles of wine. Networking he called it.

Jess briefly wondered whether he was networking tonight as she surfed through the TV channels. '*Bridgerton* or *Line of Duty* repeats?' she asked General Gordon. The decision to go with Daphne and her duke had nothing to do with the hat-retrieving stranger she'd met earlier, she told herself as the doorbell sounded.

Okay, tomorrow she would change the locks and buy one of those video ones that lets you see who's ringing without leaving the armchair.

The marquee was crammed with round tables all seating ten people. Neil consulted the plan by the door, avoiding the receiving line, although that also meant forgoing a glass of champagne, which appeared to be the prize for anyone prepared to run the gauntlet and survive kisses from Mrs Ogbourne St. George, the mother of the bride and the bride. Or, if you were a woman, from the bride's father, the groom, the best man and three groomsmen.

He didn't recognise any of the other names on his table and debated pretending a headache and making a run for it. He wanted to get back to his dog and his flat.

'Neil,' Ross said, slapping him hard on the back.

He winced. He might not have to pretend. A headache would pale into insignificance compared to a broken spine.

'I'd like you to meet a friend of mine,' Ross said, seemingly unaware of his own strength. 'He's in the process of taking over the world and needs our help.'

The man wearing an expensive suit, laughed. 'He exaggerates,' he said.

No shit.

'Not the world, just a local company,' he added.

'He wants us to act for him. Put in a bid, negotiate, do the due diligence. Make sure he's getting a bargain. You know the sort of thing.' Ross had had a lot to drink. His face was flushed, and his voice loud.

'That's great,' Neil said, quietly. 'Now is probably not the best time to discuss it. Your bride is waving at you.'

'I've sat him on your table,' Ross said, blowing a drunken kiss back to Annette. 'I have to go, but he wants it done soonest.'

The man nodded. 'I've got the files in the car,' he said.

'Good man,' Ross said. 'If you can get the ball rolling …'

'Me?' Neil said.

'Well, hello here. News alert – I'm going on my honeymoon.' Ross pulled a face and wiggled his hands in front of him. 'Tell you what, I'll pick it up and run with it when I get back.' He started to walk towards the receiving line. 'We can talk then about my introduction fee, or perhaps a partnership,' he called over his shoulder.

Over my dead body. Neil clenched his fists and bit his bottom lip. Thankfully Ross didn't look back. 'I didn't catch your name,' Neil said.

'Martin.' The man extended a hand. 'Martin Cowley, managing director of MJC Computing.' His handshake was limp and sweaty.

'Neil Jackson,' Neil said, wiping his hand surreptitiously down his trousers. He didn't feel the need to mention his job title or company, presumably Martin knew it already.

The toastmaster joined the receiving party and in a booming voice announced the wedding breakfast was about to be served and asked everyone to take their seats. The receiving line broke up and everyone streamed into the marquee.

'Shall I get the files now?' Martin asked.

'No,' Neil said. 'We ought to take our seats. Are you on your own or waiting for someone?'

'Not me. I've got a free pass out this evening.' Martin grinned. 'And I've booked a room, so let's get this party started.'

Neil looked longingly at the door. This afternoon he'd briefly met a woman he'd have happily partied with all night. Four hours later, he couldn't wait to leave. He'd eat, then go and if he could get out without Martin Cowley's files, so much the better. He could get back to his growing to-do list of things which was, with Ross's attention diverted elsewhere over the last few months, fast reaching overwhelming proportions.

Their allocated table was at the furthest point diagonally from the top table, between the flap to the catering van and the flap to the toilets. Neil and Martin took their seats as others started to arrive. Everyone nodded at each other, but no one felt the need to introduce themselves. Martin picked up the bottle of red wine that sat in the middle of the table. He stared at it before calling the waiter over and asking for the wine list.

'How long have you known Ross?' Neil asked as soon as Martin had ordered a more expensive bottle and waved his American Express card about.

'Since uni,' Martin said. 'Good man, Rossie. Got a vision – someone you'd always want on your team.'

Not sure he shared the same view; Neil was saved from answering by the waiter returning with a bottle of wine, a napkin draped over his arm. Martin made a great show of smelling, swirling and tasting the wine, before nodding wisely and asking the waiter to fill Neil's glass too. Neil let him splash a little wine into it, before stretching a hand over the glass. 'Thanks, I'm driving,' he said before turning to Martin. 'Why don't you tell me about your plans?'

Martin grinned, the red wine had already stained his lips and teeth. 'It's likely to be a hostile takeover,' he said. 'I want it done anonymously and fast.'

Chapter Five

'I take it the big night didn't go well,' Jess said, pulling her thick long sweater tighter round her, as if it was an invisibility blanket she could hide behind as Sarah flounced into her sitting room and made for the sofa.

'Have you done something in here?' she asked, flopping down, tucking her legs underneath and stroking General Gordon. 'It feels sort of minimalistic. Have you had a clear out?'

There wasn't enough room for the two of them and a cat on the sofa, so Jess picked up the bottle of wine, poured them both a glass and moved to the armchair. Bloody cat was a traitor. He was purring now, couldn't have looked more delighted at being stroked by someone so utterly gorgeous.

'I take it "Mr Right" has turned out to be "Mr as Fucked Up as All the Others"?'

'Understatement.' Sarah raised her eyes theatrically, bringing a dimple to Jess's left cheek as she stifled a laugh. 'Life's so unfair.'

The girl was wasted in accounts, she should have been on the stage. Jess fought back the urge to come up with a cliché or the "Life's a bitch and then you die" line Maggie came out with at least once a week when a supplier chased payment of an invoice or complained about the delay.

'We were supposed to have been "official".' Sarah took a sip of her wine and looked at the glass. 'Since date three.'

Jess sighed and sat back, her evening with the Duke of Hastings put on hold. 'Ryan was okay with that?' she asked.

Sarah looked a picture of unhappiness. She sniffed. 'We'd agreed we were in a relationship.' She pouted. 'Don't look at me. I didn't get heavy. He was the one who insisted we got on so well, we should delete our dating apps and live happily ever after.'

'He said that?'

'Yes.' Sarah's lips achieved full pout. 'Well, the bit about deleting the app anyway.'

'I guess you did, he didn't,' Jess said. 'And you had no idea he was still swiping anything with two legs and a fanny?'

'It's not funny.'

‘I’m not laughing.’ Jess topped up the glasses. ‘What happened?’

‘This woman marched across the pub, slapped her glass down on our table, pointed at me and said, “You need to know, I’m here and I’m not going anywhere”.’ Sarah cringed. ‘She wagged her fingers at me in a threatening way. Ryan told her to sit down and she said, “Have you told her to get lost and leave you alone?”’ Sarah’s eyes glistened. Tears looked like they were threatening to start.

The last thing Jess wanted to do was to upset her any more, but sometimes she despaired of Sarah’s inability to think badly of anyone. Ryan was a plonker. She deserved better.

‘You believe this girl turning up out of the blue was a coincidence?’ Jess asked, quietly.

‘I do.’ Sarah nodded. ‘She was there with Harry.’

Jess looked at her questioningly.

‘You know, Harry Roberts, the geek from Customer Services? Graphic T-shirts and jeans guy?’

‘She’s seeing him as well as Ryan?’ Jess asked.

‘Don’t be daft. She’s his sister. He recognised Ryan from a picture she showed him earlier, then she checked his location on her phone.’

‘You mean she was stalking him?’

‘No,’ Sarah said, sounding like she was talking to a complete idiot. ‘Most online dating apps show you the location of your matches, so you can see if there’s anyone close.’

‘Creepy,’ Jess said. ‘Relationships should be about chemistry, not reading someone’s profile, staring at old pictures, and certainly not about right swiping the occasional sex monster on your phone or worse.’

‘Chemistry – that’s the dinosaur in you coming out. Have you ever used a dating app? It’s all done on algorithms these days,’ Sarah said. ‘Which have been scientifically proven to be the best way to meet and connect with like-minded people.’

‘Says who? Look what’s happened to you. Half the excitement of a new relationship should be the first meeting. That moment when you catch sight of someone for the first time, and they see you. You look into his eyes and find yourself wondering if they are blue or grey, as you watch the sun playing with the highlights in his hair.

‘Really?’

'Yeah, okay what I am trying to say is there should be an instant attraction and sparks should fly. Did Ryan ever make you feel like that?'

Sarah stopped, her glass of wine on its way to her mouth. It was difficult to tell from her face what she thought.

'Did he ever make you feel warm inside? As if your nervous system has come alive. Your heart skips a beat,' Jess went on. 'There are smiles, and eye contact that goes on a smidgeon too long. You don't get that from poring over page after page of possible dates, do you?'

Sarah's eyes were locked on Jess, who shifted uncomfortably as memories of the hat-retrieving stranger flooded back.

'That's what happened with you, is it?' Sarah asked, clearly losing the battle with her facial muscles to smother a smirk. 'When you met your own dream boy?'

'What do you mean?' Jess said, her colour and temperature rising.

'You told Maggie and me you met Martin on a management course. You never said anything about lust at first sight. Now you're saying your eyes met over a spreadsheet and passion levels rose, as you realised pivot tables were never going to be the same again.'

'I didn't say that,' Jess said.

Sarah laughed and took another sip of wine.

It was really, really nothing like that. Yes, they'd met on a management course. But they'd spent three days in the same conference room without acknowledging one another, then by accident had ended up next to each other on the same train home. Jess had spent the entire journey helping Martin sort out some budgets he'd struggled with, partly because he'd spread out all over her small, fold-down table as well as his own and was making such odd noises, she couldn't concentrate on her book.

They'd been so wrapped in the figures that they'd missed their stop and ended up in Bristol Temple Meads some seventy miles away.

Martin hadn't been pleased, especially as the first train back to Redford wasn't due for a couple of hours.

They'd gone for a meal. Jess couldn't remember where, or whether the food was any good. Truth be known it felt more like a business meeting or interview than anything else.

Martin took her number when they got back to Redford and a few days later rang to pick her brains on another financial matter. This time he offered to take her to lunch as a thank you and because she hadn't been able to think of any reason why not, she'd gone.

Twelve years later, here she was, back to square one. On her own. Her and the cat. But no way would she ever download a piece of software to find her perfect match and if that meant being single for the rest of her life, so be it.

She needed to get off the subject of her own love life and quickly. 'So, you had no idea Ryan was seeing someone else?' she asked. She probably looked like a boiled beetroot; she certainly felt like one.

'Do you think I'd have spent a fortune on a dress, Prosecco and condoms if I had?' Sarah asked.

'You slept with him?' Jess frowned.

'Hang on, high horse on the loose.' Sarah fiddled with the stem of her glass. 'No, but I think Harry's sister has. She doesn't have a six-date rule. She doesn't seem to have any rules.'

'Seven,' said Jess. 'It's a seven-date rule which we set for your own good. But I'm guessing dress, Prosecco, condoms meant you'd thought about it.'

The pout was back. 'I'm grown up and Ryan is seriously hot.'

'Was. Past tense. It's over. He's shagging someone else.'

'Thanks.' An odd gurgling noise seemed to rise from the sofa. 'Sorry, that's my stomach,' Sarah said. 'I don't suppose you've got anything to eat?'

'You've been out for a meal.'

'I left before the food arrived. I find a harridan wiggling a finger in your face and telling you, if you don't get out of her space, she's going to make your life hell, tends to curb the appetite.' Sarah rubbed her stomach. 'But only temporarily it seems.'

'What did Harry say?'

'He told her to wind her neck in. I got up. I'm not sure he didn't think I was about to lay the witch out, because he moved all the glasses off the table and offered to walk me home. Oh God.' Sarah buried her face into a cushion. 'Everyone at work is going to know, aren't they?'

'Maggie and I won't say anything.'

'Harry might.'

'He doesn't look the sort.'

'Izzie will wheedle it out of him. I can imagine her face.'

'Try not to. It's late and you don't want nightmares.' Jess glanced at her watch. 'Do you need a bed for the night?'

Sarah nodded. 'Won't Martin mind?'

Jess bristled defensively and swallowed the last of her wine. 'He's away at the moment,' she said.

Chapter Six

Few things made Jess really bad-tempered, but first thing on a Monday morning, someone parking in her spot at work ranked on the crimes against humanity scale along with pinching her named food from the company fridge.

Anymoore's designated car park spaces were a privilege that came with seniority and length of service. In a car park, shared with three other companies, which was always full, they were considered to be a more valuable staff benefit than discounted gym membership.

Jess parked in the visitor's spot and noted down the offender's registration number. She asked reception to arrange to have it moved on her way past. Hopefully, the embarrassment of being called to move it would mean the perpetrator would see the error of their ways and never darken her spot again.

'Looking good, Jess,' the receptionist said. 'You must have had a great weekend.' She tilted her head in a questioning sort of way.

'Cracking,' Jess replied, handing over the car's registration details.

Which wasn't far from the truth; it hadn't been bad. She'd enjoyed the time on her own once Sarah had gone. Sunday had been stressful; she'd spent the morning worrying whether Martin's mother would turn up for their usual lunch date, but although he hadn't told Jess he was leaving her, seemingly he had managed to relay the fact to his mother.

And the afternoon had been spent being stared at by a locksmith who wanted to know why she wanted to change every lock in the place and not falling for the "I lost my key ring" line, but as it was a call-out and he was charging her shedloads of money, he didn't challenge her lie.

On Saturday, for the most part, she'd busied herself with wedding photo edits, but with every new image, Friday's stranger popped into her head, sending electric shocks through nerve endings and a rush of arousal to places that hadn't been aroused in a long time. Hormones and emotions played such havoc with her concentration that the job took longer than anticipated, still when she finally shut down the computer late evening, she had to admit she was pleased with the final result.

'You look well today,' the receptionist said.

At times like this, Jess wished she could conjure up a pithy reply to put the girl firmly back in her box, without appearing openly rude.

Was the woman trying to imply Jess had laid her make-up on a bit thick this morning? She didn't think she'd done anything much different, well apart from the eyeliner and the mascara. She'd gone for subtle, nothing outlandish or worthy of the "you look well" comment, which in the international language of womankind, everybody knows means "What the fuck were you thinking?".

'You can hide a lot behind a smile?' her mother had always told her. Only these days "painting on a smile" required oodles of foundation, blusher and lipstick and today, eyeliner and mascara. Everyone noticing something different was the one thing she'd hoped to avoid. It wasn't that she didn't intend to tell people her relationship status had changed; she wasn't ready to do it yet.

Could the receptionist see through her facade? Did she look like a woman who'd been dumped? Was that what the girl was trying to say, in a rather blunt, up-close and personal sort of way?

Well, she had been. Her trouble was after nearly a week on her own she didn't feel as if her heart had been ripped out. She ought to be missing him, but she wasn't. When she got her head around what Martin's departure meant, perhaps she could deal with everyone's sympathy and questions. In a caring, family company like Anymoore Ltd there was likely to be plenty of both. Heaven knows what everyone would think if they knew she was a recently abandoned woman lusting over a brooding, classically handsome hat-retrieving stranger.

'Thanks,' she said, because what else could she say? Jess's lips curved into a smile as she skipped up the stairs to the first floor. Thinking about "Neil darling" was enough to send a warm flush through her body.

Sarah was sat at her desk sorting the post when Jess reached the office, but their perfunctory greetings were cut short by Frank, two paces behind her.

'Oh good, you're here,' he said, making both women jump.

'Morning boss,' Jess said, dumping her handbag on her desk. 'How was your weekend?'

Frank waved a hand that could have meant any number of things. 'Last year's accounts and this year's projections, where are they? I have a meeting first thing,' he said. 'I need them.'

Jess opened a drawer in one of the filing cabinets running along the wall behind her desk and extracted two folders. 'Give me five minutes then I can run through the figures with you.' She pulled up her diary on her phone. 'How long do we have? Only, I wasn't aware we had a meeting this morning. I've got nothing in the calendar.'

'We?' Frank looked confused.

'If you're discussing company finances, you'll want me there.'

'No.' Frank made a grab for the folders. 'This is nothing for you to worry about.'

Jess's head shot up. An oxymoron if ever she'd heard one. She was definitely concerned. If she had any doubts, the fact he looked so sheepish confirmed her suspicions. He was up to something. She'd worked for Frank for fifteen years, knew him probably better than he knew himself. She put her hands on her hips and shot him her look.

'I'll be okay,' he said, looking suitably embarrassed. 'It's only a preliminary chat,' he muttered and left the room.

'What's that all about?' she said to the door, as it shut behind him. 'Did he say anything on Friday?'

'Nope,' Sarah said, sorting the opened pile of post into smaller piles.

The accounts department might be one of the smaller areas, along with Human Resources, but at least they had the advantages of walls and a door, whereas every other department, in a bid to encourage team building, was open plan.

Sarah sat with her back to the window and Maggie usually had her back to the wall and the white board, which she took great pleasure in updating on a regular basis. Today her desk was empty.

'No Maggie?' Jess asked.

'Trick question, right?' Sarah said, without looking up from her pile of envelopes.

Jess narrowed her eyes.

The office door opened, and Harry Roberts from Customer Services entered; wearing a shirt with a collar and a pair of smart trousers, he looked less geeky than usual. Jess noticed even Sarah did a double take before she blushed.

'I've moved the car,' he said.

'You parked in my spot?' Jess glared at him.

'Whoa, lady, not me,' Harry said, holding his hands up. 'I cycled in this morning. Izzie asked me to move her car and let you know when I had.' He saw Sarah, took a step towards her. 'Sarah …'

'I'm making drinks,' she said and shot out of her chair. 'Can't stop.'

'I wanted to check you're all right?' he said.

'Why wouldn't I be?' Sarah glared at him.

'Friday night …'

'Don't go there.'

'We should talk.'

'I mean it. I have nothing to say.'

'Please Sarah, talk to me, if not now, then later?' There was a note of desperation in Harry's voice.

'Okay,' Sarah said, slowly. 'I'll call you as soon as I've had a cup of Earl Grey.'

Harry smiled. 'I'll wait.'

'Don't bother.' Jess walked over to Maggie's whiteboard and checked it for any clue as to the woman's absence. No one had noted any time off. 'Sarah only drinks coffee.'

'She is pissed with me then.' Harry's shoulders slumped. He looked genuinely upset.

'I think she's got more of a problem with your sister,' Jess said. 'Look, give her a day or two – she'll calm down. Sarah never holds grudges for long.'

'Yeah right.'

Jess turned, hands on hips, and stared at the coat stand and then back at the desk.

'Have you lost something?'

'Maggie. I've never known her be late and if she's not well, she'd have phoned by now.'

'Maybe she got caught up in the accident this morning,' Harry said.

'What?'

'Something happened in the High Street, involving a car and a bicycle. Police closed the road. I mean, I'm sure it's not …'

Jess froze. Maggie always came by bike. An elderly affair with a wicker basket on the front.

‘I’d better get back.’ Harry left the office before she had a chance to thank him for moving the car.

Jess bit her lip and rang Maggie’s landline and mobile. No answer so she left messages on both.

‘Still no Maggie?’ Sarah said, backing into the office carrying a tray and three mugs.

‘Do you know what happened in the High Street this morning?’

Sarah shrugged. ‘I walked …’

The phone on Jess’s desk rang and she grabbed at it. ‘Jess Willersey speaking.’

She listened as the woman on the other end who, having checked she was talking to the accountant, started venting in a high-pitched, gabbling sort of way. She was clearly upset and didn’t feel the need to stop for breath or to give Jess a chance to answer.

Sarah watched her.

Jess shook her head. ‘Not Maggie,’ she mouthed.

‘Thank you for letting me know,’ Jess said, when the woman stopped her tirade long enough for her to get a word in. ‘But it’s really not a problem – we don’t require your services any more.’ She replaced the receiver as the agitated monologue started again, getting higher and louder before being cut off.

‘What have you done to upset her?’ Sarah asked, putting one of the mugs on Jess’s desk.

‘Not me.’ Jess ran her hands through her hair and rubbed her eyes. ‘That was the employment agency.’

‘Oops.’ Sarah winced and handed her a tissue. ‘You’re a bit smudged,’ she added in response to Jess’s surprised expression.

‘I should’ve been told you asked last week’s temp not to come back.’

‘You were photographing a wedding.’ Sarah shrugged. ‘And she was bloody awful. Even you have to admit she was clueless. Friday, she spent the whole morning explaining the problems Maggie could expect from childbirth if she ever got pregnant. Things, she said, she wished someone had told her, before she fell pregnant with her daughter. Maggie is sixty-two. If she got pregnant, she’d need a darn site more than gas and air. Then she spun us a line about how companies usually realised her management potential early in her placements and didn’t waste her talents making her perform such archaic administrative functions as filing. It couldn't have been 10 o'clock before Maggie told her not to come back after lunch.'

'Okay.' Jess smiled. 'We're better off without her, but what about the one before her?'

'Ate pencils. Went through three on her first day. God knows how many she'd have got through once she was up to speed. She'd have been through the stationary cupboard in a matter of weeks. Bankrupted us in months. Ask Maggie.' As if she realised Jess couldn't, Sarah stopped and looked at Maggie's empty desk. 'When she gets in, she'll tell you.'

'And the one before her?'

'Body piercing and obscene tattoos.'

'Said who?'

'The guy who fixed the air conditioning.'

'No, please don't tell me.' Jess used her phone's camera app as a mirror. She might need to rethink the eye make-up at work thing. Sarah was right, except it was a little more serious than a smudge – she looked like a flaming panda. She spat on the tissue and scrubbed round each eye. 'Okay, I'll look for another agency.'

'I'll do it if you like. I know what we need.'

Jess looked over her phone at her colleague. 'Thanks, but no thanks. We need accounts help not a male stripper – a completely different skill set. Best leave it with me.' She picked up her car keys. 'But there's something I have to do first.' She needed to move her car from the visitor's space. It wouldn't take much longer to pop over and check Maggie was okay, would it?

Chapter Seven

Neil had been born and grown up in Redford and now lived less than ten miles away, so had no need for his satnav. Even with the road closures the radio mentioned, he knew the roads well enough to be able to avoid the problem with the High Street.

Redford had expanded over the years, throwing out new estates in every direction. If it grew any larger, it would soon start to swallow up some of the surrounding villages. Bluebell Field industrial estate was a recent addition, but as a young boy he'd played on the very field with his gang. Other gangs of boys his age might have played Cowboys and Indians, war games or climbed trees, but Neil's gang dug holes. They had a plan. They were going to build and make a den somewhere adults or other gangs would never be welcome.

For several weeks they'd tunnelled and dug. The field sprouted a new hill as the soil excavated was left in a heap. One morning, they arrived to find the tunnel had collapsed overnight. Neil had been all for starting another. He'd been outvoted in favour of rolling down the mud pile. Life, he'd reflected that day, as he had on so many since, could be full of disappointments.

His secondary school used the field in later years for cross-country runs. The Sunday football team used it for their home games. The travelling fair, twice a year, positioned itself there, as did the annual donkey derby. It metamorphosed into a skate park for a while, then briefly a park and ride, until it was finally transformed into an industrial estate.

Anymoore Ltd, he saw from the files, had moved into one of the newly built prefabricated buildings about three years ago.

He had always preferred to deal with customers on a face-to-face basis, rather than hold endless virtual meetings, so the more local the better. Local also meant he could avoid overnight stays, something of a necessity these days, mainly due to the Newfoundland currently sprawled out behind him and snoring.

'No chance of either of us overheating today,' he said, as the weather forecaster cheerfully declared the weekend's heatwave to be well and truly over with today's temperatures expected to hit the mid-teens only.

When his wife left him two years ago, the only thing he'd fought for was his dog. He'd given up the widescreen television, the sound bar and the newest car. His mother said, on a fairly regular basis, if he'd fought half as hard to save his marriage as he had to keep the dog, they'd still be together. He doubted it. Another month down the line and she'd have found something else to moan about. When she announced she was moving in with the guy from work, he didn't beat his chest, or threaten his love rival. Instead he bought her out of the flat and kept the dog. It was the only relationship he'd had since she left and it seemed to suit Dudley as much as it suited him. He certainly was in no hurry to get involved with anyone else. Until last Friday, he'd not met anyone he'd even looked twice at since, let alone tried to vault a wall to save … from a hat. He winced; yeah, that hadn't been clever.

Something about the way the wedding photographer had smiled at him twisted his insides and made him feel like an adolescent with rampaging hormones.

The closed roads added five minutes or so to his journey, but he'd left in plenty of time. As he turned into the industrial estate, a map showed him where to find Anymoore Ltd. Following the road round, he pulled into a paved area in front of the offices and parked in an empty visitor's space. He had twenty minutes to spare, long enough to whizz Dudley round the field, while he tried to rid himself of inappropriate thoughts and remind himself of the proposal he intended to put to the managing director.

Had Ross not been away on his honeymoon, Neil would have asked him to come along too. After all, this was Ross's initial contact and he appeared to have done a whole lot of preliminary work. Neil guessed he'd probably written a large part of the proposal too; there were phrases in it that could only have come from him. And Ross had arranged this morning's meeting with Anymoore Ltd's owner and managing director, something he had conveniently forgotten to mention at the wedding.

There were a lot of documents in the file and it had taken Neil most of the weekend to review them.

His new client, MJC Computing, came across as efficient. Nothing in the report indicated when it had been introduced to Jackson Consultancy or how – apart from a brief reference to a long-term development plan

Ross had helped with. As a result of which MJC had concluded the best way forward was a complete reorganisation of its structure and a rationalisation of its services. The goal was to expand and offer a more comprehensive range of software and hardware solutions or "The Complete Package", one of Ross's favourite phrases and which Neil kept coming across in the file.

MJC had decided that in order to provide the company with the necessary experience and contacts it was lacking, it should take over an existing company already in this line of work. The report identified Anymoore Ltd as the one it wanted.

Neil's job was to determine, before anyone spent any more time working on the proposal, whether the company would be interested in selling. If he received a favourable reaction, he'd conduct an assessment to make sure the business fitted MJC's requirements and help negotiate a fair valuation that suited both sides.

He knew from MJC's report that Anymoore Ltd was owned one hundred per cent by Frank Moore. It was likely to be a tricky meeting. There were no other shareholders to keep happy, but in his experience most people had highly inflated ideas of what their businesses were worth.

The building in front of him was clean, tidy and situated behind a small lake. In the centre of which, on a small island, sat a wooden duck house and two mallards basking in the early morning sun. On the face of it, it didn't look like a failing company.

He put Dudley back in the car and made sure he was settled. The tailgate guard he'd had fitted meant he could leave the boot open to provide air, but not the means of escape.

'Why this company?' he muttered, as he straightened his tie and picked up his case from the back seat, because according to the files he'd spent the weekend reading, this was MJC's only choice.

The receptionist looked up as he opened the door. She gave him a beaming smile, signalled she was on the phone and made a face he assumed was asking if he could wait until she'd finished her conversation.

'Oh God, Jess, tell her we're sorry. I'll tell Frank.' She offered Neil a pen, pushed a visitor's book over the desk towards him and waved a right hand in a gesture Neil took to mean, he was expected to sign it.

Sarah groaned.

'Look you can tell me to sod off,' Harry said, holding his hands up in front of him as he walked into the middle of the accounts' office.

'Okay, sod …'

'Jess suggested I give you a couple of days, but I can't because I need to know you're okay.'

Sarah shut down the dating website she was searching and scowled at him over the top of her screen. She wished for a hole in the ground to swallow her up, a wall she could walk through, or a beam-me-up box, anything to get her away from the office and quick. She didn't care what or where, so long as it was far away. If she'd been offered a time machine, with no guarantee of ever being able to get back to the present, she'd have got in and taken her chances.

'Never been better,' she said. 'And you?' Because it seemed polite to ask.

'Yeah, me too.'

It was the sort of conversation she'd normally have with someone over her shoulder as she kept walking. Except Harry stood in the middle of the office looking like nothing short of a rugby tackle would shift him.

'She knew he'd be there,' he said.

'Don't care. It's a bridge over troubled water.'

'Water under the bridge.' Harry grinned.

'What?'

'Water under the bridge is the cliché you're looking for. The other is a Simon and Garfunkel song with dodgy lyrics. That crap my sister told you about me seeing Ryan's picture on her phone then recognising the man at the bar, was bollocks.'

'So, she was stalking him?'

'I don't know.' Harry shrugged. He didn't look as geeky as usual. His shirt suited him. His trousers were straight-cut jeans and finished off with a pair of brown shoes. Casual but smart. 'I wanted you to know us being there had nothing to do with me. It was her idea not mine and she didn't mention what she had in mind,' he added.

Sarah "hmphed" and didn't say a word. She was good at lengthy silences.

'You won't take Ryan back, will you?' Harry asked, eventually.

'God, no.' She was good at lengthy silences, unless people asked ridiculous questions in which case she had to react. She'd rather have stuck red-hot needles in her eyes than take Ryan back but she didn't say as much. She didn't know Harry well, but he didn't look like the sort who would think psychotic tendencies were an attractive trait in a colleague. 'Your sister is welcome to him. Tell her not to worry, I won't queer her pitch.'

'That's not why I'm asking,' he said.

'Actually, I'm totally over him.' Sarah blushed again, glad there was only her in the office. She could imagine Jess's face.

'Good. I know it's none of my business.'

Was he blushing too?

He was.

'No, but thanks anyway.'

'You're right not to like Earl Grey tea,' he said, turning to the door. 'It's disgusting, tried it once – I'm not convinced it's even tea.' Hand on the door, he turned back and said, 'You really are better off without him, although what you ever saw in an overgrown mummy's boy with a disgusting temper and crippling financial debts, I have to admit, is beyond me.'

His eyes were bright and a dimple twitched in his cheek she'd never noticed before.

Chapter Eight

Jess knew Maggie loved her garden, but the sheer variety of colour and plants took her breath away. Flowers wound their way around her porch and front gate. The lawn had stripes mowed into it.

The cottage was picturesque in a posh garden magazine sort of way. Wisteria crept up the front walls, although it seemed to obscure bits of the downstairs windows. Martin would have cut it back.

When Maggie spoke of her home, there was always something that needed doing. Jess had pictured one of the more run-down ex-council houses at the other end of the road. Not something as quaint and beautifully maintained as Meadow View Cottage and set in such a gorgeous garden.

Funny how you can work with someone for so long, know exactly what their favourite biscuits are, how many sugars they take in tea and yet not have the faintest idea what their house looks like. The two of them had worked together almost as long as Jess had been at Anymoore, but never been in each other's houses.

The cottage tucked behind a large, modern-looking house, was currently the last house at the end of a cul-de-sac, although judging by the building site hoardings bordering one side of Maggie's garden, it wasn't going to be the case for much longer. Presumably they hid the meadow which, according to a large sign, was about to become nineteen executive, two- or three-bedroomed apartments and twenty-five three- and four-bedroomed detached houses starting from … *How much?*

Now she came to think of it, she remembered Maggie telling them last year the developers wanted to buy her out. Seeing her home now, Jess understood why: presumably, they could put a huge number of houses on Maggie's plot. They must have thought they could, judging by the amount of money she said they'd offered her – nearly enough to buy one of their new properties. She'd refused it, much to Sarah's horror.

'What's money to me at my age?' she'd said. 'It's not like I have family to leave it to.'

'You could leave it to me,' Sarah said. Jess suspected she was only half joking. Sarah was always short of money.

'Where would I live in the meantime because I'm not planning on going anywhere anytime soon,' Maggie said.

Jess made a mental note to have a look at the plans when she got home, not that there was the remotest chance her share of the house would allow her to buy anything there. She sighed. Where to live was a problem she'd have to address at some point. She couldn't afford to buy Martin out even if she wanted to.

The windows were wide open, the curtains pulled. Someone had been in the cottage earlier. If she was to find a body, chances were, it wouldn't have decomposed. Maggie surely wouldn't have left her windows open if she had set off for work. Redford was hardly crime central, but no point in taking any chances. Which left the hundred-and-one-dollar question – why hadn't she set off?

Jess parked on the drive and frowned. The stillness made her uncomfortable. She closed her eyes and tried a calming breath. Okay, no car outside the house, but Maggie was the sort to garage her car, plus she cycled most places so that didn't mean anything.

Jess swallowed and drummed her fingernails against the steering wheel and contemplated going back to work and ringing Maggie again from there. She might've been in the bathroom earlier, that's why she hadn't answered. Maybe she'd overslept. She'd probably feel silly enough without a nosy colleague turning up and demanding to know what was wrong. Yup, going back to the office would be the sensible thing to do, wouldn't it? Maggie was probably there already, completely unaware of the panic she'd caused. Jess could have something to eat to quell the empty feeling in her stomach. Alternatively, she could man up.

She climbed out of the car, stared at the house, pulled her handbag strap firmly onto her shoulder and marched up to the front door with as much purpose as she could muster.

The bell made an absurd sound. Maggie's present last Christmas in the office lucky dip. Even knowing what the tuneless jingles were supposed to be, Jess smiled at the memory of Frank holding his hands against his ears and saying, 'No, don't tell me. It's on the tip of my tongue.'

The sight of a person approaching the door through the bevelled glass quickly extinguished any humour and brought her sharply back to the present.

'Jess,' Maggie said, drawing the bolt across and opening the door enough to peer round. 'Oh God, I'm sorry, I should've rung.'

'Look, I was passing, and what with the accident in the High Street and then Harry said it was a bike …' The words came out in a jumble and Jess wasn't even sure it was her talking. She took a deep breath. 'What I am trying to say is, are you okay? I … we were worried.'

Maggie opened the door wider and stared. 'You're wearing eye make-up? You look different.'

So do you.

Jess stared back at the older woman standing in front of her. She was pretty sure she'd never seen Maggie without her grey hair pinned into a bun on the back of her head or without her "lippy" on. She was wearing nightwear and nothing on her feet. Her face was puffy, her eyes red. Something was wrong. Jess's heart rate speeded up. 'Can I come in?' she asked, trying to make her voice sound a lot brighter than she felt.

Maggie hesitated briefly, then took a step back and opened the door properly. 'It's Mother,' she said quietly.

'Has she got worse?'

'You could say that,' Maggie muttered, following her down the hall.

Jess knew Maggie's mum had been taken into a nursing home about six weeks ago. It had taken ages to arrange and for what felt like months in the run-up to the move, Maggie had spent all her free time investigating the merits of all the various Redford care homes, before she settled on Treetops. More recently she'd cut her hours down to three days a week so she could help her settle in. But lately, she'd seemed more positive; it sounded as if Mrs Simpson was adapting nicely. 'She'll be all right,' Jess said.

Maggie wound her outer layer tightly about her. Difficult to fathom whether it was a dressing gown or an elderly coat. Either way it wasn't a good look.

'Actually, she won't,' she said, sniffing. 'I got a call about five this morning from Treetops. The home manager. She died early this morning.'

'*Oh my God.*' Jess flinched. 'I'm so sorry.' She leant against the door frame for support, unable to think of what else to say.

'It's not your fault.'

'Come here.' Dropping her handbag, Jess gathered Maggie into a hug. 'You've had a shock.'

Maggie started to relax into the embrace. 'I don't think at ninety, death is completely unexpected. Her dementia had got worse, she was away with the fairies most of the time. I lost her a long time ago. Often, she didn't recognise me, or if she did'—Maggie shrugged—'she would be plain rude, but that's nothing new. She's been rude to me for the last sixty-two years. Yesterday was particularly fractious.' Her voice broke, as if she had a lump in her throat, the words difficult to get out. 'Still I had no reason to think I wouldn't see her again when I left Treetops. I thought a good night's sleep would do us both good. Seems I was wrong.' A tear slid down Maggie's cheek.

Jess prided herself on being able to cope in a crisis. Her family referred to it as "eldest child syndrome". With hindsight, there had been times in her life when empathy rather than organisation should probably have been called for, but this was not one of them. She led Maggie through to the sitting room, sat her down in an elderly, leather wing chair, tidied a pile of newspapers on the table and fluffed up some cushions around her. There were a lot of cushions.

While the cottage was beautifully maintained, decorated and updated, the soft furnishings wouldn't have looked out of place in a sixties' horror movie. Lace doilies decorated the various heavy wooden pieces of furniture. All the chairs had cushions with what looked like home-made quilted cushion covers sprinkled all over them. White linen antimacassars sat on the chair arms and backs. Maggie talked while Jess straightened. She would lay money she'd find a crocheted doll toilet roll holder in the toilet. Someone, probably Maggie's mother, had been terribly busy with a crochet hook.

The fact some people could produce such delicately made pieces of work was amazing. The only thing Jess's mother ever produced was knitted dishcloths. Martin hated them. They were a distinctive if rather unhealthy grey colour and assumed a slimy texture the minute they encountered anything remotely wet. His mistake had been telling her mother he didn't think they were hygienic. He had received two every Christmas ever since.

She found a pair of slippers and checked the heating. 'I'll ring the office then make a cup of tea,' she said, trying to press the numbers on her mobile as she stroked Maggie's hand.

'Tea's in the caddy by the cooker,' Maggie called out as Jess, now in the kitchen, filled the kettle. 'Have a biscuit if you like. There should be some in the cupboard.'

Jess rummaged, finally pulled out two packets, one yellow, one green, and walking over to the sitting room door asked, 'Do you mean these?'

'Choose whichever you fancy,' Maggie said, nodding.

Jess was normally the first to agree sell-by dates were overrated marketing ploys, but the biscuits even through their packaging felt squidgy. 'They're two years past their sell-by date. Shall I just throw them away?'

'Crisp them up in the oven.' Maggie's voice broke and she promptly burst into tears. 'If I'd known you were coming, I'd have baked something.'

The sobs were loud and uncontrollable. Jess crossed the room quickly. 'It's fine. I'm not hungry.'

'Do you know what hurts?' Maggie sniffed and wiped her eyes on a tissue she'd retrieved from one of her pockets. 'She didn't say goodbye.'

Jess waited until Maggie seemed calmer before she took the biscuits back to the kitchen. Stamping on the pedal of the bin, she threw both packets away and carried two mugs of tea through to the sitting room. One she set down on a lacy coaster on the coffee table in front of Maggie, who looked at it as if she wasn't sure what it was.

'She only needed to hang on another couple of hours. I'd have been there by seven. I always stop in on my way to work to help her with her breakfast.'

'I'm sure it wasn't intentional.' Jess wrapped her hands round her mug, glad of the coffee's warmth.

'You don't know her. I hoped when the time came, we could put our differences behind us. But we never did and it's too late now.'

From the odd comments Maggie would let slip from time to time, Jess knew the women's relationship had never been easy.

'I've looked after her most of my life. She should've said goodbye, shouldn't she?' Maggie's shoulders sagged and thinking she was about to cry again, Jess put her mug on the table and squeezed her arm.

‘I’ve always known she didn’t love me. She told me as much. Nothing I ever did was right. When she went into the home that was my fault too.’

Jess wanted to say something, anything, tell her she was wrong, that she knew how she felt, but she didn’t. She couldn’t. Her own mother had taken early retirement and was still very much in possession of all her marbles.

‘One day I went to visit her, she was staring out of a window, smiling. She looked so beautiful and alive. Then she must’ve seen my reflection in the window. Her eyes clouded over and she returned to her usual monosyllabic self. I tried telling her about my day at work. She insisted she couldn’t hear what I was saying. Told me I wasn’t talking clearly enough, but when someone called the inmates for supper, she upped and went.’

‘Patients not …’

‘Mother didn’t suffer. It was quick, the manager told me. He thought I might find that a comfort. I should be glad she doesn’t have to carry on living some sort of bizarre half-life.’ Maggie paused. ‘But I’m not. I keep thinking about me. I’m all alone.’ She sobbed. Her whole body shaking. ‘I have no one left.’

Jess hugged her again. ‘Not true,’ she said. ‘You have Sarah and me. And we have you—’ She stopped, aware she was starting to sound like a dodgy country and western number.

The sound of the front door being clicked shut woke Maggie, but she waited until she heard Jess’s car leaving before she checked her watch and got up from her chair. It was gone eleven, she must have dozed off. She remembered Jess sitting with her and stroking her hand, as she told her about Sarah’s latest date disaster.

A blanket had been wrapped around her legs. She walked into the kitchen and instantly realised how stressed Jess must’ve been. The whole place had been tidied to within an inch of its life. She’d worked with the woman long enough to know that when things weren’t right, Jess tidied. It was her stress mechanism. Quite manically at times. On the kitchen table stood two pints of milk, a new packet of chocolate biscuits, an envelope and a note from Jess telling her she’d made an appointment at the Register Office for Maggie to register her mother’s death that afternoon, with a proviso that if she needed any help Maggie should call her. Maggie looked at the white envelope. Jess had collected the medical certificate of cause of death from the surgery and must've shopped for milk and biscuits at the same time. Her kindness brought a lump to Maggie's throat; a smile played around the corners of her mouth as she recalled Jess's suggestion that they should help Sarah choose her next few dates.

'She always gets it so wrong,' Jess had said.

'Because she goes for the same type every time,' Maggie had agreed.

'Good-looking, wild-boy types, but the minute they start beating their chest and acting in character, she gets hurt. If we put our heads together, I'm sure we could come up with more suitable matches.'

'You, maybe,' Maggie said, surprised. 'I'm hardly the right person to ask.'

'Nonsense. We probably know her as well as anyone.' What do you consider essential "must have" qualities for her next date?'

'What, you mean like kind face, nice eyes, that sort of thing?'

'A sense of humour is essential.'

'As is a large bank account and having only served a short prison sentence.'

'Oh God, do you remember him?'

'Poor girl.' Maggie shook her head. 'Sarah thought she'd been stood up until she got a letter from Belmarsh inviting her to visit.'

'We need to find out what she thinks she needs,' Jess said.

'Easier said than done.'

'When you were Sarah's age, what were you looking for in a man?'

Maggie shook her head. 'I wasn't.'

'I didn't mean …' Jess coloured.

'It's okay. I wasn't looking for anyone – I was in a relationship. I had found Mr Right. He had nice eyes, definitely a good sense of humour, kind face.'

Jess stared at her, open-mouthed.

'We were in love. I thought we'd be happy forever.'

Jess nodded. 'Then I guess you started to take one another for granted. The little things that used to amuse you started to annoy you. The way he couldn't load the dishwasher properly, men never can. Don't you hate that? I mean, how difficult is it to work out, plates in the narrow vertical bits, bowls in the wider bits?'

'We didn't have a dishwasher.'

'Then, what? You drifted apart?'

'Not really …'

'It happens to everyone. You spend longer greeting the cat than you do your partner. You tell yourself everything's okay, it's normal. You've got into a bit of a routine. But it's not just a routine, more a rut and a flaming deep one. You can't remember the last time you sat and chatted over a meal without him checking his social media accounts. And if he'd rather spend an evening in his office with the door shut than an evening watching *Britain's Got Talent* or *Strictly Come Dancing*, then you justify it on the grounds he's overworked.'

'I'd rather spend the evening in the garden or the kitchen than watching either of those, too.'

Jess bit her bottom lip and frowned. 'You don't mean that.'

'I don't have a cat, or any social media accounts.'

'So, what happened with you and Mr Right?'

'Ray.' Maggie walked over to the sideboard and picked up a photograph of a young man in army uniform. She rubbed the glass against her dressing gown and looked down at the face smiling back at her. It never ceased to make her heart skip a beat, even after all this time. 'He was killed in the Falklands. Never came back.' She handed the photo to Jess. This, and a few letters, is all I have left.'

Jess's mouth opened and shut. 'You never said,' she said, eventually.

'Not something that comes up in everyday conversation. I never had a father, so apart from Ray, the only man who has been any influence in my life was my grandfather and although I loved him dearly, he was a cantankerous old sod. Although, in infant school, I had a friend called Kevin – everybody said we made a cute couple. He used to stand on the doorstep and let me kick his knees. Not sure why or what went wrong with that relationship, but one day he went off and never came back. So, you see, I'm not the person best placed to select anybody's ideal partner.'

The phone went and Jess looked relieved about the interruption. 'I'll get it,' she said. Maggie would have been happy for it to ring through to answerphone.

'It might be work.'

Chapter Nine

'I realise this will probably have come as something of a shock,' Neil said.

Frank stood looking out of his office window.

'I'm not asking you to give me a definite answer, just an indication whether selling the company would be something you might consider.'

Frank sighed. 'If you'd asked me a year ago, I'd have said no,' he said, turning back.

Neil knew from the file, Frank was in his mid-sixties. Looking at him now, if he'd been asked to guess, he would have put him a few years older.

'But over the last few months, if I'm honest then yes it's something I've considered. I guess I've finally realised the company I created has not only grown legs but is now more than capable of walking without me. I don't program any more. I'm rarely asked to help with any marketing campaign. Increasingly I seem to get drawn into all sorts of red tape and bureaucracy. My meetings these days are more likely to be with Health and Safety officers, than customers. Risk assessments bore me rigid. My customers would rather deal with younger members of staff than me. I can't understand half of what my computer engineers are talking about.' He clasped his hands behind his back and turned back to the window again. 'I've been left behind.'

Neil didn't speak. Watching Ross in action, at times he felt the same. 'Of course, I can't guarantee you a quick release. My client's offer would be dependent on you staying on the board for a period of time after takeover.'

'Why would they want me to stay?'

'It's common practice. It shows your customers and staff it was an amicable takeover, gives everyone time to settle down. After a set time it's up to you to decide whether you wish to renegotiate your contract or leave. I can't speculate as to the likelihood of my client wanting you to stay.'

'What about the staff?'

'Once the takeover is agreed we would enter into full consultations with them and the unions. Initially, any who want to stay will be transferred to similar positions within the new company with no loss of benefits.'

The standard line, in keeping with current employment law.

'However,' Neil added, 'in the future there may be a degree of "rightsizing".' He hated that bloody expression. He'd rather call it for what it was. 'There may be areas where there is duplication of work, accounts for example. It's unlikely the new company will need an accounts department much larger than the one they have now.' He flicked through the notes. He didn't have an existing organisation chart for MJC Computing so he couldn't tell how big their existing department was, but the folder Martin Cowley had presented him with at the wedding contained a note in Ross's neat handwriting saying MJC considered the number of administrative staff in Anymoore Ltd disproportionate for the size of the new combined business. It was planning on taking advice but figured it would need less than half of the accounts and human resources. There appeared to be no evidence to support this conclusion and it wasn't relevant to preliminary discussions, so he hadn't challenged Martin on the point yet.

'Obviously, when the details are announced, anyone who is not a hundred per cent behind the move will be able to leave in accordance with the terms of their current contract.'

Frank nodded.

'Look, there's a lot for you to take in. I certainly don't want to rush you into making a decision you'll regret later,' Neil said. 'I'll leave you my details, have a think and if you'd like to progress things, give me a call.'

He handed over a business card and a brochure about Jackson Consultancy.

Frank flicked the edge of the card. 'I'm interested,' he said.

'Are you sure?' He'd never make a salesman.

Frank nodded. 'What happens next?'

'If you're happy to let me take the accounts, I can work on putting together a detailed proposal. I would suggest we try and get together later in the week, talk through the offer and any questions either of us may have. If you're not interested, there may be other companies they would be interested in talking to.'

Not that he'd come across anything in the files to give any indication that was the case. He hoped Ross and Martin had considered other avenues. That's what he would have recommended.

Maggie clutched the envelope from the doctor in her hand and sat in the Register Office waiting room facing three grey doors, each with an official notice on it about the latest virus going around. How you blow your nose, what you should do with your tissues and how long you should wash your hands for. There were antiseptic gel dispensers on both walls. She pushed the button, a blob of gel shot out at an unusual angle and landed on her coat.

She sat down, on the verge of tears, and dabbed at it with her handkerchief. Why on earth hadn't she rung the home manager and asked for help? He'd offered to accompany her, something he'd probably done a thousand times before with grieving relatives. He was being kind and she'd immediately regretted saying no.

She had been unsure of what she should wear to register a death and opted for black in the end. A pair of trousers, matching sweater and a pair of patent court shoes. She'd walked rather than cycled in, somehow cycling hadn't felt appropriate and she'd decided against any form of headgear, although she'd always wanted a black veil and headdress like Spanish women wore on formal occasions. Whatever was it called?

She did what Sarah told her she should do when she wanted to know something specific and googled "Spanish head gear for death". An enquiry that brought up a number of very strange images. A balaclava or skull mask weren't quite what she had in mind.

She snapped her phone shut as one of the office doors opened. A man came out.

'Registration appointment for Simpson,' he said, looking directly at her. It took Maggie a moment or two to realise he was talking to her although she was the only one waiting.

'Registration appointment for Simpson,' he repeated.

This time she stood up.

'My name is Luke,' he said. 'I'm a registration officer and will be registering your mother's death. I see you have the certificate from the doctor. Can I take that?'

Maggie looked at the envelope and nodded. He reached out. She reached out. He took hold of it. She tightened her grip. He pulled. She couldn't let go.

'It's all right,' he said gently. 'Why don't you come in and sit down. I need to check some details and then we can go through everything together.'

He looked through all the documents she'd brought in. Taking inordinate care, unfolding and reading each one. The ones he didn't need he refolded and put in a pile on one side. 'And is this you?' he asked, spreading out the ragged document Maggie recognised as her own birth certificate on the desk. She nodded.

'It's the only one I have,' Maggie said.

'It's okay,' Luke said. 'I'm not going to keep it.'

'I'm not suggesting …' She sighed. 'It's all I have to prove I am my mother's daughter,' she said.

'That makes sense.' He nodded. 'Unfortunately, this is a short certificate. It proves your nationality but little else. A full certificate shows your parents and proves you are related to Rose. I don't need to see it today. You've told me who you are and I'm happy to take your word for it.'

If he'd known Rose in real life, he would have seen the similarities. All her life, people had told her how much she looked like her mother. Rose would have snorted and said, 'You'd be so lucky.' Why couldn't she have inherited the nice bits. True, her hair curled naturally too, but whereas Rose pretty much kept her colour through to her death, Maggie's was mainly grey. Rose had elegant hands, long fingers and strong nails. Maggie's fingers were chunky, and her nails frequently chewed.

'Do you have brothers or sisters to help with the arrangements?' the registrar asked.

She stared blankly. 'I'm an only child,' she said.

'I'm sorry to hear that. It must have been hard and sounds like she was ill a while. It is still a terrible shock.' He had a kind face. Not a young man. Maggie guessed he had a version of the same sympathetic conversation with people at least half a dozen times a day.

'Not really,' she said. 'The outcome was inevitable, just quicker than we thought. She lost a lot of weight, there was nothing of her in the end.

When the dementia got bad, she didn't want to eat. The doctor prescribed protein drinks and lots of sweet things.' Maggie remembered the cake she'd baked yesterday evening to take in today.

Luke's printer spewed out various sheets of paper; the noise returned Maggie to the present. He signed each page and put them in a folder. He tapped something into his computer and stared at his screen, positioned at such an angle Maggie couldn't make out what he was looking at. He pulled a form out of a drawer and filled in a number of boxes. When he'd finished, he pushed it across the desk to Maggie. 'If you want a full birth certificate, hand this into the office downstairs. They will be able to produce one for you.'

'Mantilla,' said Maggie. 'That's the word I was looking for.'

Chapter Ten

'I'm sixty-five,' Frank said, running his hands through his hair.

'A statement, not an excuse.' Jess placed a mug of tea on his "*I'm only here to help*" coaster, in front of him. 'Maggie's not far behind and she's not talking about retiring. Things aren't bad. It's a bit quiet, but we've been through sticky times before. That's why you expanded the customer service and marketing side of things to develop new business.'

'It's only an estimate,' Frank said, tapping the document on his desk. 'But it's reasonable. He based it on the published accounts and an estimate for the current year. He's gone away with the current accounts and is putting a proposal together. Nice chap. Said he couldn't think of any reason why a firm offer would be substantially less. It's not as if Brexit has affected us. Our forecasts for this year and next are still roughly in line with expectations.'

'It's nothing special. Surely goodwill and years of experience count for something. If you are thinking of selling, speak to our auditors. Get a proper valuation done.'

'They want a quick decision.'

'Of course they do, but you don't have to roll over and play dead. Take your time. If they want Anymoore that badly, they'll wait. You need to think about whether it's what you want.'

Frank dropped his head and sighed. 'I've worked since I was sixteen years old. Work has already cost me two marriages. I don't want to jeopardise my third. I love my wife. I want to spend time with her, go places, do things, and I'm tired. I'd like to buy a boat and take off for the Caribbean. You can't tell me if it came down to a choice between spending the rest of your life, calculator in hand or camera in hand, you'd choose to go down the accountancy route again.'

'This isn't about me …'

'No, it's about me. And honestly, I've had enough of red tape and office politics. I sit all day in my office worrying about work schedules, budgets and targets. Customers don't pick up the phone to speak to me about a programming issue these days, they want the younger generation. I'm seen as old school because I prefer face-to-face meetings, not teleconferences.

'I'm a dinosaur when it comes to social media. I don't "WhatsApp" every bloody idea I have, paste endless photos on Instagram or Facebook of my walk to work in the morning, or my breakfast.

'I don't understand what half the techies are talking about, so I sit here and smile when they start spouting about avatars, or wiki, or webinar issues, but in reality, it goes way over my head. I talk in English, not acronyms or smiley face thingys.'

'Emojis.'

'Whatever. It might as well be a completely different language. I'm too old to change.'

'I'm sure, in the top ten things to do before you die, learn a language is up there.'

'Bollocks.' Frank smiled. 'No, it's time. Maybe this has given me the push I needed. There's a yacht out there waiting for me to take ownership of and sail away. Screwdriver emoji. End of.'

'Screw what?' Jess pushed her hair back behind an ear. This wasn't what she was expecting to hear today. Life kept getting weirder and weirder.

'My point exactly,' Frank said. 'Go on, calculator or camera?'

It would be the camera every time. Of course it would. Jess looked down at her own hands; she could do with a manicure. But in Frank's place, she'd probably jump at the offer too. She didn't blame him, but she'd given fifteen years of her life to the company.

They worked well together. He referred to her as "the power behind the throne". An exaggeration, but she liked to think part of his success was down to her. Maybe it was time to bite the bullet too, but after Friday's wedding, did she want to consider even a part-time career as a photographer?

It was hardly the right time to consider it. She was on her own, had no idea what was happening with Martin, or where she was going to live, and now it looked as though she might need to update her CV and look for another job.

Frank was watching her, waiting for a response.

She wanted him to be happy. He was a kind and fair man. He might have had his pound of flesh over the years, but it had been his encouragement that had got her through her accountancy exams when she'd considered giving up. He was the voice of reason when she had big decisions to make. She'd miss him.

Jess squinted at her boss. 'Boat beats Harley-Davidson, I suppose. But isn't this some sort of mid-life crisis?'

'A bit late.' Frank grinned. 'I'm talking permanent retirement here and how I want to spend whatever time I have left. In some ways I see this as taking a leaf out of your book.'

'My book?' Jess spluttered on a mouthful of tea and stared up at him. 'You don't want to do that.'

'Don't put yourself down. You've always gone after what you wanted. You pursued your accountancy exams, even though I couldn't afford to give you time off. And you had the guts to get off your arse and study photography. How did the wedding go, by the way?'

'I'm delivering the photos after work. They look great. I'm chuffed. Not bad for a first time. I'm hoping the newly-weds like them enough to pay me. At the moment, I am substantially out of pocket.'

'They will.' Frank drummed his fingers on the A4 document. Jess's hands itched to take it.

'The management consultant thought their client would be willing to take on my staff, under existing terms and conditions. They are prepared to guarantee employment, to every employee who wants to transfer, for at least six months.'

'That's what all businesses say. Let me guess. They have no immediate plans to change the name of the company either. But I'd lay money the minute the new MD has his feet under your desk, he'll start talking in clichés about rightsizing and integration.'

'I will make sure everyone is treated fairly.'

'How will you do that?' Jess gave in and snatched up the proposal, ignoring Frank's surprise as she flicked through it. It looked professional enough.

'They want to retain me in a consultancy position to ensure a smooth transition.'

Jess opened the document. '"My client appreciates the considerable amount of time and effort it has taken to build up Anymoore Ltd.",' she read aloud. '"It is their intention to, initially, run this company as a division of their existing business and continue to grow its market share over the coming year".'

The proposal was littered with words such as "assets" and "liabilities", sprinkled with phrases like "compensation" and "goodwill", and a fair amount of management and company "know-how" mixed in.

Jess frowned as she skimmed through. The management consultancy firm's logo was printed on each page, but no mention of the company behind the offer.

Jess stared at the last page, dwelling on the figures. The amount someone was prepared to pay for Frank's life's work. She wasn't impressed, but she knew what Frank's answer was going to be. He didn't need more time; he'd made up his mind. He was only telling her out of courtesy.

'Who's the company?'

Frank shook his head. 'It doesn't say.'

'You have asked, haven't you?' She turned on him, hands on her hips.

'The consultant says they prefer to remain anonymous at this stage.'

'You must have some thoughts as to who it is. A customer?'

'No one springs to mind.'

Jess felt exasperated. If someone made an offer like that to her, she would need to know everything about them before she'd even consider it. 'Did the consultant say what size company it was?' she asked. There must be a clue somewhere, he'd just missed it.

'I didn't ask.' Frank looked out of the window and sighed. 'I don't know who it is. He turned back and looked up at her. 'They've made me an offer. Maybe, it's not as much as I would have liked, but I think I'm going to take it anyway.'

'Frank, they came looking for you. You have something they want. Nobody ever accepts the first offer.' Trust me, I'm your accountant, was on the tip of her tongue. 'They won't be expecting you to accept it. It's a starting point. Now you've got to counter with a higher figure. Play hard to get.'

He yawned. 'Of course, you're right.'

Jess frowned. She knew he had no intention of arguing.

When her father wanted to make a point, he would hold her chin and stare into her eyes. That way she couldn't turn her head and look away.

She wanted to get hold of Frank's chin, stare him out and make him see reason. He was looking at his desk, his blotter, his keyboard. The one thing he wasn't looking at was her.

'No,' Sarah said, 'I can't promise when you will get paid—Oi!' she added as the telephone was unceremoniously snatched from her hand, and a large Tupperware container landed in her lap, propelling her wheeled chair backwards across the room. 'Oi,' she said again, coming to a stop before Jess's desk.

'How can I help?' Maggie said into the phone. 'Mr Whitehead, how's your wife?'

She typed something into Sarah's computer and pulled up an account. 'I'm sorry for the confusion. We've had such terrible problems lately with temporary staff, but I am back now and I can assure you that you are definitely on this week's payment run.'

Sarah crossed her arms and frowned. 'You're not supposed to use my computer,' she hissed. 'Security issues and all that. Didn't you read the email?' She lifted the corner of the plastic box. It smelled like lemon cake. She inhaled and let the delicious aroma assault her nostrils.

She had to hand it to Maggie though. The man on the other end of the phone was no longer shouting or threatening to put their account on hold.

'Yes, we're definitely having one. The money will be in your account on Friday as usual. I'll email the remittance advice. Give my regards to your wife.'

Sarah put her hand in the cake box, only to have her wrist smacked. Jeez, that woman had eyes in the back of her head. 'You're supposed to be off all week,' she said as Maggie put the phone down. 'Jess said she'd given you compassionate leave.'

'She did,' Maggie said. 'She just didn't tell me what I was supposed to do with it. Besides I have some phone calls I need to make, and a lot are premium-rate numbers. I might as well do them from work.'

'If she gave me a week off, I could think of plenty of things to do.'

'I baked a cake.'

Sarah took a large wedge. 'Want a bit?' she asked, pointing at the cake and raising her eyes.

'Actually, I was planning on taking it into Treetops after work,'

Maggie said. 'Oh hell, why not? Half the size of yours,' she said. 'Where's Jess?'

'Frank's office. He had a meeting earlier with a great looking guy and when he came out, just said, "I need to see Jess as soon as she gets back". They've been tucked up in his room with the door shut ever since she came back from yours. Jess said you had to register the death. How did it go?'

'I now have a certificate and assorted paperwork for a dead mother and discovered I have a biological father.' She unbuttoned her coat.

The piece of cake on the way to Sarah's mouth, ended up back in the Tupperware box. 'You've got a what? Say that bit again.'

Maggie hung up her coat and stared at the plant on her desk. 'I had a father.'

'You're joking, right?' Sarah pushed back from her desk and stared at the woman. 'Of course you had a father. Everyone does. I know you're not married, but surely you've heard about the birds and bees?'

'According to my mother he was a one-night stand who took advantage of her. As far as she was concerned, he didn't exist. She had no idea who he was. He was a taboo subject, guaranteed to bring on a raft of pursed lips and unnecessary aggro, so never mentioned.'

Maggie spread a small red square certificate out on the desk. 'Until today, all I knew was that I was Margaret Rose Simpson, born in Redford, female – no mention of parents.'

'And you never asked?'

'You might come from a loving family who talk through everything, but I didn't,' Maggie said. 'Most of the time Mum and I passed like ships in the night, barely civil. I've lived in my grandparents' house all my life. When they died, they left it to me, with provisions about looking after my mother. For the last forty years it has been mother and me. She never bothered about much apart from daytime TV, or her next meal, but no, I guessed it was a relationship she'd rather forget.'

'Are you sure she never mentioned him?'

'Yes, I'm sure. I'd have certainly remembered if someone had said, "Maggie, meet Arthur Francis Warburton ..."'

'Arthur who?'

'Warburton. I am starting to have senior moments. I forget little bits of information, like what I was about to do, why I was going upstairs in the middle of the day, the odd shopping items, but something as huge as a father, would probably have stuck.'

Sarah picked up the certificate, studied it as she ate the rest of her cake in silence. 'So he wasn't a one-night stand then?'

'What makes you say that?' Maggie said, as she sorted through a pile of mail.

'He hung around long enough to sign your birth certificate. Seriously, wow, this is like an episode of that programme. Any moment now, Davina McColl could turn up and announce she has found your other family.'

'Hardly.' Maggie snorted.

'What are you going to do with this now?' Sarah asked, wiping her hand on a tissue.

'Send it to the bank,' Maggie said, discarding a number of envelopes and glossy pages. 'They're the ones who need it.'

Sarah sat upright and glared at Maggie. Boy, she could be obtuse at times. 'How come you can be so calm? You've had a big shock and you're treating it like a little thing your mother forgot to tell you – like the dentist rang, or the washing machine's broken.'

'I'm not due for a check-up for another three months and she never went anywhere near the washing machine.'

'You know what I mean,' Sarah said.

'I do,' Maggie agreed. 'But it's been a day of shocks. Mother's dead, the biscuits are past their sell-by date, and I've discovered I have a father, but believe me, they all pale into insignificance beside the big one.'

Sarah stopped rubbing her hands. 'Which would be?'

'My twin brother wasn't stillborn.'

'You had a twin?' Sarah pushed back from her desk and stared at Maggie. 'Yeah right, so where is he now?'

Maggie shook her head. 'I don't know, but now I know he didn't die at birth. He was adopted.' She spread two certificates out in front of Sarah. One for Margaret Rose Simpson born 12.24 a.m. and one for Stephen Arthur Simpson born 12.04 a.m.

'Were you identical?'

'I've never met him.' Maggie chuckled. 'He was my brother, so I think not. Otherwise, he would have been my sister.'

'What will you do? Will you look for him? I know it's not straightforward, but there must be adoption registers. Couldn't you check through them? Or, I could ring ITV? Seriously, we could get Davina on the case? I'm sure she'd love a family as screwed up as yours.'

'I don't think so.' Maggie's answer was spoken softly but firmly; this wasn't a subject open for negotiation. She and Sarah had worked together long enough for Sarah to realise this conversation had reached the end of the road.

Usually.

'What are you going to do?'

'I need to make an appointment with the undertaker who has Mother. Mother had a funeral plan with the one in town, Forever Dead or something. The home arranged for them to collect her. I need to let them know what I want them to do with her now.'

'Green,' said Jess walking back into the office, a bundle of papers in her hand. 'Forever Green not dead,' she added. 'It's been run by the Green family for years. I was at school with their son.' Jess frowned. 'What are you doing here? You're supposed to be on compassionate leave.'

'Told you,' Sarah muttered.

'I'm back and full-time, which means we're back up to fighting strength. No need for temps.'

'*Temp 'as fugit*, as they say in Rome,' Sarah said.

'Do they indeed?' Jess dropped the pile of papers she was holding onto her desk and stared, first at Sarah, then at Maggie.

'The temp has flown,' Sarah said, with all seriousness. 'Maggie is teaching me Latin.'

Jess smiled at the monitor on her desk. 'Did Maggie mention her entire Roman vocabulary comes from *Life of Brian*?'

'That's unfair,' Maggie said, collecting the mugs from the desk. '*Quod licet bovi, non licet bon jovi.*'

Sarah looked up, questioningly.

'What's good for a cow, is probably not so good for Bon Jovi.' Maggie shrugged and left the room humming.

Jess looked through the bucket list on the "50 things to do before you die" website, while she waited for Neil Jackson to call her back. She'd left a message on his mobile suggesting a meeting the following morning.

Most of the ideas were not practical if you were concerned about your carbon footprint, or worried about your fitness or bravery levels.

Stood on death's doorstep with just time to fulfil her wish list, would she rush out and run the London Marathon, abseil down The Shard, or make an extreme bungee jump over water? Unlikely.

She googled zorbing. That looked like sheer madness. And she'd never considered writing a book or learning the guitar. Her list was already a lot more manageable.

'I've made an appointment for you with Forever Green for tomorrow morning at 11.00 a.m.,' Sarah said to Maggie. 'You'll have to take an early lunch.'

'Hang on a minute,' Jess said.

'She has to go,' Sarah said. 'They've collected her mother but need to discuss the funeral arrangements.'

'Why? They're undertakers,' Maggie said. 'They should know about this sort of thing. They need to tell me when and where, and I'll turn up.'

'It doesn't work like that,' Jess said, quietly.

'Doesn't it?' Maggie looked up and blinked. 'What can I tell them? I've never been to a funeral.'

The woman who had sat on the opposite side of the room, in a tweed skirt, white blouse and home-made cardigan, whatever the weather, for the last fifteen years looked sad. The woman, who ensured the company had a credit rating of one hundred per cent, who had suppliers wrapped around her finger, looked so totally out of her depth that Jess wanted to cross the room, throw her arms around her and comfort her. But such a public display of emotion would probably add to Maggie's distress.

'Sarah will go with you,' she said. Neil Jackson hadn't rung back; she would have to apologise about tomorrow's meeting and suggest another time.

Sarah's face twisted into a surprised expression that wouldn't have looked out of place on *60 Minute Makeover* had she come home to find Peter Andre hiding behind a large pot plant with a bottle of Prosecco – but a tad over the top in the current situation.

Maggie nodded and Sarah flicked through a pile of purchase orders before she found the one she needed. She scanned it carefully and stapled it to an invoice and delivery note. She appeared deep in concentration. It was unnaturally quiet. Having worked with both women long enough, Jess knew Sarah never did anything quietly other than think.

'You've never arranged a funeral?' Sarah said, eventually, still thumbing through sheets of paper.

'Have you?'

'No, but I'm less than half your age.'

'My day job is in accounts, I get home at night and until last week, I was looking after a sick mother or at least visiting her,' Maggie said. 'I garden, I cook, I do housework, but strange as it may seem, I don't have time for a secondary career in funeral direction. Unless you include Mr Nelson.'

'Definitely,' Sarah said, looking up. 'Why wouldn't we? Can you remember the arrangements for his funeral?'

'I'll try.' Maggie looked at her watch, stood up and started collecting the used mugs from the desks. 'It was a long time ago.'

'The coffin?'

'It was lovely, lined with silk. You finished?' she asked Jess, pointing at the mug on her desk. Her expression gave nothing away as she put it on the tray and wiped Jess's desk.

'Aren't you a little curious about Mr Nelson?' Sarah asked as Maggie manhandled the tray through the door and it clicked shut behind her.

'Enormously,' Jess said.

'I might go and see if she wants a hand,' Sarah whispered, as Jess's telephone rang.

'Hello,' said the voice on the other end of the line.

Jess's stomach fell. 'Martin,' she said, quietly.

'You've changed the locks.'

Chapter Eleven

Jess parked in a service yard behind the High Street shops. It was full considering most of the shops and local businesses had long since closed. It was Tuesday, so no late night shopping, and still far too early for Templeton's nightlife to be out and about. Hosni's Palace, an Egyptian restaurant, was on the corner. Some of the girls in the office had talked about it. She hadn't been there, but couldn't miss the flashing neon sign, advertising "Whirling Dervishes", "As much as you can eat", and a spicy aromatic smell coming from the right direction. She felt hungry. Maybe she could persuade Sarah and Maggie to try it one evening. An accounts department night out.

She shifted her heavy bag onto her shoulder, where it immediately started to hurt, hardly surprising considering she'd stuffed it full of albums, CDs and all the photos from her first wedding assignment.

She hoped Darren and Leanne would like the pictures. The last two evenings had been spent checking every single one and, where necessary, Photoshopping any issues out. She'd printed off a proof-book with thumbnails of everything and created a DVD with all the images set to music, on the off-chance Leanne would actually change her mind about only wanting fifty pictures when she saw the rest.

Looking at the finished result, she felt proud. There weren't any images which looked as though they had been taken by a rookie photographer or that she wouldn't be happy to include in her portfolio and show others. Maybe she could do it again. It had been a learning experience. There were many things she might do differently, but she had learnt a lot.

The service yard was a ten-minute walk away from Darren and Leanne's, but it wasn't a walk she minded, despite the weight of her shoulder bag.

According to the map on her phone, she should be able to walk down the side of the dual carriageway, cut through a short alley and come out in Prescott Close opposite Darren and Leanne's house.

The graffiti must be new if the lingering smell of aerosol paint was anything to go by. Some street art Jess admired. She was all for free expression, but these tags were fairly basic and the slogans daubed on the side of the house at the end of the alley weren't just unsightly; if she did subscribe to the view "bombing for peace was like shagging for virginity", it wasn't something she'd dream of spraying across a wall. Although, with a can of black paint and a few minutes, she could correct the spelling.

Prescott Close, as she turned in, was packed with cars, in most places parked two abreast; the ones with less than four tyres dumped on the grass verges. Children played football in the road, seemingly using the cars as goal posts. Jess winced at the sound of yet another wing mirror being bent by the impact of a large inflated rubber ball.

Darren was at home, at least his bike was. It was parked on the six-foot square of grass that in Prescott Close amounted to a large front garden and chained to the pole holding up a porch roof, suggesting he trusted his neighbours as much as she did. Its position required her to make a rather complicated gymnastic manoeuvre in order to ring the bell. Jess was sure they were in, even when there was no movement for the first couple of minutes. Sure enough, as she was about to give up, she heard Leanne scream, 'It's all right, it's only the photographer.'

The door was opened by Darren, wearing a towel round his waist. Jess winced and made a point of staring at his head. 'Hi,' she said, cautiously. 'I've brought your wedding pictures. I thought you'd want to see them as soon as possible. But if it's not convenient …'

'Not really. I'm on my honeymoon,' Darren produced such a wide grin she was aware of a tongue stud. 'And a man has to do what a man has to do.'

Jess shuddered but was saved from a response by Leanne pounding down the stairs and yanking Darren out of the way.

'Course I want to see them,' she said, thankfully wearing what looked like a dressing gown. 'Come in.'

Chapter Twelve

Martin's email sat in Jess's inbox between an offer for private health care and one from the post room reminding everyone post had to be with them by four in the afternoon.

Martin's email was time-stamped two minutes after she'd put the phone down on him yesterday. She should've expected it after their brief exchange.

'You've changed the locks,' he'd said.

No niceties. No small talk. No questions about her well-being. He'd gone straight to the point.

'All of them.'

She'd taken a deep breath, pinched the bridge of her nose and closed her eyes. 'Yes.'

Where was Maggie's flaming stress ball when she needed something to squeeze? 'I got someone in to do it properly though,' she added defensively, knowing how much Martin hated things not being done right. At least she could head that criticism off at the pass.

He grunted, probably fighting back an urge to make some unpleasant quip. His eyebrow and left side of his mouth would have been twitching. They always did when he was annoyed. Any minute he'd start tapping his fingers.

'I couldn't get in,' he said, eventually. The sentence accompanied by a rhythmical tap.

Frankly, that was a relief, otherwise she'd have had to think about claiming her money back under the terms of the locksmith's "totally secure" guarantee.'

'It's my house.' The tapping got faster and louder.

'Our house,' Jess said. Her words spat out with a steely undertone to them. Her way of warning any sensible person she wasn't happy and they should back off.

'I need—'

Martin was never great at reading the signs.

'Drop me an email with your requirements. I will consider your request and let you know my decision. Within ten working days,' she added, under her breath, her finger poised to disconnect the call.

'You're not—'

'Thank you for your call.'

The next two minutes she spent blocking his number. Martin clearly spent his time crafting a long, loquacious message which he must have sent to both of her email addresses, work and home.

The subject line had one word: "Meeting". Just the word, no punctuation.

'Maggie's triffid is looking good,' Sarah said, throwing her bag across her desk. The strap causing her prized photograph to wobble and fall.

Jess looked up from her computer screen and watched as Sarah scooped it up and checked for damage.

"Dear Sarah. Glad you came. Love you lots too" was scrawled across the middle of a picture of four broody-looking, dark-haired men. The last word, an unrecognisable scrawl was apparently the name of a band Jess had never heard of.

Sarah wiped the picture glass against her jumper and kissed it, before she set if back down in the middle of her desk.

Maggie had no photos on her desk, only the pot plant. Jess was also relieved to see it was still alive. Or at least more alive than it had been yesterday morning, after a weekend in a centrally heated office.

Maggie hadn't commented on the bucket they'd dumped and left it in when she returned that afternoon. Jess ought to find out what the plant was. She didn't believe it was cannabis whatever the guy from technical said. Although if anyone was going to know what cannabis looked like he seemed the sort.

'You okay?' Sarah asked.

'Uh huh,' Jess said.

'Did you get the money?'

'What money?' She dealt with her work emails and deleted the usual junk until only Martin's sat in her inbox. She could mark it as spam, pretend she'd never received it, but somehow she didn't think he was going to go away.

Her foot twitched.

What if he wanted to come home? Jess rubbed at her toes and bit her lip. She needed to know. She double-clicked the message.

‘I’ll make drinks,’ Sarah said. ‘Then you can tell me about the money.’

‘What money?’

No introduction, no salutations. Straight in, but that was Martin, never one to waste time on perfunctory greetings, small talk, or for that matter foreplay of any kind.

The disclaimer on the bottom that said what to do if you weren’t the person he’d sent the email to filled up so much of the screen, it only left enough room for the one line that very succinctly said: “Need to talk. Advise first window for meet. M”.

Picking up a pair of scissors, Jess wished they were a lot sharper and that part of his anatomy was within close range. Any part, she wasn’t fussy.

No kisses, but then there hadn’t been any form of intimate contact between the two of them for a very long time.

She flipped a page on her desk diary. “Today was a total waste of make-up”, the slogan read.

‘You’re not bloody wrong,’ she muttered.

She stared at the email and then at her diary. Diaries didn’t have windows, they had pages. They were not airless dungeons. She wished she could think of some clever sarcastic reply, but she couldn’t.

Some of the pages in her diary were covered with ink, appointments or comments and some weren’t. Okay, apart from work, most weren’t, but she was blowed if she was going to tell him. If he’d decided he’d made a dreadful mistake and wanted to come home, she needed time to think. A week perhaps. She flicked the page. Maybe two; she turned another. Maybe a month, even a year. She didn’t want him back. Not this week, not next week, not ever. She had to tell him that. Then stick to her guns. Say “No” and mean it. Perhaps she would practise. She knew from experience; it wasn’t a word that came easily. If and when it did, the first “Oh please” usually had her doing a U-turn and agreeing to anything anyway.

It would be so much easier to kill or at least permanently maim him. Not something they’d covered in the Learning for Life lessons at school. Maybe they did these days. Divorce and murder had increased considerably since her days in the classroom. She opened up her internet browser and googled, “How to murder your husband” – that should have the technical department concerned. She expected the usual company message about the content having been considered unsuitable for access. It didn’t happen. Instantly over three million results popped up. On the first page alone, she discovered a killer cookbook and invitation to a film seminar guaranteeing to teach any upset housewife how to reclaim her single status quickly and easily.

Upset! She wasn’t upset she was bloody livid. The scissors in her hand were opening and shutting – fast.

‘Okay mad woman, step away from those scissors.’ Sarah put a cup of tea on her desk. In her haste to clear her screen before Sarah saw what she was looking at, Jess snapped the scissors shut. It was one thing wanting to kill Martin, but she didn’t want to advertise the fact. The scissors closed with little resistance, but the computer screen didn’t change.

Sarah giggled. ‘That told it.’

The computer mouse sat on its blue mat, but the wire that stretched across the desk had been cleanly cut through. The mouse end was no longer attached to the computer end. Shit.

‘Great scissors, so sharp.’ Jess dared not look at Sarah. She put them back in her desk tidy and used her keyboard to shut the browser down.

‘Do you want me to see if IT has a spare mouse?’ Sarah sort of squeaked.

And a hand grenade, supply of weedkiller or hosepipe that will fit over the exhaust of Martin’s car. ‘Thanks.’

Sarah was on the phone straight away while Jess typed a brief reply to her ex, sending it before she could change her mind, then deleted both the original and reply.

‘Thanks gorgeous, I knew I could rely on you.’ Sarah blew a kiss and put the phone down. ‘Sorted.’

‘Thanks.’

‘Should I take it they didn’t like the pictures?’

Jess stared at her assistant. ‘What?’

‘Leanne and Darren,’ Sarah said. ‘You won’t talk about the money and something’s clearly wrong. I guess they didn’t like the photos. Didn’t they pay you anything?’

Darren, oh my God, he’d be brilliant. ‘Leanne said she loved the pictures.' Jess pulled a cheque from her pocket. '£150.00.' She waved the small piece of paper in front of Sarah.

'You weren't going to settle for anything less than …'

Jess screwed up her nose and shrugged. 'She drove a hard bargain.' At one point it looked like she wasn't going to get any money, so £150 was good. It had been a learning curve; an experience and you couldn't put a value on that. At least that's what she told herself. 'I'm happy,' she said firmly, although she was anything but.

Neil hadn't been concentrating. He missed the shortcut they usually took back to the office. They ended up walking down the disused railway line which ran past the yacht club. A big mistake – Dudley was attracted to water like magnets to one another. By the time Neil realised how close they were to the pond, Dudley was knee-deep in water and refusing to come out. A wet Newfoundland in a small office wasn't a great idea at the best of times. At least Ross was away on honeymoon and couldn't moan too much, although it might be an idea to stock up with air freshener before he got back.

The morning was beautiful, the sky blue and the early morning fog had started to clear. The view from the top of the bridleway had been stunning. For a few minutes, Neil allowed himself to forget about the proposal he'd been working on pretty much solidly since Friday night.

Which was good, because it had unsettled him.

He'd expected resistance. How would he feel if someone walked into his office and offered him a merger with an anonymous company? He'd have thrown them out by their ear. Frank Moore had seemed grateful to be given a way out. He didn't even seem to think the price would be a problem. It wasn't completely derogatory, but hardly a fair reflection of the company's worth. To that extent Neil had been certain he must have missed something and spent yesterday afternoon and evening checking and rechecking his calculations. Only to find nothing to suggest the figures were anything other than had been reported.

Now he felt guilty for going in with such a low bid. He had never expected it would be accepted. Okay so Frank hadn't said categorically he would take it; he said he needed to talk it over with his accountant. Who, according to the annual reports, was a Jessica Willersey. Neil hoped she could talk some sense into her boss.

It would be normal practice for a counter-offer to be made. For both parties to puff out their chests, make a bit of a song and dance, then agree on something in the middle.

Martin Cowley had suggested it could be a hostile takeover, but as a private limited company with only one shareholder that was never likely.

What if the accountant woman didn't talk Frank into suggesting a higher price or threatening to put the company up for sale and inviting tenders? Could he revise the price upwards in light of the current forecasts and accounts?

He'd not discussed terms with Martin and the original price he'd suggested was at the low end of his budget.

Neil could argue he'd insisted on an exclusivity agreement which had come at a heavy cost while they made all the necessary arrangements for finance and went through due diligence. He'd be right to insist on one. If other companies found out the company was up for sale at a ridiculously low price, they'd be all over Anymoore with better offers.

Counter his own counter-offer. Bloody hell that would be a first. He was well known for his negotiating abilities. His clients loved him for always ensuring they got the best deals. And this would be a fantastic deal. But he'd liked Frank from the moment he met him. Whereas something about Martin Cowley made him uncomfortable.

There had to be a relationship between Frank and Martin he wasn't aware of. A disgruntled ex-employee perhaps? He'd promised his client complete anonymity until contracts were signed so he doubted he'd get a straight answer from Martin. Online enquiries about both companies met with few results. There had been images of Frank when he'd accepted the Redford Business of the Year award, on behalf of Anymoore, the previous year.

He wondered how difficult it would be to persuade Martin that Frank should stay for a reasonable period after the sale to ensure a smooth handover. By the time they reached the small office block, Dudley allowed Neil to rub him down with a towel. It was one of his favourite pastimes; squirming, grabbing the towel and making it as awkward for Neil as possible. Neil couldn't help but smile.

There were six messages from his telephone answering service. Four from Martin Cowley wanting to know what was happening, one from his father, reminding him his mother expected him for lunch on Sunday, and one from Jess Willersey, wanting to arrange a meeting for that morning.

Chapter Thirteen

Muzak played as Sarah led Maggie into the shop, giving the impression they were about to enter a lift rather than a funeral parlour.

A woman in a dark suit, her hair tied back, took them through to a small office with a sofa and poured them a cup of tea. She sat behind a desk, moved a pot of silk flowers out of the way, and explained she was a funeral arranger, with so much head tilting and wide eyes Sarah worried she had balance issues.

'We understand Maggie's mum had a funeral plan,' Sarah said. 'So, everything is paid for?'

'There may be some extras you'd like to talk about.' The woman addressed Maggie rather than Sarah as she pulled from a desk drawer a foolscap brown file and flicked through it. 'We pride ourselves in giving our clients the best help in planning their end of life arrangements to make sure they embark on the next stage of their journey with dignity.'

'Can I see?' Maggie asked, holding her hand out for the file.

'We will go through the options together,' the woman said, moving the file well out of Maggie's reach. 'That way I can talk you through Ms Simpson's wishes, although I am sure there won't be any surprises.'

'No need.' Maggie's arm shot out and she had the file before the woman had a chance to answer, but her calm, sympathetic air slipped along with her false smile.

'Let me get this straight,' Sarah said as she read over Maggie's shoulder. 'You've been paid for the full works, a funeral, a hearse, a limousine, a celebrant, an obscene flower arrangement and a pile of leaflets.'

'Service sheets,' the funeral arranger said. 'Rose was specific about most things. There is an amount of money set aside for a celebrant; she hadn't decided at that time who she wanted to do it.'

'I will,' Sarah said. 'That means you pay me that amount doesn't it?'

The woman had stopped pretending to be kind or caring. 'If that's what the family want,' she snapped.

'And the flowers and the service sheets, Maggie would like to do those too.'

Maggie sat on the chair next to her, squeaking in a slightly alarming way. Sarah patted her knee.

'So, you can give those amounts back too?'

The woman moved a pile of brochures off the desk.

'And the limousine? We're in walking distance of the crematorium – that seems an extortionate amount to pay for someone to drive us round the corner.'

'You don't have to use the car, but that amount would be non-refundable,' the woman said.

'Fine,' Sarah said. 'In that case we will let you know who we need collecting and where from nearer the time.'

'Talking of which,' the woman said, 'we should look at dates.'

'Four weeks,' Sarah said.

'Four weeks?' Maggie repeated, looking slightly surprised.

'Don't worry. We could do it sooner ...' The woman opened a diary. She looked across at Maggie and smiled. 'I know how you feel. You're not alone. Most people want their beloved to begin the next part of their journey as soon as possible. And we can certainly accommodate ...'

'She's not alone. Jess and I are with her,' Sarah said. 'Can you do Wednesday in four weeks' time or not?'

Jess looked at the plate of expensive lemon and white chocolate cookies on the meeting room table. Her stomach rumbled although her appetite was suppressed by the feeling they were a bribe. Frank was trying to soften her up with a plateful of her favourite biscuits so she didn't make a fuss. He was going to take the money on offer. And sooner rather than later. He didn't want anyone sticking spokes into his wheel. He'd had one of the receptionists investigating boat shows this morning. He was already planning a future away from Anymoore Ltd.

Neil Jackson sounded charming on the phone. He apologised for not getting back to her earlier and said he'd like to meet as soon as possible to discuss the next steps. Maybe she should hide the biscuits until she heard what he had to say. She wasn't about to roll over and play dead. He had some serious questions to answer. And if his answers weren't satisfactory, he wasn't getting a cookie.

She placed her files on the meeting room table, choosing a seat from where she could see out of the window and moved the biscuits so anyone sitting opposite might struggle to reach them. She placed the proposal on the table. She had gone through it at least three times since yesterday. There were pencil marks in the margins and a number of multicoloured post-it notes highlighting areas she wanted clarification on. Not least, who the acquiring company was and why this company was in their sights.

She'd tried to talk Frank into asking for more. Jackson Consultancy had made various assumptions which weren't correct. At least the acquirer should pay a fair rate. And if the company wasn't prepared to up the offer then she'd tell Jackson Consultancy, Anymoore wasn't interested in selling. And no biscuits.

Empty threats, she knew. She didn't like the feeling the staff were about to be shafted and if Frank wasn't prepared to ask for a more realistic selling price, then she wanted the redundancy package increased and guaranteed for any staff not wishing to transfer. The company couldn't ensure jobs for life, but a golden parachute deal seemed like the right thing to do. Especially as one of those jobs could well be her own.

A company of any size would have its own accounts department. She'd probably be downgraded. Or pushed sideways for a while then got rid of as soon as possible. The writing was on the wall. She wasn't negotiating a boat deal for Frank, she was negotiating a complete career change for herself.

Leanne had liked the photographs and agreed to some extras. Okay, the price they'd settled on wasn't a fortune but should at least clear the parking fine she'd managed to pick up. Jess smiled. Neil Jackson should thank his lucky stars he wasn't trying to agree the sale with Leanne. She drove a hard bargain.

Leanne said she'd recommend Jess to some of her friends. Darren suggested she could pay them a commission for any recommendations they inspired. After all, word of mouth is cheaper and more reliable than any other form of advertising. Okay, she could have been more enthusiastic about that. If wedding photography was going to become an income stream, could she afford to turn down any work?

She bit into one of the cookies before she realised she'd even picked it up. The bitter lemon and sweet chocolate sensation made her smile. She closed her eyes and savoured the taste and took another bite. Then another and another. The biscuit was soon gone, and Jess opened her eyes to find she was no longer alone.

Instead she must have died and gone to heaven. Her insides started dancing. Her temperature began to rise.

Staring down at her was the hat-rescuer from the wedding. 'Sorry,' he said. 'I didn't mean to wake you.'

'I wasn't asleep,' she said, embarrassed. 'I was eating a biscuit.'

'Jess, you're here already,' Frank said, pushing past the gorgeous man in the doorway, his eyes focussed on the plate of biscuits – no doubt counting them. He knew her too well. 'This is Neil Jackson, from Jackson Consultancy.'

The demigod took a step towards her and held out a hand. 'Pleased to meet you properly.' He smiled. His hand felt real. The tingles running up her arm felt real. 'How did the photos turn out?' he asked.

Chapter Fourteen

Sarah pushed open the library door. Jeez, this place was like a crèche for old people. A line of them sat staring at ancient-looking computers.

She followed the handwritten signs to Family History and walked up to a large desk where an elderly man sat in front of a similarly aged woman. They were studying a document together.

A bell sounded and a crackly voice reminded everyone the library would shut at six. Sarah's watch told her she had half an hour before she'd be thrown out, but she wasn't banking on being there that long.

She'd done well to get there at all. She'd expected Jess to insist she made up the time from this morning; the woman was a stickler for punctuality. She didn't make a great deal of fuss if you were a few minutes late, as long as you made the time up. And the appointment at the funeral directors had meant both she and Maggie had effectively taken a two-hour lunch break. So, she'd expected some argument when she'd said "Goodbye". At least a token protest. She'd spent most of the afternoon thinking up excuses, but Jess had just smiled and said, "See you tomorrow". Weird.

Document-man pushed his glasses up on top of his head and lifted the papers closer to his face, presumably to have a better look. Sarah let out a loud sigh and fiddled with her notebook. Why couldn't the woman give him a photocopy, or better still let him take it back to one of the other tables?

No one else was waiting in the queue, if there had been, it would have been karma and not meant to happen. Sarah would call it a day and disappear. It was a ridiculous idea. But then the day was getting more ridiculous by the minute. Had she really agreed to conduct a funeral for Maggie's mother? A woman she didn't know from Adam. She knew little about Maggie either, other than her being sixty-two, having green fingers and being an ace when it came to filing systems. She didn't suffer fools gladly and liked her tea strong.

She'd need a lot more if she was going to be able to produce a passable funeral service for Maggie's mother. If the tables were turned, would Maggie fare better if asked about her?

The only funeral Sarah had attended had been her mother's sister. Was it a bad thing she couldn't remember any of it? Only that they went to the pub at the end of the road for the wake afterwards and there had been some row as to what Aunty Claire would have wanted done with her car and jewellery which ended up with her mother and her other aunt coming to blows and having to be separated by her father. Then Aunty Claire's husband, too drunk to care, made inappropriate comments along the lines of, "May the best woman win" and being prepared to be the victor's prize.

Maybe while she was in the library, she could find a "Funeral arranging for dummies" book to borrow.

Even weirder, at some point that afternoon, she'd agreed to let Maggie and Jess arrange five dates for her. She'd promised she wouldn't date anyone else until she'd been on at least one date with all of their five. Where had that come from? Even they'd looked surprised as she'd agreed. It was a moment of madness. Where were they going to find five potential dates? What if it took them ages? Did they seriously expect her to hang about and not date anyone else? The only stipulations they'd accepted were no one from work, no one older than her by more than ten years and no criminal record. Two months. She would give them a time limit of two months. She'd tell them tomorrow. She couldn't put her love life on hold indefinitely. After that they had to agree she could date whomever she chose.

A younger man walked behind the counter, put some cards back in a small drawer and turned around.

'Can I help?' He smiled. Sarah turned and checked because it would be her luck that he was talking to someone else. No one else there.

'Err yes,' she said. 'I hope so.' He wasn't someone who could rely on his good looks to help him sail through life, but he'd a cute smile.

He indicated a chair in front of the desk. She grabbed her bag and moved forward.

'I'm um looking for someone,' she said. *And you look well interesting.* 'Only I don't know where to start, so if you could point me in the right direction ...'

'Who have you lost?' he asked as he entered something into his computer, stared at his screen for a minute before focussing on her.

Nice eyes.

'Not me,' she said, nervously under his intense stare. *I've promised I won't look at another man for two months without my colleagues' permission.* 'Asking for a friend.'

He nodded. 'And this friend, what do they know about the missing person?'

'Just his name.'

'Good start, unless it's John Smith.' His eyes creased as he smiled again.

She swallowed. 'Arthur Francis Warburton.'

'Date of birth? Place he lived? Or might have lived?'

The bell sounded with the reminder that it was early closing and the request that documents be taken back to the collection points.

The woman next to her was gathering up the man's documents. He'd stopped looking interested in the papers and was now watching Sarah.

'I don't know.' She pushed her chair back and went to get up. 'Look, it was a bad idea. Sorry, for wasting your time.'

'Please,' the man said. 'You're not. It's a bit more of a challenge than usual. Why are you asking?'

'He's my friend's father,' Sarah said. 'I was trying to help.'

'And they …'

'She. She didn't know he existed until yesterday when she discovered his name on her birth certificate.'

'Okay,' he said, pulling a notepad across the desk. 'So what age is your friend and where was she born.'

Sarah found the photograph she'd taken of Maggie's certificate and passed her phone across.

'Five minutes,' the tannoy announced, interrupting her thoughts.

'I can come back,' Sarah said. *In two months' time.*

'It's all right, you're here now.' He reached for her phone, his hand briefly touching hers.

A jolt of warmth ran up her arm. Then she noticed the ring on his wedding finger. 'Good,' she said, putting on an overly bright smile, to cover the disappointment she felt.

This was ridiculous. Why on earth was she there? She wasn't sure how Maggie would react if she knew what she was doing now. She'd justified it on the basis of if it was me, I'd want to know. She hadn't even asked Jess for advice. Well, you could hardly approach your boss and say, hey, I've photographed Maggie's birth certificate with my phone when she wasn't looking, and now I'm going to see if I can find her dad.

The man scratched his nose. 'The certificate format changed after 1968. Prior to that there were multiple entries on each page of the register book. It had been like that since registration began in 1837, but from 1969, one entry per page and those gave a little more information – parents' place of birth, that sort of thing. All the important details. We know both parents signed the register page, so they weren't married. Arthur's middle name might help us find him more easily. So now comes the interesting bit.' He typed furiously onto his computer keyboard. 'Yes, I thought so.'

He looked pleased with himself. Sarah wished he'd share his findings with her, so she could get out of there.

The man looked up. 'Local family,' he said. 'He lived in Templeton until he died.'

No one at work knew Martin had left. That was okay – Jess wasn't ready to talk about it yet. It wasn't something she could just drop into regular conversation. 'Have you received the goods received notes from maintenance yet, oh and by the way, Martin's gone.'

She looked down at her notepad, now covered with an interesting doodle, but not the list Maggie had asked her for.

Concentrate.

She knew Sarah wouldn't be happy until she knew every last detail about the break-up. Maggie might pretend not to be interested, but little passed her by.

She didn't mention Martin often, but she couldn't leave it much longer. Neither woman was stupid. They must have noticed something had changed, especially if he was going to start leaving messages with the switchboard about estate agents needing her keys to value the house, and she was going to spend her afternoons mooning about a stranger. Only he wasn't a stranger any more. She knew his name. Neil Jackson. It suited him.

She'd tried to come across as the ultimate professional while they sat together and discussed his proposal. Tricky, after he'd accused her of being asleep when he arrived and a difficult act to pull off when your brain goes fuzzy and disconnects from your mouth; or when every nerve in your body tells you you're in close proximity to an incredibly hot man.

'Earth to Jess.'

Maggie was watching her. 'Are you away with the fairies? Did you hear a word I said?'

'I'm listening,' Jess said defensively, chewing the end of her pen. She looked down at the sheet of paper, full of writing – all crossed out for one reason or another. 'We're looking for a professional man, six-foot-tall, give or take three inches, twenty-five to thirty years of age. Who doesn't live with his mother.'

'With a decent-sized bank account,' Maggie said. 'No criminal record.'

'Which star sign is she looking for?'

Maggie raised an eyebrow. 'That requirement changes on a daily basis. Personally, I'd steer clear of Gemini and Scorpio, but it's not me you're talking about.'

'Skills?' Jess put her pen down. 'If we were, what would you say about your talents?'

'Nothing special.' Maggie shook her head. 'Nobody would be interested in my ability to take minutes or keep the filing up to date. And if they were, they're probably not the sort of person I'd want to meet.'

Jess smiled. 'Don't put yourself down. Have you seen Sarah's minute-taking recently?'

Maggie smiled back. 'Didn't she just draw pin people having a punch up last month? Which I'm sure more than adequately reflected the tone of the meeting.' She sounded as if she was fighting not to laugh.

Jess didn't bother hiding her amusement either. 'The tone maybe, just not the points raised. But back to Sarah's personal statement. How about "Can't cook, won't cook; but cocktails and cookies with an adventurous fun-loving man are my idea of a perfect meal"?'

Maggie shrugged.

'Good sense of humour essential.'

'Athletic build, under thirty, professional, required for a …'

'Go on, you were doing well up until that point.' Jess stared out of the window.

'Loving, playful individual, who needs firm handling to reach her full potential,' Maggie mumbled.

The car park had all but cleared. Jess checked her watch; nearly six o'clock. 'You realise who would make a perfect match for Sarah, don't you?' she said.

Maggie clicked the top of her pen. 'Young Harry in Customer Services. Except he's on the top of her definite "not if he was the last man on earth" list.'

'If we so much as suggest a date with him, she'll have a hissy fit and we won't hear the last of it. It's been hard enough to persuade her to let us choose her next five dates.'

'She doesn't think I know what she needs anyway. How could I? I'm old enough to be her mother.'

'Sarah thinks of you as a friend and colleague, you know she does,' Jess said. 'She values your opinion. This isn't about age …'

'Her mother is actually younger than me.'

'And even flakier than Sarah from what I can gather. The woman drinks heavily and has had a stream of unsuitable men on the go. Sarah left home as soon as she could. I don't think it's a rift that's ever healed properly. She trusts you. It's your approval she needs.'

Maggie studied her biro. 'I don't want her getting hurt again,' she said, quietly. 'Or ending up lonely.'

She didn't say "like me" but the way her shoulders drooped made it clear that's what she meant.

'She has so much life.'

'Come on, we can pick this up in the morning.' Jess squeezed Maggie's arm. 'Are you busy this evening?'

'I might take some of mother's books to Treetops. They're likely to have more use for them than me.'

Jess watched Maggie clear her desk and go. Age-wise, there were three years between Maggie and Frank, but while he was longing to pilot his own yacht around the Caribbean, Maggie wanted to keep working until she dropped.

Jess sighed and pulled the merger proposal towards her. She needed to be sure provision had been made for them all in the new company. This wasn't a matter of financial compensation; this was a matter of mental well-being, wasn't it? She drummed her fingers on the table, itching to let them phone the number on the business card. She wanted to talk to Neil Jackson. Never mind her future, there was something about him she wanted to get to know better.

Chapter Fifteen

Maggie could put the three pairs of pants that, from the name written in black felt pen across the back of them, plainly didn't belong to her mother, in an envelope and send them back to the nursing home anonymously. Then she could spend the evening watching *Great British Bake Off*, or some other cookery programme, with a sherry and maybe have an early night. No one would expect anything else.

Her mother had been dead for two days. She'd been at Treetops for the best part of two months. But before then, she was usually in bed by eight. Evenings weren't something they'd ever spent together. So why did the emptiness suddenly hang so heavy?

Maggie added the pants to the box in the hall and picked up her car keys.

When she'd cleared her mother's room, she'd mentioned her mother's book collection to John, the care home manager. He'd said they could never get enough books. She hoped he was right; she'd filled four boxes already, hardbacks and paperbacks, large print and small print. For all her faults, her mother was an avid reader.

The car was reserved for high days, holidays or hospital appointments. Maggie never went far, and the bicycle was her preferred mode of transport whatever the weather and the cycle paths around Redford made even night-time travel safe. She'd never joined the gym, even with the corporate membership discount her length of service afforded her. She didn't see the point. Her daily exercise was her bike. No worries about parking spaces; always a lamp post she could padlock it to, and she relished the extra time a journey took. The bike shop in town took care of any repairs and the small basket which sat proudly in front of her handlebars was big enough for a small amount of shopping, but tonight, filling it with her own bodyweight in books was not an option.

A tense psychological thriller fell out of one of the boxes. She flicked through it and snorted. 'Give me a romance any day,' she muttered, loading it and the boxes into the car. She turned the key in the ignition and gave her usual silent prayer that the car engine would remember how to work and not let her down. It did and roared into life.

Treetops was a one-storey building, not a tree house. It sat at the end of a private road, lined by elm trees. In the gaps, where a storm and Dutch elm disease had destroyed a number of trees some years back, bushes had been planted, their random colour and sizes adding to the charm of the quiet drive.

Maggie always enjoyed the three minutes it took her to cycle from the gates to the house. Today, even at the recommended ten miles per hour, she did it in a fraction of the time. It was almost half past six when she pulled into the one empty parking space next to a red Ford.

'Put them down there will you?' John, the home manager, said as she staggered in with the first box. 'Afraid I can't help.' He held up his hands, both covered in something white that looked a lot like flour.

Maggie put the box down in the space he indicated. 'Have you been cooking?'

'Been?' He raised his eyes. 'I still am. The chef didn't turn up this morning and it's Tuesday.'

'Tuesday?'

'They have roast on Tuesdays. If they don't, things get ugly and – well how difficult can a roast be?'

'For how many?'

'Thirty. Before you say anything, I know. Bloody impossible.'

Maggie smiled.

'Frankly I'm running a bit behind.' He shrugged and looked at the large clock over the kitchen door. 'See, it's gone half six – most are already at their tables. I will be at least another half an hour – they'll riot. I know they will. You'll read all about it in the nationals later in the week: "Home Manager savaged by Violent Nonagenarians".'

Maggie looked through the hatch into the dining room and giggled. A toothless crone grinned back at her and another elderly man hobbled across the room, heading for a table by the window. 'That lot riot?'

'It's not a pretty sight.' John started back towards the kitchen.

'Have you got any sherry?' Maggie asked.

'Good idea, we'll get drunk.' He pushed open the kitchen door with his shoulder and held it so Maggie could follow him into the room. A roasting tray of blackened potatoes sat on top of the oven.

'Not us. Give them a sherry. A small one. It can be an aperitif.'

Maggie opened the door to the dining room a crack so she could see in. More people were taking their seats, some immediately started fiddling with serviettes, or the salt and pepper shakers. John came up behind her. He was so close, his breath warmed the back of her neck.

One of the table sitters spotted a movement at the door and started making her way towards the kitchen at breakneck speed, waving a walking stick around in front of her. Maggie backed up, straight into John.

'Sherry or riots, you're right,' he said. 'It's in the cupboard over there. There are glasses in the corridor. I don't suppose …'

'Absolutely not. Give me your apron, you deal with that lot. I'll sort out the kitchen.'

'I could kiss you,' he said and the lines on his face seemed to fall away as he smiled at her. 'You're an angel.'

Maggie blushed. No one had ever said they could kiss her before. 'Go on with you. Now go and let me finish cremating the potatoes.' She turned away before he could say anything else, conscious of a warm feeling sneaking up through her body.

Maggie put the last clean plate on the trolley and the last tea towel into the laundry basket. It was nearly nine by the time they'd cleared the meal away, washed up and laid the tables ready for the following morning's breakfast. The residents, still awake, were in the lounge playing bingo.

'You have no idea how grateful I am.' John handed her a mug of tea. 'Let's go through to my office.'

She followed him along a maze of corridors until he showed her into a dingy room. Its only window overlooked the car park. The office, he said, used to be a bedroom, but it was the room furthest away from the kitchen and the constant smell of cabbage, so he'd claimed it as soon as he started there.

'It's supposed to be only temporary,' he said as he switched on a light.

'What happened to the old manager's room,' she asked, remembering how large and well-lit it used to be. He looked at her and sighed, clearly debating whether to say anything or not. 'An elderly couple. They wanted to be together. Well, we're not a workhouse. And this isn't too bad. I don't spend long in here. And it does have one benefit.'

Maggie took a sip of her tea and raised an eyebrow. 'It does?'

'I get some down time as frivolous things don't often merit the journey.'

John pulled out a chair and indicated she should sit. 'Thanks for the books, by the way. I'll put them out in the day room tomorrow. How are you coping?'

Maggie didn't like talking about herself or answering direct questions. 'Fine,' she said, staring at the mug, so she didn't have to make eye contact with him.

'Any news about the arrangements yet?' he asked.

'You mean funeral arrangements? It's going to be at the crematorium in four weeks' time.'

'Would you mind if I came and I expect a number of staff will want to be there too.'

'Really?' Maggie looked up; he was smiling at her.

'I know you two didn't have the closest of relationships,' he said. 'But it's difficult when a family member dies, there is always so much to do and sort out. You should allow yourself time to grieve. If you ever want to talk, you know where I am.'

They drank their tea in silence. Maggie enjoyed the companionship, but she didn't need therapy. She didn't want to admit she felt empty, but otherwise not upset. If anything, it was a relief. Did that make her a terrible person? "Not the closest of relationships". John didn't know the half of it. She finished the drink quicker than she would've liked. But once it was finished, she felt a little awkward sitting there with an empty mug, so she made to get up.

'Look, let me take you out for a meal to say thank you properly for tonight,' John said, suddenly.

'There's no need, I enjoyed it,' Maggie said.

John looked as if he was about to argue when the doorknob rattled and the door swung open. Both of them turned as an elderly woman clutching a letter in one hand made a beeline for John.

'Edna, whatever's wrong?' he asked.

'This.' She held the letter still, only long enough for John to take it.

'It's addressed to you,' he said. 'It looks like your neighbour's writing. It doesn't look like there's anything wrong. I don't think you need to worry. If there had been I'm sure she would've phoned.'

‘What?’

‘If something was wrong, she would have phoned,’ John said, this time louder. Much louder.

‘I know that, I know that,’ Edna said, her voice seemed to drip sarcasm.

‘So why have you given it to me?’ he asked.

‘What?’

John lifted up the woman’s hair and shouted the question in her ear.

She turned and faced him. ‘I’ve lost my glasses. You’ll have to read it. Something might be wrong.’ Turning back, she tilted her head slightly and looked at Maggie. ‘Your new strumpet, I suppose,’ she said. ‘Do you speak English?’ she added, this time addressing the question slowly and loudly to Maggie.

For the first time in as long as she could remember, Maggie laughed. And once she’d started, she couldn’t stop.

Chapter Sixteen

Sarah followed the nine o'clock funeral party into the crematorium chapel and sat in a middle row. She didn't want to look out of place. She picked up a service sheet and concentrated on it, to avoid engaging in conversation with her neighbours.

Robert Timothy Latton, ninety years old. The picture was of a much younger man, clearly taken many years ago. He looked kind. An organist played an upbeat number which according to the service sheet was the "Maple Leaf Rag".

The doors at the back of the chapel opened. Sarah turned around to watch as they were asked to stand for the arrival of the coffin.

A woman in a navy dress, walked next to a man in striped trousers and a top hat. She carried a folder and looked straight ahead but matched his stride step for step. Behind them six men carried the coffin on their shoulders. They reached the front of the chapel and slid the coffin on to what looked like a table with rollers built in. The woman and the top-hatted man stepped to one side. The six men took a step back; everyone bowed. The woman walked to the lectern and arranged her folder as the bearers and the top-hatted man left the room. Once the door had closed, the woman nodded to the organist who came to the end of the phrase he was playing. Sarah watched expectantly as the woman smiled at the congregation.

'Good morning, please be seated,' she said and waited before continuing. 'My name is Audrey. I am an independent celebrant and Robert's family has asked me to lead this service today. It is, of course, my pleasure and privilege to do so.'

The woman, Audrey, left a generous pause as she checked the folder in front of her, before saying, 'Ladies and Gentlemen, I would like to wish you all a warm welcome here today to celebrate the life of Robert Timothy Latton, a kind, generous man who lived life with both a smile and a story to tell. A man who liked his tea sweet and his wine white and medium-dry.'

Another pause. A number of the congregation chuckled. Sarah guessed they could all remember sharing a glass or two with him. She wished she had a pencil; she could do with making notes.

'We are here today to acknowledge and remember everything Robert meant to each one of us as we give thanks for his life and say our goodbyes.

'We think at this time of those closest to him – especially his younger sisters.' Audrey smiled at two ladies sitting in the front row. 'Ladies, we will hold you in our thoughts and prayers over the coming months as you come to terms with your loss.'

She looked up at the congregation. 'As a child,' she said, 'several hundred years ago, in his own words, Robert was the lead singer in his local church choir, but he was not religious and saw death as an unknown quantity. He didn't think of it as something to be afraid of. Neither had he ruled out the possibility of being reunited in spirit with loved ones, particularly his beloved wife Eileen, whom he lost to ovarian cancer and all his adored dogs, nor the possibility that the end of life might be just that – and bring with it the possibility of welcome eternal rest. Robert didn't know the answer and neither do we. We only know everything that is born, dies. You all have your own thoughts and beliefs on what happens next. Whatever the outcome, the Robert we knew will never die, but live forever in all our hearts and memories.

'Our service today was created with his input. We will listen to music, hear about his life and listen to some poems as we bring him centre-stage one last time. Robert will stay with us throughout the entire service. Only once everyone has departed will he continue on his final journey. The curtains will not be closed and at the end of the service, his sisters will say their goodbyes by placing flowers on his coffin and invite you, on your way out to do the same.'

The eulogy charted Robert's life. There were two poems and a Katherine Jenkins song played while the congregation reflected on their own memories. Goodbyes were said and everyone invited back to the family home to share refreshments, memories and a glass or two of Pinot Grigio.

Audrey asked the congregation to join in with Robert's favourite song, Dean Martin's rendition of "Little Ole Wine Drinker Me", on their way out. The man with the top hat was back. He opened the door of the chapel, waited until Dean had sung the first chorus, before handing flowers to the sisters and indicating where they should place them on their way out.

Sarah checked her watch. The service took twenty minutes from start to finish. She took her place in the line of family and friends who shuffled past the celebrant. 'Thank you for coming,' she said to Sarah and then immediately turned her attention to the next person.

Maggie hadn't looked convinced she could do it, but having seen what was involved, Sarah knew she could. In fact, she'd been surprised by how moving she found the service. She meant it when she told Audrey it was a lovely ceremony. She would need to sit down with Maggie and talk about her mother's life but figured she could put together a decent tribute and service sheet. The money they saved from the celebrant, printing and flowers should more than cover the wake afterwards.

Sarah briefly considered taking Robert's family up on their offer to return to his family home to see what sort of food might be needed, but she ought to get back to work. Doctor's appointment excuses should never be extended beyond a credible length and she needed to have a quick word with the crematorium office.

Chapter Seventeen

It took Jess a second to orientate herself when she got to the park entrance. The smell of bacon wafted across to her. Some runners were about. And a few dog walkers.

She wasn't sure until she saw him walking towards her that she'd got the right gate. If her eyes hadn't recognised him immediately, the butterflies dancing round her stomach and the warm tingly sensation running everywhere else, intimated the rest of her body had.

'Hi,' Neil said, raising a hand with a dog lead in it. 'Thanks for coming.'

At first, he looked to be on his own. There were a number of loose dogs, any one of which could have been his. Jess didn't think the long-haired dachshund was his. He turned in the direction of the trees and whistled. There followed a sound of snapping branches, and suddenly the largest, fluffiest dog she'd ever seen pushed his way out of the undergrowth. He looked across to Neil, wagged his tail, but didn't hurry to join him, although he did set off in the right direction at a lolloping pace.

'Can I get you something to eat or drink?' Neil said as he got closer. His dog, seemingly less concerned about personal space, walked straight up to her, leaned against her leg and pushed a wet nose into her hand.

'Dudley, meet Jess.'

She bent down and stroked the dog's head. 'Hello, Dudley. Have you finished your walk?' The question was answered with a wag of the tail.

'Almost,' Neil added. 'We normally get a coffee at this point, maybe a bacon roll. In fine weather we go back to that bench up there by the bridge and eat it while I check my emails before we walk back.'

Jess looked to where he was pointing.

'How are you for time? Can I tempt you to join us?'

Jess nodded. Food would be sensible. She skimmed the menu on reaching the van, but the smell of bacon was too strong to ignore. 'A bacon roll, please,' she said.

'Make that two,' Neil said.

She reached into her bag for her purse, but he stopped her.

'My treat. It's the least I can do after dragging you out of the office.

It's just that I'm tied up most of the day and it sounded urgent. And if this old man doesn't get his daily exercise, all hell can break loose.'

Dudley was at Neil's feet with his eyes shut. Jess couldn't imagine him being responsible for anything breaking loose. 'You didn't drag me.' She smiled. 'I like the idea of an alfresco meeting. Who knows, it may catch on.'

'I'd like that,' Neil said, his lips curving into a smile, which if she hadn't been leaning against the coffee van at the time would probably have floored her.

'It's always tricky to find an office at Anymoore when you need one.'

The man in the van wrapped two bacon rolls in serviettes and put them on the counter next to two cardboard drinks containers. He wiped his hands on his apron and handed Neil a credit card machine. 'Milk and sugar on the table,' he added, as the machine sprung into life and generated a receipt. Jess took that as their cue to move out of the way and gathered up the cups. Yesterday, Neil had taken his coffee white, so she added milk to both cups.

The sky was grey with no sign of the sun, but Jess felt pleasantly warm as they walked up to the bench on the bridge. The ramshackle bridge looked like it had seen better days and was off the beaten track. A signpost they passed indicated that the pale golden track was the circular route round the lake, while the bridge itself, the bench and the waste bin were marked as a picnic area. The view was spectacular. Jess felt relaxed and happy as they ate their rolls in friendly silence.

'You get used to seeing the same people day in, day out,' Neil said. 'See the man over there with the headband on? He's a high court judge. I overheard him in a restaurant once telling his companions that he runs two laps of the lake every morning. He doesn't. He only does one at the most and at more of a walk than a run. Dudley's better at recognising people than I am. Dog walkers only tend to know each other by their dogs' names. See that little white Yorkshire terrier? That's Jethro and the man over there, he's his owner. He's known to most people as Mr Jethro.'

Dudley pricked up his ears, turned his head in the direction Neil pointed and was off.

'Do you need to go after him? Shall I hold your drink?'

Neil shook his head. 'Mr Jethro carries treats. Dudley will be given three and then come back.' They sat and watched as Dudley sat in front of the man, looking fixedly at his hand, the Yorkshire terrier sat beside him. Treats were counted out. The man held up his hands to indicate no more and looked over. Neil raised his own in greeting.

'He's gorgeous,' Jess said.

'Who? Mr Jethro?' Neil's head snapped round to face her. 'Don't tell me you are some sort of fetish queen who likes middle-aged men in lycra.' His grin told her he was teasing and made her feel even warmer.

'Dudley,' she said and playfully punched his arm.

'Be careful,' Neil said. 'At this rate, he'll insist on coming home with you.'

'Mr Jethro?' Jess grinned. 'In my dreams.'

Neil wound down the car window to get some fresh air and to stop the rest of the windows from steaming up.

'You're telling me, we've been given the green light to go ahead?'

Another day, another wet Newfoundland. The second time Dudley had gone after a stick, he'd excelled himself, going for total submersion in the lake, to the point that even Neil started to worry. Thankfully, just when it looked as if Jess planned on jumping in to rescue his dog, Dudley emerged holding not the stick, but a deflated football, and covered in algae. He'd looked exceptionally pleased with himself.

Neil had been relieved, but equally had enjoyed the sensation of Jess clinging to his arm, and of warmth spreading through his body. It twisted his stomach into strange knots and went the instant she took her hand away to make a fuss of his dog.

'I am saying,' Neil clarified, 'if you are prepared to make the offer suggested, I've been led to believe it will be favourably received.' His good mood and humour had since been dampened almost as much as Dudley, not by an expanse of water, but by the conversation with Martin Cowley.

'How do we push this forward?' Cowley said.

Neil sighed. 'There are a number of conditions.'

'Is Ross there?'

'He's on his honeymoon. I don't think any of us thought this would move so quickly, but the owner is keen to sell for the right price. I will list out the conditions and the offer I think you should make. If you want to go ahead, I'm happy to push it forward for you and get contracts drawn up. Or if you'd rather, you can wait for Ross to get back and we can discuss it then.'

Neil puffed. No way was he going to let Ross in on the deal at this stage. He could manage the merger when he got back, but Neil wanted to make sure contracts were in place before then. He'd made certain promises to Jess and he wasn't going to let her down.

'I've told them I would expect to make a formal offer before the end of this week and asked for a week's exclusivity to enable us to carry out due diligence and make sure everything stacks up, but the company has indicated it is only prepared to sell at the price we discussed subject to their staff receiving certain guarantees.'

'I told you how much I was prepared to pay. You're suggesting more.'

'Your calculations were based on last year's accounts. The offer isn't a great deal more because the owner is keen for a quick sale too, but he is insisting on using a higher Profit/Earnings ratio to determine the price and a guaranteed exit package for existing staff who don't wish to transfer, put in place.'

'Guaranteed?'

That had been Neil's reaction when Jess first suggested it. 'Effectively a golden parachute clause. Your intention should be to merge two companies and not make anyone redundant, but we know there's no point in the administrative functions of two companies doubling up, that there are bound to be some adjustments down the line. Staff are given time to decide whether they are a hundred per cent behind the transfer or wish to leave. It's a win-win situation. Those that want to jump ship get a generous package and you get a fully committed work force at an extremely competitive price.'

Neil didn't know Jess well enough to ask if she might take that option rather than transfer. She had refused to divulge any names. Until everything was signed, sealed and delivered, it wasn't appropriate to discuss any member of staff. 'Most staff would be glad to work for a new dynamic company, so I don't anticipate the majority of them being interested in leaving,' she'd said.

Martin didn't say anything.

Neil could picture him at the other end of the phone getting hot under the collar. Time to strike the killer blow. 'I understand there's been interest from other quarters.'

'Other quarters?'

'I spoke to the accountant who mentioned Frank is talking to someone else.' *Okay, what Jess had actually said, was Frank had an appointment with a financial consultant about his retirement.*

'That's why I suggest an exclusivity agreement and we get an offer on the table as soon as possible if you are serious about …'

'Of course, I'm bloody serious. This is a company I can take to the next level.'

'All the more reason to put forward a sensible offer.' *Was this a good time to mention that the building was a single floor?*

'Do they know who I am?'

'Not from me.' Neil rubbed the bridge of his nose. 'Perhaps if you explained why this company …'

'No.'

Neil would have dearly loved to put down the phone and walk away. He'd had difficult clients before. He tried to believe he was hanging on because this was Ross's friend. 'Okay,' he said, slowly. 'I agreed I wouldn't mention your name in connection with the merger and I haven't. Obviously if and when contracts are signed, that information will be there for all to see.'

He could tell the man Jackson Consultancy wasn't interested in representing him and walk away. But Martin would find another company. They'd probably make the lower offer and someone else would end up dealing with Jess Willersey.

Neil's father's mantra of "never mix business with pleasure" sounded in his head. This week had had a number of pleasurable moments. He smiled at the thought of Jess with her eyes shut, eating cookies. And Jess sitting on the bench, coffee in one hand, bacon roll in the other looking happy and relaxed.

Chapter Eighteen

'I'm telling you this is Jess's house – 42 Broadwater Close.' Sarah dropped the leaflet on Maggie's desk. She kept one eye on the office door. 'I recognised it, so I went in and asked for details. I told them my parents were looking to move into the area.'

The woman hadn't looked convinced when Sarah asked about the three-bedroomed house in the window but had taken her name and address and handed over a pile of glossy brochures for a number of houses that she felt "may interest your parents too".

'That's why you're late, is it?' Maggie looked at the leaflet, and went back to the *Redford Chronicle*. 'I thought you must've gone down with something. It's been like an upper deck of the bleeding Marie Celeste here this morning.'

'You've not been busy if you've got time to read the local paper,' Sarah said. 'Anything interesting?'

Maggie sniffed and moved the paper to one side of her desk. 'Where have you been? And don't tell me the estate agents.'

'Oh, you know, things to do.' Picking up the date stamp, Sarah turned her attention to the pile of envelopes on her desk. It wasn't the right time to discuss her crematorium visit.

Don't look up. She couldn't afford to catch Maggie's eye; she had a way of wheedling information out of her. Concentrate on the post. She opened and stamped the first half a dozen letters before she asked, 'Where's Jess?'

'A meeting. Didn't seem to think it would take long, but I haven't seen her since first thing this morning.'

The sounds coming from the other side of the desk sounded as if Maggie had picked up the paper and was flicking through it again.

'Do you think she's showing people round her house?'

'No. She said she was meeting that consultant fellow again.'

'Has she mentioned anything to you about moving?'

'What's this – twenty questions?' Maggie was focussed entirely on the paper

'What's in the paper?'

'Nothing.' Maggie shut the paper quickly, but not before Sarah realised it was either the advertisements or obituaries she was reading.

'Have the funeral directors put your mother's obituary in there?'

'No.'

'Are you looking for another job?'

'Don't be ridiculous.' Maggie stood up and fussed with the pot plant on her desk.

Sarah knew her well enough to recognise a distraction technique when she saw it. She was interested in something in the paper that for some reason she was keeping quiet about.

'Have you finished the post yet?' Maggie asked as she removed a dead leaf.

Change the subject. Sarah smiled. Okay, she could play that game too. She'd wait until Maggie left the room and then take a look.

'Perhaps they're having financial difficulties. Maybe they're going to downsize. What is that plant by the way?'

'Scarlet Hibiscus,' Maggie said, cutting off another two leaves. You went over to Jess's last weekend, didn't you? Are you sure you didn't see an estate agent's board?'

'No,' Sarah said, indignantly. 'I'm not completely stupid.'

'Nothing complete about you.' Maggie moved the plant back to its normal spot and sat back down as if waiting for a response.

Sarah stamped two more pieces of post harder than before. 'They were having a clear out. One room was completely empty. Jess said something about decorating.'

'Sounds plausible. I clear out a room if I'm decorating. What did Martin say?'

'He wasn't there.' Sarah frowned. 'Jess said he was away for the weekend, but I think he's gone for good. Either that or he's buried in the garden.'

'Just finish the post Miss Marple. Pass me the invoices, you check the statements.'

'We should tell her we know, shouldn't we?' Sarah passed the largest pile across the desk.

'What, that we think she's killed Martin? That should go down well.'

'You could bring him into the conversation. See how she reacts.'

‘What you mean like – Jess, how many people have you killed?’

‘No.’ Sarah frowned. ‘You’ll need to be more subtle than that.’

‘Okay,’ Maggie said. ‘I have an invoice here for spanners. I wonder how much Martin pays for his?’

‘What do we need spanners for?’ Sarah’s head shot up. ‘Who ordered them?’

Maggie grinned. ‘So, come on, why are you late today?’

Shit. The boardroom was full.

Jess had forgotten the management meeting had been rescheduled for 10.30 a.m.

Everyone looked animated enough. They were in full swing, clearly coping, they didn’t need her. Frank knew about the meeting with Neil, just not where it was.

It had been nice. Jess smiled. More than nice. They could’ve had the conversation on the phone, except he was out walking and the signal in the park kept cutting out. They’d lost the connection for the third time when she received a text. ‘Bench on the bridge – fifteen minutes?’ It was on her way back to the office that she’d wondered if he’d meant the signal was better there and he’d ring her when he got there, but face to face was easier. He’d looked pleased to see her and she’d have been back in plenty of time if he hadn’t suggested a walk round the lake after their bacon roll.

To be fair, it wasn’t far. The bit that delayed her was persuading Dudley back out of the water. Remembering the dog, stood in the middle of the lake, wagging his tail slowly, a large branch in his mouth, made her chuckle. He’d come close enough for Neil to grab one end, but it had taken both of them pulling to free it. They’d ended up collapsed on the bank, soaked but laughing, something which seemed to delight the dog even more.

Jess took her hand off the door handle and the door clattered shut, everyone inside looked up and stopped talking.

Frank beckoned her in.

Double shit.

‘Morning.’ Jess forced a smile.

Frank nodded. His confused expression implied he’d noticed she’d been home and got changed. She’d had to; algae splattered trousers weren't a great look, whatever Neil said. No one else said a word, even Sarah didn't look up. *Not a good sign.*

Frank waited until she'd sat down before he looked down at his pad. 'Okay, next item on the agenda, number four – car park lighting. Who wants to kick off?'

Something caught Jess's tights as she pulled her chair up to the table. A ladder shot up her leg with frightening speed. *Triple shit.*

'Have I missed much?' she whispered to Sarah as Izzie launched into a vitriolic rant, using words like dangerous, policy, responsibility and health and safety.

'Yes,' Sarah said and pushed a pad across to Jess. 'You're late and were supposed to be taking the minutes.'

The date was written on the top corner of the page, but nothing else.

'Anything happened I should know about?' she asked.

Sarah shrugged. From the way she was slouched in her chair, she probably had a magazine on her lap, either that or she'd contracted some strange spinal disease overnight. She would've said, wouldn't she? Was that why she'd needed time off? A doctor's appointment? Her text message hadn't said why she was going to be late.

'Everything okay this morning?' she asked quietly, trying not to attract attention.

'No, it's flaming not.' Sarah's eyes blazed.

Izzie stopped mid rant and looked round. 'I think you'll find I'm right.' She glowered at Sarah. 'If you'll let me finish.'

'Was the advert in the *Redford Chronicle* your idea or Maggie's?' Sarah hissed.

'I have no idea what you're talking about,' Jess muttered, through gritted teeth and a forced smile.

'How about "Wanted Perfect Partner for Adventurous, Fun and Food-Loving Girl".'

Jess froze. Oh my God, Maggie had only gone and done it. They'd talked about advertising, but they'd been joking, hadn't they? They'd talked about setting up profiles on dating sites and accosting strange men in the street with flimsy excuses of market research. *Please tell me Maggie hadn't done that.*

'We do not have an endless pot of money,' Frank said as Jess reached into her handbag for a pen.

'You're being very cavalier,' Izzie carried on. 'Adequate lighting is essential, especially at this time of year.'

'Last month, new carpet in reception was essential.' Jess dumped the contents of her handbag on the table. 'The month before, a new microwave was essential.' She picked up a pen and shovelled the rest back into her bag.

'Only males between twenty-five and thirty, bearing more than a passing resemblance to Timmy Mallett need apply,' Sarah mumbled.

'What?' Jess mouthed at Sarah.

'The car park …' said Izzie.

'Is perfectly safe,' Jess said, still staring at Sarah. 'Shouldn't that be Tommy Mallet? Isn't he the one you've got a bit of a crush on?'

'Exactly,' Sarah mouthed back. 'Maggie said, "What's one misspelled word between friends?" The paper has only been out for twelve hours and she's already had ninety-two responses.'

'Health and safety—' Izzie said.

'Checked the lights last month,' Jess said, interrupting. 'They meet all the standards, so they've given them a clean bill of health and advised they should be checked again in a year's time.' Impressive, maybe she could get Maggie to write an advert for her wedding photography services.

'I almost fell this week.'

'Last month you "almost" tripped on a carpet tile.' Jess snarled, fighting an urge to mention sensible shoes would be a more practical option. Although, knowing Izzie's expensive tastes in clothes and handbags, changing the lights would probably be cheaper. 'There is only one way we could afford additional lights.'

Izzie nodded. 'You have to do it.'

'We'd have to take money out of another budget.'

Frank stared at her.

'We'd have to lose the Christmas party,' she said.

Sarah was staring too, as if she was public enemy number one, number two and three combined. The party had been Sarah's life's work for months. She'd booked Grey Towers and found an ABBA tribute band. She was on the verge of agreeing menus. She clearly thought Jess was bluffing, but in case, shot her the sort of look that said, "Do it bitch and die".

'I don't know off hand what the cancellation policies are. With less than three months to go, I'd imagine we'd lose at least our deposit possibly the rest of the monies paid, but we could always have a chat with them – they might give us something back. Shall we put it to the vote.'

A room full of surprised faces glared at her. Jess wasn't feeling the love. 'Lights, no party. If I propose, can you second, Frank?'

He nodded slowly.

'All those in favour …'

Izzie raised a hand.

'Against?'

Everyone else, even Sarah, raised theirs.

'That's settled then.'

'Which brings us to item five, any other business.' Frank raised his voice to be heard above the noise. 'Nothing happened in your meeting this morning Jess, did it, to change what we discussed?'

She shook her head.

'In that case …' Frank paused and swallowed. 'I should tell you I've decided to sell the company.'

"MD announced his intention to sell the company. Everyone," Jess wrote, then added, "Most people expressed surprise". Considering how vocal, Izzie had been all morning, it was strange she remained silent. Even Sarah sat bolt upright, dropped her magazine and managed a "No".

'That'll take a while, won't it?' someone said.

'I suppose so,' Frank agreed, cracking his knuckles. A sure sign Jess knew he was lying.

'What will you do?' the woman from contracts asked.

Frank shook his head. 'Don't know yet.' But as he said it, he'd started to stretch his fingers.

Jess could feel another crack coming on.

Chapter Nineteen

'I didn't get any message.' Maggie frowned, her heart sank. The nervous anticipation she'd felt when she recognised the care home's number on her phone and realised who was ringing vanished faster than balloons at a hedgehog's birthday party. 'I guess you're crying off.'

'It's not like that,' John said. 'Well not exactly. I do want to take you out. Just not this evening.' He made a noise that sounded like a sigh.

A sound like china breaking made Maggie jump. 'That sounds expensive.'

'It's all kicking off here. The bloody chef has walked out. I've asked the gardener to give me a hand boiling some soup and buttering slices of bread, only I think it might've lost something in the translation. Look, can we take a rain check? Reschedule?' Another crash. 'I don't want you to think … Oh God. Please no. He's only gone and set the smoke alarm off.'

And he was gone.

'Great.' Maggie put the phone back in its cradle. She'd been stood up; her mother was right. Whatever his reasons, she'd been let down. Left in the lurch. Dumped. Like Sarah after the hot date that had gone disastrously wrong. Except, unlike Sarah, she was never going to chance another date. Why would anyone want to spend time with a middle-aged spinster who'd been recently orphaned?

She kicked off her shoes and walked into her bedroom.

John had suggested a rain check and to be fair he sounded upset. It wasn't as if she had a full social calendar.

Maggie removed her new dress, rehung it on its padded coat hanger and changed into a pair of comfy trousers and an oversized jumper. The perfect outfit for another Friday night at home, whether planning cleaning, cooking, gardening or flopping in front of the telly. She'd enjoyed wearing her new dress – briefly. It felt nice, not too clingy.

She'd lost weight with all the recent running around. That, and not having to cook traditional meat and two veg every night. She couldn't be described as thin, but the dress was a size smaller than she'd normally have gone for and hung beautifully.

The shop assistant said it made her look ten years younger, but the woman neither knew how old she was, nor knew her ten years ago. The comment was part of her sales patter, like her "You can't go wrong with black" comment, but still Maggie was pleased with both the dress and the scarf the woman made her buy when she mentioned she might team it with a cardigan. She smiled recollecting the undisguised horror that flashed across the woman's face before she pulled out a drawer full of scarves which she said could be used to add colour or jazz up the outfit.

The dress made her feel elegant, not glamorous.

She wasn't a glamorous person. Her clothes were always chosen for practical purposes and longevity. She had a limited budget and didn't need a huge wardrobe. Everything was washable and she washed them regularly. The black dress and scarf needed to be dry-cleaned, that alone felt frivolous. The only things she'd ever taken to the dry cleaners before were curtains.

She had been looking forward to spending an evening wearing the dress. Okay, and spending an evening with John. He had a nice face and smiled a lot which made his eyes sparkle.

The possibility of an empty evening loomed large. She needed to think about something to eat and decide on which murder series repeat she could stomach watching. Thank God she hadn't mentioned at work that she'd planned on going out tonight. The cross-examination on Monday would have been every bit as bad as being stood up. She'd have to go over every detail.

What would they have done if it had happened to them? Jess didn't count. She and Martin had been an item forever. On evenings when she worked late and Martin was out, Maggie was certain she didn't cook a proper meal, probably settling for toast, or a sandwich. Jess had a thing about fish finger sandwiches or shrimp paste.

Sarah, on the other hand, would probably drown her sorrows, watch some rubbish on TV and send out for a pizza and a bottle of wine. Tonight, she'd take a leaf out of Sarah's book: a takeaway and evening of *Love Island*. That should have her mother turning in her grave although technically she wasn't there yet. Maggie picked up her handbag and noticed her mobile tucked in its usual pocket. The screen was flashing, apparently with four text messages. All from John and growing increasingly desperate. The last one had been left after they'd spoken: *I am sorry. You have no idea how much I hate chefs at the moment.*

'If the mountain won't come to …' she muttered and picked up her car keys.

Chapter Twenty

On Saturday morning, Jess sat at her kitchen table trying to update her CV, while the estate agent fussed around the place, getting it ready for what he termed "a photo shoot". "Deadline driven and proficient in scheduling, reporting and budget management," she typed.

'Don't mind me,' he'd said. 'You won't even know we're here.'

She did. It was increasingly difficult to concentrate on transferable skills, which made her claim to be able to "operate effectively in challenging, fast-paced environments" somewhat spurious.

He'd been through every room, running his fingers over surfaces, presumably checking to make sure it was clean. Jess was relieved she'd spent last night giving the house a thorough clean from top to bottom. So far, if he wanted to catch her out, he'd been disappointed.

"Excellent attention to detail …"

A vase of silk flowers had been placed on the kitchen worktop, three extra cushions on the settee, a selection of country life magazines spread over the coffee table and a bowl of plastic fruit adorned the sideboard in the dining room.

'A little house dressing,' the estate agent called it. 'We do this all the time, trust me,' he added.

Trust him.

He was an estate agent for pity's sake. Trusting him was the last thing she planned on doing.

"Great leadership and presentation skills, although sometimes lacking the finishing touches …"

'It helps potential buyers see the bigger picture.' He'd even folded the ends of the toilet paper into a point.

She badly wanted a cup of tea, but he'd hidden the kettle somewhere and she couldn't bring herself to ask.

"Strong verbal communications" – *sometimes.*

General Gordon had disappeared over the neighbour's fence as soon as the man had turned up. She was tempted to follow him.

"Self-motivated; powerful negotiator; exceptional risk assessment and analysis skills …" Maybe she wouldn't follow the cat.

‘I know you hoped for a quick sale.’

Did she?

‘I’m pleased to say there’s been a lot of interest,’ the man said, ‘considering we only posted details on our website yesterday.

‘Before you’ve done the photos?’

‘Under the banner “Coming Soon”. We like to create a bit of a buzz.’ He flicked through his iPad and showed her a picture of the front of her house, clearly taken yesterday, because it had the “For Sale” sign that magically appeared in her garden sometime yesterday while she was at work.

‘We’ll get the photos uploaded this afternoon. I’m hoping to have good news for you very soon.’

She needed to get out of there. If General Gordon wasn’t hanging around, neither was she. Jess put her laptop and camera in her car as a young woman drew up. She wound down a window and stared at the house. It was difficult to judge from her expression whether she liked what she saw or not.

‘Photographer,’ the estate agent said, pushing Jess out of the way as he raced down the drive.

‘You’re early,’ he said, a smile pasted on his face. ‘Not a problem, don’t sit out there, come in, come in.’

Jess wondered about staying to watch. She’d never done much architectural photography. There was an art to getting the light right. She could probably learn a lot.

‘I think you’re going to love this one. Current owners have looked after it and there’s plenty of space. You’re not going to have to take photographs from under the furniture to make the rooms look a reasonable size.’

Or maybe not. Jess fetched her handbag. ‘Every door is unlocked,’ she told the estate agent. ‘I’m not going far. Ring me before you’re ready to leave and I’ll come back.’

The car park was empty apart from the weekend call-centre staff’s cars outside Anymoore when Jess arrived. She toyed with the idea of spending the day in the office catching up, but her most pressing concern at the moment should be finding somewhere to live and she was struggling to focus on anything else. Or she could take her camera into the woods.

She checked her watch. Sarah would be meeting her first date at midday, perhaps she could wander into town, have a look in estate agents' windows and casually walk past the café, see how they were getting on or whether she'd actually turned up. Sarah hadn't exactly been over the moon with the idea.

'Let me get this straight,' Sarah had said. 'You want me to meet someone you've chosen.'

'That's our agreement,' Maggie said. 'Five dates. He is number one. You don't have to spend all afternoon with him. Have a cup of coffee. If you don't like him, we'll look for number two.'

'Shouldn't we have had some discussion about this, you know, before …?'

'We did. You told us what you were looking for and he ticks all the boxes apart from the looks. I told him that was a typing mistake.'

'Did he believe you?'

'You were just below a freestanding hooker. What do you think?'

'You've arranged for me to meet him in person?'

'And that's a problem?' Maggie asked.

'That's not how these things work these days. We should be sending each other messages. If we think we've got something in common, we'd swap numbers and talk. Then and only then if we both felt a connection would we talk about meeting up.'

'Sounds a lot of effort to me,' Maggie said. 'I didn't know what you'd be wearing, so I told him you'd be carrying a copy of *Pride and Prejudice*.'

'Ha,' Sarah said, folding her arms. 'I don't …' A large book landed with a thump on the desk, inches from her.

'How do you know he's not a serial killer?'

'You're meeting in a public place. Someone will help if he starts attacking you or at least film your demise.'

'Thanks,' Sarah said. 'Then upload it onto the internet, I suppose.'

'Yep,' said Maggie. 'Seems to be how it works these days. But look on the bright side, phones these days take great pictures. The police should have no trouble catching him from that.'

'What do you know about this man?'

'Right height, age, describes himself as adventurous. Not been in a relationship for some time. Thought you sounded nice. What more do you want?'

'You haven't forgotten lunch tomorrow, have you?' Neil's mother asked.

He moved the phone far enough away from his ear so she couldn't hear his sigh.

'Your dad said he spoke to you earlier in the week and your sister has finished reviewing the contract you asked her to look at.'

He had planned a long morning walk with Dudley and a lazy afternoon. The conversation with his father about lunch had completely slipped his mind.

'What time?' Neil asked, trying to inject a little enthusiasm in his answer.

'One. She's bringing the boys over too.'

Great. That meant the afternoon could be written off. His father would retire to his office as soon as lunch was over and he'd be left to entertain two overactive children while Sophie caught up with their mother in the kitchen under the pretence of washing-up, although everyone knew they'd sit down with a cup of tea as soon as the dishwasher was stacked.

'The boys are excited about seeing Dudley. Try to make sure he's not wet or muddy when you arrive. Will it just be you? No one else you'd like to bring?'

'Just me.'

'You know Sophie's friend Fiona is going through a divorce? Sophie's partner is helping her.'

'She's not coming?'

'Don't be silly, it's a family lunch, unless …'

Fiona had been Sophie's friend since school. They had been inseparable then and still were by the sound of it. Fiona had been through many disastrous relationships. Neil knew when most of them ended because his mother would drop less than subtle hints. His own love life had hardly been the thing of storybooks, but at least being married stopped the hints.

Emma was the sister of a work colleague. After three years, he'd bowed to peer pressure and asked her to marry him. A year later they married. The marriage hadn't lasted as long as the engagement and had left him with the crippling mortgage he'd taken on to buy her out of his flat and the Newfoundland, who was currently on the sofa pretending to be asleep. Neil rattled his car keys and Dudley sprung to attention. His tail wagging enthusiastically, he stretched and stood by the door.

Having parked at the office, Neil decided on a circular loop through the woods avoiding the footpaths with stiles too high for a Newfoundland to clear. He plugged his earphones in, selected "Darkness on the Edge of Town" from his music library and set off in the direction of the forestry commission woods. He never bored of their variety. Bluebell tracks and primroses in the spring, gave way to ferns growing in the shade of the beech trees, which right now were changing into the most glorious golden colour. He could lose himself for hours in these woods. Today, with Springsteen's help, he would forget Anymoore's merger for a couple of hours. His sister would want to talk about it tomorrow. She provided legal advice to the Jackson Consultancy, which she rarely remembered to invoice for – something Neil was profoundly grateful for.

His parents had backed both their children, every step of the way in their chosen careers, and when Neil had announced he wanted to be an accountant not a solicitor like his father, there had been no guilt trips or negativity. When Sophie announced she wanted to branch into civil and property law after her degree, they'd been equally encouraging. His mother, having trained as a legal secretary, was often called, by one or other of them, to help with urgent jobs.

He'd had an interesting conversation with his father during the week. He'd mentioned Ross wanted a partnership and his father had snorted and said, 'No way. I hope you told him where to get off.'

His reaction had surprised Neil. True, he wasn't ecstatic about the idea either, but he'd always planned on expanding eventually and that would undoubtedly mean taking on a new partner at some point.

'He brought you a lead – one lead,' his father said. 'He's been with you for five minutes and hasn't exactly been worth his weight in gold – has he? How much money has he offered to put in? Nothing – I thought as much.'

His father was right. Even allowing for the distraction of the wedding. Ross had big ideas about where the company should be going. He had an impressive CV, great references and came across well at interview which is how he got the job in the first place. But in the year he'd been with the firm, he'd cost it a lot more than he'd generated in income.

Whether even Ross with all his "exceptional leadership and project management skills" was qualified to do half the things he'd added to the Jackson Consultancy website was a matter for debate. Jackson Consultancy now offered a "Comprehensive range of services, essential for all companies, whatever their size". Neil hadn't a clue what an agile scrum master was and hoped no one ever asked them to provide one. He'd not played rugby since school and the games master had never described him as agile.

Neil didn't like to think badly of anyone. The fee Martin Cowley had agreed for a successful transfer was handsome, so if not a partnership, maybe he would be able to afford to pay a bonus.

He needed to have a word with Ross about Tanya, when he got back from his honeymoon. Ross treated their part-time admin assistant, as his personal secretary and dogsbody which she'd complained to Neil about more than once.

And he didn't like Dudley.

"Something in the Night" finished as Neil rounded the corner by the reservoir.

Dudley ignored a collie who clearly wanted to play, raised his head, sniffed for a second and took off. Instead of heading in their usual direction to the small lake, he bolted down into the woods along one of the smaller paths.

'Just don't roll in mud,' Neil called after him, nodding at the collie's owner.

Dudley had a limited boredom threshold. He'd be back, Neil told himself.

Bruce was halfway through "Racing in the Street" when Neil's phone interrupted the track. He'd answered it before he realised it was an unknown number. He didn't speak immediately, expecting a robotic voice to enquire if he wanted to claim damages after a recent accident he was supposed to have had.

'I have Dudley,' a voice said. 'Where are you?' His stomach leapt. *It couldn't be.* His mood soared.

‘By the reservoir,’ he said.

‘Okay,’ the voice said. ‘Don’t move, we’re on our way.’

He couldn’t. His insides had turned to goo.

He tried to work out which way they would be coming from, fighting the urge to run towards them and gather her up in his arms. Emma had never made him feel like this. Fiona certainly didn’t have the same effect. Okay, be honest with yourself Jackson, there’s no way you’re handing project management of the Anymoore merger to Ross.

They came into view. Dudley was letting Jess hold one end of an impossibly large stick.

She raised her other hand as soon as she saw Neil and smiled.

He took one look at them both and winced. They looked like they’d been mud wrestling.

‘Guess who found me,’ she said, letting go of the stick and wiping a dirty hand across her face.

Neil pulled a tissue from his pocket and tried to wipe some of the mud away.

‘Spit on it and scrub a bit harder.’

She was so close; it was all he could do to breathe.

‘Oh God, I’m so sorry,’ he said, and rubbed a little harder.

Jess closed her eyes and let him.

‘It feels like I’m five years old and having my face cleaned before I am allowed into Grannie’s house,’ she said. ‘I’m afraid we had a bit of an accident on the side of a puddle. Not the best angle for photos of reflections as it happens. Although I think you’ll agree our stick is very photogenic. Dudley certainly seems to think so. He was really keen to show it to you.’

‘I am sorry,’ Neil said weakly.

She giggled. ‘You’ve already said that. Were you worried when he disappeared like that?’

‘I owe you.’ Neil noticed she tilted her head when she asked a question. She had the most amazing brown eyes. They reminded him of the chocolate-covered toffees, he used to enjoy as a child. The ones with the woman’s face on the wrapper. He wondered whatever happened to them. He couldn’t remember the last time he’d had them or chocolate nuts and raisins for that matter. When he looked up again, she was staring back.

‘Cool,’ she said. ‘I’ll think about a suitable payback.’

Chapter Twenty-One

Sarah had already decided to play it cool. She ambled up to her desk on Monday morning, a bit slower than most mornings, dumped her handbag in her bottom drawer but didn't say a word.

That would infuriate them. She'd already ignored calls from Maggie on Saturday and Jess on Sunday.

'Have you heard? How did we do?' Sarah heard Jess ask as she walked into the office. Jess was sat on Maggie's desk, swinging her legs. They seemed to be examining Maggie's computer when she'd walked in. But both were clearly desperate to hear what had happened on Saturday. Let them sweat.

They probably expected her to gush enthusiastically about her wonderful weekend. Well it wasn't wonderful. They could wait.

Sarah hung her jacket over the back of her chair and asked if anyone wanted a drink. No one answered. If they thought not needing one was going to speed her up, they were so very wrong.

Harry Roberts removed the teabags from four mugs as Sarah entered the kitchen. Tempting though it was to walk straight back out again, she stayed. He concentrated on squeezing each bag against the side of its mug. It took a while before he looked round.

'Hi,' he said. 'How are you?'

'Do you play dragons and prisons?' Sarah asked, filling the kettle.

'*Dungeons & Dragons*.' He smiled.

'I take it that's a yes then.' She was surprised at how disappointed that made her feel.

'Absolutely not,' Harry said, drying his hands. 'I spend the majority of my time in the real world. I like it there, so no need to spend my spare time cocooned in my bedroom, pretending to be a twenty-third level law-breaking, barbarian halfling or whatever, however much wisdom and charisma he might have.'

He rinsed the spoon and put it on the draining board. 'Do you want the teabags? Earl Grey, wasn't it?' He turned his brown eyes on her.

Sarah swallowed. 'Coffee, please,' she said.

'Of course, my mistake.' He handed her down a jar of instant. His eyes gleamed and a hint of a smile played round the corners of his mouth.

Spooning coffee into her mug, she watched him pick up his four and leave.

He was okay, she decided. So far no one had mentioned the incident with Ryan, which must mean he hadn't told anyone. Not bad looking either but then having spent an hour on Saturday lunchtime with Nigel, her judgement was probably clouded. That was an hour of her life she'd never get back. What on earth were they thinking?

If she'd been asked what she'd hoped for, it would be pleasant conversation with an interesting and sexy person. Saturday's date wasn't. On a looks scale, she would score him a six. Not the ugliest fruit on the tree, but not someone she would crush over.

Conversation wasn't a problem. He had an opinion on everything, one, he'd been perfectly willing to share without needing any sort of response, or reaction from her. Up until that moment, she had no idea *Dungeons & Dragons* was such an all-consuming pastime. Nigel was looking for someone with a similar obsession he'd said. He didn't think it might put potential girlfriends off. On the contrary he saw it as "a great way of learning about people's personalities, work out who you're compatible with and who you aren't".

'Imagine spending the rest of your life with someone who would happily chop down a goblin without thinking about it,' he'd said.

'Too right,' Sarah replied. 'Bring on those damn goblins. Let me and my axe at them.' She'd made her excuses and gone to the library.

'Okay, describe your thinking,' Sarah said, returning to the office and not looking at either Jess or Maggie. 'Justify your thought process so I can decide how angry to be.' She took a sip of her coffee and sat down. 'Let's start with the name "Nigel". Not the sort of name usually associated with someone in their twenties, whatever he told you. And he wasn't. I spent an hour on Saturday with a forty-six-year-old virgin called Nigel, who only left the sanctuary of his bedroom because he thought I must be into *Dungeons & Dragons* after how you'd described me. What the bloody hell did you tell him?'

'I know lots of nice Nigels.' Maggie tilted her chin up.

'Go on,' Sarah said. 'I'm listening.'

'Nigel Havers, Nigel Slater.'

'Your generation not mine.'

'Nigel Farage,' Jess added.

'You're not helping.' Sarah put her best cross face on. 'Okay, let's do this the other way round. What qualities did he have that you thought I'd go for?'

'Intelligence,' Jess said.

'No.' Maggie winced. 'Just that he liked adventure.'

'He's into role-playing games with flaming monks and dwarves. He lives with his mother and has a moustache clearly modelled on Adolf Hitler. He voted for Brexit. Okay, ground rules,' Sarah said.

Both women watched her expectantly.

'I know you have my best interests at heart.'

'There's a "but" coming,' Maggie said. 'I can feel it.'

'Own transport a must – and we're not talking pushbikes or bus pass here. I'm a sociable person. I like cinema, clubbing and meals out. I want someone with the same interests.

'Walking and food are not hobbies. They are things you do. You walk to buy food. You eat to stay alive. I don't describe driving to work as a hobby, why would anyone describe walking as one?'

'You said you liked food.'

'I want to be wined, dined and treated like a lady, not to have discussions about whether broccoli or cabbage is better.

'I want someone I can laugh with, because he's got a sense of humour, not *at*, because he's downright weird.

'I'm Libra, definitely not compatible with a Cancer or Capricorn.

'I'm not looking for someone to go climbing trees with. Fishing and football bore me. I want to come top of someone's list of favourite things not third or fourth behind washing the car and dinner with his mother.'

'Nigel had a car then?'

'I'm speaking hypothetically, forget Nigel. I threatened his goblins and if I had to spend any longer with him, I'd have probably been tempted to take him out with a Kalashnikov, or whatever they use in *Dragons & Dungeons*.'

'Walking's good for you,' Maggie said.

'Not for me,' Sarah said. 'It makes my feet hurt and me cross.'

'You could buy proper shoes,' Maggie said, lifting up her phone and punching in a number.

'Or pick friends who will choose more suitable dates. We said five and you're one down. I'll go on the next four because that's what we agreed, but after that you have to agree to butt out of my love life.

'Look, I know you mean well, but I want a normal guy. One I don't mind looking at. One who doesn't talk with his mouth full— Oh God. Now look what you've done. I'm starting to sound like my mother!'

Jess crawled under Maggie's desk, to check the computer cables. After Sarah's outburst, the last thing she needed this morning was to be patronised by technical support. She let Maggie make that call.

'It worked on Friday. If it hadn't, I'd have rung you on Friday,' Maggie said, her telephone tucked between ear and neck. 'No, I don't have a call reference logged.'

'Someone here to see you,' Frank shouted. 'What exactly are you doing down there? Have you lost something?'

Why do people always ask such ridiculous questions? Jess frowned. She could hear Maggie bang the phone down. 'Sarah, if I pull on each lead, can you check they're plugged in and switched on?'

'Uh huh,' Sarah said, sounding decidedly distracted.

'This one.' Jess pulled.

It was all quiet above the desk. 'For God's sake, will someone check the bloody plug is in the electric socket and switched on?' she said.

'It's a bit loose,' a male voice said. 'Is that better?'

Jess twisted her head to see where the voice came from and found she was looking into the face of a sitting Newfoundland dog, who wagged its tail and held out a paw, as if inviting her to shake it. A green light came on and the computer whirred into life, but her attempt to back out and regain control was somewhat impaired by the dog. All she could see behind him was a pair of smart, dark coloured trousers and the bottom of a blue checked shirt.

'Hello again,' Jess said slowly. Dudley continued to wag his tail and hold out his paw, except now his head was tilted and his ears pricked.

'Frank said it was all right to bring him up. I can put him back in the car if you'd rather,' the voice said.

Jess was glad she wasn't standing. It was a bit crowded under the desk, but at least no one had witnessed how unstable hearing his voice again made her feel.

'He's fine.' She pushed herself up onto her knees, but Dudley wasn't backing off. 'Nice to see you. And you're looking a bit cleaner today,' Jess said, as she ruffled his fur, took the paw being poked at her and shook it. The dog put his paw down, but his tail was wagging so fast and furiously that his entire body swayed dangerously, and Jess was bowled over and being licked to death. At least this time they weren't in six inches of mud.

'Oh God, I'm sorry. Dudley – heel,' Neil said, between bursts of female laughter. 'Here let me help you.'

She was hauled to her feet, but even when upright Neil continued to hold her.

'Hi,' she said, quietly.

'Are you okay?'

'No broken bones,' she said, without taking her eyes off his face. 'I wasn't expecting you until this afternoon.'

'Frank thought it made sense if I made an early start.' His eyes were fixed on her face. 'Is that okay with you?'

'Is someone going to introduce us,' Sarah said.

Jess started to mutter something very unladylike.

'Neil,' he said. 'Neil Jackson.' He stretched out a hand, which Sarah grabbed and held on to for a lot longer than was professional. Jess briefly considered having to break her fingers to get her off, but luckily Dudley moved and Sarah let go, turning her attention to the dog. 'And, who's this handsome man?' she said in an annoyingly girly sounding voice.

'That's Dudley,' Neil said. 'I'm afraid my parents taught him to shake hands when he was a pup. It was funny at the time.'

'You must be the management consultant we've been warned about. How long will you be here?' Sarah said.

Was she fluttering her eyes?

'A few days,' Neil said, his answers directed at Jess and she smiled. 'I have a couple of preliminary enquiries I need to make, but providing I have access to the accounts, they shouldn't take long. At this stage, it's a matter of satisfying ourselves you're the type of business my client believes you are and that we're on the same page when it comes to price and timescale.'

'What sort of timescale have you in mind?' Jess asked.

'Realistically, these things rarely take less than six weeks. But I know both parties are keen to proceed as quickly as possible. Perhaps we could talk, over something to eat. Is there somewhere nearby where I can buy you lunch?'

Jess grimaced. 'I'm afraid there's someone I need to see,' she said. 'And I've brought sandwiches with me, but …'

Lying behind her desk amongst some plastic and paper wrappings, Dudley pretended to sleep.

'Oh God, sorry,' said Neil, as she bent down to pick up the discarded wrappings, aware the dog was watching her, with one eye open.

'They were my favourite,' she said, waving the wrappings at him. 'Chicken and coriander. I hope you enjoyed them.' He closed his eye, but the slow wag of his tail indicated he probably had.

Jess did a double take when she saw the house. When Leanne and Darren had told her they were going to decorate, she hadn't appreciated they meant outside. Graffiti covered their front wall, the bottom half of it at least. Presumably whoever had "tagged" the wall, wasn't either tall or in possession of a ladder. It had been done since she was last there. Last week, even in the evening gloom, she'd have definitely noticed the garishly coloured "The only place left to go is the future".

No one answered her knock. She picked up the letterbox and peered through. Leanne stood in the hall, peering straight back at her.

'Come on Leanne, I haven't got all day. You can't avoid me forever. You know I'll come back.' She'd seen enough films to be able to make a thinly veiled threat. Still, she was relieved when the door opened – she wasn't sure what her next line would've been.

Leanne looked embarrassed. 'I can write another cheque,' she said, fumbling around on the coffee table. Jess thought she must be looking for her cheque book, until she pulled out a packet of cigarettes.

'Is there any point?' Jess asked. 'Have you come into money, or will we be having the same conversation in a week's time?'

Leanne lit a cigarette and blew a perfect smoke ring up to the ceiling, before she answered, 'Probably.'

‘I’d rather have cash.’ That was about as likely as being abducted by aliens, being made prime minister, winning the lottery, or having a date with Neil Jackson. She shook her head to get that image out of her head.

‘I haven’t got any,’ Leanne said. ‘I could get some.’

Jess felt hopeful. ‘You could? When?’

‘End of next week. Someone owes me. Here, I know what.’ She stubbed out her cigarette, got up and left the room, closing the door behind her.

Five minutes later Jess wondered if she’d been abandoned and wasn’t sure what she was supposed to do. She picked up her handbag, knowing she needed to get back to work. She was halfway down the hall when Leanne charged down the stairs.

‘Take these as security.’ She held out a hand and uncurled her fingers to show a handful of jewellery that sparkled under the light.

‘I can’t.’

‘You must. Gran left them to me. They’re real gold. Take them then you know I will pay, otherwise I won’t get them back. And I really want them back because they’re precious.’

Jess, who knew nothing about jewellery, hesitated. ‘Keep them. I’ll come back for the cash at the end of next week.’

‘You have to take them.’ Leanne took off the necklace she was wearing too, wrapped the whole lot in a grubby handkerchief and pushed the whole lot into Jess’s handbag.

Jess had never had that much jewellery in her life. Okay, realistically it was probably costume jewellery. Pretty but worthless and she had been shafted again. Twelve years together and the only jewellery Martin had ever bought her was a watch for Christmas one year.

They argued for another five minutes, but Leanne insisted. ‘Look,’ she said, ‘I’ll pay you next week, but if I don’t pay you within a month, pawn it. That’ll cover the cost of the photos. Send me the ticket and I can get it back when I get the money.’

Jess who had never pawned anything in her life, doubted it would be that simple, but Leanne wasn’t to be moved. Jess wrote a receipt for “Jewellery of unknown value to be exchanged within one month for the sum of £150.00” to avoid confusion later, she explained.

‘You should sign it,’ Jess said.

‘No need.’ Leanne shook her head. ‘I trust you.’

Chapter Twenty-Two

'Who's Jack?' Maggie said Tuesday morning. 'She didn't look up from the wordsearch puzzle she'd partially hidden under her in-tray. So far, she'd only found nine words and the paper said thirty-four was excellent. She licked her index finger and sorted through a pile of delivery notes, found the one she was after, stapled it to the rest of its paperwork and initialled the invoice ready to be paid.

Sarah's blank expression suggested she was trying to understand the question which meant she knew who Jack was and was hiding something.

'He rang to speak to you,' Maggie said. 'I wondered who he was? You've never mentioned a Jack before.'

'The name doesn't ring a bell,' Sarah said, slowly, wiggling her mouse to wake up her computer. 'Did he leave a message?'

Maggie nodded and lifted down an overflowing file from the cupboard. She wasn't facing Sarah. She didn't need to be, she could feel the girl getting defensive and weighing up the possibilities of how much Maggie knew, so Maggie let the question hang.

'He works at the library. I'm not seeing him. I'm not cheating on my dates if that's what you think.'

Her chin would be up, her chest out.

Maggie put the file down. Right on both points. 'That's okay then,' she said, because I've arranged another date. With Andy. She slapped a piece of paper down in front of Sarah. 'You're meeting him after work this evening in the library café.'

Sarah grabbed at the piece of paper. 'That's a bit random isn't it?'

'Not really. It's late night opening and has its own car park.' Maggie had her back to her now. 'And you're meeting Jack at the library thirty minutes earlier. I could walk with you.'

'Because you're worried about my well-being or need to renew a book? What has this Andy got that you think I'm going to fall in love with?'

Maggie filed half a dozen sheets of paper and closed the file.

'He sounded genuine, is definitely not lying about his age. He emailed me a copy of his driving license. Blond hair like your ideal man, although thinning a little prematurely.' Maggie put the file back on the shelf, pretty certain that the look Sarah would be firing her wasn't a loving one. 'Drives a blue BMW. I said you'd wait in a window seat.'

'I'm changing my ideas about my ideal man,' Sarah said. She was looking out of the window. 'Do you think he's spoken for?'

Maggie looked to where she was pointing. The management consultant was getting out of his car. He opened the rear door and his large dog got out and shook himself. 'You'll have to fight our boss for that one,' she said. 'Talk of the Devil.'

'Is that Neil?' Jess asked, walking into the office and straight over to the window.

'And his dog,' Maggie said, looking out too.

'We're going to be working in Frank's office this morning,' Jess said. There was a colour to her cheeks and Maggie turned away, so Jess couldn't see her smile.

Jess added a comment to the bottom of the appraisal, signed it and groaned as she turned to the next one on the huge pile.

'The new company will want to look the personnel files over as soon as everything's signed and sealed,' Frank said. 'Help them see who they're taking on. I don't think we've got any weak links, but make sure appraisals, the organisation chart and all the training records are up to date, would you?'

Reading obliquely coded messages such as "Uses resources well" and trying to work out whether that meant delegates everything or helps themselves to the stationery cupboard when no one's looking was doing nothing to lighten her mood.

She might be sat in an office with a really hot man, but there were few things she'd rather do less than check staff appraisals, in fact nothing she could put her finger on.

Maybe toenail extraction.

She signed off Isabel's appraisal and tried to turn her attention back to the next on the pile, Douglas from facilities, but it got stuck on its way and lingered on the sexy, smouldering man opposite her.

He was busy. He was going through the annual reports and management accounts, asking the odd question and ticking items off. Frank suggested it would be easier to discuss things in some privacy and suggested they work in his office. Neil seemed to cope; it was Jess who was the emotional wreck. It took every last ounce of restraint she had to concentrate on Douglas's ideas for his own personal development and not sweep the piles of appraisals off the desk, stand up, unbutton her blouse and shout, 'Take me I'm yours'.

When Neil's phone had rung, he'd smiled apologetically and switched it off. She hadn't meant him not to answer it. She hoped he didn't think she was being rude, but his dark eyes and strong cheekbones gave nothing away. He was, as Sarah succinctly put it, "all testosterone".

There had been a succession of females in and out of the office. All of them invented a valid reason to be there. In between staff appraisal forms, Jess fielded a series of mindless questions.

She looked out of the window and watched the world go by. Or not, as it happened. If Neil looked up now, he'd probably think she was a proper airhead, still that would be preferable to finding her staring and, hell, probably dribbling.

The pond in front of the office was still, and a couple walking across the car park were in jackets. But it was impossible to judge the temperature through the double glazing. The air conditioning unit in the office was set, so whatever the time of year, you needed a vest or at the very least a cardigan, if you weren't to die of frostbite.

Jess rubbed her arms trying to get the circulation going again.

Neil stood up and stretched his legs. The movement made Jess look round. 'You off?' she asked, surprised at how disappointed she felt.

'Just need some fresh air.' He smiled. 'Dudley too.'

The dog at his feet thumped his tail but made no attempt to move.

'Look, have you brought sandwiches in today?'

'Why is he hungry?'

Neil grinned.

Jess's insides started to melt.

'Come with us. Let me buy you lunch.'

Okay, don't rush to get up. Look cool about this. He's only offered you a sandwich. 'Thanks, I could do with a walk,' Jess said. She picked up the rest of the forms, tapped them into a neat pile and put them into Frank's desk drawer and locked it.

They walked in silence across an open field. Jess was glad she'd had the foresight to pick up her sunglasses. Dudley ran off and immediately found something interesting to sniff. As they neared the end of the path, Neil, his jacket over his shoulder, suggested they head for the Wellington Arms.

'We can sit in the bar, they allow dogs in there, and have a drink with our sandwiches. Then you can tell me about Jess,' he said.

'Nothing to tell. I'm an accountant. It's common knowledge accountants are very dull indeed.'

'I'm a management consultant. That's far worse.'

'Who says?'

'It's a well-known fact. Management consultants are top of the boredom charts, then lawyers, then accountants.'

'I don't think so. How many invitations have you had to dinner parties in the last month?'

'That's not fair. You can't ask me that – I'm a good-looking single guy.'

Jess laughed. 'Says who?'

'Besides, I have Dudley – he gets constant invitations. Last month, two Labradors wanted him to give a lecture at their obedience class. Why do you think I take the useless lump everywhere I go? He's my passport to a constant whirl of social engagements.'

'How many?' She laughed.

'One,' he said. 'You?'

She'd been about to say "None" but tomorrow night she was meeting Martin. 'One,' she said, quietly.

The bar at the Wellington Arms was full by the time they arrived, but Neil steered Jess towards a table where a couple were leaving. They stopped and stroked Dudley who made a point of shaking paws with both of them, waving his tail enthusiastically.

Neil took charge of the sandwich orders while she sat with Dudley. A waitress brought over a bowl of water and Neil appeared shortly afterwards with their drinks. The sandwiches, when they arrived, were made of thick fresh home-made bread, filled with salmon, prawns and salad. Martin would have had heart failure at the sight of so much carbohydrate. Somehow that made them taste better. 'How are your enquiries going?' she asked, when the sandwich plate had been emptied.

'Are you allowed to say?'

'It's not a criminal investigation,' he said, laughing.

'That means you haven't found the Swiss bank account, or realised we only have half the number of employees we're paying?'

'No, but thanks for the tip-off. I'll start digging this afternoon.'

'Are you allowed to say who the client is yet?'

Neil shook his head. 'Not until everything's signed.'

'We are starting to know who it isn't.' Jess reached down and stroked Dudley, still lying by her chair. 'Frank's mentioned he's selling, to a number of his friends and there's a message from one of them this morning wanting to talk about the sale.'

'We have an exclusivity agreement in place,' Neil said. 'One week. If we don't have everything agreed by Friday, Frank can talk to who he likes.'

He stared at his glass. 'I probably shouldn't say anything, but I'm having a meeting tomorrow night.'

Jess watched as he took a sip of his drink.

'To discuss a heads of terms agreement. Everybody seems keen to get this done as soon as possible and is working hard to ensure it is. Everything I've seen over the last couple of days suggests you're exactly the type of company they're looking for. And Frank seems keen to sell.'

A waitress came to collect the plates and asked if the glasses were finished with. Jess checked her watch. 'I should get back,' she said.

'What about you? Are you happy about the takeover?' he asked as they walked back to the office.

The question surprised her. She wasn't sure how she felt about it. She'd been at Anymoore all her working life. It was a comfortable job. She liked the people she worked most closely with. Most of the time, it didn't stretch her capabilities or cause her too much stress. But the redundancy package was generous and being too comfortable wasn't necessarily a good thing, was it?

'You haven't answered my question,' Neil said as they walked through the car park to reception.

'Yes,' she said. 'I think I am.'

Three post-it notes had appeared on her laptop's screen while she was out. "MARTIN RANG. RING ASAP" was written in capital letters on the top one.

She would, but not while Neil sat opposite. She screwed up the message and threw it in the bin.

A message from Frank postponing their four o'clock meeting – he wouldn't be back in time.

Underneath those another in Maggie's scrawl: "Who is General Failure, and why is he so bloody concerned with my hard disk?"

Chapter Twenty-Three

Grey Towers looked dramatic. Jess drove down the long drive to the hotel. Straight out of a Jane Austen novel – a regency house set in a ring of trees. It was the sort of place a heroine would drive up to in her carriage to meet her one and only, peering shyly out of the window as the horses clattered noisily into the forecourt. A curtain would twitch at a window. It would be him. The light would come on, the door opened by a doorman. He'd be standing in the drawing room, but he'd turn as she was announced. It would be love at first sight. They wouldn't know it, but the reader would. No one was looking out, waiting for her.

The rain was positively Wagnerian. Jane Austen would have loved it. Her heroines frequently got stuck in rainstorms and had to be rescued from death's door by a hero and gently nursed back to health.

Jess had been surprised when Martin suggested they meet after work. She'd been bloody amazed when he suggested this place. It was simple, he needed to see her, he said. He'd tell her why when they met and wouldn't be drawn on the reason. She hadn't pushed it when he'd suggested Grey Towers, the posh hotel on the edge of town. She wanted to see the venue for this year's Christmas party. Not that that would be a fine dining in their restaurant kind of thing. She'd only been once before and that was with Martin. He'd taken her for her twenty-fifth birthday.

She wished she knew what he wanted. She hated surprises. She considered saying no, but not having been out for a meal since she couldn't remember when, and gift horses and all that, she'd agreed.

Sarah and Maggie had looked surprised when she'd told them. She could hardly blame them. Hell, she was shocked. Added to which she had a growing feeling she wasn't going to like what he had to say. It was just over a fortnight since he'd moved out. Maybe he wanted to move back. She hoped not. Was this his way of softening her up? Feed her nice food. Complement her on her outfit. She'd chosen a long-sleeved blue crepe dress for the evening, plain with an asymmetrical hem. Functional and attractive, rather than glamorous, but it made her feel good. She'd have to play for time. She didn't want him back, but she could hardly spoil the evening telling him that. Besides if he got the hump and walked out, she'd have to wash up for weeks.

She followed the sign and swung into the gravel car park with a satisfying crunching noise and peered again at the huge building through her rain-splattered windscreen. Her level of nervous anxiety had built steadily all afternoon. She considered turning round and going straight home. She could ring Martin from there, after all she had the new Mark Billingham novel waiting on her coffee table and a full packet of lemon puffs in the kitchen cupboard.

But she was here now and may as well get it over with.

She opened the car door, pushed it as far as it would go with her foot, shook her umbrella out into the open position, and reached for her handbag. It wasn't easy with only one hand spare and she swore under her breath as her handbag rolled away from her.

'Do you know there is nothing I fear more than a woman with an umbrella?'

Jess thought about lowering it, but changed her mind. No point getting wet.

'Here, allow me.'

The umbrella was gently removed from her outstretched hand and the car door opened further.

'Hi,' she said, in an unnaturally high-pitched squeak, because stood outside her car was her very own Jane Austen hero.

'Hi, yourself.' Neil moved to let her out, angling her brolly so she wouldn't get wet.

'What are you doing here?' Her stomach did that annoying thing it had taken to doing whenever he was anywhere close by.

'Meeting clients on neutral territory. Shall we?' His hand indicated the direction of the front door.

She nodded, not trusting any part of her body to behave enough to answer him properly.

'I have to say, you don't look as frightening as some I've seen.'

'Some who?'

'Women sporting umbrellas.'

'What about men?'

'No, men being the superiors of the species, can manoeuvre their umbrellas to avoid oncoming obstacles.'

‘Oi.’

Neil held her umbrella above her head. ‘Obviously, I can’t speak for present company, but usually women feel they own the airspace under their umbrella and woe betide anything or anyone who intrudes into that exclusion zone.’

Jess smiled. ‘That’s wholly unfair and just to prove how wrong you are, you are more than welcome to join me under here. I promise I won’t bite or declare war, providing you don’t let the rain run down the back of my neck.’

Neil offered his arm. She looped her hand through and together they managed to stay dry as they made their way to the front door. It was an impressive entrance. They stopped and looked at the art deco porch. ‘I suggested, we meet in my office,’ Neil said, shaking his head. ‘Can’t understand why they suggested this place.’

‘Maybe they’ve got more money than sense.’ Jess wished it was Neil who was taking her to dinner. ‘Where’s Dudley?’ she asked as they skipped between puddles.

‘Sulking indoors,’ Neil said. ‘But don’t worry, I’ve left him the remote control and a bag of crisps. He’ll get over it.’

‘Wow,’ Maggie said. ‘This place is amazing.’

‘I can’t believe you’ve never been before,’ John said as the waiter showed them through to the lounge. He gave them their menus and took their drinks order, returning with a plate of canapés. Maggie lost track of what they all were, but they tasted divine.

‘I don’t eat out often,’ she said. Not a complete untruth. She didn’t add, the only time I ever did was lunchtimes, with the girls from work. ‘We’re having the office Christmas party here this year.’

‘Really?’ John looked impressed. ‘That must be costing a fortune.’

‘Frank has always been very generous with our annual party,’ Maggie said and then feeling slightly uncomfortable added, ‘But I think they must do some sort of corporate deal. I understand it’s a popular place for parties and weddings.’

John nodded.

Maybe she’d invite him along as her “plus one”. That would surprise everyone. She smiled at the thought.

'Maggie,' John said.

She looked up, there was concern in his face. A waiter hovered by his side.

'Could you give us a little more time?' he asked, looking at Maggie. She nodded quickly and the waiter moved away.

'Sorry,' she said. 'I was away with the fairies.'

'Lucky fairies.'

Maggie's face broke into a smile and a warm feeling swept through her.

'Have you decided what you'd like to eat?' John asked, with an equally wide smile. 'We should think about ordering.'

'Just something small,' she said. John might have refused her offer to go "Dutch", but the prices on the menu had shocked her. 'Just a starter would be fine.'

'Nonsense woman.' John laughed. 'I am not having you watching me wade through many courses while you push a pea around your plate. Seriously, this is my treat. I promised myself the tasting menu the next time I came here. I'd like it if you would join me.'

At least, that's what Maggie thought he said. His words came out in a rush.

'I'm sorry,' he said, taking another sip of his drink. 'I'm unbelievably nervous. I can't remember the last time I took anyone out for a meal. And you look so lovely this evening.'

'Thank you.' Maggie blushed. 'Actually, I'm nervous too. It's a long time since I've been out for an evening.' The last time had been with Ray. She could pinpoint the exact date. Two days later he had left for the Falklands. It had been an evening full of promise. She had been so happy.

The conflict only lasted two months but it took from her every drop of happiness she possessed. It took Ray. She'd fought, since then, with every fibre in her body to keep any feelings of joy or pleasure at arm's length. If that meant never having to experience pain again, it was worth it. She had thrown herself into caring for her mother and hiding from the world. It wasn't easy, but she had her home, cooking, her garden and health. She coped. That's what everyone said about her. Somebody would probably engrave that on her gravestone: "Maggie Simpson coped". Time gave her stoicism, a face she could present to the world, but it was work that gave her a new lease of life. Slowly, the safety barriers she had built were starting to fall. She enjoyed the office, working with Jess and Sarah. But she hadn't told them about the evenings she'd spent at Treetops with John or how much she enjoyed them.

'As neither of us is driving,' John said, 'shall we share the chef's choice of wine? You do drink, don't you? I'm sorry I haven't even checked. Are you happy with wine?'

Maggie watched him studying the menu and explaining the various dishes. She understood what most of them were, but he looked so happy, she wasn't going to stop him.

Perhaps next week, she could return the favour. Treat him to a meal. Her budget wouldn't stretch to anywhere as grand as this. She'd pick Sarah's brains. Maybe they could try the bistro in town, or else she could cook for him. She'd like that. She'd get her books out and look for something special.

Jess did a mental run through of which knives she needed to use with which course and which glass for which wine. There were three glasses beside each place. In the event, the decision was taken out of her hands when the waiter poured the Chardonnay she'd ordered into the smaller of her two glasses and water into her tumbler.

The dining room was beautifully arranged; the tables not too close for comfort, laid with clean white linen and shiny cutlery.

Martin marched across the dining room and sat down, without stopping at the desk. He sucked a huge amount of air through his teeth and glared at her. That seemed to be his idea of a greeting tonight. She was grateful he hadn't gone for a kiss or any declarations of love.

'Have some wine,' she said.

The waiter appeared and poured him a glass. 'Shall I give you five minutes to decide on your food?' he asked, arranging the bottle back in the ice bucket. Jess nodded her thanks and picked up her menu.

'What are you doing?' Martin said. 'We're not staying and we're certainly not eating.'

'You said …'

What had he said? "Meet me at Grey Towers".

'You booked a table.'

Martin looked confused.

The waiter tried to tell her the table was booked for 8.00 not 6.00. Of course, it was no problem – the hotel wasn't full. He'd apologised, said it was the hotel's fault and taken her through to a table by the window overlooking the lake.

'You booked a table for two for eight o'clock. The hotel didn't get the time wrong after all, did they? You're meeting someone else for a meal, aren't you?'

'No, no, no,' Martin said.

The man does protest too much. 'Yeah right,' Jess said.

'I didn't come here to argue,' he said. 'The estate agent rang. We have a full-price offer on the house. Cash buyer in rented accommodation, wants to be in as soon as possible.'

'Fine,' Jess put her menu down. 'Any reason why we couldn't have had that conversation on the phone?'

'I want to make sure you're looking for somewhere to live. The estate agent said you hadn't registered with them.'

'There are estate agents all over the place,' Jess said.

'Good,' he said, slowly. 'So we just need to talk about our finances. It's worth trying to keep things as amiable as possible.'

By dragging me to a posh hotel and telling me I'm not worth the cost of a meal.

'We're not married, we don't have to worry about a divorce. We don't have to fight about whose fault it was that our relationship didn't work out but we do need to divide the proceeds from the property fairly so we can both walk away and start again. You've always been a reasonable person so I'm sure you'll agree to a fifty-fifty split. The endowment policy is in joint names, it's not worth a lot. I'll keep paying the premiums and transfer that into my name. I need your assurance that you won't be looking to make any claim on MJC Computing. My company solicitor will draw up paperwork to that effect and he will, of course, be looking after the conveyancing of the house.'

'We'll have to see about that,' Jess said. 'I'm getting quotes. That's what the estate agent suggested.'

'Someone has to do it.' Martin looked irritated.

'I'm sure your solicitor will be happy to quote for the work. If he sends me the information, I can pass it on. I'll tell my solicitor to expect the agreements as well.'

'You've got a solicitor?' A reddish colour crept up Martin's neck and was starting to rise up his cheeks. He wasn't happy. Twelve years with the same man and Jess considered she was something of an expert on his body language. She could read him like a flaming book, albeit one with no credible characters or story.

Jess nodded and picked up the menu. 'Anything else?'

Martin shook his head.

'Good, then leave £10 to cover your share of the wine.' He looked as if he was about to argue.

'Because you've always been such a reasonable person,' she added.

The red hue was impressive now. Actually, more scarlet, puce even – not an attractive colour for a man with his colouring and dress sense. But it matched nicely the blood vessel on the side of Martin's head that had become more pronounced since he'd arrived. He was fighting a losing battle to contain his temper. If they were on their own, he would have raised his voice by now, resorted to insults. Instead, he slapped a £10 note on the table and practically ran out.

'Everything all right, madam?' A waiter appeared at her side.

'Perfect, thank you. I'd like the French onion soup and the lamb shank please. By the way it will just be me for supper tonight.'

The waiter smiled as he wrote it down. 'Good choice, madam.'

He was right, it was an excellent choice. A weight had been lifted off her shoulders and she felt lighter and happier than she had in weeks. They were over. Seeing Martin crystallised the realisation that if he was the last man on earth, she didn't want him back. But if he thought she was going to roll over and sign any agreement, he had another think coming. The old Jess might have; the new Jess, who'd stood up to Darren and Leanne wouldn't.

But he was right she did need to think about a new house and packing. She wouldn't trust the estate agent he was using as far as she could throw him, but he seemed to have come up with a buyer and it sounded as if she was going to need somewhere to live sooner rather than later.

Another waiter appeared with a tray of cutlery and changed the smallest of her knives for a soup spoon and removed a small fork.

It was time she fessed up to Sarah and Maggie, told them Martin had gone. She'd justified not telling Maggie on the basis she had enough on her plate at the moment with her mother's death. She'd justified not telling Sarah because she was the biggest office gossip and telling her something like that would be like handing her a hot potato and expecting her not to drop it. The news would be round the company, if not Redford, within days if not hours. At times Sarah's ability to talk had its advantages; it could be much quicker to tell her something than send an email, but in this case, it was safer not to.

'Jess?' said a male voice in her left ear.

'Jess?' said a female voice in her right.

'Have you been stood up?' Neil asked. 'Are you waiting for anyone? Would you rather eat alone or can we join you?'

'No, no, no and yes,' Jess said, shaking her head.

'It's not some sort of special occasion or anniversary?'

Divorce and break-up parties might be fashionable according to some papers, but they were surely not something you did on your own.

'Didn't you say this afternoon you fancied a treat?' Maggie said. The length of her gaze suggested she knew exactly what Jess had said earlier. She was going to have to tell them tomorrow about Martin. But she wasn't the only one with secrets it seemed. Maggie had arrived with a man.

'This is John,' Maggie said. 'He was mother's care home manager.'

The waiter moved them to a table for four after all the introductions and handshaking had finished.

'It's no trouble,' he assured Jess, pressing Martin's £10 note into her hand while the others took their seats.

'What about you?' she asked Neil. 'What happened to your meeting?'

'Client rang me from his car,' Neil said. 'Stuck in traffic and unlikely to make it for at least an hour, so we rescheduled. I was on my way home for supper when I saw you.'

Chapter Twenty-Four

Maggie had never eaten such a delicious meal. So many different flavours perfectly combined. Jess and Neil's meals had looked delicious too.

There had been no sign of Martin when they'd arrived. Maggie assumed he and Jess had had a row and he'd stormed off? She wouldn't put it past him, but Jess hadn't looked at all upset, in fact she'd looked genuinely delighted to see them all.

John was great company. He had them crying with laughter with his tales about the care home and the residents.

Maggie told them about Sarah's latest dating mishap at the library. To be fair, Andy had looked nice, close to her ideal, well apart from the tattoo on his neck. And clean jeans would have been better, but Sarah's reaction on learning Maggie was reading to four children under five in the back of his car was a little over the top.

'I didn't ask your mother to babysit,' he protested.

'That's not the point.' Sarah pouted.

Maggie would have preferred her to argue the "mother" bit, but she didn't.

'I rang to cancel but she offered,' Andy said. 'She said she didn't want to be late, but if we wanted to meet for a quick coffee, both of you were going to the library straight after work.'

Maggie had heard enough. She wound the car window back up at that point and continued with the tales of Hairy Caterpillar. A lot of hand waving went on until Sarah stomped off.

'Two down, three to go,' Maggie told Jess, Neil and John. 'In my defence your honour, there was no mention of children on her "definitely not" list. I guess we should assume they're on it. But I don't think she should be allowed to change the goalposts at the drop of a hat, do you?'

'Who else is on this list?' John asked, when he'd stopped laughing.

Maggie took her notepad from her handbag and passed it over. Both men pored over it.

'Why are some crossed through?' Neil asked.

'I have a list of questions. If I don't like their answers, they get crossed out. Simple as that. I really do have Sarah's interests at heart.'

'What was wrong with Billy?' John asked. 'You've written "unsuitable" – is that "neckwear" you've written next to it?'

'Weird,' Maggie answered. 'Said his only ties were cats.'

'I suppose the number next to them is their age,' Neil said. 'What's with the rest of the letters?'

'First three letters are star signs – Sarah was specific. Then there's favourite food, relationship status, criminal record, pets; describe yourself in one word …'

'Did someone really describe themselves as vulgar?' John asked.

'Looks like it. Or are dogmatic, jealous, possessive and oversexed your opinions?' Neil asked.

'Possibly.' Maggie felt light-headed and warm. It was a strange feeling. It could be the wine, she wasn't used to drinking, but it probably had a lot to do with the company too.

'What about you?' Jess said, looking at Neil. 'How would you describe yourself?'

He turned to Maggie. 'Do you want to tell her?'

'Warm-hearted,' Maggie said.

'What?' Jess looked confused.

'Favourite music? Another of her questions,' Neil said. 'Oh yes, I'm on her list. "NJ, 36, Vir, Chinese, Springsteen" – that's me, isn't it?'

'You *were* on the list,' Maggie said. 'I crossed you off fairly quickly.'

'Because I liked Bruce Springsteen?'

'No,' Maggie said. 'Although the correct answer to the music question was Acres. They're Sarah's current favourite.'

'So why?' All three looked at her expectantly.

'Too old.' She tidied up her cutlery but when she looked up, they were still waiting. 'Okay, okay, I just didn't feel you were at the right point to think about entering into a new relationship with a woman.'

Neil spluttered.

Jess and John stared.

Someone, Maggie wasn't sure who said, 'What?'

'Sarah and I overheard him in the car park talking to someone on the phone about taking a relationship with a colleague to a new level,' she said, defensively and folded her serviette. 'A male colleague and he was talking about them becoming partners.'

'Do you mean Ross?' Neil asked.

'Possibly.' Maggie wished she could remember how to make the linen square into a boat.

'I was talking to my father. The jury is still out about whether I'll offer Ross a partnership. At the moment, he's on his honeymoon.' He turned to look at Jess. 'It was Ross's wedding when I met you. Tell her.'

'He was definitely at a wedding.' Jess laughed. 'Does that mean he's back on the list?'

'I bloody hope not.' He laughed back, not taking his eyes off Jess.

They sparked off each other. They were perfect together.

'What's wrong with the guy from Customer Services?' Neil asked. 'He seems keen.'

'Definitely not,' Jess and Maggie said together, and everyone dissolved into laughter.

'It's all right for you two,' Maggie said, once they'd composed themselves. 'Jess and I still have three dates to find for Sarah. And she's getting impatient.'

John mentioned the local golf club used to have a singles night, but when Neil checked on his phone it was for over fifties, so they teased John for a while.

Maggie talked about her garden, Jess about her photography and the conversation flowed easily. Maggie couldn't remember the last time she'd enjoyed an evening so much, even if it did go faster than she would've liked. The sort of night she wished could have gone on forever.

The taxi dropped her first. John walked her to her front door.

'Thank you,' he said, watching as she turned the key in the door. 'For a very enjoyable evening.' He hesitated.

What should she do now? Was she supposed to ask him in for a coffee?

'There's something I wanted to put to you earlier,' he said, looking down.

Maggie tensed, afraid of what might come next. The mood seemed to have shifted.

'I know you said you hadn't decided about your mother's wake, but would you consider holding it at Treetops? That way, a few of the residents could be involved.'

'Seriously?' It was as if someone had thrown her a lifeline. 'I'd love to.' She smiled. 'To tell the truth, I haven't even thought about trying to organise that.'

Maggie closed the door behind her. She felt too alive to think about bed. She'd had a lovely evening and it didn't sound like it was going to be the last one. John took her hand as he said goodbye. 'Could we do this again sometime soon?' he asked.

And she nodded as enthusiastically as one of those dogs that used to sit in the back window of cars as he raised her hand to his lips and kissed it.

Jess had had far too much to drink to drive, they both had, and Neil had to collect Dudley from the friends he'd called when he'd decided to eat at Grey Towers. They'd popped over and scooped the dog up, Neil promising he wouldn't be late. The earlier rain had passed through and a walk after consuming so much food seemed like a good idea.

When he suggested walking Jess home, she'd happily agreed. She didn't discover until halfway home that they lived on opposite sides of town. By any stretch of the imagination it was a lengthy diversion, but Neil just shrugged and said he didn't mind.

She couldn't remember anything before the kiss, or much after it come to that. It hadn't felt like a mile and a half, it had gone far quicker than she would've wished. The whole evening had.

Maggie and John had been perfect company. Conversation flowed easily round the table. There were jokes, laughter and incredible food.

The main course was so amazing Jess thought she'd died and gone to heaven, and judging by all the empty plates, so did everyone else.

And that was before the lemon soufflé.

'That's me,' she said, pointing to the house with an estate agent's sign in the front garden.

'You're selling up?'

Not me, just Martin. 'Already had an offer, so got to get my finger out and find somewhere to live.'

Neil stroked her cheek and tilted her chin upwards. 'It'll be all right.'

'Will it?' she murmured, closing her eyes. Any further response was impossible, as his mouth met hers. A light moan escaped his lips. A warmth swept upwards through her body as if she had caught fire. She put her arms round his neck, feeling as though she was on the verge of something dangerous. Exhilarating but dangerous. She gasped and he pulled her towards him, his fingers running through her hair. Her lips parted allowing his tongue to explore her mouth. When they pulled apart, he kept her hugged to his chest. She didn't open her eyes until he'd kissed both eyelids.

'Hi,' she said, looking up at him.

'Hi yourself.' He smiled. 'I guess this is goodnight.'

It doesn't have to be. Come in. Stay the night. Stay the rest of your life. 'Do you have time for a coffee?'

He shook his head, not taking his eyes off her. 'I'd love to, but I should collect Dudley. And the walk will do me good.'

'I'll see you soon?' Jess walked down the drive. When she got to the door, she turned and blew him a kiss.

'Right back at you,' he said, blowing one back. She watched him walk to the end of the cul-de-sac before she let herself in.

Chapter Twenty-Five

Jess opened one eye. It couldn't be six o'clock. Surely not. She couldn't have been asleep an hour, let alone any longer. It wasn't fair. It always happened. She'd got to a good bit in her dream, a bit she wanted to last forever then she'd woken up. And this morning's dream promised to be one of the best she'd had for a long time. Neil Jackson had come to rescue her.

'Hold on,' he'd said. 'I'll be right there.' Jess had been standing on the roof of her car in the middle of Redford Lake. She'd been run off the road by Martin. Neil's motor cruiser pulled up alongside, he lifted her to safety, wrapped her in a blanket and held her.

She looked up into his eyes. His green eyes. They were bright green.

Except they weren't his. His eyes weren't green, Jess knew they weren't. But the time glaring at her from the alarm clock was. Its neon glow shouted 5.45.

She shut her eyes to try to get back to sleep. She still had fifteen minutes before the alarm was supposed to go off, and in fifteen minutes, a girl could be grateful, very grateful indeed. She tried to hide under the duvet, but heard a rhythmical knock, slow at first, then building.

Jess took the stairs two at a time, not bothering to put on her dressing gown or her slippers. She didn't check her face in the mirror, although, with hindsight, she rather wished she had. But at quarter to six in the morning, the only way to make the noise stop was to open the door. She didn't stop to think about who was on the other side of it. She didn't care whether it was George Clooney or Bonnie and Clyde as long as they stopped bloody knocking.

'Tell me you're not Jehovah's Witnesses.'

A man and a woman stood on the doorstep. Both wore suits but behind them stood four others in unmistakeable police uniform. Jess squinted, not believing what she saw.

'We're not Jehovah's Witnesses,' said the woman, stepping forward, and holding out a hand with some sort of card in it. 'Redford Police. Inspector Lenham. This is DS Cobb. Can we come in?'

Jess didn't bother answering because the inspector had already walked past her and stood in her hall. She stood aside to allow DS Cobb through and then the rest of them. Her mouth opening and shutting all the time.

'We have a warrant to search your property.' A piece of paper was shoved at her. Jess took it and walked through to the kitchen, suddenly aware she wasn't wearing slippers as her feet hit the cold tiles. She turned back to the hall carpet, managing to get one foot back on it, before she bumped straight into the inspector.

'Is there anyone else here?' the woman asked, not moving.

Jess shook her head, not moving either. 'Just me and my cat.' The policemen scattered, one into the sitting room, three ran upstairs.

'I'm going to need you to stay here,' the inspector said, as Jess turned to follow them.

'Here?'

'All clear, ma'am,' came a shout from upstairs.

'Good.'

The male sergeant behind Jess said, 'Why don't you sit in the kitchen. Make yourself a cup of tea. Looks like you could do with one.'

The inspector nodded.

Jess shook her head. 'My feet are cold. I need my slippers.'

'Where are they?' the sergeant asked.

Jess explained and asked for her dressing gown too, which hung behind the door in the bathroom, if he didn't mind. He took himself upstairs.

She was sorry he'd gone because that meant it was just her and Mrs Inspector, stood on about a foot of carpet, staring at each other. At that distance, the woman had a supercilious look, a bit like the expression Martin used to wear whenever he thought he had one over on her. A sort of smug, insufferable expression, that always made Jess want to punch his lights out.

'You haven't asked why we're here,' the inspector said. 'I guess you were expecting us.'

Jess stared at her. Expecting them. No way.

'If you tell us where they are, we won't need to tear the place apart looking for them. Of course, my team try to be tidy, but well with the best will in the world you know what men are like, and this lot when they get excited …' Her voice trailed off. It was flat, sounded official but patronising as well. Jess wondered how many times she'd used that line. Was that what they taught you at police college?

The sergeant came back with Jess's slippers and dressing gown. Jess smiled her thanks for his kindness, slipped the gown on and fastened the belt as tight as she could, before she answered. She rubbed the sleep out of her eyes, then wished she hadn't. Somehow it was easier to talk to a blur. 'I don't know what you're talking about,' she said, walking into the kitchen.

Mrs Inspector looked about as if she was considering whether to buy the place rather than search it. 'The warrant is specific,' she said, sitting down at the table. 'Why don't you read it? Or do you want me to read it to you?'

'No.' Jess surprised herself with the force the words came out. 'I can read.'

'Of course you can.' The inspector turned away and talked to one of the other policemen in a hushed voice.

It's difficult to tell if someone is being sarcastic when you can't see the curl of their lip or their eyebrow halfway up the forehead.

Jess left the paper on the worktop while she made drinks. That's what her mother would recommend. She filled the kettle and took some mugs from a cupboard. 'Tea?' she asked.

'Please,' the woman said.

'Any chance of coffee?' the sergeant asked.

'What about the others?' Jess asked.

'They're fine.'

Comforted by the hot drink, Jess sat down at the table and picked up the warrant. 'It says, "stolen jewellery".'

'That's right.'

'What stolen jewellery?'

'Ma'am.' Jess was aware of movement behind her. One of the policemen put a handkerchief on the table. Jess recognised the necklace Leanne had given her poking out.

'That stolen jewellery.' Inspector Lenham put down her cup and stood up. 'Jessica Willersey, I am arresting you for theft …'

'I didn't steal it.'

'… You do not have to say anything, but it may harm your defence if you do not mention, when questioned, something which you later rely on in court.'

The rest of the words seemed to run into one another. Jess couldn't believe what was happening. Apart from the parking ticket she'd picked up photographing Darren and Leanne's wedding, she'd only ever got one speeding ticket in her life, but she'd been so embarrassed about that, she'd sent a letter of apology with her driving license and cheque. Suddenly everyone was staring at her.

'Why don't you get dressed?' the inspector said.

Chapter Twenty-Six

Neil watched the black BMW with a personalised number plate pull up outside his office and frowned. He'd been intensely grateful when Martin Cowley had been delayed the previous night, and was happy to reschedule their meeting, especially as Martin was prepared to come to his office, but something about the car bothered him.

If he'd been questioned, he would have sworn the same one had been in the hotel car park last night when he arrived. Granted, he'd been sheltering Jess from the rain and in such close proximity to the woman, his jangling brain cells had left him incapable of all rational thought, but he'd been surprised at the time to get the call from Martin saying he was stuck on the M4 and at least an hour away.

Neil rung Anymoore earlier, needing to hear Jess's voice. That wasn't the reason he gave. She hadn't been there. The receptionist asked if she could pass on a message, but he couldn't think of anything to say that wouldn't sound odd.

Two things had become increasingly clear. One, he had feelings for Jess and hoped she might be starting to feel the same way about him. She had certainly looked pleased when he'd asked if he could join her for supper in the restaurant last night. He loved hearing the sound of her laughter and they'd laughed a lot. And then the kiss. She'd closed her eyes and leant into him. He'd put his arms around her to keep her safe and held her. He smiled at the memory. Her lips were soft and warm. When they finally pulled apart, she'd opened her eyes and sighed. If only she knew how difficult it had been for him to walk away. He'd just wanted to kiss her again and again.

He straightened up, thinking about Jess Willersey before an important meeting wasn't wise. He needed to get a grip.

Two, the atmosphere in the office was better. Tanya had been in a noticeably better mood since Ross had been away. Last Friday she'd brought in home-made brownies and a doggy chew for Dudley.

They were busy. She'd worked a lot more hours than she was contracted to, but they were completely up to date.

At no point in the last fortnight had Neil got back into the office to find an answering machine full of unlistenable-to messages or the contact email account full of unanswered queries that would take him most of the evening to sort out.

Tanya had dealt with everything.

Appointments had been made. Requests for information answered and quotes sent out. Work had been billed and outstanding invoices chased.

She'd even taken on the urgent design and layout of sales brochures for one of their established companies, checking Neil was happy before she sent the proofs back to the customer. She had a good eye – he was impressed. The new brochure looked more professional than their last one. And the quote she'd secured for printing was competitive, so even with the Jackson Consultancy fee, the customer said they were still paying less than in previous years. She'd looked pleased when he'd thanked her.

'Could I have a go at the Jackson Consultancy brochures and stationery if I get time?' she asked, looking a little nervous as she put a cup of tea in front of him. 'And maybe tweak a few things on the website. I'd like to get more involved if that's okay with you. After all, I studied media and communication at university. One of our customers this week told me he wished we did web design. We could, at least I could, but apparently, he spoke to Ross about it and he recommended another company. He said they'd helped with ours.'

Neil must have looked surprised because Tanya suddenly blushed and looked embarrassed. 'I mean ours is fine,' she said. 'I think …'

'It could be better?' he prompted.

She nodded. 'Nothing serious. Updated pictures, a few more recent customers' testimonials, that sort of thing. Maybe a news section we update regularly. And we should make our policy on the use of cookies clear.'

The buzzer on the outside door sounded. 'I'll make coffee, shall I?' she said.

'What are you saying?' Neil paced round the office. 'The heads of terms and exclusivity agreement have been agreed, we're in the process of due diligence to meet the ridiculously short deadline you've set for signing of contracts. You can't now change the terms without a material reason for doing so.'

'We have one. Anymoore Ltd's lost one of its major contracts.'

'Which one?'

Martin looked like he was about to shrug, so Neil repeated the question – louder.

'Robinsons.'

Neil laughed. 'In that case the price should go up. That contract has been making a loss for two years. Losing it might dent turnover, but not profitability. Robinsons have been costing the company money for years.' He picked up the report from his desk and flicked through the pages until he found what he was looking for.

'There are six months to run on the existing contract and you will see I recommended that following the merger that contract is not renewed. The fact Robinsons have taken the decision out of Anymoore's hands I think is excellent news.'

'You are supposed to act on my behalf, and I am telling you I want to pay less.'

'The current price is on the derogatory side of low already. Have you read my report? Here look: "The company appears unaffected by the current economic downturn. It has a constant loyal customer base and a proactive project team. It has a large portfolio of diverse customers spread over different industries, for whom Anymoore deal with initial installation and ongoing maintenance of computer systems and software, providing a 24/7 support service. Six customers account for 80% of the company's turnover, but their contribution to the net profit is significantly lower than average, with two companies actually costing the company money. Both contracts have been rolled over for several years, with no significant investment in new systems and Anymoore Ltd is now maintaining obsolete software and equipment. Forecasts are based on these losses being on-going and my recommendation would be that the clients are advised it is Anymoore Ltd's intention to end the contracts at the next renewal date after acquisition."'

'My accountant has read it and I have emailed it across to Ross for his comments.'

'You've done what?'

'Ross persuaded me there is no cause to accuse you of material non-disclosure but agrees with me the offer should be lower.'

Neil ran his fingers through his hair in exasperation. 'My opinion is that the loss of that contract doesn't make the company any less attractive. My recommendation as to the price stands.'

Martin fiddled with his jacket sleeves. 'Valuation is not an exact science. At the end of the day, a business is worth what parties agree it is worth. I don't believe Anymoore Ltd is worth what we originally estimated.'

Neil heard the kettle starting to boil and Tanya getting the coffee out of the cupboard.

He couldn't see whether Tanya had spooned the coffee into two cups or one. 'Mr Cowley is leaving,' he said.

'My contract is with you.' Martin stood up. 'Please make the revised offer today, with a view to contracts being finalised before the end of next week. If you feel you can't, Ross has offered to return early from his honeymoon and take over.'

'I'll make your offer,' Neil said, 'and let you know the outcome.'

He used to watch *The Incredible Hulk* as a child and wonder how it would feel like to be so angry that you'd turn green and swell up. He might be about to find out. He needed to get out. 'Walk,' he said to Dudley, who wagged his tail at the magic word, but didn't look in any hurry to get up. 'Now!'

Chapter Twenty-Seven

'We need to clear the air.' Maggie said as she put down a box of four Belgian buns just out of Sarah's reach. 'I am sorry I didn't tell you about the children, although they were sweet, and they liked the tales of the Hairy Caterpillar.'

Sarah made a hmphing sound.

'And in the spirit of complete openness, I should tell you I went out for supper with someone last night.' Maggie took her mug and one of the buns back to her desk and sat down. 'I have taken advice on your "potentials" list and thrown it away. I am considering options for your next three dates but would be happy to receive suggestions.' She switched on her computer. The monitor only needed one slap before it remembered what it was supposed to be doing although clearly had no intention of hurrying. She nibbled the icing away from the side of her bun while she waited.

'Who?' Sarah asked eventually and reached out for a bun.

Maggie breathed a sigh of relief. Boundaries were coming down.

'Who did you go out with last night?'

'His name is John. I've helped him out in the kitchen at Treetops on a couple of occasions and he took me out to say thank you.'

'And you like him?'

'It's not like—'

'You said, no secrets.'

Maggie didn't actually remember saying that. 'Yes, I like him. It's early days and I am not getting excited, but he's suggested we hold Mum's wake at the nursing home so the less able residents can come to the do afterwards. I know you've done a lot already, but I could use your help. I've never planned a party. And I want it to be perfect.'

'Okay,' said Sarah. 'Actually, there's a lot we need to talk about regarding your mum's service. I've been to a couple of funerals, so I have some idea of how these things are done.'

Maggie jerked her eyes up from the office emails. 'That's why you keep having time off?'

Sarah nodded. 'Three now.'

'In one week. You should've said. I feel terrible now. I thought I was having a bad time – I had no idea you'd lost so many relatives or friends. Were they unexpected?'

'They were no one I knew,' Sarah said, the idea obviously amused her and she smiled. 'I turn up at funerals and watch. And I'm sorry about losing it yesterday. But four kids under five? Andy didn't need a girlfriend, he needed a nanny.'

'Hang on a minute. Let's wind back – why are you going to random strangers' funerals?' Maggie stared at Sarah. 'You can't keep changing the goalposts.'

'What goalposts?'

'The ones on your ever-growing list of essential requirements. Should I add'—she typed something on her keyboard, stared at the screen for a second or two, turned her head and stared at it again, this time at an angle—'taphophile to your list?'

'Tapho what?'

'Tombstone tourists according to Wikipedia.'

'Oh please.' Sarah rolled her eyes. 'I so wish I hadn't shown you Google. My requirements haven't changed – well, apart from the kiddy thing. But as we're having a no-holds barred, everything-on-the-table conversation this morning,' Sarah added, 'I do need to know some personal details for your mother.'

'Like what?' Maggie gritted her teeth, not liking the direction this conversation was taking one bit.

'Usual things – what she was like when she was younger, what did she do for a living, why you ended up living with your grandparents?'

Maggie frowned. 'Can't we gloss over that bit?' She made to get up; she needed to wash her hands.

'Sit,' Sarah said, fiercely.

Maggie did.

'Now tell me everything I want to know. We can decide what we leave out later.'

'I thought you wanted to talk about when contracts were to be signed.' Frank didn't sound angry, or resentful, yet Neil sensed he was hurt.

'That's what I hoped we'd be talking about, yes.'

He hadn't liked MJC's owner from the moment he'd met him.

Clearly, funding wasn't an issue. MJC were in a strong position and their bank had already agreed a loan in principle. But, at the end of the day, as Neil kept being reminded, he was working for MJC in this.

He couldn't believe the man could pull a stroke like he had this morning. Not a reasonable, rational honest man.

Frank wasn't greedy, and once the idea for the sale had been mooted, he seemed to embrace the idea of retirement enthusiastically. He hadn't even wanted to consult a solicitor else to look after his own interests. Neil was glad he'd insisted his sister Sophie's company help him.

'I'm sorry.'

Frank waved away the apology. 'At my age, I should know better than to start making plans before everything is signed sealed and delivered. I thought they were happy with the price. Do you think I'm being greedy?'

'No, I don't.' He watched Frank flick the pages of a boating magazine. 'That's what I am trying to say. When we worked out the company's value, we took into consideration your published accounts, but we also made an estimate of your projected earnings. On that basis my client made a reasonable offer, but less than I believe the company was worth.'

'How did they find out about Robinsons?' Frank looked genuinely confused. 'I know you can't tell me who your client is, but tell me how they found out?'

'I don't know. My client wouldn't say.'

Which bothered him. Martin Cowley had been cagey.

Had MJC put in a bid for the Robinsons work? They were in similar lines of business. Martin had been dismissive when he'd asked. When Ross got back to the office, he'd ask him to find out.

'When did you find out their decision?' Neil asked.

'Yesterday afternoon. Mr Robinson rang me to tell me they planned on scaling down their operations over the next couple of years and had taken a difficult decision to let us go. It was an amicable enough conversation. We've known each other many years. What should I do?'

'You want my advice?'

'Why wouldn't I?'

Neil could think of a hundred and one reasons. 'Okay, I think you should stick to your guns. The loss of the Robinson contract makes no difference. As I told my client this morning, there are potentially many cost savings which will work in the company's favour. It should not affect his offer price and I am embarrassed that he felt it did.'

Frank nodded. 'Are you telling me to refuse the offer?'

'Yes.' Neil sighed. 'I know it's not what you want to hear, but yes, I am. Your dream might be put on hold for a while, but I know of other companies within similar corporate sectors looking to expand. If you're happy, I can sound them out and put them in touch. I have no doubt we will have buyers fighting over you.'

'Will that take much longer?'

'I can't say.'

'What about the exclusivity agreement?'

'If my client wants the terms changed, so do you. They might hold an exclusivity contract, but it's linked to the current offer. I will go back and hint you've already been approached by two other companies who've heard on the grapevine you want to sell, and they want to talk terms. If you don't receive formal confirmation by the end of play today that my client is prepared to continue on the current agreed basis, then you consider the deal is off and will start talks with other interested parties.'

Frank nodded. 'Okay, do it. I should've told you about Robinsons yesterday as soon as he rang. I'm sorry.'

Great, make me feel like a complete shit. Neil would have objected had Frank's phone not began to ring.

Frank picked up the receiver. 'Hello.'

Neil stood up; they'd finished anyway.

'Jess? Why isn't she in?'

Neil picked up his briefcase. He couldn't make out the conversation but could hear a high-pitched voice on the other end of the line. As soon as he could catch Frank's eye, he'd tell him he'd ring later.

'Don't be ridiculous, Sarah. She can't be.'

The voice at the other end of the phone was talking faster and getting louder. Frank listened for a while without saying a word, his eyes growing wider, his face paler. Whoever it was, was still talking. Frank put his hand over the mouthpiece, looked up at Neil, and in a barely audible voice said, 'Jess has been arrested.'

Chapter Twenty-Eight

The room was nothing like Jess had imagined. It was smaller than anything she'd seen on any television police drama series. She couldn't remember *Midsomer Murders* ever interviewing suspects in an interview room. That's what she was, wasn't it? A prime suspect.

They were always interviewed in their homes. She wasn't even sure Midsomer had a police station.

As rooms went, this one was tiny. It had no window. On the plus side, it didn't appear to have a two-way mirrored wall either. A metal table screwed to the floor sat in the middle of the room with some sort of recording device on top.

Jess felt claustrophobic.

They'd asked her if she wanted to call a solicitor. She'd said no, but the question had shocked her – made her feel like a career criminal. She didn't have a solicitor; despite what she'd told Martin, her plan was to ask the estate agent to recommend one. The only time she'd ever had to use one was when she bought the house with Martin, and he'd found that one.

She couldn't remember the man's name or anything else about him other than he looked as nervous as a rabbit caught in headlights, every time she asked him a question, something that did nothing to inspire confidence even with something as mundane as house buying. It hadn't helped that his nose went into convulsions whenever he said certain words. Stamp duty, she remembered was a particularly vigorous twitcher. Goodness knows what it would do in this situation.

Six hours on, Jess wasn't sure it had been such a good idea to refuse. It felt like she'd been here for days rather than hours. She wasn't even sure where the questions were going. She kept repeating the same thing. No, she didn't know how valuable the jewellery was. No, she didn't know where Leanne and Darren had got it. Leanne told her it was her gran's. Would they keep her here all night, asking her the same questions until finally, exhausted she confessed? But she couldn't. She had no idea where they had got it from.

In TV programmes, the police always got their man, or woman, or child. But she wasn't it. She didn't know about any bloody jewellery.

They could wire her up to a lie detector, torture her, or threaten her cat but she still wouldn't be able to tell them otherwise.

Her fingers showed traces of having been inked when her prints had been taken. She'd washed them as best she could, but there were still black bits and they felt dirty.

She'd only had the one cup of tea at home this morning. Perhaps the torture had already started. Everyone who knew her knew she wasn't at her best in the mornings until she'd had at least two mugs.

The table in front of her had ring marks on it from hot drinks, so clearly some people had been given refreshment. Jess wondered how long she had to be here before she was offered something to drink and she could add her own ring mark to the others. There were some initials carved into the metal. How, she couldn't work out. All her possessions had been taken from her in the custody suite earlier. They hadn't searched her; they didn't have to. The inspector had watched her get dressed, so presumably she knew Jess didn't have a Swiss army knife strapped to her leg. Laid out on the table between ring marks were plastic bags, containing the jewellery they'd found earlier.

'It's not mine,' she said, when the inspector asked her if she recognised it.

'I know it's not yours. That's why we're here.' In the silence that followed, the ticking of the plastic clock on the wall above the door sounded unnaturally loud. Even the hum of the machine recording her words was audible.

'They belong to Darren and Leanne,' she said, speaking straight at the machine.

'That would be Darren Fielding would it?' The inspector turned to the sergeant. 'Do you want to tell her or shall I?'.

Jess felt relieved. They knew Darren. 'Yes, that's right. Ask him. He'll tell you Leanne gave it to me.'

The sergeant picked up one of the bags. 'We've already spoken to Mr Fielding,' he said. 'That's how we knew where to find it.'

'So, you know I didn't steal it.' Jess smiled; confident they'd soon realise the error of their ways.

Inspector Lenham looked back at her. Something in her face suggested she didn't share Jess's self-assurance. 'Darren Fielding admitted taking it, but said he was stealing it to order.'

'Did he tell you who?'

'He did indeed Ms Willersey. Darren says he stole it on your instructions.'

Jess's mouth opened and closed; nothing came out. She sat immobilised, staring at the woman opposite her.

'In fact, he says, this isn't the first time you've provided him with an address, and a shopping list, so to speak.'

'No.' The high-pitched sound that left her mouth Jess barely recognised as her own. She coughed. 'I have never suggested Darren should steal anything. I hardly know him. I met him for the first time at his wedding.'

'You're friends with his wife?'

'No.'

'Yet they invited you to their wedding?'

'They didn't invite me. I took their wedding pictures. I'm a part-time photographer.'

The inspector wrote something down on her pad.

'How come they chose you? Where do you advertise?'

Jess looked at her hands. They felt clammy and wet. She was starting to sweat in the warmth of the room. 'I don't,' she said weakly. 'Leanne overheard me talking to my colleagues in a pub – The Olde Swan. We don't normally go there, but it was close to the college.'

Inspector Lenham folded her arms. 'Go on,' she said, the undertone in her voice suggested her patience was running out.

'I'd done a photography course. Sarah and Maggie came with me for my certificate presentation. We all went for a drink afterwards and I said I was thinking about photographing weddings. I said I wanted to practise first, maybe not charge full price for the first couple. Maggie and Sarah joked I could always do theirs.

'Sarah's been on about getting married as long as I've known her, but so far, she hasn't managed to persuade anyone up the aisle. Maggie's in her sixties. Her mum has died, although now she's met John …'

'Ms Willersey, I know I said in your own time, but I knock off in two hours and I'd like to have finished taking your statement before then.'

The inspector's voice was level, she hadn't raised it but it had an edge to it, that made Jess shiver.

'Leanne overheard us talking and said I could do her wedding for £150. I said no, but Sarah gave her our work number and told her to ring in a couple of days to give her time to talk me into it which she did. I met Leanne before the wedding but Darren wasn't there.'

'Can you prove any of this?' the inspector asked.

'Maggie and Sarah, my work colleagues,' Jess said, weakly. 'Speak to them.'

Jess jumped as the door to the room opened and a woman police officer peered round. Inspector Lenham didn't turn around until the woman said, 'A word please, ma'am.'

The sergeant said something for the tape, looked at his watch, announced the time and switched off the machine as both women left the room. 'We raided The Olde Swan last week,' he said, as the door clicked shut.

Chapter Twenty-Nine

Maggie sat and stared out of the window. She felt wrung out, drained. Sarah had pushed her hard, asking endless questions about her mother or trying to find out what music she wanted played at the funeral.

'I need three pieces of music,' Sarah said. 'Think of them as your desert island moments. We won't play the whole track unless you can't think of anything for me to say, but we'll play bits of each at various points during the funeral.

Maggie wasn't religious and her mother had only ever gone to church for weddings, baptisms or, more often than not these days, funerals. She might have no idea what music people played at funerals, but she liked *Desert Island Discs*. The guests had to choose eight pieces of music, a book and an object.

"Maggie May" would be her first choice. The song of her teenage years, her grandfather used to sing it all the time. She'd always been his "Maggie" never Margaret. Her mother would roll her eyes. She was the only one who ever called her Margaret. Three syllables she could linger on were so much better when they were spat out with venom than two.

Rod Stewart, surely given the number of years he'd been around, must have sung something appropriate for a funeral. She'd wrote his name on a post-it note and passed it to Sarah.

Maggie felt alone and shivered. Loneliness was a cold feeling. What did she expect? She wondered who would be doing this for her when her turn came. Everyone she'd known and loved had gone before her.

What was her favourite food, Sarah had asked.

'Rhubarb and custard cake.' Said without hesitation.

'Favourite TV programme?'

Tricky one. Her mother watched anything and everything, wall-to-wall telly from breakfast until bedtime.

Maggie toyed with the theme tune to *Bargain Hunt*. At least it would be a piece of music her mother recognised.

Ray had called her "Square-eyed Rose" long before *Kilroy* and *Neighbours* became part of her essential viewing.

He loved his music. He'd have found the prospect of only selecting three pieces the hard bit. It was Ray who once took Maggie to the only concert she'd ever been to. Queen at the Milton Keynes Bowl. He had worshipped Queen.

Tickets were like gold dust. She never did find out how he managed to get two. Or how much he had to pay. But she had loved every minute of that evening. It might have been nearly forty years ago, but the clarity of her memories from that night still surprised her. They'd sung "Bohemian Rhapsody" and "Crazy Little Thing Called Love" all the way home.

'Our song,' Ray had said, squeezing her hand. 'It will always be our song,' he'd added.

It had been a great evening, even her mother's best burning martyr impression for the following few weeks hadn't taken the shine off her happiness.

That evening, she was on top of the world. Like that Carpenters' song. Humming the tune, she tried to remember the lyrics. *Desert Island Disc* choice maybe, but not suitable for her mother's funeral.

Her "happy ever after" lasted less than a year. Freddie Mercury only survived eight years longer than Ray.

There had been no funeral for Ray. A memorial service had been held six months later for all those who lost their lives in the conflict. It wasn't the same. If she was choosing music for Ray's service, she'd want something by Queen.

'What did Rose think happened after death?' Sarah had asked.

Maggie shrugged. 'Cremation, I suppose. That's what's happened to all our other relations. Why? Should I consider taxidermy, or freezing her in case some miracle cure is forthcoming?'

She was being facetious, but Sarah clearly wasn't happy. Hands on hips, eyes narrowed. 'What about you?' she'd asked. 'What do you believe happens after death?'

There had been a lot of questions like that. Sarah's response of 'Just answer the sodding question,' hadn't been the sympathetic ear Maggie had expected.

But memories had started to form. In some cases, just snatches. A girl, wearing a pink dress and blowing out cake candles. Her cheeks puffed out. She blew hard. So hard it hurt. A boy held her hand. He blew too. The memory faded. Maggie couldn't be sure she was the girl. Were there guinea pigs? Or was her memory playing tricks?

She certainly had a guinea pig, just one, then he was gone, and she'd cried. There had been a lot of tears. Her mother was there with other adults. 'You've lost him,' one of them said.

'He's not lost,' Maggie remembered saying, possibly with some stamping of feet involved. 'He's just not moving.'

"Memories", she wrote carefully on her pad.

Chapter Thirty

It took Jess a moment or two, once she'd walked out of the police station, to notice Neil leaning against his car. Her heart raced. She didn't care why he was there, she just wanted to run to him. She didn't, but it took all her effort to hang on to what little composure she had left and walk slowly across the road. It was market day and the high street was full, but she was bloody sure someone was watching her, probably Inspector Lenham. The woman hadn't looked happy when she'd come back into the room and told Jess she could go.

'Something has come to light,' she'd said. 'We need to make further enquiries.'

The sergeant made some remark about not leaving the country and that the clock on the wall said ten to four. Ten minutes until the inspector finished her shift, she seemed in a hurry to get going, so she collected up her papers, the jewellery and the tape and left Jess to the sergeant.

'I'll see you out,' he said as Jess collected her watch and house keys from the custody suite.

'I understand there's someone waiting for you,' he said as he typed some numbers into the keypad next to the door and pushed the door open. The sergeant made no attempt to walk through it but signalled she should. 'Been there a while.' The door closed again before she could turn around and ask him where, who, or anything else.

'Come on, get in and let's get out of here,' Neil said. 'I'm opposite a police station parked on double yellow lines.' Hardly the most romantic of greetings and he barely glanced at her as he opened the passenger door. She got in. Dudley, on the back seat, was beside himself with delight. As she did up her seat belt, he licked her face. At least someone was pleased to see her.

'You've got Sarah to thank they've bailed you,' Neil said, as he started the engine.

'I haven't been charged with anything,' Jess said. Looking out of the window, she caught sight of herself in the wing mirror and shut her eyes. *Oh God, no.*

'She found the receipt you'd tried to make Leanne sign in your desk drawer with the bounced cheque. What did the police say?'

'They will continue to make enquiries and be in touch.' Jess tried not to cry. Until that moment she'd conveniently forgotten her hair looked the same as it had when she'd got out of bed that morning. She was wearing no make-up and her decorating outfit of tracksuit trousers and one of Martin's old and shapeless jumpers. It was the first thing she could lay her hands on. She hadn't wanted to root through her wardrobe with the inspector sitting on her bed watching her every move.

'How did you know where I was?'

'I was with Frank, when Sarah rang.'

'You weren't expecting to be in today, were you?'

'Something came up.'

'I'm glad,' she muttered under her breath as they drew up to a roundabout and Neil brought the car to a halt.

'What did you say?'

Jess bit her lip, staring straight ahead. 'Nothing.'

The car behind chose that moment to honk its horn. Neil looked in his mirror and pulled away. The wheels screeched, but from his profile, he seemed to be smiling. The rest of the journey flew past and suddenly he pulled up outside her house. If she'd been quizzed on how they got there, she wouldn't have been able to say. As he turned off the engine, Jess turned to face him. He moved towards her. She closed her eyes, hoping he was about to kiss her again like he did last night when he took her breath away and made her feel special. After the day she'd had, she needed to feel special, except when the kiss came, it felt like the side of her face was being rasped. Whatever Neil's intentions, Dudley had got there first.

'Would you like a cup of tea?' she asked, recovering her composure.

'Have you eaten anything today?'

'I'm all right,' she said, her left hand opening the door.

'I know you are.' He gripped her other hand. 'But that doesn't stop …'

Dudley, realising this to be his best chance of escape, leapt over the back seat on to Jess's lap and out of the open door before either of them could stop him. He bounded up the drive towards General Gordon sat on the doorstep. There was no disguising the cat's displeasure.

'Crikey, that's one happy looking cat,' said Neil, leaning over and peering through the passenger door.

Dudley sat down, in front of General Gordon, who tilted his head and glowered at him. Dudley tilted his head too, then lifted a paw. The cat stared back, then stood up, arched his back and walked across to the dog.

'This is going to end in tears.' Jess tried to free herself from the seat belt and Neil's grip in case she had to rescue the situation.

'Hold on,' he said.

Dudley lay down and General Gordon, his tail erect, had a good sniff then sat down next to him and started washing.

'I don't ruddy believe it,' Jess said. 'That cat's been known to eat postmen for breakfast.'

It took them two hours to clear the house. Jess had forgotten about the search until she opened the front door. Neil helped.

She saw him raise his eyes when he saw the mess in the hall, and it occurred to her perhaps he thought that was how she normally lived.

She made a cup of tea, and afterwards gave him an opportunity to go, saying she wanted to get started with the tidy up. She wouldn't have blamed him if he'd gone, but he hadn't. He stayed and vacuumed the carpets as she put everything back in the drawers, cupboards or any other cubbyhole it had been dragged from.

Why didn't the police employ women in search teams? At least they'd take their shoes off when they entered a house. And if they opened a cupboard, there was perhaps a reasonable chance they'd think to shut it again, even put the contents back. Upstairs, thankfully, had been relatively untouched. She was grateful the police had found what they were looking for before they'd completely trashed the place.

Neil suggested Jess should take a shower while he went to get food.

It hadn't been his idea to go for a Chinese takeaway. He'd have happily taken her out for a meal. The idea of a quiet restaurant somewhere appealed to him, but after their cleaning marathon Jess opted for a quiet night in. She looked totally done in. He hadn't been entirely sure when she suggested a takeaway whether she meant a quiet evening in with him or without.

Only when she pulled an impressive array of takeaway menus from the hall table drawer and asked him what he fancied did he figure it must be okay to hang around.

The final choice came down to Asian fusion or Chinese. Early on, they'd ruled out pizzas, pasta, hamburgers, fried chicken or fish and chips. The final decision took longer, until Neil put both menus behind his back. 'Left or right?' he asked.

'Left,' she said, until he produced the Asian fusion menu. 'No, right,' she said, jumping up and down. 'I meant right.'

He laughed and said it had to be Asian fusion but had gone for a Chinese anyway.

'I got a set meal for two,' he said, handing over a bulging plastic bag.

'This is for two?'

'I asked them to add extra spare ribs and prawn balls.' She turned and grinned at him. He wanted to kiss her. Earlier in the car, he'd been about to kiss her when Dudley started licking her face. This time she was busy dealing with the bag on the worktop.

He sat at the bench in the kitchen and watched her take the lids off all the foil dishes to arrange them on a tray which she set down in the middle of the kitchen table. She added a spoon to each.

In the forty-five minutes it had taken for the meal to cook, she'd had a shower. She smelt minty and was wearing a long jumper and black jeans. Her hair was scraped back away from her face into a huge plastic clip. Her face looked scrubbed. She must've scrubbed hard; she'd managed to put some colour back in her cheeks. He wanted to hold her tight and protect her. No, who was he trying to kid, she stirred emotions in him that were far from protective.

'Dudley's in the lounge,' she said. 'He's in front of the fire and General G is on top of the sofa watching him. Red wine okay?'

'Red wine's perfect,' he said. 'Have you got a bottle opener?'

She opened a drawer by the cooker and passed him a corkscrew.

'You know there's a message on your phone, don't you?'

'Can you press the white button then?' she said taking two large glasses out of the cupboard.

The phone whirred and a computerised female announced she had been called that morning just before twelve.

'I've never read the instructions.' Jess looked embarrassed. Neil held out a glass of wine.

'Jess,' a man's voice cut in. She froze and stared at the machine.

'I need to arrange a time for the buyer's surveyor to come and check the property at a time to suit. Obviously, we're happy to help, but you need to let us have a key. He's keen to get moving on this and I also need details of your solicitor.'

'That's the estate agent. Wow, it sounds like everything's really going full steam ahead.' She put down her glass and picked up a fork.

The man rambled on a bit more and then left a name and number which he repeated even slower the second time round before hanging up.

The computerised voice went through another ramble about how there were no more messages and how Jess could delete the one she had if she pressed a button. Jess stabbed a pork ball and put the whole thing in her mouth. The ball was either bigger or hotter than she thought, because she seemed to be having difficulty digesting it.

Neil didn't laugh. 'Are you all right?' he asked.

She nodded, but he still had to wait a while for her to swallow before he got a proper answer.

'Sorry, I'm okay, I'm just being silly. I hoped it might take a bit longer to sell. The house was only on the market for a week. And I haven't found anywhere to live.'

Clearly she wasn't okay, because she went for a second pork ball with equal venom.

Neil stretched across the table and took hold of her arm to give it a reassuring squeeze. The gesture made her jump and she dropped the fork and the ball. For a second, she looked about to cry. She stared at him wide-eyed, but didn't move her hand. She did not move anything, she just sat there.

The pork ball made a bid for freedom, rolled straight across the table and on to the floor. He wondered about picking it up, but that would have meant letting go of her arm and he didn't want to. 'Jess,' Neil said, quietly. 'Would you rather I left?'

Her head snapped up and she stared at him.

'No.' She blinked.

He hoped she wasn't about to burst into tears, but looked around for some kitchen towel, just in case.

'No,' she said, firmly. 'I want you to stay.'

His mouth started to twist into a smile, which he tried to stop because it didn't seem appropriate. Thankfully, she couldn't see his stomach flipping. 'That's okay, then,' he said. 'Look why don't we have a drink while we warm this up in the oven, then we can start again?'

Neil put the two plates back in the oven, he felt vaguely alarmed. Jess looked as if she was working hard to keep tears away. And clearly he wasn't helping.

'Sorry,' she mumbled. 'I'm not usually like this. Wine and sympathy are a heady combination. Whatever must you think of me?'

'I think you're a strong, gorgeous woman – and you should remember that.'

'Oh I will.' She took a large sip of her wine and smiled at him. 'I am a strong … what was that other word?'

He put the food back on the table and grinned. 'Gorgeous,' he said.

'A strong gorgeous woman, who tomorrow needs to start looking for somewhere to live. But tonight, is having supper with an equally gorgeous man.'

The food, even Neil had to admit, was delicious and the nice thing about Chinese takeaway was the washing up didn't take long. Dudley and General Gordon devoured the leftovers. Dudley grudgingly left the cat's bowl alone, while making it clear that as soon as his new best friend left the room, he would finish whatever was left.

Neil carried full glasses of wine through to the sitting room.

'Why are you single?' Jess asked suddenly, flopping down on the floor next to the sofa and looking up at him.

The question seemed to come out of the blue, catching him unawares. The woman was direct, he'd give her that.

'Would it sound corny if I said I'm looking for someone special, rather than someone simply available?'

'Yep,' she made pretend vomiting gestures as she pulled her hair from the clip and let it fall loosely around her shoulders.

And I don't want to hurt any more. Probably nearer the truth. When the end came last time around, it was hard. It had been some months before he'd even told his parents Emma had gone. When he had, they assumed it was his fault. He couldn't see any point in telling them otherwise. Partly, because they wouldn't have believed him and partly because he couldn't bring himself to believe how badly he'd been hurt by her leaving.

The divorce had been drawn out and painful. Why two rational people felt the need to fight over cheese graters and fitted sheets, he still didn't comprehend. He'd made a promise two years ago not to let anyone ever get that close again and he'd kept it. He had Dudley. He didn't need anyone else. It was that determination which made him successful in business. Once he made up his mind about something or someone, he stuck to it. His mother often said it was something he'd done ever since he was a kid. She'd always bring up the time he learnt to ride a bike as an example of her philosophising: it didn't matter how many times he fell over or grazed his knees, she'd tell whichever audience she had at the time, he'd persevered.

Suddenly his leg hurt. Neil rubbed his knee. The scars were still visible as a testament to how difficult he'd found it.

'He doesn't have the same coordination or balance as his sister,' he'd heard his mother whisper one day.

It had been like that with their love interests too. His sister fell in and out of love at the drop of a hat. She always had some boy on her arm who fell for her charm, or her easy humour. Neil had envied her, until Emma came along.

There had been other girls since Emma, but none of them had ever made him feel like the girl sitting next to him. Something about her fascinated him and had done from the first moment he'd seen her.

But surely, at thirty-six he was old enough and wise enough not to believe in love at first sight – wasn't he?

Jess brushed her hair behind her ears and cocked her head as if she was waiting for a response.

'What?'

'You're after a fairy-tale romance. Is that because you see yourself as something of the Prince Charming type?'

He considered shutting her up with a kiss. 'Are you laughing at me?'

'No,' Jess said, biting her lip, clearly trying not to. 'Definitely not.'

'You don't think I could pull off the tight trouser and sequin look. Is that what you're trying to tell me? God, woman, you have a cruel streak.'

Jess giggled. 'I've dashed your ego, I am *sooo* sorry.'

He nodded, his arms folded across his chest.

Jess put a hand on his shoulder. 'Can I do anything to make it better?' she said, weakly, before bursting into another fit of laughter.

It sounded good. It made him happy to hear her laugh. Neil reached out and pushed some of her hair back behind her ear. She looked at him. Her hand felt so hot through his cotton shirt. He waited for her to say something. Anything. He stroked her face. She didn't move away, he pulled her towards him and brushed his lips against her forehead. Pulling back he looked at her. She smiled back at him, her lips slightly parted. He kissed her, softly at first. But the kiss got deeper. Sweet and gentle becoming harder and more urgent. Sliding his tongue into her mouth, he felt her gasp and her arms move round his neck.

He couldn't remember whose idea it had been to go to bed, but it had been a good one.

Naked under the duvet, the warmth of her body felt good against his.

'Tell me when it feels good,' he whispered.

'It feels good.'

He could feel her breath against his chest.

'Neil.'

He stopped breathing.

'I don't do one-night stands.'

'Good,' he said, kissing her neck. 'Neither do I.'

Chapter Thirty-One

'What?' Jess's head shot up.

'Are you going to tell us what it was like?' Sarah asked.

Surely she didn't look that obvious. All right so maybe she'd been in a better mood than usual this morning, but they had all been in the office for nearly two hours and it had started to wear off. She stopped humming when the dawning realisation of the amount of work involved in finalising the pack for the corporate lawyers dawned on her. There had been an issue over the Robinsons contract. Frank hadn't gone in to all the details, but everything was now back on track and going full speed ahead.

'They want it by when?' she'd said, when he'd asked.

'Tomorrow night.' He looked uncomfortable, as well he might. 'I know it's a tight timescale. Sorry. But they'll have to work on it all weekend if they are serious about signing contracts at the end of next week. At least you get the weekend off.'

She'd muttered about seeing what she could do, while not promising anything. Frank smiled and relaxed. She'd meet the deadline. He knew it. She knew it. She always did.

'The police station, duh. What did you think I meant?'

The trouble with Sarah was that you never knew what she did mean.

'Oh, that,' Jess said, slowly. 'Nice building. Modern. Obviously handcuffed and on the rack, it was difficult to be completely objective.' Thankfully the phone on her desk rang. She grabbed it. *Saved by the bell.*

'What?'

The company had an answering policy for external calls. "Good Morning" before twelve, "Good afternoon" after. You announced the company name, your own name and then asked the caller how you could help.

Sarah and Maggie both looked surprised at the lightning speed of her response. Jess didn't feel it was the last she'd heard of that subject but was grateful for diversion.

'Hi. It's Neil, remember me?'

It was difficult to think when your stomach was leaping all over the place like a demented bungee jumper.

'Yes,' Jess said as her insides melted and a smile found its way back to her face.

'Have you found a solicitor yet?'

Her stomach untied itself. She had hoped for something a little more romantic. 'I haven't been charged. I don't need a solicitor.' She wasn't expecting declarations of undying love, well not yet, but some recognition of last night would've been nice. "*Thanks, Jess, for my best night ever.*" Because it had been pretty spectacular. "*When can we do it again?*" sort of thing.

Neil had dropped her at Grey Towers, so she could collect her car.

For a brief moment when they'd arrived home yesterday and the drive had been empty, she'd thought the police had taken the car. Had they told her? Had she signed something to agree to them taking it, or else had Martin, had he taken it?

'The car,' she'd said weakly, looking up to find Neil grinning at her.

'We walked home last night, you remember. From Grey Towers,' he added when she looked at him blankly. 'Clearly I found the evening more memorable than you.'

It had been such a relief to find no one had clamped it or left threatening messages about parking charges on her windscreen that she'd been halfway to work before she realised, they hadn't made arrangements to meet again.

'For your house sale.'

Was he laughing at her?

'Look, here's a name and number. My sister Sophie said she'd be happy to help. She'll give you a sensible quote and look after you.'

'Thanks.' Jess wrote down the details carefully, wanting to drag the conversation out for as long as possible.

'See you soon?'

'Yes please. Thank you.' Jess heard a chuckle from the end of the phone before it went dead.

Sarah and Maggie were incredibly quiet, which meant they were either listening or concentrating hard on what they were doing. How much had they overheard? She had to tell them about Martin some time. It was getting increasingly difficult to pretend nothing was wrong. Now was as good a time as any.

‘Have you two got a minute?’ she said.

Both women appeared not to hear. She could do the normal staring thing until someone looked up and said “Sorry, were you talking to me”.

No, they could sweat a bit longer. She’d make drinks first and then tell them.

It was tempting when the office door clicked shut behind her to march straight back in and catch them in the act of discussing her. She had absolutely no doubt they would be.

Unofficially it was recognised at Anymoore that more decisions were made in the kitchen than in any meeting. In an ideal world someone would be employed to sit there all day and take minutes.

Today, the small room was crammed when Jess arrived.

‘Room for a little one,’ she asked as she squeezed past Contracts to get to the kettle, pausing briefly on her way past to ask for some customer and lease agreement information. Customer Services proved harder to negotiate – they stood between her and the worktop, huddled around a piece of paper and Izzie.

‘Excuse me,’ Jess said in the sort of tone she hoped implied urgency, authority – with a dash of sarcasm thrown in for good measure. Well it was a kitchen after all.

‘Izzie’s shown us pictures of her new house.’ Harry waved a brochure in front of her. ‘Tea for you and Maggie?’ he offered and pulled their mugs down from the cupboard. ‘And …’

‘Coffee for Sarah. Thanks.’ Jess took the brochure. She recognised the logo and colours from the fence opposite Maggie’s cottage. ‘Nice,’ she added after flipping through a few pages. She tried to sound impressed, while feeling anything but.

She needed somewhere to live. But even if she could have afforded the smallest apartment they advertised, modern properties crammed into huge estates were her idea of hell. Probably not the right time to share those feelings. She was more a cottage with climbing plants winding through trellis round the door person. A bit like Maggie’s. She looked at the artist’s impression of a wildflower meadow on the front cover. ‘I didn’t realise you’d moved.’

‘We haven’t yet.’ Izzie coloured. ‘It’s being built now. I was showing the others what it will look like. We should be in by Christmas.’

She turned a very odd shade of red.

Jess wished she'd done the First Aid refresher course when it was offered. How did the rhyme go that they'd learnt on the last one? "If it's red, raise its head." Izzie was standing up; technically her head couldn't get much higher.

'That's if her new man gets his finger out and comes up with the deposit.' Harry held up two mugs of tea. 'Do you want a tray?'

Jess nodded without taking her eyes off Izzie. The woman looked positively apoplectic. Jess wasn't sure what apoplectic meant, but in her mind it conjured up all sorts of purple images that seemed fitting.

'Are you okay?' she asked eventually.

'Mmm, yes,' Izzie said.

Jess sighed, relieved because she had no idea what she would have done if the woman had said no.

Harry had added Sarah's coffee to the tray and Jess had made her way almost back to the corridor before Izzie said, 'You're moving too aren't you? Have you found anywhere yet?'

'Did you tell Izzie, Martin's left me?' Jess slammed the coffee mug on to Sarah's desk spilling a lot of the hot brown liquid.

'Didn't know he had,' Sarah said, as she mopped up some of the spillage with a tissue. 'He's just rung. You've missed him.'

'You've spoken to him?'

'He whined on about you delaying everything and needing your solicitor's details. I assumed they were the ones on your desk and gave them to him. I told him if he got off the phone and took his finger out of his arse, he could probably get things back on track. Guess that's me off his Christmas list.'

Sarah looked over the rim of her coffee mug. 'Actually, yes, I did think he'd left you or else you'd killed him. I didn't buy that house clearance for decorating lark, but no I didn't tell Izzie or anyone else. Well apart from Maggie and only when I saw your house up for sale in the estate agent's window. We figured you'd tell us when you were ready.'

'Thanks.' Jess tidied the reports on her desk. 'And sorry about the coffee. I was going to tell you both today anyway. Izzie took the wind out of my sails, announcing to the whole company I was moving.'

'How does she know? Is she buying your house?' Sarah asked.

Jess shook her head. 'No, one of the new homes opposite Maggie.'

'I don't bloody think so, matey,' Maggie said.

'I've just seen …' Jess was on the point of arguing until she realised Maggie wasn't listening. She was busy swiping her phone, sighing loudly and muttering expletives.

'What on earth is Maggie doing?' Jess asked, circling a typo on the latest business plan and forecast report.'

'Waiting for technical support to fix her computer,' Sarah said.

'I keep getting pictures of men's penises.' Maggie frowned. 'Is there someone I should report them to? All I did was ask what his intentions were.'

'She set me up a Tinder profile.' Sarah walked around and looked over Maggie's shoulder. 'Jeez, isn't there a programme on telly that looks at deformities like that? Embarrassing bodies or something.'

'You let her do that?' Jess said with a slow, disbelieving shake of her head.

'What was I supposed to do? She's a woman on a mission. A mere "No" wasn't going to derail her. She's changed my profile three times in the last half hour. On the plus side, I no longer want to "explore the possibility of a loving relationship" and I'm not "party animal in need of regular exercise".'

'Ah this one says "nice face",' Maggie said. 'Oh no.'

'What?' Sarah and Jess asked as the office door opened and one of the technical guys walked in.

'He wants pictures of my boobs,' said Maggie, throwing her phone across the desk.

Paul stared at Maggie. 'You've got a problem?' he asked. Jess smiled, watching him stare at Maggie's chest.

Jess nodded. Hell, everybody nodded.

Paul flicked a switch on the screen. Nothing happened so he flicked it again. When nothing happened that time, he resorted to a tried and tested technical technique and banged its side as his phone rang.

'Got held up. No, nothing serious, just an annoying little delay.'

Maggie muttered something inaudible, her expression alone suggested it wasn't ladylike.

'The figures look great. I'll drop them into a spreadsheet and see what happens. Motherboard's screwed,' he said, putting his hand over the mouthpiece, and addressing Maggie. 'Need a new one. I'll let the department know.'

He listened for a moment to the voice on the other end of his phone, lifted his hand and made some encouraging noises.

'Don't muck about with dating apps. They attract all sorts of perverts,' he whispered, his hand back over the microphone. 'Try the monthly speed dating club at the community centre. Google it, well obviously you can't do it now, but she can.' He pointed at Sarah.

'Sorry Katie, no wasn't talking to you. Calm down, be more like me. I don't suffer from stress – I'm a carrier.'

Jess could hear his laughter long after the door clicked shut. She reprinted the business plan and forecast with the errors corrected and filed it with all the other financial reports from the last five years Neil had asked for. A text message arrived on her phone.

Photo exhibition at the Sports Centre this evening. I'm planning on taking a look. Hope to see you there. The number wasn't one she'd attached contact details to, but she'd used it enough over the last few days to know exactly who it belonged to and she smiled. Suddenly the Organisation Chart review didn't seem nearly as bad.

Chapter Thirty-Two

Photos covered every wall; Jess was impressed. Such variety. All through college they'd concentrated on one genre at a time. Here the images covered every subject: landscapes, animals, portraits and some so abstract she couldn't work out what they were, whichever way she angled her head.

She admired a panel of work called tramps, which had a story in every picture: the haunted looks, the empty cans. The holes in clothes. The doorways they slept in. On each picture the photographer had included a piece of text giving the tramp's name and a description of who that person was and what they had been before they ended up on the streets.

The next one on the wall was a panel of dead flowers. Jess was amazed by the colours and details. Another panel had the photographer going to great lengths to replicate classic paintings with a modern twist. Van Gogh's sunflowers had the plastic still around them and a price tag. Somebody else had recreated scenes from Cluedo. Some of the creative images made her laugh.

One of the stewards handed her a slip of paper and asked her to choose her favourite image which was going to prove to be a huge challenge.

She moved between the sections trying to take the job seriously. 'What do you think?' one woman asked.

'I love them all,' Jess said. 'It's going to be so difficult to choose. They're all so different. I wish I was so creative.'

'Do you take photos?' the woman asked.

'I finished college last year.' Jess nodded. 'I've just taken my first wedding.'

The woman screwed up her face. 'Rather you than me. I'd be more nervous than the bride. I prefer still life. If I get the angle or the light wrong on a bottle or a bowl of fruit, I can retake the shot. She indicated a panel of dead flowers. 'Those are mine,' she said. 'I'm Kate.' She held out a hand.

'I'm Jess and I loved those,' Jess said enthusiastically. 'They are beautiful, but not in the conventional way.'

The woman seemed pleased. 'They took so long.' She leant over and whispered, 'Have you any idea how long it takes to properly kill a flower and dry it out like that? My husband gets so cross. Somebody would buy me a bouquet and I'd refuse to put water in the vase to speed things up a bit. Then I'd spray them with hairspray to stop the petals falling out. I have a shed full of dead flowers. What about you? What do you take when you're not dealing with bridezillas?'

'I love photographing people.'

'With or without clothes?'

'With.' Jess giggled. 'I try to bring out something quirky or unusual about them. I find everybody is so different. I'm afraid I don't have the patience for wildlife or dead flowers.'

'Have you seen the self-portraits over there?' The woman pointed at a set of black-and-white images. 'Gina took those. She was going through medical treatment at the time and wanted to record it. She won a national award with those images.'

Jess had admired them. It was a brave decision to take pictures showing every emotion and scar let alone show them publicly.

'Some of the other members are taking a picture every day. They post them on social media. I tried it myself. You always end up with a very interesting set of pictures, but it can be unnerving to realise what projects like that say about you. That's when I realised dead plants were my bag.'

'Didn't you find it difficult?' Jess asked. She hadn't pressed the shutter on her camera since the weekend.

'There were days when I didn't feel like taking a picture, when I wasn't feeling up to scratch. But somehow the idea of giving up the project was worse. I found something satisfying about getting to the end of the day and knowing if I'd achieved nothing else, I had a picture. Some of them I revisited later, and took again, but at the end of a year, I had a fair few hundred images and dead flowers featured prominently.'

Jess stopped in front of a series of pictures that were more abstract. 'Clive's,' the woman said. 'He can't hold the camera still any more. He's got a bad shake,' she whispered conspiratorially. 'So he decided to do a project on intentional camera movement. 'Some of them are unusual, but some of them'—she rolled her eyes—'are frankly a bit weird. It's always fascinating to hear what the judge makes of them on competition nights.

Have you thought about joining the camera club? Are you local?'

'I am now,' Jess said. 'But I need to find somewhere to live, so may end up anywhere.'

The woman flapped a hand. 'Every town has a camera club these days, although Redford does have one of the best locally. Why don't you come along next Tuesday? We have a brilliant speaker coming and your first meeting is free.' She fumbled in her handbag and pulled out a small booklet, flicked through and announced a name that sounded familiar. Jess made a mental note to look him up later.

'What about you, sir? Are you thinking about joining our camera club too?' The woman spoke to someone behind her. The room had filled up and Jess was clearly in the way, so she turned to apologise to the newcomer.

Neil. Her face broke into a smile.

'I'm not creative.' He laughed. 'I leave that to the professionals.'

'Nonsense,' the woman said defensively. 'Everyone has a creative streak – they just have to learn to control their inner critic. Before you argue about not being able to afford a camera, mobile phones take great pictures. In fact I'm sure if I flicked through your camera roll, I'd find some very pleasing images.' She looked at Jess, as if she expected her to confirm her point.

'Absolutely.' She grinned.

The woman's eyes flicked between the two of them and she said, 'I'll leave you to persuade him. Hope to see you next week Jess. And don't forget, I want to see a daily picture.'

'Hi,' Neil said as soon as she'd hit on another couple. 'Sorry I'm late. I had hoped to be here earlier.'

'It's okay.' Jess waved away his apology. 'This is amazing,' she said. 'I've loved looking round and I will definitely pop along next week to the camera club.'

'Have you eaten?' he asked.

'Do you ever think of anything but food?' She chuckled.

'Asking for a friend.' Neil smiled back. 'Only Dudley wondered if you'd like to join us both in the Badger and Fir Tree to share a bowl of chips.'

Chapter Thirty-Three

'Come in, come in.' Maggie pulled Sarah in and peered round her front door before closing it.

'What's going on?' Sarah said crossly as she came to rest against the hall wall.

'Martin. He's come out of the estate opposite.'

An eyebrow twitched.

'You know, Jess's ex and he had his arm round Izzie, from customer services.'

'As in Izzy Wizzy Lets Get Busy?'

'The same. Come on, let's go buy a house.'

'We're supposed to be meeting Jess and we don't need a house.'

Maggie had already gathered up her handbag and was off.

Flags advertising late-night opening flew either side of the gatepost, and a row of little red arrows were planted along the verge, all pointing to a Portakabin tucked among the unmade roads and half-built houses. The house next door to it had all its lights on and was not only finished but furnished too.

A man stood in the doorway watching as they walked towards him. They were only halfway up the road when he flung out his arms and smiled.

'He's gorgeous,' Sarah said, starting to speed up. 'Hi,' she called in her best Marilyn Monroe throaty voice. Maggie rolled her eyes.

'If you're looking for a house, ladies'—he took a step back and held out a hand to Sarah—'you've come to the right place. Come in. Take a seat. Have something to drink, some of our nibbles. What would you like?'

Sarah made a bit of a song and dance about choosing a drink. Maggie shook her head and took a sausage roll. They were home-made, small, but tasty; she was impressed. Sarah and the salesman were sniggering about something so she took another couple.

The man's name badge told her Sarah's Adonis was Geoff.

'So Sarah, are we looking for a house for you or your mother?'

Maggie growled under her breath. 'How many houses are you

building here, Geoff?' she asked and filled a paper napkin with sausage rolls.

Sarah glared at her, but Geoff, seemingly oblivious to the women's squabble, slipped seamlessly into the professional salesman's pitch and showed them site plans, including a miniature model of the new development and a rather futuristic DVD making the place look like something out of a computer game.

'That's an awful lot of houses in such a small space,' Maggie said, putting her food parcel into her bag for later. 'Most of them don't even have garages.'

'These days it's about internal living madam, rather than external.'

'Not for a car.'

'Our hands are tied by current regulations. You'll have to speak to Boris, if you want them changed.' It was said with a smile that didn't reach his nose let alone his eyes. 'But internally'—he forced the smile a bit wider—'we like to think we've taken everyone's needs into consideration. In three storeys we have fitted everything you're ever likely to want.'

'Three?' Maggie studied the brochure he handed her. 'What if you want a loft?'

'Perhaps you'd like to see our show house, madam. I'm afraid you're just too late if you wanted this particular property. The last couple to view fell in love with it. It's sold subject to contract, but you should be able to appreciate the quality of our finishes.'

A car pulled up outside.

'That way, when you're ready, ladies.' Geoff started to sweat, his eyes flicked between them and the couple getting out of the car. Maggie didn't blame him. If he was on commission, judging by the car alone, the commission on the next sale was likely to be huge.

They stood up.

'Sarah, you will come back and tell me what you think, won't you?' Geoff moved to his place by the door. 'I'd like to take down some details.'

'You would?'

He looked back at her quickly. 'I would.'

'He's not Mr Right,' Maggie said, going through the door he indicated and ending up in a dining room.

'Good God, this is tiny,' Sarah said.

Something of an understatement. The dining room could only seat four people at any one time, one in each corner. The round table that took up most of the room had been laid with black and white china. Matching serviettes were arranged in wine glasses. In the middle sat a basket of plastic bread rolls.

Memo to Goldilocks – Eat before breaking in.

'Do you think Izzie and Martin will be happy here?' Maggie asked.

'What?'

'You'd make a lousy detective. You'd never pick up any clues. He said the couple who'd just left had reserved the show home.'

'This one?'

'Yes, Sherlock.'

Jess uploaded the photos from her latest memory card onto her computer and flicked through them. They included some she'd taken in the woods last week. One of Neil leaning against a tree and smiling. He looked relaxed and happy, and one of Dudley backlit, mid-shake, after coming out of the lake. Bloody hell that was good too. The water droplets flying everywhere had caught the light and sparkled; Dudley looked straight at her. She increased the magnification to check the pictures were sharp where they needed to be.

Neil had mentioned his assistant was in the process of updating his website because she felt it needed to be more "customer friendly". The woman was right, it hadn't been easy to navigate round when Jess last looked. She wanted to see whether Jackson Consultancy listed its clients, to see if she could guess who was so intent on acquiring Anymoore's.

She checked her images for obvious flaws and, before she changed her mind, emailed the contact details on the website, attaching both and telling Neil she was happy for him to use them and could supply higher resolution images if he needed. She felt strangely exhilarated about sharing her images until she heard the knock on the door.

Her muscles stiffened. She wasn't expecting anyone and couldn't make out who it was through the frosted glass. Just that there were only two of them standing in the gathering evening gloom.

Not the police.

Her heart took refuge in her shoes. She didn't want to open the door. But, if it was the police, she'd watched enough TV cop programmes to know they'd have one of those red things to break in with. It might be the two of them on the doorstep, but the rest of the shift would have the back covered in case she decided to make a run for it.

Here we go.

Sliding the chain into place, she opened the door a fraction and squinted through it.

'Hi.' Sarah held out a bottle of wine. 'We're going speed dating, but first we need to talk.' Behind Sarah, Jess could make out Maggie waving.

'Must be a big apology, that looks expensive,' Jess said, removing the chain and opening the door.

Collecting three glasses, she joined the other two in the sitting room. Her mood changed instantly when she saw them. Something was wrong. They were quiet. Sarah and Maggie were never quiet. They were sitting on opposite sides of the sofa and staring at their glasses.

'Okay – what is it?' Jess took a large swig of the wine and prepared for the worst.

Sarah, she noticed, took an even larger swig and told her.

'Martin and Izzie? As in Izzy Wizzy Let's Get Busy?'

Maggie and Sarah nodded.

'Are you sure? I mean what's she got that I haven't?'

'A "C" cup for a start.' Sarah offered Jess the bottle for a refill.

Maggie looked shocked. 'Martin can't be that shallow.'

'I've known worse,' Sarah said – the voice of experience. 'But I never put Martin down as a boob-man. Well he can't be …'

'What do you mean?' Jess asked indignantly. There were times you needed friends and there were times when you didn't, and this was fast becoming one of those did-not times.

'But she is blonde.'

That was it, Maggie was off her Christmas list too. Jess filled her glass to the brim, taking a large gulp without pause.

'I once heard her telling Frank,' Maggie added, 'her mother was a cordon bleu cook. And hasn't she got some sort of American business degree under her belt?'

'I suppose now you come to mention—' Sarah's last words were obliterated by the cushion Jess pressed firmly into her face. 'But if he didn't tell you he was seeing someone else, why did he say he was leaving?' she added, once she was free.

Jess got to her feet, surprised at how unsteady she felt. It occurred to her food might be a good idea. She found some olives and crisps in a cupboard and arranged them on a plate, took a handful and put the plate in the middle of the coffee table to which Maggie added half a dozen sausage rolls.

'He didn't tell me why and I didn't ask.'

'You've been together for ten years …'

'Twelve.'

'So, he says I'm off and what – you say okay?'

'That's about the strength of it.'

'That doesn't sound mature.'

'That's rich, coming from you.' Jess laughed. And I'm not mature. Two-hundred-year-old wines are mature. Mouldy cheeses are mature. I'm thirty-two years old. I'm in the prime of my life.'

'That's practically middle-aged.'

Jess picked up the cushion Sarah had put back on the sofa.

'He should've been honest enough to tell you.' Maggie's glass was empty and Sarah topped it up despite her protests.

'If he had, I'd have probably helped him pack and told her what I really thought about her new house.'

'Remember, even if Martin doesn't, we still love you and care about you,' Sarah said.

'Gee thanks. That makes me feel so much better.' Jess smiled. She was touched by their concern, but it didn't dull the shock. 'With friends like you two, who needs—'

'Cheating partners.'

They raised their glasses in a mock toast.

'Seriously,' Sarah said. 'We are always here for you. And I promise I never uttered so much as a word about your love life, prison sentence, or anything else to Izzie. Scout's honour.'

Jess knew that. Of course, Izzie would have known she was selling the house if she was involved with Martin. She didn't hate Martin for cheating on her. Love was supposed to be a two-way thing; she'd always known that. You love someone, they love you back as much – no more, no less. Anything else was some sort of crazy power struggle. If she wanted to love something and get nothing back, she'd have bought a goldfish.

Looking back, their relationship had been dead for years. Someone once said something about hindsight and vision. She was sure they had. But after two glasses of wine and a handful of crisps and olives, Jess couldn't remember who or what.

She couldn't put a day or year on the time her relationship died. At first, there'd been the petty criticisms, she'd put down to stress. The times they spent apart, well they were both busy independent people, both had careers and friends, and they needed space. Being honest, she hadn't just fallen out of love with Martin, she hated him. For lots of reasons. For the times he ignored her and refused to help around the house. For the nights she spent at friends' parties, dinner parties, etc, on her own because he didn't like her friends. For never making an effort on birthdays or anniversaries. For never asking about her day, or when he did, only to compare it in some belittling way to his own. For always having bigger crises than her. For pushing her away.

She hated him for sitting night after night in front of his computer screen with his office door shut, talking to mates by Skype or whatever social media he used. For the way he criticised her clothes, her cooking, her figure, the amount she drank. For never missing a chance to put her down in front of others.

She hated him for his reaction at last year's Redford's Business of the Year award, when Anymoore won the title for the third year running. MJC had been up for the same award and Martin thought he had it "in the bag". Two of the people he'd invited to join him on his table had been on the judging panel. When Frank asked Jess if she was going and she'd said no, he'd invited her to sit at his table. He joked about not having enough friends to get his money's worth from British Telecom's friends and family discounts and how he was struggling to fill the table that all nominees were given and said she'd be doing him a favour. He'd asked Jess to join him on the podium when he accepted the award. He gave a funny but self-deprecating speech, acknowledging all his fellow nominees, but pointing out that as a man was only as good as his team, he'd been head and shoulders above all the competition coming into the contest and was accepting the award on their behalf.

Martin disappeared after the awards and hadn't returned home until the next day. Neither of them mentioned the evening afterwards.

She hated him for never taking her out but going out regularly with friends to ever more expensive places.

Of course. Jess smiled at the thought of their Grey Towers meet. The lousy rotten swine must have planned on taking Izzie for a meal there the other night. That was why there'd been a meal booked in his name for later. A quick conversation and clearly he imagined he'd get her out of the way long before Izzie turned up.

The fact he'd started a relationship with a stick insect with boobs. She couldn't hate him for that. He hadn't lost Jess when he'd lost his inhibitions with Izzie, he'd lost her many, many years ago. Izzie didn't break up their relationship, whatever Sarah and Maggie thought. Jess and Martin had managed that all on their own.

'Do you know what hurts?' Jess asked. 'I signed off her staff appraisal form the other day and added some positive comments.' She stood up. 'Are we going out or what?'

Chapter Thirty-Four

Jess tucked her arm through Maggie's as Sarah argued all the way to the community centre about whether going speed dating counted as an actual date. The pre-fabricated building was not the most romantic venue in the world. The large wooden door, plastered with adverts for Slimming World and that weekend's Psychic Fayre opened to reveal a small bespectacled woman of Maggie's age.

Sarah had only bought two tickets. The woman pushed her glasses on to the top of her head, looked through a pile of paper and announced it wasn't an issue, when Jess offered to leave them to it.

'More men than women this week,' the woman announced. 'This will balance things nicely.'

She typed their details into a computer and handed each of them what she described as a score sheet, blue for men, yellow for girls, a pen and a badge with a number on which she insisted they put in a prominent position on their tables.

'Now, a few rules. Only a few. This is still a fun place. You're not allowed to ask anyone for a date at the table,' she said, smiling at them.

Like that's going to happen. Jess looked round the room at the group of people standing about rather uneasily.

'Don't ask for or give out a phone number.' Each statement was accompanied by a sharp push of glasses back up her nose. Her nails matched her lipstick and they both matched her dress. 'You mustn't ask how the other person is scoring you.'

'Scoring?' Maggie looked uneasy.

'Well not scoring. You just have to put a "Yes" or "No" in the box on the sheet that corresponds to each man's appropriate number and he will do the same on his sheet. At the end of the evening, hand them in and we'll compare the sheets. If any of your "yes" match, we will send you an email tomorrow morning listing all those you're matched with and their email addresses. Then it's up to you. You can get in touch if you want to. Just let us know any success stories, as we like to post them on our website. Any questions?'

What like, how soon can I get out of here?

'The evening takes about three hours and we have two comfort breaks.' The way the woman stressed "comfort" and looked at Maggie, made Jess wonder if she thought Maggie was incontinent.

'We'll be starting in about ten minutes, so why don't you girls get yourself a drink? You can always reserve one for the intervals. Just one more thing. When the bell goes, you have four minutes to find out all you need to know about your speed date. Men move on, women stay put.'

Jess looked at her card after "17" had left, inking in yet another "No". It hadn't been the worst four minutes of her life. No – that had belonged to "41". It just wasn't four minutes she wished to repeat anytime soon, however much he winked and said, I think we'll be seeing one another again, don't you? She was tempted to write yes in all the boxes just to see which ones matched her back, but thinking any of those she'd met so far, might be given her email address or phone number was too horrible a thought to contemplate.

"38" sat down. 'Hi,' he said, 'I'm Donovan. You can call me Donny.'

No, I can't. Never.

From a pocket he pulled out a shiny piece of paper. 'My crib sheet.'

'What?'

'Ten questions. I find it easier. This way I don't waste precious time or forget anything critical.'

The bell sounded.

'Right,' he said. 'We're off. I'll start then. Are you a vegetarian?'

Jess's "No" was met with such a long sigh and so much head shaking that she started apologising.

Three minutes and forty-five seconds left.

'What will you be doing in two years' time?'

'I don't know.' Another long sigh and a head shake. But she didn't. 'I'm thinking of taking a career break.'

Three minutes and counting.

'When did your last relationship end and why?' Donovan looked at her, his fingers tapping his piece of paper.

'Is your crib sheet laminated?'

He looked surprised at the way the conversation was heading. 'It preserves it.'

'Have you used it often?'

He looked slightly uncomfortable.

'Do you come every week?'

Two minutes.

He shook his head this time. 'No, they don't have one every week and Fridays usually clash with my salsa night.'

The bell rang, a lot of chairs scraped across the floor and "38" got up to be replaced by a laughing "27".

'Tell me,' he said, as soon as the bell sounded, 'if you were an animal, what sort would you be?'

'How are you getting on?' Jess found Sarah at the bar in the interval. She was smiling.

'I've just been asked what car I'd most like to drive.'

Jess grinned. 'And you said?'

'I'm happy with my Aston Martin.'

'And he said?'

'Well that's just it, he didn't. He sort of started drooling.'

'"Yes" or "No" then?'

'Definite "No". How are you getting on?'

Jess shook her head. 'I have to say it's not going well. I asked one man if he had a criminal record – I felt I had to. A couple of the conversations felt more like job interviews and one man suggested I try therapy, preferably before I engage in another relationship. And you know what – he's probably right.' She looked down at her feet. 'Look Sarah, I'm sorry. It's been a strange week. I'm going home. I'll go and tell Maggie.'

'She'll probably want to go too,' Sarah said, 'but I've got my eye on "26".'

Jess saw "26" as she made her way to the exit. He was a tall man talking to a girl with a spiral perm and an annoying giggle. She heard someone say, 'Do you prefer boxers or briefs?' She didn't wait to hear the answer.

'Did you give anyone a "Yes"?' she asked, slipping her arm through Maggie's. They made it out without anyone seemingly noticing.

'There was only one man anywhere close to my age.' Maggie laughed. 'I think he might have been the caretaker, roped in for the evening.'

They walked down the high street and stopped to look in the estate agent's window.

'How are you getting on finding somewhere to live?' Maggie asked.

'With all the stuff going on at work, I've decided to put everything into storage and rent for a while,' Jess said.

'Have you found anything?' Maggie asked.

'Two flats,' Jess said. And that was two too many.

To say the first was small would be something of a massive understatement, but that was all she could say about it. She hadn't considered where she wanted to live but was certain it wasn't in a mad air hostess's box room. She didn't know definitely the air hostess was mad, but something about the woman's hair and her manners made Jess uncomfortable. Even without the fact, she'd be expected to sleep on a pull-down sofa bed that, when open, covered most of the room's available floor space, the landlady's wild eyes had been enough to put her off completely.

At the second, she'd been put through a vigorous interview, where nothing, not even her most personal habits, were considered out of bounds.

No – she didn't smoke. No – she couldn't think of an occasion when she'd need to use the cooker or the washing machine after 10.30. No – she didn't dye her hair. No – she wouldn't clip her toenails anywhere other than the bathroom and she'd leave that as she found it, sans underwear, towels, toiletries, make-up and absolutely anything else. She absolutely must leave the plug in the sink and the toilet seat down. The room had been "feng shui-ed", but you can't be too careful when it comes to generating bad chi. And no, she wasn't in a relationship.

She'd seemingly answered all the woman's questions correctly because Carole or Caz, as her friends called her, announced, before she actually saw the room, that she hoped they'd be best friends and wanted to know when she could move in.

It had been advertised as a large room. Yes, she'd seen smaller. At a push you could fit a double bed in – probably. There were two windows, a wardrobe and a dressing table on the opposite wall in imminent danger of collapse. And it was red – pillar box red.

Carole seemed oblivious to the fact it looked as if the Texas chainsaw massacre had happened in that room. She had been colour-matched. She was summer and red was absolutely her colour, “didn’t she think?”. She held a towel to her face. Jess wasn’t sure why.

A huge television filled most of one wall in the sitting room. The only thing Carole-Caz positively must watch at all costs was *Grey’s Anatomy*. Jess could choose anything else as long as it didn’t clash with an episode. Jess resisted the urge to say that it was on so bloody often, everything would clash with it.

‘I’ve had an idea,’ Maggie said as they came to the end of her road. ‘Why don’t you move in with me?’

Chapter Thirty-Five

Ross wasn't due back until the following Monday, but he was sat at his desk and on the telephone when Neil got to the office. Neil doubted Annette was happy that their honeymoon had been cut short, he certainly wasn't. If Ross thought he'd ride into town, guns blazing at the last minute, for the final showdown and save the day, he was too bloody late.

'I think Trafford has to be the key …'

Presumably, whoever was on the receiving end of his diatribe was deaf. Neil couldn't think of any other reason why Ross should be talking so loudly. He fingered what looked like some estate agent's brochure for a new estate, as he spoke. What was happening around here? Everyone was moving.

'Of course, there's a resource contention issue, especially now it's so mission critical, but it's far too late to change horses at this point …'

Neil put his briefcase on his desk, feeling old. At school, they'd spoken in a kind of pig-Latin, a secret code everyone knew, but at least the words were English to start with and as soon as hormones and puberty kicked in, everyone decided it was childish and dropped it.

He'd hoped he had a couple more days. At some point he was going to have to address the partner issue. Neil couldn't imagine Ross was going to let the opportunity drop. The last postcard he'd received had been addressed "Hi Partner".

Neil shuddered. His father had joked that he should tell him his investor was going to pull his money out if he took on another partner and he'd need Ross's agreement he would match and replace the sum before he was willing to discuss the matter.

'Dad, the only thing you've bought for the office was the coffee maker,' he'd said. 'And I thought that was a birthday present.'

'Ross doesn't know that', his father said, when they'd talked about it over Sunday lunch. 'Most of my clients come from recommendations, but I don't offer the local criminal fraternity a partnership every time they suggest one of their mates should give me a call.'

'Maybe you should,' his mother said, as she cleared the plates. 'Jackson and Trigger-Happy McCoy has a certain ring to it.'

His father lifted one eyebrow and looked after her.

Neil smiled.

'Didn't you say Tanya's generated a lot of work too?' His mum had returned from the kitchen and placed what was probably a fruit crumble on the table, although it could equally have been a deconstructed cake.

She was right. Tanya had brought in a lot of new work. Currently, she was busy developing their online presence and social media profile. She hadn't even asked for an increase in salary, let alone a partnership.

'Be upfront,' his mother said, wiping the drip from a jug of custard before setting that on the table too. 'Don't leave him hanging on believing you're thinking about it.'

Easier said than done. They gave him no further suggestions as to how he should drop the bombshell into a conversation. "Good honeymoon? Ross, sorry no can do about the partnership." He'd had the conversation over and over in his head since.

Ross, now finishing his call, agreed to "diarise" something for next week. He put the phone down and turned to face Neil.

It looked like he was bursting to say something. Neil nodded towards the pile of papers on his desk. 'How's the house hunting going?' he asked.

Ross froze, flashing him the sort of look designed to turn him into a pile of ash or something worse but was prevented from answering by the phone on Neil's desk ringing.

Neil reached for it.

Too late.

Ross answered and got about halfway through the greeting, before a rather high-pitched peculiar noise came from the handset. Either the phone was broken, or someone was not happy. Annette? Neil had only met her occasionally before the wedding and she hadn't come across as the sort who would scream hysterically at Ross. Someone, however, would, and the rant continued.

'He's just arrived. I'll bring him up to date.'

He's talking about me. Neil strained his ears and tried to make out the other end of the conversation too. He couldn't, but Ross's response hinted he'd probably find out soon enough. He tried to look disinterested, opened his laptop and plugged the power cable into the mains.

'He needs a helicopter view of the situation. Leave it with me.'

They were in the middle of Redford. The closest a helicopter could get to the office was the bypass.

'I think Clive would be an excellent choice. He won the A.P.M business at G.P.F.G …'

Neil didn't even know who blooming Clive was. Whoever he was, he hated him.

'He phoned me, said he'd throw his cap in the ring, right from the get-go. He certainly plays with a straight bat …'

Probably not a cricketer.

'Spent yesterday afternoon revisiting some options. Had to really, now number ten's off the radar.'

Number ten. Fuck. He's a spy.

'Let's touch base offline about that … He'll persuade them to come to the party, I'm sure of it. Yes, I'll speak to him now and come back to you as soon as … Ciao.'

Ciao! Tell me I misheard.

Ross put the phone down. Neil, unwilling to ask, fixated on the welcome screen as it came up on his computer.

Perhaps it was a double-glazing company cold-calling. Perhaps Ross spewed out random words to make them think they were busy. Maybe the job had started to get to him. Maybe he was cracking up. Neil typed his user name and password into his computer and when it didn't recognise it, typed it again, relieved the second time it did and made a mental note to remember tomorrow no capitals, but aware yesterday he'd probably thought the same, tomorrow he was still unlikely to remember. Left to his own devices, passwords would be written on sticky notes and stuck all over the office. Tanya had taken them down recently and entered them on his digital calendar after dire warnings of what happened to companies who managed to lose clients' confidential information.

Ross spoke again. All Neil had done since he'd arrived was switch on his computer, even so he felt exhausted.

But if Ross was talking and he wasn't on the phone any more and there was no one else in the room, that meant …

'Neil?'

He looked up. Uh-oh, perhaps the conversation he'd done his level best to ignore for the last few minutes had been aimed at him after all.

'Sorry, run that past me again, would you?' he said, smiling. *Preferably in English.*

Ross sighed. 'I was saying,' he said. 'I have spent most of the morning on the phone to Martin Cowley.'

'That's good,' Neil said slowly. 'Everything's in place for contracts to be signed tomorrow.'

Ross frowned, clearly not what he'd been saying.

'We haven't been slacking, while you were swanning around on your honeymoon.' Neil tried to inject a note of humour into his words. 'Considering what a preposterously short timescale we were given, everyone pulled out all the stops. Anymoore Ltd's set up a virtual data room. All the company's documents were uploaded last week, and the auditors have promised that audited accounts to September will be uploaded by close of play this evening. Due diligence is almost there. Tanya is working there today, reviewing the asset register and finalising the dilapidation report.'

Ross looked at Tanya's desk as if it had only just dawned on him she wasn't there.

'I've scheduled a meeting this evening with Frank and Martin, to introduce them to each other and review everything.'

'I can't this evening …' Ross butted in.

'No reason for you to be there. We weren't expecting you back until next week.'

Ross nodded. 'I know he's keen to make his presence felt as soon as possible. He wants a full staff meeting scheduled as soon as possible, so he can introduce himself properly and outline his corporate vision to the staff.'

'It's already been agreed the existing team will continue to run the company until the end of the calendar year to give Martin a chance to get to know everyone and their jobs.'

'He wants me to be on board through this next phase.'

'Next phase? Our brief was to acquire the company, not manage it for them. That was all I quoted for. Next week we have other customers who need attention.'

'Martin sees this as a good chance to gain publicity and wants me on board to work on the PR side of things. I can't see anything pressing here that needs my attention, so I have agreed in principle …' He hesitated. 'Obviously, I said I had to run it past you.'

'Is he intending to pay for this service? How long are we talking here?'

Ross shrugged. 'How long is a piece of string?'

'Six weeks. Do a quote. Charge him the usual daily rate for thirty days. If you're working on site, charge any additional expenses and the usual company mark-up. Then I will follow up this evening. Anything else?'

'Yes,' Ross said. 'The accountant was arrested last week. Martin doesn't see a position for her in the new organisation and there may be a few others he wouldn't necessarily want in his new team.'

'That'll be his problem now. He knows the legalities.' Neil's heart lurched. 'It's too late to change any terms, so perhaps you could explain that to him when you discuss the quote for your work.'

'She should at least be suspended.'

'On what basis? I was at Anymoore when it happened. She was released without charge.'

'He wants you to make sure, in light of what happened, she isn't …'

'All staff transfer to the new company on existing terms and conditions. Because of timescales, there is an agreement between both parties. They have a month to make the decision whether they wish to work for the new company or not. Those wishing to leave have been provided for and that includes the accountant. Of course, if somewhere down the line, MJC feels there are economic, technical or operational reasons for getting rid of people, then it can, providing all staff are treated fairly and it is not getting rid of staff affected by the transfer because of the transfer.'

'He doesn't want the accountant.'

Neil wanted to scream that's not fair, but as his father used to tell him, all's fair in love and business. 'How did he find out about the arrest?'

Ross shrugged and switched on his laptop, shooting Neil an irritated look. 'That's irrelevant.' A silence settled in the room, broken only by the whirring of the fan as Ross's laptop woke up. He looked set to pounce like a wild animal.

'Fine,' Neil said, because he couldn't think of anything else to say.

Nothing professional anyway. He hated it that Ross would be on site for six weeks at Anymoore and see Jess every day.

Jess. Should he tell Frank about this latest demand? Part of him, no, all of him, hoped Jess wouldn't want to work for Martin Cowley. He was too full of his own importance. But deep down, a nagging doubt that somehow this latest demand had something to do with him, bothered Neil. *How the hell did these people know about her arrest?* The only other people who knew apart from the Redford police force were Sarah, Maggie and Frank.

Chapter Thirty-Six

The last time Neil had waited at Grey Towers for Martin Cowley, he'd been stood up and ended up having supper with Jess. He smiled. The waiter put a bottle of water on the table and asked him if he'd like to see the wine list. He poured a glass of water and said he'd wait for the others.

Supper with Frank at Grey Towers tonight, he texted. *Wish you were here?*

Having bath and Asian fusion takeaway. Then off to camera club. Wish you were here. The reply came back immediately. *P.S. Word to the wise, pastry gives Frank wind and normally, after even the smallest glass of wine, he will feel the need to show you his Shirley Bassey impression. Have fun! Xxx*

Neil grinned and a warm feeling crept through him. *Wish I was too,* he typed. *P.S. He says the same about you. Xxx*

He'd pressed send as Frank arrived. Frank didn't wait for the waiter to show him to the table. He looked around, saw Neil and walked straight across. The two shook hands.

'Jess told me we met the deadline and everything was uploaded before she went off on Friday night. Everything okay at your end?' he asked as soon as he'd sat down.

The man was nervous.

'Relax, everything is fine, and Tanya identified all the assets described,' Neil said, trying to put the man at his ease. 'Big day tomorrow. How are you feeling?'

'What you're saying is speak now or forever hold your peace.'

Neil smiled. 'Of course not.' Although, once contracts were signed, going back would be difficult. Frank slumped in his chair and stared at his hands. He looked up when the waiter handed them both a menu and asked Frank if he'd like a drink. He ordered a large glass of Pinot Grigio.

'They do a cracking steak and ale pie here,' Frank said, reading his menu. 'What are you having?'

'Not decided yet.' Neil didn't plan on eating at all. He would introduce the two men and leave them to chat over supper. He didn't mind picking up the bill, but he had somewhere else he'd far rather be.

'I have to admit it's hard.' Frank sighed. 'Harder than I dreamed it would be. I set this company up from nothing. But it's the right time and my wife is poring over cruise brochures for a round-the-world cruise as we talk. I will get home this evening and no doubt be told how much that little adventure is going to set me back. What about the buyers, are they still happy with their decision?'

Neil nodded in the direction of the door and stood up. 'You can ask him yourself,' he said. 'He's here.'

'Are you sure?' Frank glanced around.

'Let me introduce you,' Neil said.

'Frank …'

'Hello Martin,' Frank said. 'What brings you here?'

'You know each other,' Neil said, his smile slipping. Why was he surprised? Of course they knew each other. Small world and all that. Nodding acquaintances was how Martin described their relationship when he'd asked, but the supercilious grin that had spread over his face told Neil this relationship went far deeper than he'd been led to believe. Otherwise why had Martin insisted on keeping his identity secret until the last minute? He'd been played and judging by the look on Frank's face, he wasn't the only one.

Chapter Thirty-Seven

Neil, sat at his desk, put the phone down and sighed. Contracts were signed. No one had pulled out. The deal had gone through and in record time. His part in the whole charade was over.

It had been remarkably quick and straightforward, partly due to Frank's eagerness to sell and Anymoore being so easy to deal with. Normally a job well done pleased him. He should be patting himself on the back.

Except he wasn't. He was tired.

He'd had a sleepless night. Nothing to do with the Grey Towers food. The meal had been up to the usual Grey Towers standard and he couldn't blame the alcohol. He'd hardly drunk anything.

A sleepless night that had nothing to do either with his worry that one or other party might pull out at the last minute. Ross's words at his wedding, "*We expect this to be a hostile takeover*" came back loud and clear.

He put down the stapler and stared in disbelief at the mini staple art installation he appeared to have created on the side of his desk. The stapler was now empty. And so was he.

Last night Frank hadn't been happy to see Martin, and Neil had been irritated by how much Martin seemed to be enjoying the man's discomfort. He had managed to keep the conversation light throughout the meal, a meal he'd felt the need to stay and steer, despite his earlier intentions to leave at the earliest opportunity. They hadn't broached the subject of work. It seemed to be a topic they were all keen to avoid. Martin had talked about buying a new-build house as well as a new company. He'd tried making a joke about snagging lists, but it bombed.

'Don't give up the day job,' Neil had joked.

The bombshell arrived at the same time as the coffee and mignardises.

'Why me?' Frank had asked.

'You stole two of my clients – my biggest clients,' Martin had said.

'I've tendered for and won a lot of work this year and so have other companies.' Frank had shrugged. 'Are you planning on taking them over too?'

Good question Frank. MJC would have to find themselves another consulting firm if they planned on doing that, because as soon as this was signed and paid up, Neil had already decided, he was washing his hands of the matter. He didn't like Martin Cowley; he certainly wouldn't act for him again.

Jackson Consulting was professional. Neil had prided himself on always achieving high standards of great service. But sat in the middle of two warring parties last night, he'd felt a long way short of the mark.

'I don't need to,' Martin had boomed, which judging by their expressions had surprised a number of other diners as well. 'This year's Business of the Year award won't have your name on it. The company will be mine by then.'

Jeez, was this all about some local business award? Neil had shut his eyes and rubbed his forehead. Thank God he wasn't competitive.

He'd left the two men alone briefly, while he settled the bill, coming back to find them staring at each other with thunderous looks. Martin had stretched a wine-stained smile over his pale face as soon as Neil got back, then rose, told Frank he'd see him Monday and walked out.

'Monday?' Neil asked as he and Frank walked to their cars.

'He wants to make the announcement about the merger to my staff and I've told him he can be there, but I will make the announcement. What he tells them about MJC after that is up to him.'

'Was he happy with that?'

'You saw his reaction. Your guess is as good as mine.'

'How do you feel about things, now you know who?' Neil asked.

'I have no plans to pull out, if that's what you're asking,' Frank said stiffly. 'I suppose I should have considered it might be him. He was always a slippery little sucker.' He clicked the fob on his key ring. Sidelights flashed on a car in front of them. 'Legally, the golden parachute package is definitely part of the deal. Staff are safe. He can't withdraw it, can he?'

Neil shook his head. 'Part of the price he's paying covers that. It's not entirely normal. Usually anyone not wishing to join a company would resign before the transfer, but in this case, because of the timescale, you've both agreed a clause giving everyone two months to decide what they want to do. Any employee with over five years' service wishing to leave will be entitled to the enhanced redundancy as detailed, and those that do transfer will be protected by employment law.'

'What about me?' Frank said. 'Tell me, I'm not legally bound to work for that clown for the next three months.'

'That clause was designed to give you some security.' Neil had argued hard to ensure Frank was part of the package and was irritated the man wasn't more grateful. Nevertheless they'd parted on good terms, shaken hands and Frank had thanked him for everything he'd done.

The call from Martin sodding Cowley had come on his way home.

Martin thanked Neil for the evening's generosity. He didn't mention his abrupt departure.

'Is he going to pull out?' he asked.

'Frank's not prepared to negotiate,' Neil said. 'And he expects contracts to be signed within the next twenty-four hours, but no, he's not planning on pulling out.' He'd answered a few questions on relatively trivial matters and checked Martin was happy with Jackson Consultancy's quote for Ross for six weeks.

'It's bound to be hard for you without him,' Martin said.

Neil listened to him singing Ross's praises, all the way home. How thorough Ross had been with all the groundwork and how delighted Martin was that Ross was on-side and looking under the bonnet.

Wanker!

Neil hadn't answered because he couldn't think of anything polite to say. The odd pause here and there became more frequent and suggested Martin had run out of steam; Neil did nothing to encourage him. He'd wanted the conversation over while not wanting to appear rude but there was a limit to the amount of bullshit anyone could listen to without exploding. And he had a tricky parking space to manoeuvre into.

Once Martin had finally drawn breath.

Thanks for your call and good luck, had been on the tip of his tongue, but 'How did you find out about the accountant's arrest?' actually came out of his mouth.

There was more silence on the other end of the line, to the point an answer seemed unlikely. Then the voice at the other end said, 'I presume you're talking about the spot of bother my partner got into.'

The words hit him like a right hook to his solar plexus.

Pain shot through his chest. He'd thought he was having a heart attack. He hung up, not caring he hadn't said goodbye.

Martin! Of course! She'd mentioned Martin in some connection. Neil racked his brains to remember what. He hadn't given it much thought at the time.

Jess hadn't said explicitly that she wasn't involved with anyone but surely, she'd implied it by sleeping with him. He hadn't actually asked. He tried to remember what she'd told him about her love life. He'd been open about what had happened with Emma. Jess knew how hurt he'd been by his wife's betrayal and Neil's feelings about affairs. Was that all he'd been to her? Just an affair – someone to fill an emotional void while her partner was off creating a whole new business empire.

How could he have been so stupid? How could he have ever imagined that someone as vital as Jess could be single and interested in him?

He'd pictured his father, shaking his head and saying, "Comes from thinking with your dick, son, rather than your head". A phrase he'd used often when talking about clients, although as far as Neil knew, not a defence he put forward in court.

Okay, yes, Jess was incredibly sexy. He'd fancied her from the moment he'd seen her. But his feelings went far deeper than lust. She lit up his world when they were together, or he heard her voice on the phone. She made him so crazy, he wanted to wrap his arms around her and protect her from everything. He'd only known her a couple of weeks, but … He sighed. No, there was no but. His heart might be beating, but it was well and truly broken.

He had sat in the car, staring at his mobile, long after parking, willing it to materialise into Martin bloody Crowley, so he could at least punch him.

In his whole life, Neil couldn't think of anyone he'd ever wanted to thump; he wasn't big on violence. He rescued spiders. In his book every living thing deserved saving.

Then, last night, all he could think about was how good it would feel to flatten Martin Crowley.

Sat in his car, it had all started to make sense, trying to lower the price, the filtering of information. Martin had to have got it from someone on the inside. MJC had always known exactly what it wanted. It wasn't a matter of finding a company to fit the bill; Martin knew exactly which company he wanted because his partner worked for it.

Frank had said he'd only told a few people, on a strictly need to know basis about the loss of the Robinsons contract. All this time, Neil had felt guilty, convinced he must have done or said something. But the one person who would have had access to that information would've been the accountant.

She was wasted at Anymoore. She should be on the stage. Neil wondered what Jess and Martin were doing at that minute. Were they in bed together somewhere, laughing at him?

He'd shaken his head, got out of the car and locked it.

Earlier he'd listened to Martin talk about the house he was buying. At least it explained why she hadn't started to look for somewhere to live. She had somewhere, she was moving into a show house on the new estate.

The fact he couldn't imagine her living in such an impersonal place, just proved how little he knew of her.

By the time he'd reached his front door, he'd deleted her from his contacts. The biggest reason why he hadn't slept last night was history.

Chapter Thirty-Eight

'What do you mean, you've sold the company to Martin?' Jess stood on the opposite side of Frank's desk, leant over and stared down at him.

'Well strictly not him personally …' He sat, arms folded and glared back.

'Don't strictly me …'

'The contract is with his company – MJC.'

'You didn't think I'd have been the slightest bit interested in that piece of information before now? Is that why you and your bloody management consultant told me "the client wishes to remain anonymous"?'

Jess was beyond livid, so incensed, she did the air quote thing with her fingers that she couldn't abide, then put her hands behind her back.

'I didn't know until yesterday.' Frank's voice got louder. 'It was confidential. The name of the company wasn't to be disclosed until contracts were finalised. Besides, when I heard, I thought you bloody knew. You were sleeping with the guy – I wasn't.'

'What?'

'You heard me.' He stood up, mirroring her position, still not taking his eyes off her. Their faces were only a couple of feet apart. 'Imagine how ridiculous I felt when I walked in and discovered who'd bought my company. I thought you and I were friends not just colleagues. I was bloody hurt.'

'And you think because I slept with Neil, I knew all about this?'

'What are you talking about woman?' Frank ran his hand through his hair and frowned. 'Why would you sleep with him? You *live* with Martin. Have done for years. He's a weasel. I think you could do a lot better and should have dumped him years ago, but he's your problem, not mine. I just struggle to believe that at no point in one of your moments of passion did he not mention it to you.'

Tears of anger stung Jess's face. 'Moments of passion – Martin!'

Frank sank back into his chair and stared into space.

'For your information, not that it is any of your business, I can't remember the last time I shared the same bed as Martin. And …'

'Really, I'd rather—'

'He left me nearly three weeks ago.'

'Shit, Jess, I'm sorry. I didn't know.'

She shrugged, fighting back tears, not sure any longer whether they were directed at Frank, or Neil, or both. They were as bad as each other. Except she wasn't in love with Frank. 'I won't work for him.'

Frank sighed. 'Don't make any hasty decisions. You don't have to decide yet.'

'Who else knows?'

'There is an embargo on the announcement until Monday morning. There will be a staff meeting at ten o'clock. MJC are writing a press release, the contents of which I'm expected to deliver.'

Chapter Thirty-Nine

Sarah put the glossy brochure down, still not sure why it had fallen to her to cancel the Christmas party. She'd had high hopes for this one: the ABBA tribute band had been her idea and Izzie had had heart failure when she'd announced it. Sarah wondered whether she'd have brought Martin. Part of her didn't think even Izzie could be that cruel. *Hang on. Wasn't it Izzie who'd told the receptionist, when the girl had moaned about having flabby thighs, "In that case, it's lucky your stomach covers them"?*

She watched Jess walk to her car. Something was definitely wrong. She hadn't said goodbye. She'd told her about "26", but she wasn't paying attention.

Sarah casually dropped in the conversation the "fake" news his parents were time travellers and currently stuck somewhere between the Stone Age and Industrial Revolution.

Jess looked at her, a faraway look on her face, and said, 'Yes, I heard traffic was bad this morning. There must have been an accident or else the traffic lights are out again in the town centre.'

Maggie had gone with her to camera club last night. They'd seemed happy this morning and said they'd had a lovely evening. It couldn't be that.

She'd tried asking, but Jess had snapped, told her she'd find out on Monday and that she was working from home for the rest of the day.

She turned as the office door opened. Harry came in and dumped some papers on her desk. 'I've just seen Jess in the corridor. She said, to give these to you. Is she okay? She looked like she'd been crying?'

He wandered over and stood by Sarah at the window. 'What is it with everyone round here today? Has the world ended, and someone forgot to tell me? Everybody looks so miserable.'

'I'm not sure about the world, but Frank's told me to cancel the office party. Apparently, the budget is going to be used for car park lighting after all. I thought we'd bottomed that issue out at the last management meeting, but evidently not.'

'You think that's what upset her?' Harry continued to watch Jess get into her car and drive out of the car park. 'Can't help thinking that's a bit of an overreaction. I mean I know the party was supposed to be great, but …'

Sarah smiled. 'I think something happened between her and the management consultant.'

It had to be something to do with Neil. Work never had that effect on Jess. Nor Martin. And she'd been so happy lately. Even with all the extra work.

Was Neil okay? Jess looked well enough. Had she discovered he had a terminal illness and only days to live? Or, was he secretly married?

'Frank's not going to be happy. There's very little money to come back,' Sarah said. 'We haven't bought the alcohol yet, but everything else had to be paid last week. The caterers and tribute band have referred me to their cancellation policies. I can change dates and venues, but I've left it too late to cancel the bloody thing.'

'It's a shame. I heard great things about the Anymoore parties. They were legendary – one of the reasons I wanted to join the company,' Harry said.

'I never put you down as a wild party animal.' Sarah smiled.

'In my last company a tray of sandwiches, and background music while you worked was the best you could hope for. Management banned alcohol after someone in IT introduced a virus that sent begging letters to everyone's contacts and took the company three weeks to sort out. Gone are the parties when once you'd had enough wine, you'd go and photocopy your bottom.'

'Bit before my time.' Sarah chuckled. 'But I heard about the things you oldies used to get up to.'

'Oi.' He punched her playfully on the arm. 'I'll have you know I'm a bit of a dancing queen. Put on the "Macarena" and I'd be right there.' Harry went through a series of arm movements, ending with a wiggle and a spin.

'That's something I'd like to have seen. I'd have requested the band play it specially.'

'This might come as a surprise, but the "Macarena" cannot be blamed on ABBA.' Harry spoke slowly, clearly teasing her.

Sarah tried conjuring up a witty retort, but the way he looked at her emptied her brain of all cohesive thoughts.

'What about you?' he asked. 'What gets you up on the dance floor, throwing some shapes? Do women still dance round their handbags?'

'When did you last go clubbing?' She grinned. 'Most modern girls don't bother with handbags these days – once they realised that dancing on your own with a handbag for company is fine early on but that it won't hold you up when you're drunk. It never walks you home and I can't remember the last time my bag bought me a drink.'

He did have a lovely smile.

'Talking of which, how's your search for Mr Perfect going? Maggie and Jess arranged any more bad dates?'

She rolled her eyes. 'They keep accusing me of changing the goalposts. I mean, seriously, would you date a guy with four children, whose babysitter had let him down, so he invited Maggie along, thinking she was my mother, to read them a bedtime story in his car, while he bought me a cup of coffee.'

Harry's eyes sparkled.

'Actually I've been invited out. I'm being taken out for a meal. We're going to The Last Post a week tomorrow.'

'Is that place still open?'

'I hope so. I'm meeting Terry there.'

'And his appealing qualities are?'

'He likes the ringtone on my phone, thinks I'm a cool rock chick and goes to all the music festivals. He's talking about taking me to Glastonbury and Reading next year.'

'Wow,' said Harry. 'I'm impressed. Tickets for those normally sell out as soon as they go on sale. Sounds like Maggie and Jess have come up with a winner this time.'

Sarah frowned. "32" hadn't actually said he would take her. He wanted someone to go with him. She'd sort of put two and two together and come up with … Then they'd got side-tracked before she could clarify what he meant and spent the rest of their four minutes comparing the songs they had on their iPhones. There weren't many similarities – even their versions of "Memories" were different. He'd never heard of Maroon 5. He told her she'd got it wrong when she explained she'd downloaded it for a funeral, but why on earth would Maggie want a song about "wet pavements" and "smiling about the old days"? From everything she'd said, they weren't happy times. And she'd definitely said "Memories", not "Memory".

Terry wasn't perfect, but Glastonbury and Reading were a big plus. Sarah had never been to either and was fast concluding perfect guys didn't exist. Time to be more realistic, set her sights slightly lower, so as soon as he'd got up and moved on, she'd written "Yes" on her score sheet. Not in capital letters, but nevertheless clearly. Well, if music be the food of love and all that.

'Cancelling the party is probably for the best,' she said changing the subject. 'We were going to have to take precautions during the conga. Andrew, last year, refused to join in until Tracey from contracts wrestled him into submission. At least we will save a bit by not having to have St John Ambulance on standby.'

'The guy from marketing, I heard.' Harry smiled. 'He still wears a neck brace when stressed. I understood this year the moment the idea was voiced, a lot of people planned on disappearing. I wish I'd been there,' Harry said, quietly.

Sarah wanted to say something, aware he was waiting for her to answer and "I wish you were too" was forming in her brain.

'Frank said Jess is working from home for the rest of the week,' Maggie said, coming back into the room and killing the moment completely. 'What's that all about?'

Jess lay on the sofa. She'd stopped crying, but only just. She ached all over. Her eyes felt as if they'd been stabbed repeatedly with red hot needles. They felt puffy, were probably red, but she didn't care. It wasn't as if anyone else could see them, so she kept them closed.

The last time she'd cried like that was watching *Black Beauty*. Another wave of nausea swept over her. Something pressed on her stomach. She felt empty and sure it had nothing to do with horses or skipping lunch.

Perhaps she had flu. Strangely the thought cheered her, even if briefly. Maybe she was ill. *Who was she trying to kid?* She didn't have a temperature; she was just feeling sorry for herself. Her mother would have seen through it and told her to stop mooning around or told her that her generation had gone through far worse "without breaking down in such an unladylike fashion". Jess was glad she wasn't there. All she wanted to do was wallow in self-pity.

She hadn't cried when Martin left. Maybe she should have done. Maybe these feelings were the result of years of pent-up emotion. No, she hadn't missed him, not like she missed Neil. One minute Neil had been there, all was well with her world; and now, he was gone, and it wasn't. For the last couple of weeks, she'd enjoyed feelings she'd long forgotten existed, she'd felt warm and safe. But those feelings had been ripped away and replaced by the cold unpleasant insight she'd been cheated, misused and somehow it was all her own fault.

How could he?

How could she not have seen through him? There must have been pointers in the things he said or did? Perhaps when the mere mention of Neil Jackson no longer sent butterflies performing aerial gymnastics racing between her stomach and heart, when she could put some distance between him and her feelings, when she could look back with a clear head, she might be able to see the clues which had undoubtedly been there from the beginning, but which she had chosen, in a moment of self-indulgent madness, to ignore.

He'd probably be laughing right now at how easy it had been to get her to roll over and help.

Had Martin put him up to it? "Be nice to my ex-girlfriend and she'll tell you all you need to know." She wouldn't put it past him. "Sleep with her. She'll be so bloody grateful, you'll have her eating out of your hand."

Yet, as much as she hated Martin, she had no one else to blame for the situation. That was down fairly and squarely to her own inflated self-ego. Why on earth would someone like Neil Jackson ever be interested in her – a woman heading towards mid-life crises, if she wasn't already there, at breakneck speed? Neil said all the right things, but then he probably said similar things to any girl he met. He was a good actor – she'd give him that.

She needed to toughen up, take a leaf out of Sarah's book. Sarah didn't cry herself to sleep every time a relationship ended. Not that there would be any more relationships ever again, but that girl met Mr Right more times than the traffic lights at the top of Redford High Street failed. And when his halo slipped, or she discovered a serious personality disorder lurked behind his good looks, or he slept with one of her friends, Sarah didn't take it personally, she moved on. How many times had she told Jess, "There's no point in recriminations"?

'His loss,' she said, the day after she left the last Mr Right at the Badger and Fir Tree. 'Plenty more fish in the sea.' If Sarah could be so sensible, shouldn't she be a little more grown-up? Jess was old enough and wise enough to have seen through Neil blooming Jackson. She hadn't, but she certainly wasn't going to give him the satisfaction of thinking about him again.

Jess wished her stomach didn't feel so tight and uncomfortable. Perhaps her gut had twisted, or her appendix was rumbling. It was probably about to rupture. Someone would find her dead in days or weeks to come. She wondered if they'd tell Neil. Probably not because the only other person with a key was the estate agent. He'd probably ring Martin, who'd be round like a shot, take the sofa and leave her dying on the floor.

She moved her hands down to her tummy, half expecting to discover a lump, or gaping hole or some physical indication she was terminally ill, but found instead something smooth, hairy and warm.

She opened her eyes. General Gordon observed her hands with his best "Stop moving or I'll have to kill you" look.

Jess stopped. She still had the scars from the last time she'd ignored a General Gordon look.

'I don't know why you're looking so pleased with yourself – you're never going to see Dudley again.' Her eyes smarted with more tears threatening to come.

The cat blinked slowly, as if he couldn't believe she'd stooped so low as to make threats. Clearly, he didn't seem to think that as much of a problem as she did. In fact, it was so "unworryable" he shut his eyes and settled down, his tail wrapped about him like a mobile draft excluder.

Jess closed her eyes. Think of nice things.

What was that exhibition she'd read about? A Rankin retrospective at a London gallery. She couldn't remember which magazine she'd seen it advertised in, but she could probably find it on the internet. She would go and she'd ask Maggie if she wanted to go too. Perhaps they could treat themselves to afternoon tea at the National Portrait Gallery.

But first she needed to move out. She needed to pack.

Chapter Forty

Sarah sat in the library and stared at the certificate Jack had pushed across his desk. 'Does this mean what I think it does?' she asked.

He nodded. 'Maggie's brother appears to have stayed with their birth father. He was adopted, but by his natural father and his wife. They only changed his surname. He still has the same forenames.'

'So, when Maggie's parents split up, they just divvied up the kids. Can you believe anybody could do that? Bloody hell, no wonder Maggie didn't like her mother.'

'It wouldn't have been that straightforward,' Jack said. 'Families are complicated things. By the look of it, Arthur was already married when the twins were born – to someone else. Did Maggie give any indication she might have known?'

Sarah checked her notepad. Maggie had looked completely washed out by the time she'd finished questioning her. She'd pushed hard and found out a few personal details, the beginnings of a eulogy had been written, but nothing of substance.

'She knew she was a twin, but understood her brother was stillborn. Her mother never talked about her father but gave the impression she'd been the product of a one-night stand. She never questioned that until she got a copy of her own birth certificate.'

'What did her mother say?'

'Nothing, Maggie was registering her death at the time.'

'Ah,' Jack said. 'That explains the lack of knowledge.'

His findings looked promising. Sarah would have rather not spent money on certificates, but he'd said, 'You shouldn't assume anything with genealogy. Always research and confirm. You'd be surprised how many versions of my own family tree are dotted all over the internet, because people have made incorrect assumptions.'

'Arthur's death certificate has Stephen, his son, recorded as the informant.'

'Yep, and we have an address. I've checked, there appears to be someone still there with the same name.'

'Are you telling me you've found Maggie's brother and he's still alive?'

Jack nodded. 'He's certainly on the last electoral roll.' He pushed a piece of paper across the desk.

'What should I do?' Sarah asked. 'I can hardly turn up on his doorstep and announce I'm doing his mother's funeral, can I?'

'Are you?' Jack looked impressed. 'I wouldn't know where to start with something like that.'

Sarah tried to look calm. 'I think I'm almost there,' she said as casually as she could, even if it wasn't entirely true.

Maggie had at least come up with three musical options. This weekend Sarah needed to sit down and finalise plans. The funeral director had been pushing for an order of service.

'I should get going,' she said.

'I suppose you could spend the afternoon watching episodes of *Long Lost Family*, imagine yourself as Davina McCall,' Jack said.

'Hardly the same league,' Sarah said. 'She has a TV team behind her. I don't.'

'Take your camera. Maggie will want to see a picture of Stephen when you tell her. They always do. I know I would.'

'Would you?' Sarah wasn't sure. 'Do you think Davina has many instances when the photographed person is so scary looking that the person they've doorstepped tells them to "fuck off" as soon as they see the picture?'

Jack's colleague looked up and tutted. He grinned.

'I ought to tell Maggie first, oughtn't I?'

'Does she know you're looking?'

Sarah shook her head.

'I'd say don't. Stephen probably knows about being adopted. He may be upset his birth mother never tried to track him down. He's got to deal with the news she's dead. You have to face it, he might not want to see Maggie.'

'Then if he doesn't want to see her, she need never know.' Sarah nodded, thoughtfully.

'And if he does, you can have that lovely moment when Davina sits them down at the table and says, "I've got something to tell you" as she slides the photo across the table. Just make sure you have a box of tissues to hand.'

Jack's colleague looked up. 'I love that moment too,' she said. 'It always makes me cry.'

Frankly, anyone less likely to burst into floods of tears than Maggie, Sarah couldn't imagine, but she smiled sweetly.

'Come back and tell us how you got on?' the woman said, eagerly.

It made sense. Jess wasn't in the right head place to make major decisions about where she wanted to live. She'd be stretching her finances to the limit to buy a one- let alone a two-bedroomed property with a garage and garden in Redford. The flats she'd seen were awful and very few would even consider General Gordon.

It was sad but true, balancing a set of accounts used to give her a thrill, bank reconciliations excited her, but neither gave her the electric feeling she got when taking a picture that she knew had worked. Nowadays at work she was rarely asked to help find a difference, everything was computerised. She had to review final figures, check occasionally things were in the right place, but more often than not, her work involved looking at the financial implications of ongoing contracts, working out how profit could be improved, or producing risk assessments.

Deep down, she wanted to be a photographer. When Frank asked her the calculator or camera question, she hadn't hesitated. She just had no idea whether she could make it work or not as a business, but Maggie had thrown her a lifeline when she'd offered a room at a ludicrously low rent.

It would give her the breathing space to decide where her future lay. It was unlikely she could make a living from wedding photography in the foreseeable future, but the exit package from Anymoore would give her the financial cushion to give it a go.

These days everybody had a digital camera. She'd spoken to wedding photographers before who said the big money weddings weren't there any more and they struggled to make ends meet. Most of their work came from recommendations, which would only come once she'd got established: Catch 22. Leanne and Darren's wedding was hardly going to lead to many leads and after the trouble they'd caused, she wasn't sure she'd take advantage of any opportunities that came from it.

Financially, it made no sense to give up a well-paid job. The new company had to continue to employ her at her current level. Her head told her staying was the right decision, anything else was a ridiculous flight of fancy.

But her heart …

She was a trained accountant. What if she advertised as a bookkeeper, she could offer to do the books for small companies? If she did that part-time to make ends meet, the rest of the time she could be a photographer. She needed a business plan. Jess reached for her mug of tea and smiled. The tea might be cold, but she was buzzing. She switched the kettle on and rang Maggie to let her know her decision.

Chapter Forty-One

'We're stopping here?' Maggie asked. 'Aren't we cutting through the cemetery on our way into town?'

'You'll find the garden of remembrance down there,' the man at the office window pointed towards a long track. 'At the end you'll find the lychgate. That's the entrance.'

'How far are we talking?' Sarah asked, squinting to see the gate he was talking about. She wasn't dressed for a hike and wished she'd brought sensible shoes.

'Two, three minutes' walk at the most.' He held out a coloured piece of paper with a cross marked on it. 'Turn right down the first path, take the second on the left and the plot you're looking for is down there. That's another minute's walk, absolute maximum,' he said, wiggling the paper until she took it. 'They go in number order, evens one side, odd the other. You're looking for 1596. You can't miss it.'

'What exactly are we doing here?' Maggie asked.

They passed the traditional graves, some with headstones, some without. Some so new, the freshly turned earth and flowers still sat proud of the rest. Some more elaborately decorated than others. Some with angels, others with open bibles carved in black stone.

'When you said there's something I want to show you, I sort of thought it maybe a new dress. A handbag. I hope you're not expecting me to go to a funeral.'

'No.'

One white headstone had a pile of soft toys in front of it, and what looked like children's paintings stuck to it. Sarah wasn't close enough to read the name or age.

'Or perhaps you wanted to introduce me to Jack from the library …'

'He's happily married. I keep telling you.'

'Okay, one of your speed-date matches then. You've been very quiet about those. How many did you get?'

'Three.' They passed a hedge and on the other side, the headstones were smaller, closer together and all flat in the earth. Sarah kept walking until they got to the gates.

'Don't tell me. One of them wants to meet you in the crematorium. Are we about to meet "26"?'

'No.' Sarah angled the map, until it tied in with the paths ahead of her. I didn't "yes" him.'

'You said he was practically perfect.'

'Only until he started talking. Turned out he has a thing about strange creatures.'

'Should make you feel at home then.'

'His bedroom is filled with tanks full of live cockroaches. He lives with his parents and has got bearded dragons.' Sarah pointed to the path on the right. 'That way I think.'

'I told John we'd be at Treetops early afternoon to help with afternoon tea and talk about the wake.'

'What? You want me to cook?'

'Only sandwiches and scones,' Maggie said. 'You can butter bread, can't you?'

Sarah had settled on a black dress for this outing. She'd figured it appropriate for the crematorium. She certainly had no intention of going anywhere near a kitchen in it.

'This won't take long. Well,' she hesitated, 'I suppose it might. Look, there's something I should have told you.'

Maggie stopped.

Ahead of her, a man raised a hand and smiled. He had a nice face.

'There's someone I'd like you to meet.'

Maggie looked round expectantly. 'Him. Bloody hell, Sarah. He's old enough to be your father. He's got to be my age at least.'

'He's exactly your age,' Sarah said. 'Give or take twenty minutes.'

Maggie's face went through various transitions as she engaged her brain.

Sarah's stomach tightened. She was in danger of going into a full-blown panic attack. Her breathing got shallow. She debated taking her shoes off and making a run for it. Maggie would never catch her. This had seemed like such a good idea. Stephen had been so excited when she'd called and told him his sister was still alive. Every episode of *Long Lost Family* ran through her head. She imagined how Davina must have felt when she told somebody, "We've found your mother and six other members of the family you never knew you had".'

They always looked pleased, sometimes they burst into tears, but they were tears of happiness.

It had been Stephen's idea to meet at the cemetery as soon as possible; he wanted to show Maggie their father's memorial plaque.

Sarah tried to slow her breathing. Deep breaths.

Suddenly Maggie's brain must have found the gear it was looking for. She stared at the man over Sarah's head. Sarah wanted to turn around and see what he was doing, but she froze, and the way she was facing was the quickest way back to the car. She slipped one foot out of her shoe, then the other.

'Stephen?' Maggie said and started walking.

Maggie walked into the Treetops' reception, pleased to find John waiting for her. He smiled when he saw her.

'Sarah's here already,' he said. 'In the lounge.' He looked through a small round window in the swing doors. 'And she's a real hit with the residents. They're discussing ideas for your mother's wake and so far'—he shook his head and grinned—'they've told her she needs the Chippendales or a stand-up comic. Go through, I'll be there in a second.'

He turned to Stephen, who had followed her in, greeted him warmly and shook his hand. 'Mr Warburton, how lovely. Everything well with your mother-in-law, I hope.'

'She's fine,' Stephen said.

'So, what can I do for you today?'

'Nothing,' Maggie said. 'Stephen's with me.'

John's face darkened.

'Not like that.' She flushed. His reaction filled her with warmth. Reaching out, she put a hand on John's arm. He looked at her with a smile that took her breath away. 'Meet my big brother,' she said quietly. 'My birth brother,' she added happily.

'Actually'—John kissed her cheek—'now you come to mention it, there is a likeness.'

'We're twins. And do you know'—Stephen laughed—'we've lived no more than five miles apart most of our lives? We have Sarah to thank for reuniting us.'

‘So that’s what she was on about.’ John chuckled. ‘When she arrived she was rambling on about upsetting you, running away and not being sure whether you’d turn up.’

A sound of laughter came from the room and someone, probably Sarah, said, ‘You can’t be serious,’ in a loud voice.

‘You two go in and I’ll make us all a cup of tea,’ John said, giving Maggie’s waist a quick squeeze.

‘I’ll give you a hand,’ Stephen said, following him down the corridor.

‘Great.’ John nodded. ‘We’ll see if we can find some of the lemon meringue tart left over from lunch.’

Maggie watched the two men walk away before she opened the door.

Sarah looked up at the sound of the door opening, her face clouded with concern. ‘I’m sorry,’ she said. ‘I should have told you what I’d done. You have every right to hate me.’

She stood up and Maggie wrapped her in a hug. ‘Stupid girl. I don’t hate you. No one’s ever done something like that for me before.’

‘Jack from the library helped,’ Sarah said, modestly.

‘I would never have looked for Stephen, even if I’d considered he might be alive. I’d never have dreamt he’d be interested in getting to know me.’ Tears pricked at Maggie’s eyes. ‘He’s a lovely man. We have so much to catch up on.’ She sniffed, seriously in danger of bursting into floods of tears. Sarah’s eyes looked moist too, clearly she wasn’t far behind.

‘I want a cuddle,’ an elderly woman rose to her feet and waddled across the room, her arms outstretched. ‘I’ve always liked a good cuddle.’ Sarah caught Maggie’s eye and they both giggled.

‘We’ve been helping your daughter plan Rose’s party,’ another woman said.

Sarah nodded. ‘They’ve given me some great ideas for food and things.’ Her head jerked up. ‘Do you know why they call them wakes?’

Maggie shook her head.

‘Edna told me people had to sit with the dead body for forty-eight hours after a person died in case the bodysnatchers came. Others would bring them food and try and keep them awake. That’s right, isn’t it ladies?’

‘And drink,’ Edna said.

A lot of nodding went on.

'What sort of food?' Maggie said.

Sarah shrugged. 'When were pizzas invented? Did they have takeaways in those days?'

A lot of mumbling and frowning.

'I meant for mother's wake.'

'Vodka,' Edna said. 'And gin.'

'We …' Sarah looked around. If she hoped for encouragement, she got it. Heads all around her continued to nod. 'We thought it would be nice to have a good old-fashioned afternoon high tea. Ham salad …'

'With boiled new potatoes.'

Maggie couldn't see who said that. Sarah appeared to have developed a talent for ventriloquism, except with a whole row of puppets not one.

'Bread and butter.'

'White, not brown.'

'Pickled onions,' another voice piped up.

'Now you mention it, we'd like pizza too.'

'And sausage rolls, scotch eggs, chicken goujons, vegetable samosas,' Sarah read from her pad. 'And scones …'

'Jam first then clotted cream.'

'And a Victoria sponge cake to finish.' Sarah looked up. 'Have I forgotten anything?'

'Drinks,' Edna said.

'Sorry. Yes. Sherry, when we get back from the crematorium. Maybe some spirits for those who want them.' She looked at Edna as she spoke. 'Then wine with the meal. Tea and coffee with the scones and champagne with the cakes. After tea, we're going to have a good old sing-song around the piano. Edna is going to play for us.'

'She's never played the piano in her life,' John said, setting a tray of tea down on one of the coffee tables. 'Have you Edna?'

'I've got a week to learn.' She sniffed. 'How hard can it be?'

'Rose would've loved that.'

'What colour rose are we talking about?' the cuddle woman asked. 'I only like pink smelly ones. They remind me of my Bert.'

Chapter Forty-Two

Unless Neil had missed an email, telephone call, or text message over the weekend, Ross shouldn't have been in the office. It was Monday morning. He was supposed to be at Anymoore Ltd. He was contracted to MJC.

'Martin Cowley would be delighted to give an exclusive interview.'

Neil's head hurt, but with or without the hangover, the very mention of Cowley, made his blood boil. He slammed his briefcase down on his desk. Dudley followed him in and disappeared into his basket, his tail at half mast, clearly worried whatever had made his master mad was his fault.

Ross, on the other hand, was far too wrapped up with schmoozing somebody on the phone to notice his mood. The person on the other end of the line clearly wasn't as delighted by the one-off opportunity being offered to them. Ross had to do some serious grovelling.

'Mr Cowley feels a prestigious paper, such as yours, would be the ideal platform to launch this exclusive.'

Bollocks, does he.

Ross looked up and Neil had the childish urge to pretend to vomit – just as he and Sophie used to do whenever his father came home and said, "How's my darling girl?" before he kissed Neil's mother. Something that after forty years of marriage, his father still did.

Neil always imagined one day that would be him. A scene that would often play in his head of coming home to a cottage in the country, the smell of home-cooked food and the woman he loved, while their children made retching sounds round the scrubbed pine table.

Whoa – stop that thought! Press delete. Step away from the cottage scenario.

He didn't have a darling girl. And never would have, because he was categorically, never going to get involved with anyone again. Dudley was under strict instructions to kill him if he ever so much as contemplated another relationship.

Bloody women.

He could give up consultancy; maybe set up a Newfoundland dog rescue charity.

'Mr Cowley appreciates how busy you are.'

Neil was angry, not just with Martin, or Jess. The man opposite him seriously pissed him off.

Ross had blown any chance of a partnership. How could he have not known Martin's connection with the company? He could protest all he liked. The "old acquaintance"; "Someone I knew at university"; "Ran into each other again recently and got talking, went out for supper a couple of times. Martin talked through his idea of merging with Anymoore Ltd, showed me the figures and I recommended you as someone ideally qualified to take charge and push the deal through."

Neil hung his jacket on the back of his chair, moved his briefcase to the floor and saw a white envelope sitting in the middle of his desk.

Ross put down the phone, wrote something in his diary and stood up. He stared straight at the envelope in the middle of Neil's desk too but didn't mention it. 'I'm off to Anymoore. You haven't forgotten you're meeting a potential new client at 9.30 in Templeton? And Tanya's not in today.'

Shit. Of course, I've flaming well forgotten. Neil opened his top drawer, thankful that, despite Ross's tidying, his emergency razor, toothbrush and a tie were still there. Ten minutes before he needed to set off, he would at least try to look a little like a serious businessman.

'Shall I take the dog?' Ross said. 'I can always dump him in the accounts office. You did say they were always happy to look after him.'

'If you're sure,' Neil found himself saying.

'I should get going,' Ross said, staring at the envelope. 'You need to open that.'

'Yes,' Neil said, a little concerned he'd managed to wind up in some parallel universe, where Ross had metamorphosed into a kind, considerate person, happy to look after his dog.

He handed over Dudley's lead before the man had a chance to change his mind.

If he was to get to Templeton in the next thirty minutes, he needed to set off shortly too.

Two aspirins, and a quick wash and brush up, or "cat's lick and a promise" as his mother would have called it when he was a teenager, later and Neil fiddled with the envelope. It had his full name and address on it.

No stamp, or official-looking "To Pay" written across it to suggest the post office wanted him to remortgage the office for the privilege of discovering the contents. It had been hand delivered. A little bubble of excitement rose in his stomach; maybe, just maybe it was her. Not that she could say anything he wanted to hear. Time was running out and curiosity got the better of him. He tore it open.

Definitely hand delivered; it had probably only travelled ten feet, twelve maximum, in all its life. Ross planned to leave at Christmas. He would be joining MJC as their Promotions Director.

Neil walked across to the kitchen and the window looking out over the car park. That explained why he'd offered to take Dudley and was so keen for Neil to open the envelope.

Ross never took Dudley anywhere if he could avoid it. That alone should have unnerved him. It had unnerved Dudley. They hadn't got far. Dudley, Neil saw from the window, made a point of stopping at every lamp post and peering back over his shoulder. Clearly, he expected any minute that Neil, realising he'd been kidnapped, would come running to save him. Everything would be all right if he could delay getting into the car a few minutes longer.

The letter went on at some length to describe the plan Ross had agreed with MJC for smoothing the takeover. He planned to work his notice out at Anymoore. He would ensure Jackson Consultancy was paid as agreed. He trusted this would be acceptable.

Neil folded the letter and put it back in its envelope and propped it against his phone. Some of that morning's tension disappeared. Jackson Consultancy services would survive. No need to rush out and look for another Ross anytime soon, possibly anytime ever.

For the first time since last Tuesday night, Neil relaxed. He smoothed his hair down, ran his tongue over his teeth and pulled his tie into place and went to meet a potential customer. The idea of getting involved in something new pleased him.

'Don't think I didn't mean every word I said on Friday,' Jess said.

Frank sat in his office. 'You're here,' he said.

'Where else am I supposed to be? I'm still employed, aren't I? Or is there something you forgot to tell me?'

'You didn't have to come in.'

He better not bloody grin. One grin and I'm out of here. 'I'm considering my options at the moment. But if I do decide to jump, let's be clear, I get the full package and salary for my full notice period.'

'Goes without saying.' Frank shrugged. 'Are you sure you want to be here?'

Of course she wasn't sure. She'd thought about little else over the weekend. She didn't know where she wanted to be. She would move in with Maggie, who no doubt thought, when she made the offer, it would be a temporary thing, six months tops, while Jess worked out where she wanted to live and what she could afford. If she threw her toys out of the pram now and stormed off, no mortgage provider would entertain her.

She needed to stay long enough to secure a loan so that by the time the bank found out, she would have her feet well and truly under a table in her new home.

'I might need time off.'

Frank held his hands palm up. 'No problem – take as much as you need.'

'There's something else – Neil Jackson.'

Frank eyed her cautiously.

'I don't want to see him again ever.' When Jess was a child and told a lie that big, she would cross her fingers behind her back. She did now. 'If you need him to come back, give me warning and I'll make myself scarce.' She didn't uncross her fingers. Her father always knew about her little trick. He used to pretend he'd dropped some money on the floor. He never had, but she'd turn and look every time.

Of course she wanted to see Neil again. Half of her wanted to tear him limb from limb for the way he'd treated her. But the other half of her loved the fact that he'd walked her home from Grey Towers because he wanted to make sure she got there. That he'd waited at the end of her drive to make sure she got safely in the door before he walked off. That he'd rescued her from the police station. Hardly a jail breakout, but he'd come for her.

They'd spent the night together, surely that meant … No, okay, maybe not. And his dog liked her; he couldn't have been in on the act, could he? It was one thing to be crossed by a cheating, lying toad, it was another to be double-crossed by a Newfoundland.

'Martin's coming in today. He's going to announce the takeover.'

'That's fine,' Jess said, fingers still crossed. 'I look forward to hearing what he has to say.'

Frank shifted in his seat. He looked nervous. Jess nodded to him and walked back to her office.

Dudley, under her desk, squeaked when he saw her, his tail wagging furiously.

Neil? Despite Frank's assurances, was he in the building?

Her heart raced and she had to concentrate on breathing.

'Someone called Ross brought him in,' Sarah said. 'He asked if we were okay to look after him.'

'Ross?' She didn't look up; she didn't want to catch Sarah's eye.

'Neil's partner.'

'Oh,' she said, trying hard to sound disinterested as she stroked the dog, who rolled over and let her.

'There's to be a meeting at 10.00 in the boardroom. Martin's here too.' Sarah put some cheques in her in tray that needed signing.

'I know.'

'You do?'

'Where is he now?'

'Izzie is showing them both around.'

The phone rang and Sarah picked up, her eyes on Jess.

'Good morning, Anymoore Accounts, Sarah speaking,' she said, still staring. 'How can I help you?'

Jess couldn't hear what was said, but Sarah's frown deepened.

'How many Fs are there in discount?' she said eventually. The tinny sound stopped for a second and then the person on the other end must've said something because Sarah smiled. 'Yup, my point exactly.' She slammed the receiver down. 'Wanker!' she added.

Jess wasn't sure whether she meant the caller or Martin but allowed herself a small smile anyway.

Chapter Forty-Three

Martin and another man walked into the office shortly before the meeting started.

Jess recognised the face from the pictures on Neil's website.

So, this was Ross.

Martin, dressed in what looked like a new suit, saw her and stopped. Ross, wreathed in smiles, clearly didn't notice Martin missing from his side until he was in the middle of the room, but he must've had an idea who she was because his smile died the moment he noticed her.

Ross and Sarah both disappeared: Sarah to get some printing done, Ross looking uncomfortable, saying he needed to check the boardroom.

Luckily, Dudley didn't feel the need to desert his post too. It felt good to have someone on her side. A throaty grumble replaced his delighted squeak of earlier. Clearly a dog with exceptionally good taste.

'Jess.'

'Martin.' Good to get the formalities out of the way.

He started across the office. 'Look.'

The throaty grumble got louder as he got closer, so he stopped, looking confused at the noise and where it had come from.

Jess kept her face as blank as she could but put her hand down to stroke Dudley. He rewarded her with a lick. 'Sorry, I don't understand. Look at what, Martin?'

He looked uncomfortable. *Good, let him squirm.*

'Jess.'

'We've done that bit. You remember who I am. I know who you are.'

'Are you coming to the meeting?'

'You bet, I'll be there.' *Wouldn't miss this show for the world.* She grinned.

'Are you planning on making things difficult?'

'Oh honey, is that what you're worried about?' She tilted her head, amused to see below her desk, Dudley mirrored her actions. 'I don't need to make things difficult for you. You've managed to do that all on your own.'

He frowned. 'That's …'

'Actually, seeing as you're here, we need to discuss furniture. There are a few items left in the house. I understand you've a love nest to furnish, so presumably you'll need some of it.'

'Love nest?'

'One of the new houses in Redford, or so I've heard.'

'How did you …?'

'These things always get out. I'm moving at the weekend and will leave the keys with the estate agent then. Anything I leave behind, you're welcome to and if you could make arrangements for anything you don't want, I'd appreciate it. And Martin?'

'Yes.'

'My solicitor has advised me not to accept the fifty-fifty split you're proposing. She has written to your solicitor this morning putting forward a counter-offer. She pointed out the additional mortgage went straight into your company and should be repaid in full before any split is discussed. And I'd like the endowment policy transferred to my name. I assume you won't be awkward. I think it's important to keep these things as amicable as possible, don't you?'

Martin spluttered but didn't have a chance to respond. The door opened and Ross appeared, tapping his watch. 'Better get going?' he said.

Jess got up too. 'We'll walk with you,' she said. 'Come on Dudley.' She picked up her camera.

'Where do you think you're going with those?' Martin said.

'Boardroom.' She walked through the door Ross held open.

The room resembled a police press conference. A long table in the front with three chairs, glasses and bottles of water.

Jess had heard in serious criminal cases that the police encouraged a similar sort of set-up. But this wasn't a tearful appeal for a missing child or call for witnesses to a cruel and brutal murder.

Martin took his place in the middle, Frank on one side, looked uncomfortable, Ross on the other, fussed over Martin.

Normally, people headed for the back row and only when that was full did they start making their way forward. Jess and Dudley made for the front row. He needed space and she might as well do something useful. If the Camera Club's speaker last Tuesday had been right, maybe she could send some images to the local paper. If they printed them, she could buy the paper and add them to her portfolio to show potential clients.

She checked her ISO and shutter speed were sufficient, made some minor adjustments and settled back.

Martin said something and Dudley growled. It cheered her a little, then Sarah came and sat next to her and she started to feel better still.

Izzie strode into the room, clearly thought better of joining Jess and Sarah in a front-row seat and took her place in the row behind with some of her customer services team. Harry, however, was not as easily put off and took the seat on Sarah's other side.

The conference started with Frank giving a moving speech. Jess felt a tear prick her eye as he talked about the people he'd worked with over the years.

'You're all family to me,' he said. 'Let's face it, I've worked with some of you longer than I've been with any of my wives.'

He thanked everyone for their tolerance and support.

'MJC are lucky to be acquiring this company,' he added. 'You've all ensured we're in a great place going forward. You don't need a fusty old pensioner telling you what computers need these days. You need a new dynamic leadership team if you're going to progress at the same rate we have been. I know you all know that, even if you're all too kind to voice it, to my face, anyway. I can't tell you what to do'—he stared straight at Jess—'but what I can say through a lifetime of experience,' he added, quietly, 'is never give up on your dreams. Fear of failure and the unknown may hold most people back, but you are not most people.'

Tears ran down Jess's cheeks and she reached for a tissue.

'You are talented, and you deserve to be happy. Believe in yourself. Don't listen when anyone tries to tell you different. Give it your best and you will find a way to achieve everything you want. Your dreams are out there for the taking. And it's your turn now. Go for them.'

Someone clapped, applause built until everyone stood. Jess moved to the side of the room and took some pictures of the staff. Many of them were crying too. Tears built in Frank's eyes. She moved and took a couple shots of him, closing the aperture down, so he appeared perfectly in focus, but chatting behind him, heads together, Martin and Ross were blurred. A quick glance at the back of her screen and she knew she had a good shot. She looked up and blew Frank a kiss. He blew her one back and, sitting down, he passed the floor to Martin.

Martin's wide smile vanished as he caught sight of Dudley with his teeth bared. The dog wore the sort of look that suggested should Martin make a move, any move, he would take great pleasure in sinking his teeth into his leg. Jess sank down on one knee and took a couple of pictures of Dudley, before focussing on Martin.

'I think I should make it clear both Frank and I see this as a joining of two companies. MJC invested heavily in this merger to make sure it works. The current economic environment has reinforced the need for strong companies willing to look forward, and both Frank and I realised MJC would become stronger as a result of this merger.'

"A photojournalist should have a keen eye and the ability to respond quickly to the situation unfolding in front of them". Wasn't that what the speaker at the Camera Club had said?

Jess took another picture of Frank, a man who didn't look like he'd been consulted, or even told about the vision he was supposed to be having.

'I don't want to hear talk about redundancies,' Martin said.

'Of course, you don't,' someone heckled. Jess wasn't quick enough to catch who had spoken up but took a picture of a lot of people nodding and not looking happy.

Martin checked the table in front of him. He read, following the words with his finger – not a speech from the heart like Frank's.

'Obviously, eventually we will consider the need for staff in all areas and all levels, but the last thing we want to do is lose any of our skilled and valued workforce.'

"Sometimes you will be taking portraits, sometimes detail shots."

Jess stood on a chair and focussed in on Martin's finger as it travelled over his page.

'There will be disruption and minor changes to the ways you have worked in the past, inevitable I'm afraid, as we evaluate where we are and where we're going, but I ask you to bear with us, because I see this merger as a positive move for everyone.' Martin got to the end of his speech, folded up his sheet of paper and looked up.

Jess took a picture, but there was no standing ovation. Not a single clap.

Jess watched Izzie through her viewfinder. She managed to turn what looked like a clap into a peculiar hand gesture Marcel Marceau would have been proud of. Jess captured it perfectly.

Martin sat down and nodded at Ross, who got up. He smiled at everyone and then banged on for a good five minutes about motivational training.

He would be organising various courses over the next couple of weeks to keep everyone on the boil ready for D-day.

'That would be doomsday.' Harry grinned.

Ross ignored him, but with an expression that said he'd heard. He went on to say he would email everyone with the course details and times. 'In the meantime,' he asked, 'does anyone have any questions?'

Big. Mistake.

Three times Marketing asked how much Martin had paid for the business. Customer Services wanted to know how long their jobs were safe for and if it was going to be Anymoore's HR department or MJC's who would be involved in the evaluation process. Technical wanted to know if their terms and conditions were the same, but when the part-time receptionist started bellyaching on about TUPE and appropriate consultation periods, Jess decided Dudley needed a walk.

There were still a lot of questions, judging by the heckling and raised hands. Martin couldn't shut them down without looking autocratic and uncaring so they'd be there for some time. She knew the deal; the only thing she wasn't sure about was whether she wanted to be a part of Martin's vision or not.

She planned on slipping out quietly. She said goodbye to Sarah and picked up Dudley's lead. Until she whispered, 'Walkies', she didn't realise how much of Dudley was under Harry's chair.

Dudley stood up and jettisoned Harry back a row into Izzie's lap. Izzie screamed. Martin came running.

"But above all the best photojournalists are the ones in the right place at the right time."

Jess switched to burst mode, aimed her camera and held the shutter button down so it would take multiple shots.

Martin seemed to have lost any semblance of the sense of humour he might once have had. Jess couldn't remember it ever being great, even in their early years, but today his sense of cause and effect seemed to have joined it.

Shouting, 'Get off her, tosser!' was unlikely to endear himself to Harry let alone the rest of Customer Services.

Dudley bared his teeth and growled, making Martin hesitate to Izzie's annoyance.

As she managed to leave, Jess saw Sarah rush to Harry's assistance. Taking a final look at the chaos, she mouthed "Sorry" to Frank and left.

A familiar-looking man stood in reception and turned as she came through the double doors.

'Hi,' she said. 'Can I help you?'

'I'm …'

'Gary Mansfield from the *Redford Chronicle*,' she said, excitedly. 'I remember. I heard you speak at the Camera Club last week. Great lecture by the way.'

'Thanks.' He smiled.

She held out a hand. 'Jess Willersey. I'm the accountant here and budding photojournalist.' She pointed to the camera hanging from her neck. 'How can I help?'

'I'm looking for'—he consulted his notebook—'Martin Cowley. I'm here to do an interview.'

'Yes, of course. If you could sign the visitor's book.' Jess pointed to the black book on the desk and passed him a pen.

She watched over his shoulder as he wrote slowly in neat italic writing.

'What angle are you planning to take?'

'Oh, you know – local man made good, comes to aid of failing company,' he said. 'Nothing earth-shattering but it's a quiet news week here in Redford.'

'I think that's what's known these days as "fake news",' she said.

'That's the angle he's peddling,' Gary said as Dudley flopped down and sighed, clearly not happy at the distraction. 'Are you telling me I'm about to be fed a line?'

Jess stroked the dog's head. 'Look, there's a staff meeting going on. It's overrun and looks like it might go on a while. Are you pushed for time?'

Gary looked at his watch and shrugged. 'I've got a council summit at 12.30, photos of the new council chamber but …'

'I'm Martin's ex. If you don't mind walking Dudley round the field with me, I could fill you in on Anymoore and some of Martin's history – some personal details might interest your readers. Martin's such a modest man. He hates talking about himself. And …' She bit her lip.

'You okay?' Gary said, putting the cap back on the pen.

She nodded. 'I took some pictures at the meeting,' she said. 'Would you be interested in seeing them?'

'You bet,' he said. 'I wasn't allowed in on that. That's why you found me loitering in reception.'

The mere mention of a walk and field had Dudley already pulling her towards the front door. 'Then, if the meeting isn't finished by the time we get back, I'll make you a cup of coffee and show you.'

'Any I print, I'll credit you with,' he said, smiling. 'Great way to start a portfolio.'

'I know,' Jess said. 'You said that's how you got started.'

'Dudley's wet,' Neil said, as his dog charged through the office to greet him. 'You didn't have to walk him.'

'I didn't,' Ross hissed through clenched teeth. 'Jess did.'

Even her bloody name made his insides twist and blood rush through his body.

'She took him round the lake. Some woman and her child threw bread for the ducks apparently and Dudley joined them.'

Neil bit the inside of his lip to stop himself laughing. The look on Ross's face told him this was no laughing matter. 'Anyone hurt?'

'The inside of my car smells like a sewer.'

Harsh! Stagnant pond maybe, but sewer never. Neil put his hand down and patted the top of the dog's head. It was the only bit that looked completely dry.

'That is categorically the last time I take that creature anywhere. I am not a dog walker. I think I may even be allergic to them.' As if to make a point, Ross made a show of blowing his nose.

'Did the meeting go well?' The sparkle in Dudley's eye was definitely missing from Ross's.

No answer. Which probably meant no. If it had gone as planned, he'd be crowing about how successful it had been.

Neil didn't push for an answer. He wished he could pick up the phone and ask Jess. He missed hearing her voice and the way she laughed at something silly. He'd love to hear her take on the meeting, but then he remembered, she and Martin were in it together.

'Sarah asked me to give you this.' Ross handed him a letter. Neil's name was printed on the envelope, but in neat blue handwriting and underlined with a kiss. Seeing the envelope reminded him they still hadn't addressed the issue of Ross's resignation.

'We need to talk about your letter,' he said as he slipped a knife under the flap and pulled out an order of service for Maggie's mother's funeral the week after next and a note to say that Maggie hoped he'd be able to join her at the wake afterwards at Treetops nursing home.

Neil put it on his desk to remind him he should send it back tomorrow, apologise but claim a prior engagement. He would make something up.

Dudley, in the middle of the office floor, steamed quietly. Ross was right: not a pleasant smell.

Chapter Forty-Four

"Mystery of Scout Hut Fire solved seventeen years on", read the *Redford Chronicle*'s headline. The standfirst, underneath in slightly smaller text, went on to say, "Our editor uncovers the truth". The accompanying small picture of a man, face partially obscured by a camera, had the caption, "Gary Mansfield".

Neil had been about to turn over when he saw the picture of Martin Cowley, outside the office of Anymoore. He smiled broadly from the middle of the front page. He had one arm draped round his "new promotions director".

"Martin Cowley, as he is now", the caption read.

Confused, Neil scanned the article. A second picture of three boys, a bit further down, not so big and in black and white. And underneath, "Martin Cowley, aged 16, and two other boys, to receive bravery awards from the mayor after raising the alarm and helping scouts to safety."

Great, the man was a hero. Every one bloody loved him. Neil couldn't resist reading the article anyway.

"In the course of interviewing the new managing director of the recently acquired Anymoore Ltd, it wasn't just Martin Cowley's business skills that came to light.

"Martin's company MJC has completed a takeover of established computer firm Anymoore Ltd on the industrial estate outside Redford. Funnily enough, this new acquisition is only a stone's throw from where the scout hut used to be.

"Redford's older residents might recall that, back in the days when Redford Road was just that and not a dual carriageway, the hut had pride of place between the bus stop and the café, now a fast food outlet and garage".

A grainy black and white picture of what looked like a corrugated iron building was captioned "Scout Hut".

"The *Chronicle* can reveal to you today that the fire that destroyed the building seventeen years ago wasn't the freak accident as hitherto claimed, but the results of high spirits and teenage pranks of a group of teenage boys, including none other than the same adolescent boy later celebrated for raising the alarm and helping the patrol leaders lead their charges to safety, seventeen years ago.

"While Martin Cowley refused on Monday to talk about the incident, one of his co-conspirators was not so reticent and in an exclusive interview with the journal, revealed what Martin failed to mention back then, or at any time since, was that if he hadn't been showing off and setting light to his farts that night, the hut might not have caught fire in the first place.

"Horrified scout chiefs yesterday removed the plaque from the wall of their new headquarters which commemorated that night and Cowley's courage."

Another picture showed a man in uniform, a scout leader, clearly looking horrified. On the wall behind him there were two holes and a slightly discoloured surface to suggest there had once been something else there.

"Ross Littleton, MJC's new promotions director said it all happened a long time ago and Cowley, very young at the time, would rather put his teenage activities behind him. No pun intended, but when our editor pointed out it sounded as if that was exactly what Martin had been doing, the new director became abusive."

An interview with a man, another of the boys involved, followed the story. He said he was relieved everything was out in the open. It had been difficult for him to live with the guilt for so long. When asked if he wasn't secretly relieved that it wasn't one of his farts which caused the problems, the man said, "It couldn't have been. Only Martin's were ever that impressive."

The paper had an inset by some council official saying anyone affected by pyromania could ring a helpline and gave a number. An appeal asked for anyone with any further information to contact the paper on a given number.

Neil put down the paper and realised he ached: he'd laughed so much.

Who said "No publicity is bad publicity"? Way to go Ross.

The *Chronicle*, the article said, would be handing a dossier of all its evidence to the police. And readers were asked to text "Yes" or "No" to a particular number depending on whether or not they wanted Martin charged with criminal damage. The result, the paper promised, would be printed next week. Underneath was the usual small text about the cost of sending a message. Neil didn't care how much it would cost him. He picked up his mobile and texted: *Yes* to the number the paper mentioned. As soon as that one had gone through, he sent another, to make sure.

But it was the final line, the one that said Martin had recently left his girlfriend of twelve years, a promising wedding photographer – who had taken the photo above and some further pictures on Page 5 – for another woman, that set his pulse racing.

For another woman. Neil turned the pages and read the article on Page 5, about "Beloved boss's moving speech on handover". It contained a picture of Frank, a faraway look in his eyes, looking out over a room full of people, all on their feet and clapping, except one woman. He recognised her. She worked for Anymoore. He screwed up his eyes, trying to drag her from his memory, his recollection clouded by a feeling, the most awful, awful feeling that maybe, maybe, he'd jumped to the wrong conclusion. *Oh shit! What have I done?*

Neil picked up his mobile.

Chapter Forty-Five

"32" had a name: Terry. They'd flirted through odd emails, conversations, texts, before he'd suggested The Last Post. He described it as one of his favourite places and reserved a table for 7.00 p.m.

Sarah had googled the place earlier. It had been described as a traditional restaurant. "Authentic English food, cooked the way you like it". Just for good measure, she'd googled Terry too. It hadn't been an unqualified success: there were two Terry Pucklechurchs, neither with a picture.

On the speed-dating evening, and in chats since, they'd covered other topics like what do you do for fun? What luxury item would you take to a desert island? What was the first record you bought? If you only had a week left to live, what would be the first thing you'd do? But nothing as sensitive or heavyweight as what do you do for a living? Still, it should make an interesting conversation opener. So, are you Terry Pucklechurch, based near Swindon, "offering person-to-person computer service designed to make your experience with electronic equipment a pleasurable one", or Terry Pucklechurch, "PhD student, researching long-distance lorry drivers' health and lifestyle behaviour issues"?

When Sarah arrived, she could hardly miss him. Only two tables were occupied. One in the middle of the room had a couple who appeared to be mid-argument and at the other, tucked more discreetly against the window, was Terry.

The last time she'd seen him, he'd been wearing an open-necked cotton shirt and jeans, but tonight he'd dressed up. He wore a tie. Sadly, he also appeared to be wearing a sleeveless knitted top over his shirt. *A tank top.* She remembered pictures of her father sporting similar before he married her mother.

Back then, they were supposed to be considered cool. Perhaps nowadays, the more tasteful ones could make a comeback. Nah, and his wasn't tasteful.

If he'd come wearing the complete seventies ensemble, the huge lapels, patterned shirts, bell-bottomed trousers and platform shoes, she'd have thought he was doing retro-chic. No, she wouldn't. Who was she trying to kid? She'd still think he looked like a complete loser. But on their first proper date, she needed to give him the benefit of the doubt. Perhaps he needed a good woman, someone to take him in hand and guide him. And what Sarah didn't know about shopping wasn't worth knowing.

Terry stood up when she arrived. It would have been a chivalrous gesture if he hadn't knocked the table, rattled all the glasses and scraped his chair across the floor, with such a teeth-on-edge sound that the other couple stopped mid-argument to stare.

'How about a cocktail?' he asked, waving a plastic card, as a waitress appeared with a glass of fluorescent blue liquid, decorated with fruit, paper umbrellas and a straw.

'Go on – it's happy hour.'

'Just a sparkling water, please,' Sarah said. 'I'm driving,' she added, unnerved that now he was looking at her over the rim of his glass.

Oh God, please don't let him be winking.

The waitress put a menu in front of them, laminated too. Classy.

'Wow, this place looks like it's stuck in a time warp of some sort, doesn't it.' Sarah smiled.

'I love it,' he said. 'My parents always recommended it. They used to come here all the time.'

He stretched the word "used" out in such a way that perhaps she should ask what had happened to them.

His 'Are your parents still alive?' comment, that followed his next slurp of cocktail, did nothing to calm her rising fears. Some of the bluish froth from the top of his cocktail attached itself round his mouth and gave him an even stranger look.

'Excuse me. I need the loo,' she mouthed.

He winked. 'Going to powder your nose,' he said. 'Isn't that what ladies are supposed to say? Your nose looks perfectly lovely the way it is.' And another bloody wink.

The "Ladies" were at the back of the restaurant, next to the kitchen. She considered making an excuse like she'd left her lights on, and then she could make a run for it. But they were sitting next to a window overlooking the car park. She could see she hadn't.

Only one thing for it. She pulled out her mobile phone. The signal flicked between one bar and no service at all. Still her best chance. She typed in the message. *The Last Post – Help!* and pressed send. It was no good. The message came straight back: *Message failure, try later.* She couldn't wait. She put down the toilet seat and climbed on top of it. Holding the phone up as high as she could, she pressed resend as the door to the toilets opened and the woman from the other table came in. She hesitated, looked at Sarah as if she was a cushion short of a suite and, shaking her head, went into the other cubicle, locking the door firmly behind her. If that wasn't embarrassing enough, she hadn't closed the door from the restaurant properly, so over the top of her cubicle she could see Terry watching her. He lifted an arm and waved.

'Thanks for helping to get all my stuff packed up.' Jess arranged three mugs on a tray. 'I didn't realise I had so much. I probably could have done with the week off, not just a couple of days. I couldn't have done it without you.'

'You could bring more furniture with you?' Maggie said. 'I've got plenty of room, especially now all the medical equipment's been cleared out of Mother's room.'

Jess shook her head. 'There are a few precious bits I'm going to put into storage while I'm at yours, but the rest I expect will go to a charity shop.' She spooned a teaspoonful of coffee into all of them and a splash of milk.

'Treetops could use the bookcases and the wardrobes,' John said. 'If you're sure you want shot.'

'Be my guest,' Jess said, standing aside to let him carry the tray through to the sitting room. 'The muffins should be ready in about five minutes.'

'You've been cooking?' Maggie grinned, a twinkle in her eye as she watched John walk into the room – a look that Jess would have been blind not to notice. 'Does that mean you've finally realised the way to a man's heart is through his stomach?'

'No.' Jess handed her one of the mugs. 'I'm still at the straight-through-the-ribs-with-a-knife stage.' She handed John another mug.

'What happened to Neil?' he asked. 'The two of you made a great couple.'

Maggie drew a finger across her neck theatrically and widened her eyes. 'We don't talk about him,' she said.

'We don't?'

The timer on the cooker went off. 'Muffins,' Jess said, grateful for the excuse. 'I'll get them.'

Walking back into the kitchen, she smiled. The way John spoke to Maggie, the looks between them that lingered a little longer than strictly necessary, Jess was tempted to break out into a chorus of "People Will Say We're In Love" but she couldn't remember the tune or words and she didn't want everyone to know how sad she'd become watching romantic films at every opportunity. Still, she hummed the one line she knew when she returned to the sitting room, minutes later, with a plateful of warm white chocolate and raspberry muffins.

'*Redford Chronicle* made interesting reading.' Maggie's eyes lit up. 'They've printed some of your pictures and given you full credit for them.'

'I don't think I've enjoyed reading the local rag so much for a long time.' John laughed.

Jess blushed. 'I'd better get a copy tomorrow,' she said. 'How were the pictures?'

'They were fabulous,' Maggie said. 'The one of Frank is amazing.' She sighed. 'Listening to Gary Mansfield's talk last week at Camera Club, I have to admit I didn't understand what he meant about telling a story through pictures but seeing that one of Frank made me realise exactly what he was talking about. Everyone I've spoken to has admired them.'

Okay, as soon as she'd said goodbye, she'd go to the all-night convenience store in town. They were bound to have copies.

'Maggie and I have been talking about her plans. What about yours?' John helped himself to a second muffin. 'Isn't now a good time to start a photography business?'

Jess was saved from answering by an annoying electronic sounding tune. Maggie and John stopped talking.

It sounded familiar if muffled.

It seemed to come from the sofa.

'Sorry Maggie, I think you might be sitting on my phone,' Jess said.

By the time Maggie handed her the mobile, it had stopped ringing. The message received light flashed.

'Prawn Cocktail.' The waitress held up a sundae dish full of green lettuce covered with a bright pink sauce and what looked like soil.

Sarah nodded. A plate was set down in front of her; it also held a fork and a slice of lemon. Prawn cocktail – it wasn't just Terry doing retro-chic.

Sarah didn't know exactly how big prawns should be, but surely they should be visible to the naked eye.

Terry ordered pâté. That was a little bigger and more obvious. He insisted they should have three courses. The restaurant had a special meal deal going on.

'That's why I suggested this place,' he said as he considered the menu. 'Too good to miss out on. What are you having?'

A hepatitis injection.

'I don't have a huge appetite,' Sarah said, imagining stopping at a fast-food outlet on the way home, as soon as she could get away. 'I might just have a main course.'

'Don't be ridiculous,' Terry said. 'Can't have you going hungry later.'

She didn't want to antagonise him in case he was a serial killer. Besides she hadn't eaten since breakfast. She stabbed around in the pink sauce until a prawn wedged itself between the tines of her fork. As she lifted it to her mouth, it occurred to her it was the same size as a maggot. Her appetite deserted her. She put the fork down and took another sip of her sparkling water as the door to the restaurant opened and three more diners walked in.

Dudley looked positively overjoyed as Neil pulled up three feet away from General Gordon, who clearly wasn't about to move. The sign in Jess's garden still said sold, subject to contract. He wondered how the sale was progressing. Had she found somewhere to live? Was she going to stay in Redford? The house looked dark, unnaturally quiet, no lights on. She must be out.

He'd knock. Just in case.

Neil opened his driver's door and Dudley somehow managed to launch himself into the front seat and Neil's lap.

Just in case of what? Just in case she was sat in the dark pretending to be out? Just in case she was asleep?

'You need to go on a diet, dog.'

The comment was met with his face being thumped repeatedly by a tail wagging furiously. General Gordon, still in the road, turned his head and looked at them. He made no attempt to run.

Dudley escaped and in his over enthusiastic greeting got too close. General Gordon hissed, rolled over, stood up, smacked Dudley's nose with his paw. Then walked underneath the dog and struck him again with his tail. They both walked up to the house and sat on the doorstep.

'Why can't I have that effect on you?' Neil followed them up the drive. Seeing the cat cheered him nearly as much as it had Dudley. She couldn't have moved. She'd never leave him behind.

His first knock went unanswered, as did his second. Absolutely no movement from inside at all. If she was there and pretending to be out, she was doing a great job. He'd like to peer through the letterbox, make sure she wasn't flat out in the hall, but an old couple in beige raincoats stood on the other side of the close watching him. Dotted all over the place were neighbourhood watch stickers. He assumed those two were part of the watch brigade. Any suspicious movement and he'd probably be surrounded by an army of beige-coated pensioners with clipboards demanding details and making citizens' arrests.

He returned to the car, opened the passenger door and called Dudley.

A car kerb-crawled down the other side of the road, presumably looking at numbers. The old couple turned. The woman was writing something down. Neil hoped none of the houses got burgled any time soon: no doubt the police would know of his visit, even if Jess didn't.

Dudley wasn't disobedient as such, but never hurried if he didn't need to.

Neil wished he'd gone with his first instinct and phoned. Except, how could he have explained? She might have put the phone down. 'I just wanted to say thank you for walking my dog,' sounded lame even to him.

'I saw the piece in the paper about your ex, and I realised I'd been mistaken about you helping him to buy the company' – that one raised trust issues.

If she hadn't known Martin was buying the company, she must have thought Neil knew. She probably believed he'd tricked her into helping him and that presented an entirely different problem.

No choice: it would have to be the tried and tested face-to-face. 'I was just passing. I've been a complete pillock. I'm sorry and I've missed you.'

The car cruised back down the street and stopped behind Neil.

Dudley, who had been heading slowly back to the car, saw the newcomer arrive and headed straight for him.

'Hello, mate,' the man said. 'You look cleaner than the last time I saw you.'

Dudley licked his hand.

'Is your friend in?'

He was talking about Jess.

'I've got a surprise for her.'

How stupid had he been? Just because he missed her, didn't mean she missed him. They hadn't seen each other for a week. He watched the man walk up to the door and knock. She'd moved on.

Still no answer.

Dudley walked back down the drive and climbed into Neil's car. The man looked over and raised a hand. Neil nodded back, reached over and shut the door behind his dog, watching as the guy wrote something on a piece of paper he'd pulled out from a pocket, then stuck it into Jess's letterbox.

Chapter Forty-Six

'Maggie! Look, it's Sarah,' said Jess.

'So it is.' Maggie grinned.

'My goodness,' said John. 'Fancy meeting you here.'

Jess giggled at Sarah's face. She wasn't sure how she would describe that expression. Shock. Relief. A combination of the two. 'Of all the restaurants in all the world – well Redford – we had to walk into yours.'

Sarah lowered her eyebrows. 'Yes, fancy that.'

'Do you two lovebirds want to be on your own?' Maggie grinned. 'Or would you mind if we join you?'

Sarah's date tried to swallow a mouthful of food and nodded, which could mean either.

'Can we sit at this table?' Jess asked the waitress. 'I'm afraid we haven't booked.'

The girl shrugged and looked round the empty room, as if about to point out a better table, but all three were seated by then. She took a lighter from out of her trouser pocket and lit another candle. 'Do you want something to drink?'

'Would you like a thick lip?' Sarah muttered. The guy opposite her put down his knife and fork and stood up.

'Hi, I'm Terry. Sarah's new boyfriend. Her significant other. Her plus one.' He wiped his hands on his trousers rather than his serviette and shook hands with each of them.

The colour drained from Sarah's face.

'Oh,' said Maggie, her face a picture of innocence. 'So, you two are, what's the expression? Going steady? And what date number are we up to?'

'It's our first.' Terry smiled. 'If you discount all the foreplay.

'He's talking about emails, text messages and phone calls, nothing else,' Sarah said, her face now as white as the tablecloth.

'Early days, but I'd like to think I'm speaking for both of us when I say that we're together for the long haul.'

'Are you sure we're not interrupting a lovers' tête-à-tête'? We can sit the other side of the room if you'd prefer,' Maggie asked.

Terry assured them it was fine. 'It's great to meet Sarah's friends.' He ordered another cocktail at the same time as the waitress took the rest of their drink orders.

Plastic menus were produced. 'You have to have the three courses,' Terry said. 'That's such a good deal.'

'Just scampi for me,' Maggie said. 'I don't think I could manage three courses.'

The way John fussed about her made Jess jealous. Maggie looked back at him with a light in her eye. The sort of light that suggested she knew she'd found someone special – her soulmate, and although she hated herself for it, Jess envied her that feeling.

'I recognise you from speed dating, don't I?' Terry said, waving his half empty cocktail glass at Jess. 'I gave you a solid yes. I guess you preferred someone else.'

'I didn't tick anyone's box I'm afraid,' Jess said. 'I was there to keep Sarah company. I'm not looking for love.'

He winked at her. 'Your secret's safe with me.'

'I seem to remember you had an interesting line in questions.'

Terry looked pleased. 'I try to be original. Make you think. Remind me, if you were a Smartie, what colour would you be?'

Please don't tell me that was you.

A strange noise came from her left. John appeared to have choked on his drink and was turning an odd colour.

Don't die now. You promised you'd help me move tomorrow.

Luckily, Maggie stepped in, before she had to remember how to do the Heimlich manoeuvre.

Maggie stroked his back. Sarah passed him her glass of water. But while everything was happening around him, Terry didn't take his eyes off Jess.

'Go on then, what colour?' he asked.

Yes it was.

'Lilac,' she murmured.

'Sarah said "white".' Terry reached out to grasp her hand. 'Didn't you darling?' Sarah recoiled with such speed her knife flew out of her hand and clattered to the floor. She dived under the table to get it back.

'I don't remember white Smarties,' Maggie said, still watching John.

'They're all white, once you lick the colour off,' said a disembodied voice from under the table.

Jess opened the front door to her house and turned back to wave Sarah and Maggie off. Jess and Maggie both lived on Sarah's way home, so it had made sense for Sarah to drive them back and meant John could drive straight back to Treetops, in time to set the alarms, but he hadn't look cheered by the thought as he'd helped Maggie into Sarah's car.

Maggie had looked gloomy too as she watched him walk to his.

Terry didn't come out to say goodbye. He'd wanted another cocktail, but assured Sarah he'd email her in the morning with ideas for their next rendezvous. Sarah looked suitably mortified. Ah, love's young dream.

From the back seat Jess had enjoyed the banter as Sarah and Maggie, in the front, sniped at each other, in a friendly argumentative sort of way.

'You two are worse than any married couple,' she'd joked at one point.

'Do you know what they made me do at work while you were away today?' Sarah asked, looking at Jess in her mirror.

Jess shook her head.

'Take a psychoanalytical test to find my true personality. It's important to make sure there's a good colour balance within the working environment if we are to take the company to the next level. Apparently, they're really expensive and can only be carried out by professionals who have been trained to analyse the results.'

'And you are?' Maggie asked.

'A natural born leader who inspires others through hard work and a positive mental attitude to life.'

'Guess they'll be wanting their money back on that then,' Maggie said.

Sarah muttered something that Jess hadn't been able to hear, but the force used for the next gear change suggested it hadn't been polite.

Sarah said she'd caught the end of one of Martin and Ross's conversations; apparently Ross's wife wondered if Izzie wanted the number of a good cleaner.

'I could let her have the barcode for Harpic Black,' Maggie sniffed.

Jess chuckled and sat back, lost in her own thoughts for the rest of the journey. What had Martin told Ross and Neil about her? Ross had been civil enough so far, but she hadn't heard a word from Neil.

His assistant, Tanya, had thanked her for the pictures and they were up on his website. They looked good and she saw they now sported a copyright symbol on the bottom of each one next to a JWP monogram. Tanya had also taken to doing a daily Dudley post. Observations from below desk, she called it.

Jess sent a couple of pictures from Monday's staff meeting and told her she liked the website.

Tanya promised Jess that she would be happy to help her set up one for her own business when she was ready.

Sarah's car had turned out of Broadwater Close by the time Jess turned to go indoors and noticed the scrap of paper on the mat. She bent down to pick it up, assuming it was something one of them had dropped on the way out earlier. General Gordon wove in and out of her legs, which for the cat amounted to affection. It might be cupboard love, but she tickled him behind his ears as she read the note.

'It's from Gary Mansfield, the editor of the *Redford Chronicle*,' she said in answer to the cat's miaow. 'He says the article is out and has received a lot of interest. Shit. I meant to get a paper on the way back. The *Chronicle* has been inundated with calls all day from nutters claiming they've seen Martin setting light to everything from a firework to their garden sheds.'

The cat sat with his head tilted watching her every move. She put down the note and took a tin of cat food out of the fridge.

General Gordon miaowed loudly. Probably a "get on with it" miaow rather than an "I hope the bloke got his comeuppance and will die a long and painful death" sort of miaow. Jess forked some food onto a plate before she picked up the note again.

'Gary also received a call from some friends of his. They've been let down by their photographer. He's double booked and can't help because it's this Saturday and he's got a family celebration that he can't get out of.'

"I've recommended you," Jess read. "I hope you don't mind. Give them a ring first thing in the morning and let them know one way or the other. It is a second wedding, a small affair. I've told them what I'd charge and said you'd charge the same. They're more than happy with that. Half now, half when the photos are delivered."

How much do I charge? Jess spooned some more cat food into General Gordon's bowl.

Chapter Forty-Seven

Jess already had several pictures of the empty Register Office ceremony room and their silk flower arrangements that she'd taken at Darren and Leanne's wedding. The room looked the same. She relaxed. She'd taken some great detail shots then, which she could use again.

The ceremony was beautiful. The bride walked down the aisle to the strains of Oleta Adams singing "Get Here".

Jess captured the groom's admiring look as he watched his bride walk towards him. It had to be one of her favourite pictures of the day, that and the bride's expression as the ring was slid onto her finger and the groom told her he wanted her to wear it always so that part of him would always be close to her.

Jess felt jealous, jealous no one in her life wanted to say that to her. They looked happy; she knew they'd grow old together. They'd been through the process before and knew how devastating it was when things went wrong. But they were prepared to take another chance. She'd seen the glow in the bride's eyes and the way her smile widened every time she looked at her new husband.

Only one man had ever made Jess feel like that.

A friend of the bride stood up, moved to the front of the Register Office. As she passed the couple, she squeezed the bride's arm. "How do I love thee," she read, "Let me count the ways".

By the end of the fourth line, Jess searched for something to wipe away tears that streamed down her cheeks. She caught the registrar's eye. The woman was in the same boat. She nodded to a pile of tissues, picked a couple up and handed one to Jess.

As she backed down the narrow path and signalled for them to walk towards her, she couldn't help casting a glance over the wall. No wedding party followed them. No missing hat. No good-looking man in a dark suit trying to vault the wall.

Until that moment, she hadn't believed in love at first sight. She'd certainly fallen that day hopelessly head over heels. Something about Neil had made her heart sing. She'd hoped he felt the same but hadn't waited to find out. She'd rushed straight in.

She'd told him she didn't want a one-night stand, yet that was all she got. Maybe she should have listened to the advice they'd given Sarah. If she'd taken longer to get to know him, waited until at least the seventh proper date before she leapt into bed with him, would she have realised he didn't feel the same? She was an adult; she knew how these things worked. She only had herself to blame for the hurt she was feeling.

Maggie was cooking when Jess arrived at Meadow View. The smell of garlic and spices greeted her as she opened the door to her new home. She inhaled deeply, enjoying the aroma before calling out to announce her arrival.

Maggie, apron on, came out of the kitchen, wiped her hands, and smiled warmly. 'You must be ready for a cup of tea.'

If she'd been asked a month ago about living with a colleague, Jess would have laughed or made some sarcastic comment. But, to have someone who, when you got in, was genuinely interested in your day gave her a lovely warm feeling. She'd never had that before. General Gordon was curled up in a tight ball in the middle of a collection of cushions and blankets, a picture of happiness and relaxation.

They took their tea back to the office, Maggie's mother's room, now with a desk, bookcases, Maggie's knitting basket and a sofa, rather than a hospital bed. It smelt of new paint and looked fresh and bright. Maggie sat on the sofa and Jess dumped her bags on the floor under the desk and fired up the computer.

She downloaded the pictures from her camera while Maggie watched.

'Do you feel sad?' she asked. 'When you see them so happy, knowing your pictures will probably last much longer than their marriage.'

'In this case no. They'll be together forever.' Jess looked at the pictures as they came up, delighted she'd captured the atmosphere of the day.

The bride had been a dream to work with, happy to be ordered about and Jess took far more pictures than she'd planned. The whole party arrived together in a stretch limousine and were happy to wind the windows down and pose. They didn't want traditional, they wanted fun photographs. She'd set up one of the bride and groom in the front seat of the car, guests hanging out the back window and the chauffeur pretending to run behind. There were some of the bride and groom taking selfies with the guests in the background.

Neither the bride nor groom's parents were alive, so their wedding guests were friends and colleagues, and everyone was happy to have their photos taken, dressed in their very best outfits.

The bride's sister was her bridesmaid. As well as the conventional shots, Jess had got some lovely shots of the two women, heads almost touching, clearly sharing precious moments, unaware they were being photographed. The groom was keen to show off his socks. Jess took a picture of all the men from the knee down, raising their trousers and showing off their socks, with the groom in the middle.

'They are lovely pictures,' Maggie said, as Jess ran through them on the computer.

Jess wondered if she could detect a trace of surprise in her voice, but Maggie was smiling.

'That one'—she pointed to an image of the groom looking at the rings—'would look good in black and white.'

She was right. A couple of clicks of a button later and Jess had desaturated it – and the result took her breath away. She printed it and took the result to the kitchen where Maggie was putting final touches to their supper. The older woman looked approvingly at the image.

'I said I would show Gary tomorrow,' Jess said, as she laid the table. 'He's due back tonight and they're his friends. I need to make sure he's happy with them.'

'Does this mean you are going to give photography a go?' Maggie asked. 'Give up the finance?'

Jess took a deep breath. 'I think so.' Today had given her a buzz. She'd loved every minute and seeing the result had left her feeling genuinely satisfied. 'What about you?' she said, helping herself to a plateful of goulash and rice. 'Are you planning on working for Martin?'

'Actually …' Maggie looked sheepish. 'I've asked John if I can work at Treetops. I love cooking and I'm fond of most old people. It seems it's just my mother I disliked.'

'And he bit your hand off?'

'He was surprised,' Maggie said. 'He said we should talk about it after the funeral.'

Her face clouded with an expression Jess couldn't figure. She certainly wasn't bursting with happiness. On the other hand, she wasn't crying. She'd shut down.

Jess sighed. Maggie used to do that at work sometimes when she was faced with something difficult. It was if she needed to distance herself from the problems and her emotions. 'But,' she said, 'I am leaving Anymoore.'

Chapter Forty-Eight

Gary opened the door to Jess, dressed in shorts and flip-flops. She immediately felt overdressed in jeans and a leather jacket, but it was October and the foggy day could hardly be described as unseasonably warm.

'Did you have any difficulty parking?' he asked, looking down on a street crowded with weekend shoppers before shutting the door behind her.

'Maggie dropped me off. She's going to the supermarket and has a few errands to run. If she finishes before me, I'll walk back.'

'Is that it?' Gary pointed at the USB stick in her hand. 'Can I see?'

She nodded and followed him into a big open-plan space with a kitchen at one end and a telly at the other. The flat was minimalist in a bachelor rather than an interior designer sort of way. The computer and equipment along one wall suggested a boy who loved his toys.

The computer was switched on and the stick plugged into the drive before he offered her a drink. 'Tea? Coffee? Alcohol?'

'Tea,' she said, watching the computer starting to load and the screen flicker into life.

'Builders, Earl Grey, Herbal or I've got some Apple stuff I brought back from Turkey.'

She looked at him and grinned. 'You don't strike me as an Earl Grey or herbal tea sort of man.'

'Okay, okay, I'm not. But there's a Starbucks in the high street – I could pop out if you wanted one.'

'Builder's tea's fine.'

'Now where's that teabag I used earlier.' He looked at her face and laughed. 'Only joking.'

Gary viewed the pictures as a slide show, looked at each one, sometimes he paused and studied the picture on the screen for longer than others. Jess bit her lip. She couldn't read his expression. She'd wanted him to check the photos before she gave them to her clients. She'd asked for his honest opinion.

He didn't comment until he'd been through them all.

Her stomach clenched in nervous anticipation as he turned and looked at her.

'I'm impressed,' he said. 'You have a real talent for capturing the moment. They will be more than happy with these.'

Jess swelled with pride. She valued Maggie's comments, but to have approval from a professional was special.

'Wedding photography, like photojournalism, requires a whole range of skills,' he said. 'I don't need to tell you – you heard my talk the week before last. And you're a natural. But your photographic skills will be tested to the limit at times.' He sipped his tea. 'And you will have to call on every ounce of creative streak and calm temperament.'

Gary showed her some of the pictures he'd taken yesterday at his family celebrations and made another cup of tea while they shared experiences. He told her about a wedding he'd done where the groom in his early thirties was already on his third wife. His child from the first marriage was bridesmaid. A top local venue had been booked which cost the couple a fortune. They had the whole works then hadn't paid him for the photos.

Jess told him about Leanne and Darrren's wedding. 'It was supposed to be steam punk.' She laughed, but when she looked up, Gary had put his drink down and was leaning against the wall, studying her. 'About a month ago?' he asked, his eyebrows in danger of joining in the middle.

Great. Jess froze. Of course he knew about it, he was the editor of the *Chronicle*. He'd probably heard about it from the police. A story of local interest.

She felt uncomfortable for the first time since she'd arrived. 'Look, I should be going. Thanks for the recommendation – I'll deliver the photographs this afternoon.'

'Hey, wait,' Gary said as a picture flicked up on his screen. 'See these. They're pictures from the last wedding I shot. You must've been the photographer at the other wedding. Your crowd looked far more interesting.'

Jess walked over and looked at the pictures he was showing her then took another look. 'The posh wedding. Neil's partner's wedding. You were the photographer,' she said, slowly. 'I was in awe of you that day – you looked so professional.'

'Hey, I am a professional.' He laughed. 'And I scrub up well. I hope they paid you a fortune for their pictures. It looked a, shall we say, challenging wedding? I'd love to see your images sometime.'

Jess told him about the cheque, the jewellery, the parking ticket, the arrest and the fact she was still on police bail.

Gary was crying with laughter by the time she'd finished.

'It's not funny,' she protested. But his laughter was infectious.

'Prison probably won't be that bad,' he said. 'Three meals a day. Seriously, do make sure you keep any pictures of Darren and Leanne,' he said. 'When it's over, promise me the *Chronicle* gets an exclusive.'

She scratched her cheek.

'I'm serious,' he said. 'Well, not about the exclusive, but I'm hoping we can work together in the future.'

He shut down his computer and returned her USB stick. 'The other day you mentioned leaving Anymoore. I'd love to be able to say, "Come and work with me". Frankly, we could do with someone with your talent on board at the paper. But just now, we don't have any vacancies or the budget.'

Jess nodded. 'It's okay, I wasn't angling for a job. I haven't decided what I'm going to do.'

'You have to do photography,' he said. 'It might be tough to start, but it won't get any easier if you delay. You need to bite the bullet and get out there. Get your name known. Pictures like that, people will be fighting to get you before you know what's hit you.'

'Thank you,' she said. 'It's kind …'

'It's not kind of me. I'm a businessman and I recognise talent. I am always getting asked to do more than I can cope with on my own and often need to call on a freelance photographer.'

Jess looked at her watch, unsure where this conversation was heading.

'You're great. I like what I've seen. There's a real originality about your images compared to some of the muppets I've used in the past. I can't promise you regular work, but I would like to use you next time something comes up.'

She'd missed her lift with Maggie, but Jess felt she could float all the way home.

Chapter Forty-Nine

Jess took a pile of tissues and mopped up the tea Sarah had managed to slop over her desk when she set the mug down.

'How was your first weekend in your new home?' Sarah asked, seemingly oblivious to the mess she'd made. 'Maggie said you did another wedding. Did you get the photos to them?'

'Good, Yes and Yes.'

'And did they pay?'

'£2,000.' Jess grinned. 'Straight into my bank. And it's there – I checked this morning.'

'Have you seen our new boss?' Harry came through the door carrying a file.

'Who?' Sarah looked up.

'Martin blooming Cowley. Oops, sorry Jess.'

She waved away his embarrassment. 'Is he here?'

Harry nodded. 'Down by the fountain. He appears to have brought a TV crew with him. They're filming a "damage limitation exercise" according to Izzie for tonight's local news.' He walked across to the window. 'Look.'

Neither of them needed further encouragement.

'Is that some sort of new workout he's doing?' Jess watched her ex walk from the front door of the building to the fountain. He looked like he was power walking the speed he was going, and the way his arms were moving about.

Harry joined them. 'He's been round that square at least five times now. They keep making him do it again.'

'What's with the arm movements?'

'He's supposed to be giving it some fizz,' Harry said, laughing. 'I heard them talking when I arrived.' He cleared his throat and put on a high-pitched voice, '"You're making the whole thing seem too ordinary, Martin, too pedestrian. We need passion. Don't make it sound as if you're reading a script. Fizz – we need fizz. Now after three, fizz for the camera".'

'That's his idea of fizz,' Sarah said.

‘That’s Martin’s idea of everything,’ Jess said. A man in a blue waistcoat, holding a clipboard, walked up to Martin and said something. He listened intently. They both consulted the clipboard. Both of them nodded; the man with the waistcoat moved aside. Someone with a clapperboard clicked it and Martin set off. This time with a strangely exaggerated walk Monty Python would have struggled to pull off, and his hands rotating at the end of his arms like out of control windmills.

The sound of the combined laughter from the accounts department travelled through the glass because Martin stopped and looked up. They all took a step back. The man in the waistcoat went over. Jess hoped the TV company wasn’t in a hurry to get it “in the can”.

She was on her way back to her desk when she saw a dark coloured saloon car pull up. A woman climbed out of the passenger seat, said something to the driver and started to walk to the building. The waistcoated man must have asked her not to walk in front of the fountain because she stopped and watched the proceedings.

Shit, double shit and triple shit. Today wasn’t one of her bail days. Jess picked up her handbag and rang through to reception.

‘My visitor has just arrived,’ she said. ‘Please tell her I’m on my way down. No need for them to sign in.’

The last thing she wanted was for the whole company to know who the woman in the smart suit was.

Sarah looked at the telephone in her hand. *Sick Joke Jess. Yeah, you had me fooled.* It was a bad dream. It had to be. *Okay, tell me you’re joking. Game over.*

‘Why are you ringing me?’

‘I have the right to a phone call. I’m making it. I didn’t know who else to ring.’

‘What do you want me to do?’ Sarah asked, hesitantly.

A pause. Jess, when she spoke again, seemed to have difficulty in controlling her voice. ‘I don’t know, I’m sorry. I guess you should tell Frank I won’t be in today, possibly not for the rest of the week. Possibly not ever.’

‘Don’t be silly,’ Sarah said, going for a firm tone. ‘You’ll be back in no time.’

'Not this time,' Jess cried down the line as Ross stuck his head round the office door.

'Effective time management training. Have you forgotten?'

'Something has come up. Look, Jess, I've got to go.' Sarah put the phone down.

'You should be in the boardroom.'

The patronising look Ross shot her was enough to make her blood boil. She stretched herself up to her full height. Okay, she was only five foot four, but Ross took a step back anyway.

'Before I go anywhere, I need to speak to your partner. Where will I find him?'

'I don't have a partner,' Ross said, a rather supercilious expression starting to spread over his face. 'In case you've forgotten, I work for MJC, as do you.'

'Neil,' she snapped, deepening her tone. It seemed to have the desired effect.

'He's not—'

'You're not flaming partners. You said.' She moved towards him. 'You used to work for him and I need his mobile. As soon as I've spoken to him, I will join the rest of the company in the boardroom. The ball's in your court.' She bit her lip. He was the new promotions director, getting their relationship off on the wrong foot by calling him Buster, wasn't the most career-enhancing thing she could think of doing.

Ross swallowed. 'I have his card.' He took his wallet out of his pocket and pulled out a business card that he threw across the desk. 'His mobile's on it.'

Neil put the finishing touch to the spreadsheet and sat back in his chair, staring at the computer. The figures worked; the client should be happy. He checked a couple of the calculations, made sure he'd included all possible costs. He checked his notes. On the basis of the results, he'd made a couple of recommendations which he explained with the normal proviso that these were his suggestions only and further evidence should be sought before acting on them.

Everything looked okay. No surprises. He pressed print and got up to make a cup of coffee while the machine whirred into life.

Dudley stretched and opened one eye, so he stroked the dog's head on his way past. They had the office to themselves today.

He'd already cleared Ross's desk. Technically, Ross was still an employee, but he would be on site at MJC for the rest of his notice period and Jackson Consultancy would be charging them for him. There was no reason for him to come back into the office, so Neil insisted he returned his keys.

Ross had made a bit of a fuss at first, until Neil reminded him of his contractual obligations. Once Martin had agreed to pay Jackson Consultancy a daily rate for him up until Christmas, providing Neil agreed not to invoke the clause that forbade Ross working for a client for at least three years after he left the company, he wound his neck in.

Tanya had already changed all the company's digital passwords and shut down Ross's email account.

The calendar on his old desk registered the previous Monday. Neil pulled off the pages for the rest of the week and flicked through the next month; it was empty.

He screwed up the diary pages and lobbed them at the bin on his way past and missed. If only he could train Dudley to pick up paper balls and deposit them in the waste bin. He dropped down to his knees and retrieved the ball from under his desk, along with two others. It looked like Ross wasn't such a hot shot aim either.

What did Jess make of Ross's "personal development" courses? Her face could never hide what she really thought, even when her words sounded enthusiastic. He wondered whether Ross realised that yet, after all he probably saw her on a daily basis. Neil sighed. He hadn't seen her in nearly a fortnight.

He wondered how it was going with the new guy. With her house sale. Had she found somewhere to live? He made a coffee as he waited for the printer to finish and debated ringing his sister. At least then he'd know.

Yeah, like she'd tell him.

She'd witter on about client confidentiality and data protection and he'd be made to feel stupid for even considering she might spill the beans. She hadn't said anything yesterday over Sunday lunch with his parents.

His hand hovered over the phone for too long, the moment passed and he went back to the kitchen. Rooting through the fridge, he found the Mars bar that he'd uncharitably blamed Ross for pinching a couple of weeks before his wedding. It must have been there all the time. He unwrapped it carefully. But, with ears as sensitive to rustling food packaging as sound mirrors to enemy aircraft, Dudley lifted his head, and the big fella padded into the kitchen to investigate.

'Guess what I've found.'

Dudley tilted his head as if he was trying to consider an answer and Neil stroked it.

He took a bite of the chocolate bar just as his mobile sounded.

'While you're considering that one, here's another. Why do completely rational, sensible people always feel the need to talk to dogs?'

He recognised Anymoore accounts' number and smiled. Only one person that could be. 'Thank goodness!' he said. 'About time. Someone to talk to! Mind you, if you're trying to sell me double-glazing, you should know I live on a houseboat.'

'Do you?'

'Jess?' Someone had told him or else he'd read somewhere that you could hear someone smile on the phone. He wondered if she could hear he was smiling now.

'Sorry. No, it's Sarah.'

He stopped smiling.

'It's because of her I'm ringing.'

Smiling to frowning in less than a second. 'What's happened?'

'Jess once said, you told her, if she ever needed to pick up the phone and talk to a good guy, she could always ring you.'

He wondered what else she'd told Sarah.

'Neil, she really needs a good guy.'

'What about Frank? Why can't he help?'

'They've sacked him. He's gone.'

'They can't.'

'In the interests of a smooth transition or something,' Sarah said.

He wanted to say you must be mistaken, but those words had Ross and Martin *bloody* Cowley's name all over them.

'What's happened?' Then came the strangest sounds. *Was she crying*? At first, he was relieved he was at the other end of the phone because a woman crying was too much to bear. But she'd said it was because of Jess she'd rung. Something had happened.

'Stay there. I'm on my way.'

He looked at the papers sitting on his printer. The proposal had to be in the post today. He'd drop it in to the Post Office on his way back from Anymoore. Dudley, sensing something wasn't right, was primed and ready for action by the door. As an afterthought, Neil grabbed the rest of the Mars bar.

Chapter Fifty

Sarah sat in the back of the boardroom as Ross spouted on about effective time management and how he categorised his work into four – "theoretical" with finger movements – piles. She'd bet his underwear drawers were as effectively sorted. She was doodling on the back of her name card when Harry nudged her.

'What?' she said, looked up and realised the whole room was staring at her.

'One example, Sarah.' Ross was smiling at her in his smug way.

'Something on "one of your piles" today,' Harry hissed.

What like; my boss is in prison? I've got a eulogy to write for a funeral later this week and I'm sitting in this oxymoronically named effective time management meeting worried sick that in less than a month's time, I'm either going to be redundant or working for the dickhead at the front of the room. Or the fact my love life is pants.

'Have you paid the pro-forma for the car park lights?' Harry said, under his breath.

Sarah shot him a grateful look. *Shit she'd forgotten about that.* 'Car park lighting payment needs to be made by lunchtime.'

'How would you classify that? Urgent, important. Urgent, not important. Not urgent, but important or not urgent, not important.'

'It needs to be paid,' Sarah repeated. 'Otherwise, they won't start work tomorrow.'

'I guess, if they don't, they can't guarantee when they'll next be able to fit us in?' Ross didn't seem to need an answer to the question. 'If that happens, I expect there will be a lot of anxious staff won't there? Because they may be in danger. Isn't that right?' Others nodded now. Sarah hated them all. Clearly, they'd decided which side their toast was buttered. She wondered how many of them knew it had cost them their office party. Perhaps this would be a good time to tell them.

'That makes it important and urgent then, doesn't it, Sarah?' He asked her the question, so why did he look at the rest of the room when he spoke? Suddenly, he spun round. 'Shouldn't you have done it already?'

Something was nagging inside her head. Didn't the company say they would ring and confirm account details for the transfer? It was eleven o'clock and they hadn't – unless they'd left a message on the answerphone. Bugger, she hadn't checked.

'Why haven't you?' Ross repeated, still smiling but the smile now looked as if it had been glued on – and in the wrong place.

'You told me I had to come to this training session,' Sarah said, getting up. 'And the company was concerned my request for their bank details could be a scam. They wanted to ring me back with all the information I would need. I guess they will have done that by now. I should go and check because I promised the money would be with them this morning.'

Ross's, 'It can wait until the course finishes', was the last thing she heard as the boardroom door closed behind her.

Dumping the course notes on her desk, she picked up a notepad. But it caught some papers which ended up scattered over the floor. They weren't hers. Nothing she recognised. A whole lot of sheets with figures, projections, budgets and graphs. A covering letter with Neil's company logo was addressed to a local firm saying he hoped the figures were to their satisfaction and he'd be happy to discuss them further, etc. etc. He must have been on his way to deliver them when Sarah called and then forgotten them when he'd raced out. He'd spoken to someone on the phone as soon as she could coherently explain what had happened and then he'd shot out of the building like a man possessed.

'Leave it with me,' he said. 'I know a man who can help.' Words that were music to her ears.

Sarah tried to sort the papers into a sensible order. It was the least she could do, then for good measure she put them into a folder.

The office answerphone came through on Maggie's line. The flashing light indicated it had recorded at least ten messages before it stopped counting. Hopefully one of them was the car park contractor with their bank details. Sarah pulled over a chair and pressed play. This could take a while.

Jess swallowed as Inspector Lenham introduced herself, her colleague and Jess for the tape.

'You've moved.'

Jess nodded.

'And for the benefit of the tape.'

'Yes.'

'You didn't think to tell us.'

Clearly not or presumably you wouldn't have dragged me in here to tell me I had.

'I'm sorry, it was all done in a bit of a rush. I moved in with a colleague at the weekend.'

'What about your furniture?'

'Mostly at Treetops – the nursing home. Some personal things I've taken with me. Sentimental items like books, clothes and pictures I've put into storage for the time being.'

'Sounds like you're getting ready to do a runner. Like your friend Leanne.'

'Leanne?' Jess repeated, only in her case the word sounded strangled.

'Where is she?'

'I have no idea.' Suddenly it made sense.

Jess started to sweat and must've looked a little uncomfortable because the woman asked, 'Are you sure you don't want a solicitor Miss Willersey?'

Sarah groaned. There were twelve messages, including one which sounded like the caller was … singing.

How the bloody hell had he got the number? Surely there must be another speed dating event coming up soon. At the end, Terry left a number and said he hoped to hear from her soon.

In your dreams, sunshine. Sarah deleted it and moved on to the next message.

It was from the hotel thanking her for her time on Friday and confirming arrangements were in place. 'No need to ring back,' a cheerful voice said, 'unless there's a problem. We'll see you tomorrow.'

Sarah pressed delete. She looked at her watch. It was 11.30. She needed to get the payment made. Writing the other messages on post-it notes, she stuck them round the office. Most of them could wait. The tenth, or eleventh one, made her sit up straight. It was important; it could change everything.

The twelfth was the bank details she was waiting for.

She fiddled around for a while trying to work out how she could make a copy of the all important call, then unplugged the phone, making sure she'd packed up all the wires connected to it and put it into her bag.

She processed the bank transfer for car park lighting, emailed to say it was on its way and that she'd send a remittance advice soon, and put on her coat.

Martin was in the corridor as she shut the office door. 'Aren't you supposed to be in training this morning? All non-management staff are supposed to be there.'

He had a way with words.

'Problem with the bank,' she said quickly. 'The fraud department need to see my ID before they can transfer our payment for car park lighting.'

He looked concerned. 'Isn't that something Jess should be dealing with?'

'She's with the auditors,' Sarah said, grateful he didn't know her mannerisms well enough to know when she was lying and boy was she lying now!'

'Should I come with you? I am the new MD.'

'No.'

He looked surprised at her outburst.

'Look, I'm in a rush. There are forms I must complete, and I need to prove I am who I say I am, but I'm named on the account, so there should be no problem. If I rock up with some guy they don't know, they may suspect something is going on and it may delay things even more. Payment has to be made by midday. I've spoken to the suppliers, they are adamant. Late payment, no work.'

She didn't think she sounded convincing, but Martin turned and shut Frank's office door.

Sarah leant against the wall, closed her eyes and let out a breath. Thank goodness he hadn't noticed she was leaving the building with a folder of papers and a piece of office equipment in her bag.

'A few words with my client. In private. Please.'

The tall man who swept into Jess's cell had a manner about him that broached no argument. Still, she was relieved to see the two police constables look at one another and retreat. She was tempted to follow them, until she realised it was her, he was talking about.

'I'm your client?'

'I've been asked to represent you. Now, Miss Willersey, you'd better tell me what brings us both here.'

He patted his chest, removed a pen from his shirt pocket, sat down on the narrow bed and put his briefcase on his lap. He rested a pad on top of it; checked the pen worked and looked at his watch. At the top of the paper he wrote the date and time.

'Are you legal aid?' Jess asked when he looked like he was finally settled.

'No.' He looked shocked. Great! Now she'd upset him too.

'Jackson Associates.'

The name was familiar; she couldn't place it.

'Richard Jackson.'

'Neil's father?'

It came out with more force and louder than she'd intended. The outburst was enough to make him stare at her.

'Yes, Neil's father.' It was said slowly as if she wasn't quite the full shilling. 'Now, according to my son, they arrested you on suspicion of stealing various items of jewellery.'

Neil knew she was there. Her heart started to race.

'Originally, yes. But now Leanne's disappeared, I've moved and Darren's on remand. He wants to cut a deal and has told them I masterminded the whole shebang. Except they haven't told me what the whole shebang is. They keep asking if there's something I want to tell them and where Leanne is. I don't know. I didn't know her well. I photographed her wedding, but I've only met her a handful of times. You don't think she's dead, do you? Do they think I've killed her?'

The brief flick of his head, she took to mean no. He didn't stop writing and he didn't say a word.

The cell was tiny. In her old house, the under stairs storage cupboard was bigger than the room they were in. If they told her what it was that she was supposed to have done, she'd probably confess to get out of the place.

Richard Jackson finished writing and looked up.

'Did Neil ask you to come?' It was out before she could stop it.

'Yes.'

Something about the way he looked at her made her feel like a child. She tried to remember what Neil had said about his father.

She knew the man sharing her cell was disappointed his son hadn't followed him into the family profession. She couldn't remember him ever telling her what the family profession was. If he'd told her his father was a solicitor, she'd forgotten. She knew his sister was; she was doing her house conveyancing.

'What have you told them so far about your involvement?'

'How did Neil know I was here?'

'I assumed from our brief conversation you'd told him. If that's not the case, then I don't know.' This time he swivelled round to stare at her. 'Miss Willersey, the police only have a certain length of time in which they can question you before they have to release you or charge you. I assume they will not want to waste too much of it, so if you can start to answer my questions, then at least I can know how best to proceed. Presumably, you're not guilty and you do need my help, or else my son is so in love with you that he has been blinded to everything else.'

Whoa! Who mentioned anything about love? 'What do you mean?'

'I may be old, and I don't know what my son has told you about me, but I'm not as green as I'm cabbage-looking. I've known my son all of his thirty-six years. I can recognise most of his moods and emotions. Now please, if I am to do a reasonable job, do you think you could answer my questions?'

The sound of a key being turned in the lock interrupted them and the door was flung open.

'I said ten minutes, lad.'

'You've had fifteen,' the PC who opened the door, now filled the space. 'The boss wants a word. Come on let's go.'

Chapter Fifty-One

'She's out and the police have dropped the charges.'

Those words sounded good.

'Mind you, it took them long enough. Another hour in that stuffy room would have had me confessing to the whole damn mess, let alone Jessica.'

'Thanks Dad. I knew you could do it!' Neil said. And he did. They might not be terribly close; it had always been his mother he ran to when he had a problem as a child. His mother who attended parents' evenings, school plays and sports days – his father was usually stuck in a court somewhere and couldn't make it. But the man was widely feted as a good solicitor. Not long ago the local paper would always have at least one mention of him. Now, in his early sixties, he was winding down and not taking on new clients. Preferring to refer them to his younger partners. He'd never been on the legal aid list and wasn't a duty solicitor. The police never called him to some anonymous person they'd arrested in the early hours, slightly worse for drink, but his old clients still managed to get themselves arrested, although these days the hours seemed more civilised. Something he would say that was down to the fact most of them were as old as him and needed their sleep too.

'Nothing to do with me. She's done nothing wrong. No reason for me to miss my golf game.'

Neil felt guilty for asking. Golf mornings were sacrosanct. He'd never asked his father to miss one before, but then he couldn't remember the last time he'd asked his dad for help. If he'd realised it was a golf day, he wasn't sure he would have been brave enough to ask. His father hadn't turned around and argued he was on the first green preparing to tee off when Neil tracked him down. He had simply taken the details; it was only as he was packing up his clubs and Neil heard him apologise to his playing partner that he remembered it was Monday and where he was.

'Is that what you wanted me to say?'

Neil felt uncomfortable, the euphoria he'd felt seconds ago replaced with a nauseous feeling. 'I, er …'

'She's right, isn't she? She said if you'd believed she was innocent, you wouldn't have sent in the big guns.'

'I didn't know what else to do.'

'I like her. She's got far more spirit than any of the other women you felt the need to introduce your mother and I to.'

'I thought you liked Emma.'

There was a loaded silence. 'In fact,' his dad said, 'your mother's thinking of asking Jess to photograph our anniversary celebrations.'

Neil knew he was supposed to say something, but he couldn't think what. 'I thought they had a statement from the groom implicating her.' Whatever his father thought of him, Jess was safe that was all that mattered.

'When you've been around as long as I have, you'll know the likes of Darren Fielding would implicate the whole bloody Royal Family if he felt it would reduce his sentence. His statement was rather blown out of the water when a girl, Jessica works with, brought in an office phone.'

'Sarah?'

'Possibly. The Leanne woman had left a message for Jessica over the weekend, apologising for getting her into the mess in the first place and saying she'd taken cash round to Jess's house, but it looked empty. She'd posted it through the letter box, so she wanted her to know it was there. She was going away to stay with her mother in Sheffield and didn't know when she'd be back but hoped Jess didn't think too badly of her.

'The police thought it was a hoax at first. For a start, they had to go back to the office and practically rewire the whole telephone system to be able to listen to it. There were other strange messages on the machine. Some guy singing a rather tuneless version of the Temptations' "Ain't Too Proud to Beg". Jess had left the key with the estate agent when she moved out, so they had to get in touch with him, but when they opened the house, they found the cash and Leanne's copy of the receipt Jessica had written out for the jewellery in the first place.'

'Was she all right?'

The silence at the other end of the phone was broken by a sigh.

Images of *Midnight Express* and that second Bridget Jones film flashed through Neil's mind. 'Dad?'

'She's had a shock, son. Nothing more, nothing less. As soon as she's put some distance between herself and that place and had a good night's sleep, I'm sure she'll be fine.'

Neil exhaled loudly.

'And what about you, son?'

Chapter Fifty-Two

'Neil? Edward here.'

Neil scratched his head.

Bloody hell, he'd forgotten to post the proposal! Where on earth was it? Shit! He'd left it on Sarah's desk yesterday. 'I am …'

'We are seriously impressed and would like you on board for this one. Not to mention your new assistant. Cute you dark horse. I was relieved to hear you're shot of that last guy.'

New Assistant? Tanya was away for a week; it couldn't have been her. Neil looked down at Dudley, sleeping under his desk. As new assistants went, he wasn't overly useful and wasn't what Neil would have called "cute", especially since his morning walk and whatever it was he'd rolled in.

'He was so far up his own arse he needed a torch. And worse, he gave the impression he expected everyone else to join him up there.' Edward chuckled. 'I understand you're branching out into managing clients' social media. We'd certainly be interested in looking at that. Excellent website you've got, by the way. As to bringing a senior man on board for a couple of months to manage everything is a great idea. And with his previous experience, and availability, Frank sounds like he would be perfect. Maybe you could introduce us.'

Whoa. Stop. Rewind.

The caller display on Jess's phone said Frank. Maybe he'd broken a leg or managed to lock himself in his office. It wouldn't be the first time – the lock, not the leg. She hadn't seen him this morning, but there must be a good reason why he'd picked up the phone and not made the twenty-yard journey across the corridor to the accounts' office. According to the diary Tuesday was the Team Building seminar. Sarah had gone already, but she couldn't imagine it being Frank's sort of thing.

'Frank?'

'No, Martin. Can you come to my office? We need to have a meeting.'

Jess waited for the "Please".

'Jess?'

Clearly it wasn't going to come.

'Yes.'

'Good.' And the phone went dead.

'No, you tosser. Yes as in "Yes, it's Jess", not "Yes, I'm coming".' The receiver didn't respond. She put it back in its cradle, drained her mug of tea, checked her calendar and mobile phone for messages. When she couldn't delay any longer, she walked across the corridor. It was eighteen yards, if the number of paces was anything to go by.

'You need to sign a compromise agreement.' Martin pushed a large document across Frank's desk.

Except it wasn't Frank's desk any more. Something was wrong. Frank's precious photo of his dream boat had been moved.

'I took the liberty of having my solicitor draw it up.'

Frank's management toy swing thingy with all its broken strings was missing. 'Where's Frank?'

Martin kept pushing at the document. If Jess didn't take it, it was going to end up in her lap.

'Frank decided this morning to take a few days off,' Martin said, rubbing his nose hard and so fast that if it didn't catch fire, he was likely to end up with some pretty nasty burns. All the time, he was looking at Ross, seemingly for reassurance. But you can't live with someone for years without knowing most of his annoying little avoidance tactics. He wasn't telling the whole truth.

'How many?' It came out like a growl.

Martin opened his mouth, but nothing came out.

'It doesn't matter. There are things we need to sort out,' Ross said, standing up and taking over the pushing of the document.

Jess moved her chair out of the way and placed the wastepaper basket in front of the desk. It was full of old files, underneath the top one she could see the edge of Frank's management toy.

'Ross, would you mind? I need a couple of minutes with my ex.' Jess placed unnatural stress on the "need", the "my", and the "ex". 'Personal issues,' she added.

Ross looked at Martin, who was starting to fade, colour draining from his face.

'There's a personal matter I need to pull off the back-burner and run past him. You know how it is?' After so long together, she had a wealth of clichés to draw on if necessary. Ross stared at Martin, who stared at her. At this rate they could be here all day.

She stood up and opened the door. 'Martin, tell Ross he can go. He's waiting for your signal. I'm sure neither of us would feel particularly comfortable flying our dirty washing from the flagpole with him watching.' She blew Martin a kiss. His paling effect was immediately replaced by a maroon blush.

Ross took Martin's next incoherent sentence to be a dismissal. *Great. They've started speaking in code. Soon, they'll be doing salutes with oddly spaced fingers.* Ross left. He wasn't happy. That much was clear by the way he resorted to the very British pissed-off response of slamming the door. Which he did with such force that the whole stud wall vibrated.

'You need to think about anger management courses for him.' Jess crossed her legs, pushed the document back into the centre of the desk. 'He's got a real problem.' Then for good measure, she crossed her arms as well. All her personal barriers, well and truly up. 'Right,' she said. 'Talk.'

By the end of his first sentence, she wanted to lean across the desk, slap him and say I said talk not whine, but it was in her own interests not to wind him up. She let him ramble on. Some fifteen minutes later, he paused for breath and she fought the urge to say "Pardon?" and let him repeat everything. Instead she held up a hand, 'Right. My turn now.'

He was sweating. What on earth does Izzie see in him?

'Izzie is telling everyone you are getting married early next year.'

He had the grace to look embarrassed.

'It occurs to me you don't need minor things like our financial settlement or the odd lawsuit to get in the way.'

He shook his head. His eyes followed her every move.

'My co-operation comes at a price. I will sign your compromise agreement, providing it is for the full amount detailed in the redundancy clause of the contract.'

'How do you know about that?' He narrowed his eyes.

'I wrote it – I know exactly what it says,' she said. 'Don't interrupt. I will go whenever you want me to, but Maggie gets the same deal too. I know she tried to hand her notice in yesterday and you told her she was such an important asset to the company that you wouldn't hear of her leaving.'

'Ross has earmarked her as a candidate for rightsizing; she's cheap and efficient and will probably want to retire in the next five years. We're going to let her stay. She'll probably resign next year, and that won't cost us as much.'

'She goes now, gets the same package as me, or no wedding.'

He swallowed. 'I suppose, we could. It makes sense – new broom and all that. Is that it?'

'Secondly.'

'There's more?'

'Shut up and listen. You transfer the car to my name and sign the paperwork from my solicitor …'

'I've been—'

'Before the end of the week. And three …'

A sharp rap and Ross stuck his head round the door without waiting to be invited in. 'I don't want to interfere Martin, but you need—'

Jess had walked across the office and now slammed the door in his face. *Damn it. That felt good.* 'And three …'

Chapter Fifty-Three

The boardroom was set up for the team-building seminar. Most people had already arrived. Nothing much seemed to be happening. Through the window, Sarah could see Harry talking on his mobile in the car park. He was agitated and paced quickly up and down like a German extra in some bad war movie. Whoever was on the other end of his phone didn't seem to understand the point he was trying to make. She hoped he'd hurry up. She'd save a seat for him.

Ross walked into the room, apologised for the delay and announced they would be ready to start in five minutes, but in the meantime if anyone wanted to get a cup of coffee etc etc. Sarah sighed. She could have done without the delay. Customer Services headed for the kitchen. She stayed put, debating whether anyone would notice if she wasn't there. Her work was piling up; this was the third bloody seminar Ross had arranged in little over a week. She'd already been time managed and motivated. But this one, he'd told all staff in a long email, was vitally important. This was the one that would give them the tools they needed to build effective teams, to get rid of the "them-and-us" culture that had festered within the company for too long. At the end of this session, he was confident, he said, they would be able to develop and maintain inter-departmental relationships. Sarah overheard someone from Technical asking whether this meant they'd be able to sleep with Customer Services, or was that privilege only afforded to the new management team?

Harry slipped back into the room, during the five-minute break, that had turned into ten, but if he saw it, he ignored the space Sarah saved for him. He chose to sit with his own department instead. He couldn't avoid her for long – they'd been put in the same team for the first practical session when Ross divided the room into two, based on their individual answers to a rather obscure question about the position of a dot on a cube. He'd split them into predominantly left-brained or predominantly right-brained groups. The collective murmuring of "What the fuck?" had him raising his voice to explain the exercise had been designed to show them what could be achieved if people of all abilities worked together as a team.

'He didn't just say that, did he?' someone said. 'Is he calling some of us thick?'

'Abilities is the wrong word,' Izzie shot up. 'What Ross meant was those of you who are more analytical and methodical are said to be left-brained, more creative or artistic people are considered right-brained, and a good team should be a mixture of both.'

'Exactly,' Ross said. 'Thank you Izzie. And we all know what T-E-A-M stands for, don't we?'

'Take Ecstasy and ...'

Ross glared at the speaker. 'Together Everyone Achieves More,' he said, clearly agitated and annoyed. 'And that's what we're going to prove.'

Each person was given a sheet of paper with twelve statements about the residents of one street and fifteen minutes as a team to decide who the occupants of five houses were, the colour of their front doors, their pets and who milk should be delivered to.

Sarah took her place next to Harry. 'Are you okay for tomorrow?' she whispered, while their self-appointed team leader drew up some sort of complicated grid thingy on a flip chart in front of them.

'I'll be there,' he said, not taking his eyes off the flip chart.

For the last couple of months, if she'd been asked, Sarah would've said one of the things she liked best about Harry was that he didn't beat about the bush. He came straight out and said what was on his mind.

He made her laugh, not that she'd admit it to Jess or Maggie, but she had started looking forward to seeing him at work. He'd asked how she got on at The Last Post and fell about when she told him what had happened. And yesterday, when he'd helped her out at the seminar, and looked at her for a tad longer than necessary, she'd felt a rush like pins and needles through her body and been sorry she'd had to dash off. She hoped today he'd look at her like that again, make her feel special and then she'd know he was interested. Except he hadn't, so clearly, he wasn't.

It was like she'd been completely anaesthetised or run over by a truck. Every last pin or needle had been squeezed out. She was beyond pain. Empty, devoid of all feeling. Words too. No clever, witty reply. Nothing. Sarah looked at her sheet of paper without seeing what it said.

‘Thanks for the order of service,’ he said. She nodded and then he told the guy at the front of the group with the flip chart and the Sharpie, that house number two had the green door.

Sarah walked back to her office at lunchtime, glad to be away from the others. She needed to see Jess. A friendly face, someone she could rely on to say something nice or kind. Someone to tell her, her feelings for Harry were reciprocated, that some sort of chemistry existed between them and she hadn’t imagined it. Jess wasn’t there.

Ross followed her into the office.

‘That was an interesting point you made, Sarah,’ he said. ‘The one about knocking on each door and asking whether the occupant was lactose intolerant,’ he added, when she looked at him blankly.

Martin sat at Jess’s desk, looking for all the world like he’d been caught red-handed going through her drawers.

‘Where is she?’ Sarah asked. Jess’s desk looked sterile. Even the photograph of General Gordon stuck to the bottom of her monitor had vanished.

‘Jess doesn’t work here any more,’ Martin said, looking shiftier than usual.

She’d never been able to see why Jess got involved with him. Something about him made Sarah itch to punch him every time he opened his mouth.

‘We’ve come to a mutually convenient arrangement.’

‘You’ve sacked her.’

‘Let’s say she decided she didn’t want to be part of our future,’ he said.

‘Let’s not,’ Sarah said. It had been a bad morning and she wasn’t taking any more crap from anyone, whatever the left-hand or right-hand side of her brain said. ‘I saw her this morning. If she was thinking of leaving, she would’ve said.’ They’d had a conversation about the funeral and who needed to be where and what time. Sarah would’ve remembered, if Jess had said, “By the way I’m out of here.”

‘You’ve sacked her, haven’t you?’

‘No, no, no.’ Martin’s denial was accompanied by violent head shaking.

One no, she might have believed.

Two suggested something wasn't right.

But three. Three meant he was lying.

'She would have said goodbye.'

'No time. You were in the seminar. She left you a note. On your desk under the keyboard, along with a message from some guy called Ryan.' Martin flapped his hand in the direction of her desk.

Ryan? Sarah only knew one Ryan. It couldn't be. He wouldn't ring. Not after all this time.

'Her departure does leave us a little short in the department.' Martin laughed.

'Maggie's off, sorting out the last minute arrangements for her mother's funeral, so what you're saying is that this week it's just me?' Sarah looked at him with contempt.

'Not just this week.'

Sarah noticed an edge to his voice.

'Maggie has gone too. But as soon as the takeover is finalised, we'd like you to recruit your own operational team.' Martin wasn't looking at her; he was staring straight over her shoulder. Ross must be stood directly behind her. She was in the middle of a pillock sandwich. She sidestepped so she could see them both.

Ross walked round Jess's desk and stood behind Martin.

'I think what Martin's trying to say, Sarah, is we'd like you to accept a temporary promotion.'

Sarah put her hands on the desk and leant towards him, until their faces were only a few feet apart. 'Martin didn't mention temporary anything.' Okay, so he hadn't mentioned promotion as such, but Sarah wasn't going to split hairs.

'After six months or so, I don't see why we couldn't make it permanent,' Martin said, moving back into Ross, who took a step backwards too.

'Promotion to what?' She wasn't going to look away.

'Accounts and Finance …'

She straightened up.

'Operations Associate,' Martin said.

Ross seemed as surprised as she was. He broke the stare first. Hah, it might be a small victory, but it was hers.

'We identified you on day one as someone with potential. Someone we'd be prepared to invest in,' Martin said.

'I'm not a flaming hedge fund'. Sarah folded her arms and looked at Martin.

Martin shrugged. 'Job opportunities like this don't grow on trees.'

'You could work all your life and not be given an opportunity like this,' Ross confirmed.

It was like some sort of bizarre double act. Verbal tennis.

'A fancy title like that must come with a significant pay increase.' Sarah's gaze flicked from Ross to Martin and waited. Ross looked at Martin. Martin looked at Ross and then they both nodded.

'You need to decide what's important in life and then go for it,' Martin said.

'It's a matter of priorities,' Ross added.

Whose? She should be happy. They'd offered her promotion, but somehow it felt like she'd been handed a double-edged sword and now they were waiting for her to fall on top of it.

She couldn't be bothered to argue. 'I need time to decide.'

Martin froze for a second, clearly not expecting her to refuse. '

Ross came to the rescue. 'There's no hurry. Take twenty-four hours.'

'I'm doing a collection for Maggie and Jess.' Sarah crossed her arms firmly, daring either of them to refuse.

Martin stood up. 'Nice touch,' he said. 'I'm sure they'd appreciate it.'

'Good, why don't you both give me your contribution now.'

Martin clearly didn't think he should, but Sarah held out her hand, effectively blocking his exit so unless he either broke her arm or she moved it, he wasn't leaving the room. It seemed to take him a while to grasp that fact. Odd, when according to Ross, his brain was in the right place to make analytical decisions. Eventually, he reached for his pocket and put £1 in her hand and when she didn't move, he followed it with a second. She swung round and held out the same hand in front of Ross. He pulled £5 from a trouser pocket and waved it in front of her.

'I'm sorry I don't have change,' he said.

'Neither do I.' Sarah snatched the note before he had the chance to take it back. 'I'll split it between them.'

Her phone beeped with a text from a number she didn't recognise.

Sarah, I'm sorry. I made a mistake. Tell me what I have to do to make it up to you. Flowers? Dinner? Wild, promiscuous sex? Whatever it takes. Believe me, babe, you're the one I want. Ring me. Ryan xxxx

'Anything else?' She threw the phone into her handbag.

'Twenty-four hours,' Martin said. Both men were watching her as she walked to the door.

She stared straight back. 'I'm going to lunch.'

'Twenty-four hours, Sarah,' Martin said. 'Not a minute more, not a minute less.'

She needed to get out of the office and was halfway across reception when the receptionist called her back.

'What?'

The girl was hidden behind a large arrangement of flowers on the desk. As bunches went, Sarah was impressed. It wasn't overly large and it was bright without being gaudy. The sort of flower arrangement she'd like to receive.

'They're for you.' The girl smiled.

'It's not my birthday.'

'Must be a secret admirer then.'

'No, it bloody mustn't,' she muttered and rang Ryan. It took ages before his automated message cut in. She didn't know whether she was glad or not that he hadn't answered. She left him a message, short and to the point. She mentioned hell freezing over and where he could stick his flowers, one by bloody one. Tears streamed down her face as she left the office, pointedly ignoring the receptionist's questions about what she wanted done with the flowers.

What a mess!

She used to think promotion, declarations of love and bunches of flowers were all things she wanted. In the space of an hour, she'd got them all and she wasn't sure she wanted any of them.

The tears were falling so hard by the time she reached her car she couldn't find her car keys in her bag. She turned the contents out on the ground and squatted down to sort through them. She was sobbing so loudly she didn't hear someone calling her name. She found the keys, put everything back in her bag and straightened to find Harry by her side, holding the flowers from reception.

'You forgot these.'

'I don't want them.' Sarah hugged herself so she didn't do something she might regret, like throwing herself into his arms and crying on his shoulder.

'They're not from Ryan, they're from Neil,' he said, quietly. 'The management consultant guy.'

'How did you …?'

'I was in the car park when he brought them in. I was talking to my sister on the phone. She's dumped Ryan. Things hadn't been good. He said if she hadn't, he would've dumped her because he wanted to ask you out again. He implied you'd been chasing and pestering him for a while now.'

'Oh yeah right.'

'She knows how I feel about you. She wanted me to know how things stood so I didn't make a fool of myself. If you still have feelings for him, I won't stand in your way.'

'What?' Sarah said, so startled, she stopped hugging herself and her bag slid down her arm.

'If you …'

'No, the bit before that. The bit about you. How you feel.'

'I was coming to that.' Harry smiled, his voice low and soft.

'Good.' Her heart pounded.

'The receptionist told everyone about your outburst in reception. I thought maybe I might have a chance so I grabbed the flowers and ran.'

'Why?' Sarah swallowed, trying not to cry.

'Why do you think, you daft creature?' He put the flowers on the bonnet of her car and pulled her close into him. She tilted her face up to get a better look at his face and he kissed her, softly at first, then she kissed him back and everything got a lot more intense.

'Are you sure both sides of your brain know what you're doing?' she murmured.

Chapter Fifty-Four

The dress didn't fit as snugly as it had in the shop. Maggie had lost even more weight over the last couple of weeks. The shop assistant had been right about the colour though; it seemed to warm her face.

Material moved with every step she took and changed colour in the bedroom lights. She'd had her hair done at the salon in town. It was cut, washed and massaged by the salon director while piped music flowed. Her mother would have had a heart attack if she'd known she'd spent everything Sarah managed to claw back from the undertakers to pay for it. The hairdresser gave her a coffee and a magazine while her hair was brushed and dried into a soft, feathered style Maggie would never dream of trying.

'Trust me, I'll make you look special,' he said, and had been as good as his word. In the last two hours, she'd examined practically every hair in the bathroom mirrors and without exception loved them all. She hoped that when she washed it next time, she'd be able to recreate the look.

She'd even done the whole make-up thing, from foundation right through to mascara and lip gloss. She recreated the look the woman had shown her or tried to. She hadn't done a bad job even if it had taken her ages.

She hardly recognised the person staring back from the mirror. Everything she wore, apart from the pearl hanging on a fine gold chain, Rose's pearl, was new. She felt reborn.

And she had Stephen. They talked for hours and had so much in common. She asked him about her cake and candle memory. He'd looked blank at first, but then his memory started to come back too. At least once in their childhood they must have met up.

'Was that the birthday I got a guinea pig?' he'd said.

'I had a guinea pig too.' She laughed.

It felt too good to be true: she had everything she'd ever wanted. Her mother, by dying, gave her more than she dreamed possible. She didn't know how long she had to enjoy everything, but she was going to live every day from now on as if it were her last. She wasn't alone, she had friends – Jess, Sarah and John and a brother.

‘Limousine’s here,’ Jess called out. ‘And so’s Stephen.’

Stephen wolf-whistled when he saw her. She looked away so he didn’t see the tears that threatened to spill out of her eyes with extreme happiness.

Following the hearse to Treetops took ages. They must have been the only vehicles not to exceed the twenty-mile-an-hour speed limit on the Redford Road and Maggie was amused to see the Community Speedwatch volunteers drop their guns in a mock salute as they went past.

‘Everything ready for later?’ she asked, as John climbed in and kissed her. She’d have liked to have popped in and checked for herself, but he was waiting outside when they arrived and insisted they should get going.

He hadn’t wanted her there first thing either to help prepare sandwiches. ‘You’ll get in the way and must have more than enough to do at home,’ he’d said firmly.

She didn’t know what, so she baked four cakes. The funeral director looked concerned when she told him to drop them off at Treetops. He grudgingly put them in the back of the immaculately clean car but hadn’t been able to get rid of them quickly enough when they reached the nursing home, handing them to the first old dear who came out to admire the car.

‘Everything is fine,’ John said.

Her mother used to say “Fine” when Maggie asked her how she was, or if she wanted to do something; it was a word she hated. It could mean anything, and she’d no idea what it meant in this case.

It felt like John was shutting her out. He’d not commented on how she looked and he’d still not given her an answer about the kitchen job. He’d not said he’d advertised for a replacement and he had let her help yesterday.

She’d even given him an out: ‘I understand if you want a qualified cook and can’t afford to pay me. Why don’t I volunteer for a couple days a week? It would give me something to do. Jess made sure I got the redundancy package and because I’ve been there so long and am practically part of the furniture, it’s generous. Added to which, her rent means I don’t have to worry financially.’

‘Leave it with me,’ he said. She tightened her eyes, resisting the urge to shout, ‘I need to do this. I need to see you. I’m starting to like you a lot!’

'Fine,' she said and winced; the word came out sharper than intended.

John tilted his head. 'It's all under control. Really. You've got Sarah to thank. I don't know how she did it, but I think you'll approve.'

'You've let Sarah take control of the catering?' Jess shook her head in disbelief. 'Are you completely mad?'

'Not just the food, but the entertainment too,' he said. His smile and Jess's look of stunned amazement did nothing to reassure her as the hearse and the limousine stopped at the crematorium gates.

Maggie dreaded this moment. She hated being the centre of attention: ideally, she would slip in unseen. John seemed to sense her nerves and squeezed her hand. He hadn't let go of it, since he got in the car.

The funeral director climbed out, but their passenger doors at the back of the limousine stayed locked so they remained in the car. Probably a good thing. Seeing such a huge crowd, she was tempted to make a run for it.

'Bloody hell,' said Stephen. 'Who are all these people?'

'I thought you said your mother wasn't popular,' John said.

Jess and Maggie looked at each other. 'Sarah,' they mouthed.

Sarah stood outside the chapel, dressed in a black suit and holding a black folder.

The funeral director started to walk in front of the hearse with an exaggerated slowness, his eyes cast down, top hat clutched theatrically against his chest. It was a walk designed to attract attention and it did.

Maggie recognised a few faces as everyone turned to watch.

'There's Frank,' Jess said. 'And isn't that Harry from customer services?'

'That's the credit controller from Robinsons,' Maggie said. 'What's she doing here? And aren't they … How did all our suppliers find out?'

Everybody stared as they pulled up under the archway outside a double wooden door and Maggie felt her face flush, but they were familiar faces and smiled at her. These people didn't know her mother; they were there for her.

'Are you all right?' John asked, as the funeral director finally opened the door and let them out, his eyes fixed on the pall-bearers who were lifting the coffin from the back of the hearse. It was smaller than Maggie imagined.

'Okay?' Sarah said. 'We're going to get everybody in first.'

Maggie nodded.

'The chapel is ready if you are.'

Maggie nodded again.

'Ladies and gentlemen.' Sarah spoke with authority and looked so grown up and sophisticated. 'Please take your seats.'

Her mother would be pleased. "A dignified service at the crematorium" was what she wanted. Maggie took a deep breath; this was her moment. Twenty minutes of embarrassment was a small price to pay if it meant she didn't have to spend the rest of her life worrying if, when her time came twenty or perhaps thirty years from now, her mother would be waiting with a face looking like she'd chewed her way through a bowl of lemons, saying, "It was the last thing you could've done for me, but you couldn't be bothered, could you? But then, why change the habits of a lifetime?"

Maggie caught sight of a couple of members of the post room and smiled. She was sure they'd never met her mother. She was among friends. A tear pricked at her eye. John handed her a tissue. He wasn't standing with the carers from the home but with her – and her brother. She felt overwhelmed with emotion, so she blew her nose.

She caught sight of Frank walking in and Jess caught him up.

Sarah stepped forward. 'Please be upstanding,' she said.

'Why do people always say that?' Maggie asked. 'Why can't they say, stand up?'

John smiled as Sarah nodded to the man by the door.

'Nobody says down-sitting.'

Music started to play. The procession started to move.

'Do you realise this will be the only time she's ever arrived anywhere before me?' Maggie said, as they followed the coffin down the aisle.

'Great choice of music,' Stephen whispered. 'I wasn't expecting that.'

Six pall-bearers carried the coffin into the crematorium. Their measured steps in time with each other if not the music. Maggie's bunch of freesias sitting on the top, added little to the weight.

John tightened his grip on her arm.

'When Mr Nelson died,' Maggie said under her breath, 'I cried for a week.'

He patted her hand. 'Who?' he said.

'Her guinea pig,' Stephen said. 'I had Mrs Nelson,' he added when Maggie looked surprised. And I cried for at least ten days. Made her a lovely coffin though, lined it with silk.'

On one of the front pews sat a woman wearing an old-fashioned black suit and a hat. The hat had the most ridiculous feathers on it that waved with every movement she made. And she made a lot. She appeared to be sobbing uncontrollably, feathers bounced all over the place. If she can cry for my mother, Maggie thought, why can't I? The feather dance took on even more fervour as the coffin passed. Maggie wondered if the woman was crying, or whether she had the shakes.

The pallbearers placed the coffin on the catafalque and moved away, leaving Maggie, John and Stephen alone in the middle of the aisle. Her face started to colour and she started to sweat. *Breathe*.

Frank stood up and came out of the "Reserved for Family" pew. Taking her arm, he guided them in. Jess smiled.

Sarah stood at the lectern and winked.

'Ladies and gentlemen,' she said. Maggie wasn't about to admit it, least of all to the two of them, but she was glad they were both there.

Chapter Fifty-Five

At breakfast Neil decided the last place in the world he wanted to be today was Maggie's mother's funeral. He'd justified the decision on any number of counts, none of which included the real reason – Jess.

Get over her and fast. Face the facts Jackson, she's not that into you. And you've only got yourself to blame. You had your chance and blew it. She's seeing someone else now, so the least you could do is be happy for her.

If he was being completely paranoid, he would have said Dudley wasn't happy either these days. Maybe they needed a break – both of them.

'Hi Dad, how's things? If it's okay with you and Mum, I'll come over today, maybe have lunch with you both.'

'What are you running away from this time?'

'I'm …'

'Don't give me that. Your mother's lunch is not something I look forward to. I certainly wouldn't expect anyone to volunteer to drive halfway across the county for one. How's Jess?'

'I don't …'

'Sort yourself out son.'

Thirty-six years old and a conversation with his father still made him feel like he'd done something wicked and deserved to be chastised. The only difference now was that he no longer had homework that needed to be finished or exams to pass. He hadn't smashed up his first car or lost his front-door key. And the only broken thing round here was his heart. He couldn't even remonstrate; his father had already put the phone down.

Dudley let out a sigh and collapsed theatrically on the ground.

'Come on, let's walk.'

No immediate crisis in the office needed his attention. He could afford the rest of the week off. He stood up. Dudley didn't move for a second or two but then his tail started wagging, slow at first but picking up speed.

The woods beckoned.

'We need some quality man time together.' Neil picked up the lead from the coat stand and held the door open. 'Want to play sticks?'

The nice thing about dog walking is that you can lose yourself for miles, often not see another person. You can talk to yourself: if anyone notices, they assume you're talking to the dog.

Two hours later, endorphins flowing freely, Neil opened the door to the office. An order of service, like the one he'd torn up yesterday, had been pushed through the letterbox. He checked the bin: yes, definitely one in there. The second was about to join it until he noticed the writing on the back.

There are only so many times you can read words trying to make sense of them.

"Thought you might like to know about this. I'm sorry I missed you. Jess."

He spent half an hour kicking himself for not being there when she pushed it under the door. He was sorry he missed her too. He checked his watch. He had fifteen minutes. He left his car; it was quicker to walk.

'You're going to have to wait here,' he told Dudley. 'Be back as soon as I can. If you answer the phone, don't be rude to clients.'

He cut through town and arrived as the limousine pulled up. He could see Sarah by the main door and caught sight of Jess and Maggie in the middle of a mass of people. He lost sight of them as the crowd moved forward and took their places in the crematorium. It was packed. He managed to squeeze into the last row and then had to squeeze in a bit further as someone squeezed in next to him. The man looked familiar.

'Hi, are you the guy with the big dog?' his neighbour whispered. 'Didn't I see you last week in Broadwater Close?'

'That's right and yes, Dudley's mine.' Of course, he looked familiar. He was the guy Neil watched last week posting something through Jess's letter box. 'Neil Jackson.' He moved a shoulder a fraction and tried to extend a hand. He didn't get far. Crushed together, shaking hands wasn't an option.

'Gary Mansfield,' the man said. 'Say "Hello" to him for me. Great dog. I met him last week when I visited Anymoore to interview their new owner.'

'You're the reporter from the *Redford Chronicle.*' Neil said as the cogs in his brain started to whirr into gear.

'Editor, reporter, photographer.' Gary shrugged.

‘Great report on the scout hut by the way.’

Chapter Fifty-Six

'A warm welcome to you all.' Sarah paused. Row upon row of faces looked back at her. She wished she'd had a stiff drink. Another deep breath and she started, slowly at first. 'We are here today to reflect upon and celebrate the life of Rose.'

She swallowed; her eyes scanned the first few rows until they found Harry. He smiled encouragingly and she relaxed – a little.

'We are delighted to see you all this morning. We came into Maggie's choice of music, "Memories", and as the song says, a "Toast to those here today" and to all of you watching the webcast at Treetops, a toast to you too. We'll see you shortly.' Sarah waved at the red light at the end of the chapel indicating filming had started. 'I know it means a great deal to both Maggie and Stephen that so many of you have come to comfort and support them as they say goodbye to their mother.'

She focussed on Maggie, standing between John and Stephen, a hand in each of theirs. 'Please be down-sitting.' Maggie's laughter, when it came, was somewhere between a snigger and a snort.

A bit of shuffling went on as everyone sat.

'Rose was never a regular churchgoer,' Sarah said, 'often sharing her view that "when you're dead, you're dead", a view of the afterlife that could perhaps be attributed more to Monty Python's dead parrot sketch than God, but Maggie and Stephen find it comforting to think she might finally be reunited with her beloved parents.

'I'm sure you all know what an amazing woman Maggie is: a genuine, dependable person who sees her role in life as looking after people. For more years than she cares to remember, she looked after Rose's needs, while also managing to hold down a full-time job. She is always ready to help anyone, freely giving her time and advice to anyone in need. Me, probably, more than most. For that, Maggie, I will always be grateful.' Sarah blew her a kiss. 'But there is a caveat,' she said looking back at everyone else. 'Maggie has her own unique style of humour. It's sort of a Marmite thing: you either love it or hate it. I never met her mother, but having been introduced recently to her brother Stephen, I guess it's genetic. I'm not sure which parent is responsible, but if it was you Rose, be assured your bad jokes, sarcasm and wit will live on. There were chuckles from around the room.' Harry grinned and gave her a thumbs up.

'On a more serious note, Rose spent her last months in Treetops where she was cared for and never alone. She died peacefully in her sleep. No one could ask for more. Today, Stephen will read a poem, we will share what we have discovered about Rose's life and honour her memory with Rod Stewart singing "Forever Young" before committing her body to the transformational flames of cremation.'

The next fifteen minutes passed quickly. Sarah read from the script she'd prepared, read and reread at least three times since she woke up. She checked her watch from time to time. She wasn't overrunning. There were laughs in the right places and the faces looking back encouraged her to keep going.

Finally, as the curtains closed around the coffin and she'd asked everyone to keep a moment's silence for the safe transition of Rose's soul to whatever lay ahead, she gathered up her folder and took her place back at the front of the chapel.

'Thank you all for coming, but please don't rush off. Maggie and Stephen would like you to join them back at Treetops, where refreshments will be served to not only celebrate Maggie's mother's life with those who shared her last months, but also to share memories with Stephen and Maggie.'

She hesitated. 'I understand from the funeral directors it's normal at services like this to have a retiring collection, which is fortunate, because I didn't know how else I could arrange one. There is a box on your way out. It may not be common knowledge yet but Jess is leaving Anymoore and embarking on a photographic career. She's excellent – very reasonable rates – make sure you get a card: you never know when you'll need a good photographer. And Maggie is hoping to go into catering, although I understand her contract terms are still to be agreed.' She glanced at John. 'Our final piece of music was left up to me – something by Queen, was all Maggie said. I love this song. It makes me feel good – hopefully you will too! Feel free to sing along as you leave the chapel.'

Sarah nodded at the chapel attendant and heard the opening bars of one of Queen's early classics burst forth as she left the chapel.

Jess walked out into the flower garden humming "Another One Bites the Dust". The chapel attendant had let the music play on, until everyone left the chapel. John and Stephen pretended to play air guitars, Maggie seemed to remember most of the words. A few of the others seemed to too, while everyone else joined in with the chorus.

'Can you believe that?' Jess asked, as they reached a large collection of flowers next to a little stand that said simply "Rose Simpson". 'Sarah is holding Harry's hand?' she added, not waiting for a reply. 'They seem to be "together".'

'Does that mean we're off the hook?' Maggie asked, looking towards where Jess was pointing. 'Do you think we should remind her about the sex rule?'

Jess blushed. 'Let's leave them be,' she said quietly. 'Harry won't hurt her.' She moved away so Maggie and Stephen could greet the guests as they came out of the chapel.

'Lovely flowers,' one of the guests said. Jess agreed.

Maggie's bunch of freesias from the coffin had been put there too. It was the only arrangement without a small white card attached. There were flowers from suppliers and a circular pink and white wreath from Anymoore. Sarah must have arranged that – Jess couldn't imagine Martin thinking flowers would be a good idea for a funeral. He'd never given her any, not even a guilty bunch from a garage on the way home to make up for something he'd forgotten to do. But the biggest by far was an enormous bouquet of red roses from Edna and Dennis.

'Has Maggie mentioned an Edna and Dennis?' Stephen asked, voicing the question Jess had been chewing over. 'Are they someone I should be looking out for?'

'Not that I can remember. Could they be relatives?'

'None I know of,' Stephen said, as Maggie shook hands with one of the care assistants, who was on her day off, but felt she had to come because Rose was always so nice to her. 'But I guess there's a lot we still have to find out about each other.'

'Tell us about the music,' Frank said, as Maggie joined them.

'Let's say one should always check whether you're both on the same page with the plural or singular,' she said. 'I have to admit I like Sarah's version better.'

'Me too.' Frank laughed. 'Much more appropriate.' He kissed Maggie's cheek. 'And I don't think you'll ever be "smiling alone".'

Maggie coloured slightly.

Jess hoped he was right.

'I'm not leaving all these flowers behind, you'll all have to bring a bouquet or wreath back with you,' Maggie said.

Sarah came across. 'The funeral director's going to get the limousine and bring it round,' she said. 'And guess what?'

Whenever Sarah said, "Guess what?" it wasn't an invitation. More a signal she had news coming.

'He only wants me to give him a ring.' Her face had lit up.

'Don't do it.' Jess looked at Maggie who looked back and nodded. 'We don't think you should.'

'You are joking, right?' Sarah said, her eyes darkening.

'Are you or are you not seeing Harry?' Jess asked.

'What's that got to do with it? If you're planning on lecturing me about the seven-date thing, don't bother. It's too late.' Sarah blinked and stuck out her chin.

'Forget about sex.'

'Yeah, right. I don't think so.' Sarah gave a hollow laugh and folded her arms.

People were watching now. Jess really hoped Sarah wasn't about to make a scene, maybe they should have left the conversation until later. Oh well, too late now. She cleared her throat. 'You seem sort of serious about each other.'

'We are.'

'Good, so then I don't think you should jeopardise that relationship by ringing the first guy that asks.'

Sarah laughed. This time it sounded real.

'Not for a date – he's offered me another funeral,' she said, her eyes bright. 'He thinks I've got a talent for this. He's going to give me details when I ring.'

'That's great.' Relief swept through Jess and she smiled. 'And it was a fantastic service. You did so well.'

'Thanks.' But Sarah was studying Maggie's face.

'It was brilliant,' she said. 'Jess is right. He's right. It was lovely and everyone has said so. Thank you.'

'Harry was going to be our choice for date five anyway,' Jess said.

Sarah stuck her nose in the air. 'That was totally against the rules. No one from work, you remember.'

'The funeral director is making faces at us,' Maggie said, gesturing towards the limousine. 'We should get going.'

'Sorry,' said Sarah, wrinkling her nose. 'Tea and sympathy – not my sort of thing. I'll go back to the office, hold the fort.'

'You are joking, I hope.'

'Of course I am.' Sarah laughed. 'I wouldn't miss it for the world. I've ordered vodka and red bull in specially.'

Maggie grinned. 'Now you're talking. Come in the posh car with us then?'

'I don't have a choice. Harry's driven John back to Treetops to make sure everything's ready.' She picked up the huge bouquet of red roses, tucked her free hand inside Maggie's arm. 'Who are Edna and Dennis?' she asked.

Chapter Fifty-Seven

Treetops clearly didn't want anyone getting lost. Jess stopped to study the huge board with arrows drawn on it, positioned inside the reception.

'The wake's in the lounge down the hall,' a male voice said as an arm snaked around her waist. 'That colour suits you. You look amazing.'

She looked up and smiled. 'Why thank you, sir.' Gary's arm gave her confidence.

'Shall we go through?'

The lights had been dimmed but were not out completely. Coloured patterns reminiscent of seventies' discos danced across the walls in time to the music and from the middle of the ceiling hung a huge glitter ball.

At one end of the room, instruments were set up on a stage, awaiting a band. Wing chairs were crammed in round the walls and most of the chairs had an occupant watching the proceedings. A handful of people danced in the middle. The constant stream of people coming in needed to navigate round them. The conservatory was set up as a bar.

A glass of Prosecco was thrust into Jess's hand. She took a swig, grateful for the sensation, as the bubbles hit the back of her mouth.

They tried to follow Maggie and John across to a less densely populated corner of the room, but as they reached the middle, a man with a camera slung round his neck asked whether they'd like to have their picture taken as part of the band. He waved a hand at a board with full-sized pictures of four headless white spangled suited bodies painted on it in one corner of the room. Jess assumed they were supposed to be ABBA, except the faces on one of the women and one of the men were holes. It reminded her of similar boards on Brighton Pier, back in the days when as a child, she'd spent numerous summer holidays staying with relatives there. She was pretty certain if you'd had a camera in those days, you could've taken your own picture free. She couldn't remember whether her parents had, but she did remember how she and her sisters used to climb up and peer through the face holes, not caring which one was the baby in the frilled bonnet, the overweight mother or the father in a red and white swimming suit. Her mother would laugh and say, 'Oh don't you all look a scream' and they'd all giggle too.

She and Gary both said 'No' and laughed. Gary steered her past the man, already off in search of a more willing target.

'We've missed a trick there.' He grinned. 'Let's lock him in a cupboard. We could work this joint. Make some serious money. I don't suppose you've got your camera in the car?'

'Sorry, came in the limo.'

'Sorry,' Sarah repeated, grabbing hold of Jess's free hand and dragging her back through the room. 'Need a quick word.'

'That's an ABBA tribute band?' Jess shouted to be heard.

'How did they get there?' Sarah asked, sarcastically.

'I assume that's the band for the office party that you couldn't cancel?' Jess pulled her arm to stop her and Sarah laughed.

'Small print, date or venue changes okay, but no chance of money back. They're doing a set before and after tea.'

'Lovely party,' an elderly woman said, tugging Sarah's other arm. 'Lovely songs. Lovely drink. When do we get to do our dance?'

'Let's save that for after tea?' Sarah said, smiling. 'Can you remember your moves?'

The woman walked off waving arms in all directions.

'Do you think Maggie needs a hand?' Jess asked. 'Should we go and see if she's all right?'

'No, wait.'

'What is it?' Jess asked.

'There's something I need to tell you,' Sarah said. 'I can't hear myself think in here. Can we go somewhere quieter?'

'Conference in the corridor?'

She nodded and they stepped out into the carpeted hall. Jess was relieved Sarah took charge. Her sense of direction could only ever be relied upon if a signpost pointed her way.

'You're a dark horse,' Sarah said, as soon as they'd taken a turn and the music faded behind them.

'I'm not with Gary, if that's what you're thinking.' Jess looked down at her feet, appalled to realise she was close to tears.

Neil hadn't come. It was stupid to even think he might.

'Gary's offered me some work and wants to run an article on Darren and Leanne. It's a professional relationship, that's all.' She bit her lip. 'I won't stay much longer. I could do with unpacking and sorting myself out.'

'It's early yet, you're not going anywhere.' Sarah clutched her elbow. 'You won't want to miss the food, seriously it's gorgeous. Grey Towers are doing the catering.'

'You're joking? Maggie's paying for that?'

'Not exactly.' Sarah grimaced. 'They're offsetting the office party funds against it. Don't look at me like that. Martin told me to do what I could. I cleared it with Frank. He said it was the least the company could do as it wouldn't be funding any leaving parties.'

Jess smiled. 'Okay, okay, I'll stay a little longer. Grey Towers' food is to die for.'

'He'll be here. I know he will.'

'Who?' Jess clenched her teeth.

'Don't play games with me,' Sarah said. 'Neil, of course.'

'Oh him.' Jess tried to sound casual.

'I haven't spoken to him since Monday, but the way he sprang into action when I told him you were in trouble was impressive. He wouldn't have done that if he didn't care for you.'

'So why hasn't he called?'

'I suppose you've been calling him all the time. God – you two, someone ought to bang your heads together. You know he was at the funeral?'

He came. Jess's glass stopped halfway to her mouth. She could mention she'd called at his office earlier. What was the point? There was nothing to tell. The office had been shut. She'd sat on the stairs for a minute or two and then in a moment of madness left her order of service. She wrote a short note on it. She couldn't even remember what she'd said.

She'd told Maggie yesterday she wanted to thank him for his help in getting his father to take her case. She'd spent most of yesterday practising conversations. Going over and over in her head what she wanted to say. Which seemed to be variations along the lines of "I am sorry I doubted you. I love you; I miss you; I want you back." With an "I'll understand if you never want to see me again, but I've got to know" thrown in for good measure. And the occasional "I'm miserable without you, can we try again?" Except they were all sentiments likely to have any self-respecting man running for the hills.

Jess sighed. She'd finally plucked up the courage and went round to his office. Somehow his not being there was worse than him shutting the door in her face. It hadn't given her the closure she'd hoped for.

'He'll come,' Sarah said.

'And you know that how?'

'Frank,' Sarah said.

'Let's change the subject,' Jess said. Where's your Harry? What have you done with Mr Wonderful?'

'In the conservatory, talking to the man from Robinsons. I think he might be getting a job offer.'

Jess tucked her arm through Sarah's. 'I want to hear all about him.'

'But he's not actually what I wanted to talk to you about,' Sarah said.

Jess looked at her. 'In which case, we probably both need another drink.'

Neil stood in the middle of the lounge feeling self-conscious. He'd already been forced into one group dance and asked for a cuddle. This was unlike any wake he'd ever attended and except for the fact that he recognised some of the people from the funeral, he'd have thought he'd mistaken the location. If you discounted the band, it didn't seem to be fancy dress which was something. His eyes had scanned the people milling about in various groups a dozen times, desperate for a glimpse of Jess and disappointed each time to find she wasn't there. He wished now he'd brought Dudley: he would have sniffed her out in an instant.

Coming had seemed like a good idea earlier, but the realisation she wasn't here and the confidence he felt thinking she was missing him as much as he missed her was deserting him faster than Ross had done. Harry, from customer services, stood in the middle of a group of people, some of whom Neil recognised from Anymoore. A girl noticed him and waved. Her movement, slight as it was, made one of the group turn round and look. Neil recognised him but couldn't place him.

As he drained his glass and put it down on one of the tables, a waiter appeared from nowhere, whisked it up and offered him another drink. He wasn't given a chance to refuse before another glass was pressed into his hand. Oh well, he wasn't driving. One more couldn't hurt. He'd give it another ten minutes.

'Neil.' John appeared by his side. 'Come and join us. Maggie's over there. We've got something to tell you.'

Maggie was smiling, except the smile was bigger than any smile he'd even seen her smile before. Beaming would be a better description.

'Meet Treetops' new catering manager,' John said.

'Congratulations.' Neil kissed Maggie's cheek and shook John's hand. Both of them stood grinning at him and he couldn't help grinning back.

'I gave him an ultimatum,' Maggie said. 'I told him I loved being here with him and cooking. I thought I could do a reasonable job looking after the kitchens and the menus, but clearly, he didn't agree. I could take the hint and I wouldn't ask again.'

'I was distraught,' said John. 'I thought she was saying she didn't want to see me any more. I got a bit emotional. Silly really.' He took a sip of his drink. 'But I can't imagine life without her rhubarb and custard cake.'

'It was always Mum's favourite,' Maggie said. 'I'd make one whenever I had enough rhubarb.'

'Sounds lovely,' Neil said.

'Better than lovely.' John laughed. 'Absolutely amazing.'

'Go on with you.' Maggie giggled.

'It's so long, since I've done the whole dating shenanigans,' John said. 'This wonderful woman came into my life like a bolt from the blue and I tried to pluck up courage to ask her out properly, but somehow could never find the right words and then she tells me she only wants to work for me. What's a simple man to think?' He raised his hands in a hopeless gesture.

'Miscommunication,' Maggie said, taking hold of his hand. 'I think we're all guilty of that from time to time.' Her eyes sparkled, but something behind the look she gave him made Neil feel she wasn't just talking about herself.

'Jess,' Gary called, as soon as she walked back into the room. He was stood talking to three people. 'Have you got a minute?'

Not now.

Jess walked up to him. Two drinks in a short space of time had made her feel light-headed and she could see Neil with Maggie and John. He was here. Tall, solid and handsome. Remembering what it felt like to have his arms around her, she wanted to be held again, but Gary was waiting. She smiled and made her way across to him, hoping to catch the eye of the waiter with the Prosecco.

Gary put an arm round her. 'We've been asked to photograph a wedding next year.'

The three turned around. And there they were. See no evil, speak no evil, hear no evil. Martin, Ross and Isabel.

'Izzie here saw Annette's photos and cajoled Martin into forgiving me for the article. They're planning a June wedding. They want us to photograph it.'

'No, not her,' Izzie said, pointedly. 'Just you.'

'I don't work alone these days,' Gary said. 'Jess is my second camera. We're a team.'

'No.' Martin looked uncomfortable. 'You can't mean her.'

'Of course I mean her. Redford's most promising new photographer.'

Redford's only up and coming photographer.

'You'll be lucky to get her. If I were you, I'd make sure you've secured the date sooner rather than later. She's already turning work down.'

'She is?'

I am?

'Do you have a date in mind?' Gary asked.

Martin shook his head.

In the corner, Jess could see Neil, deep in conversation with Maggie, John and Frank. He was really here. She needed to go to him.

'Let Gary know as soon as you do.' She met Martin's eye, cold and defiant.

And I'll make sure I'm busy.

'There's someone over there'—Martin took a step back—'I need to talk to.' The speed with which he disappeared was impressive.

'I doubt you'll hear from them again,' Jess said to Gary as Izzie and Ross followed him across the room. 'Looks like I've just cost you a really lucrative job.'

Neil took a long swig of his drink. Jess was stood on the other side of the room with the guy from the *Redford Chronicle*'s arm around her waist. His muscles tightened. He'd joked with the man earlier. Exchanged pleasantries. Gary, that was his name.

The pain felt physical. He really was hurting.

She'd moved on, he had to accept that. Why wouldn't she? He didn't blame her. He couldn't. There was no one else. This was all down to him. He'd blocked her number and acted like a prize plonker.

American Fried Chicken and an afternoon in with Dudley channel-surfing became a far more attractive proposition than staying. Maggie and John were still talking; he'd stopped listening.

'Neil.' Sarah now appeared by his side.

'I'm not staying. Just came to say great service, well done,' he said. 'In fact, I've been here too long already. I should get going. It's been fun, but I have an early start.' He took another swig. The words sounded as false to him as they obviously did to Sarah.

'She's not seeing him,' she said, quietly. 'She's going to do some work for him that's all.'

'Really?' Neil blinked, but didn't say anything else.

'Truly,' Sarah said, smiling.

He had to give his heart a chance to stop beating so fast. His temperature a chance to return to normal and his nerves time to finish their dance. Another swig, all but finished his glass. Sarah couldn't have said anything he wanted to hear more. He didn't take his eyes off Jess. She moved away from the photographer and was talking to an old lady, who said something, using exaggerated arm movements. Jess nodded and the woman made a beeline for the stage. One of the singers came to the edge and bent down to listen. After a while, he nodded, turned to the rest of the band and they had a discussion between them.

Jess watched the band for a moment before she turned and locked eyes with Neil. It felt as if there was no one else in the room. She necked the rest of her drink and started walking towards him. Lucky, because if she'd headed off in any other direction, he'd have had to resort to chasing after her, slinging her over his shoulder and taking her home.

'Hello Neil,' she said.

Chapter Fifty-Eight

'Hello Jess.'

Just hearing him say her name felt good. Neil took her hand and she closed her eyes. The room was turning. Big mistake.

'Get out of my way.' It felt as if their hands had been torn apart.

Not exactly the declaration of love she hoped for. Popping her eyes wide open and rubbing her wrist, she found Martin had transported himself back across the room and positioned himself between her and Neil.

'What are you doing here?' she asked, standing her ground.

'None of your business.' He stared over her left shoulder, hopping from foot to foot as if debating whether to manhandle her out of the way. 'Sarah, have you reached a decision? I have a shareholder meeting later. Can I make the announcement there?'

'Get lost Martin. This isn't a work do and nobody here wants to listen to anything you have to say,' Jess said. She missed the warmth from Neil's hand, but three glasses of Prosecco gave her the courage to stay exactly where she was and confront her demons, just like that thing that had to happen in fairy tales before you got to the happy-ever-after bit, even if the demon was an annoying little twit. 'You weren't invited,' she added. Ross and Izzie stood in the doorway, their noses in the air.

'Shut up. I'm talking to Sarah.' Martin turned and looked at her. Anger blazed in his eyes.

'Were you invited? Do you have an invitation?'

'For God's sake, Jess.' Martin looked stunned. 'This is a funeral. People come to pay their respects. You don't invite people to a funeral.'

'You weren't at the funeral,' Neil said. 'This is Maggie's mother's wake. It is a private do. Numbers are strictly monitored and it's invited guests only, so if you don't have an invitation, you'd best finish your drink and leave.'

'And take those two with you,' Jess said. She'd lost all her inhibitions.

Martin turned to look at Ross and Izzie for support. They didn't move.

'Don't forget, if you're going to make a scene, the press is here and we have cameras,' Jess said.

‘I need to speak to Sarah,’ Martin said, spitting the words out.

And I need to speak to Neil. Suddenly Ross was there too. Why couldn’t they all disappear? She had things she wanted to say, things she needed to say to Neil, before her inhibitions realised they were lost and found their way back.

Uh oh, now Harry was there too. Over all their heads, Neil smiled at her. She shrugged and smiled back, feeling a warm sensation creep through her body that had nothing to do with Prosecco.

‘Are you going to be our new Accounts and Finance Operations Associate or not?’ Martin asked. I gave you twenty-four hours yesterday. That time is up.’

The room seemed to have gone quiet, everyone waiting for Sarah to answer.

‘Not,’ Frank said, from behind her. ‘She asked me for redundancy, and I’ve agreed.’

‘He can’t agree anything.’ Martin turned an odd shade of puce that could be a reflection from the glitter ball, but Jess didn’t think so. ‘He doesn’t work for us.’

‘He does,’ Neil said. ‘His contract was quite specific – until you’ve paid all outstanding monies, he is still Managing Director.’

‘I checked with Neil earlier and we spoke to the solicitors,’ Frank said.

‘You won’t get an offer this good from anyone else,’ Martin said, inches away from Sarah.

‘Possibly not.’ Neil stepped forward, pulling Jess with him. ‘But, Sarah, before you make a decision – I’d like you to come and work with me.’

‘So, Tanya’s walked out too?’ Ross grinned. ‘It was only a matter of time.’

‘She’s been promoted,’ Neil said. ‘In fact, she’s taking over your old job, Ross.’

‘Don’t be silly.’ Ross smirked. ‘She doesn’t have my qualifications.’

Jess hated people who smirked.

‘She has a first-class honours degree from a red brick university, over ten years’ experience in a business environment and a masters in business administration. Remind me, what are your qualifications?’ Neil paused, and Ross looked uncomfortable. 'But any of your skills she's lacking, I feel she more than makes up for with her personality and experience.'

Good, reasoned argument.

'And Dudley likes her.'

Not the most grown-up comment in the world, but I like your style.

'The clients like her.'

'Can I do it part-time?' Sarah took hold of Harry's hand.

'What? Which job?'

Jess wasn't sure who'd asked the question, but she, sure as hell, wanted to know too.

'Yours.' Sarah pointed to Neil. 'Because I want to help Jess with her business, and I want to do funerals too.'

Jess laughed. 'Don't be silly. All I've got is a camera. I'm hardly in a position to offer you any job security.'

'Precisely. You need someone to run the business side for you, especially if you're going to spend all your days photographing weddings or corporate brochures.'

'I'm not,' Jess said, knowing full well her diary was empty.

'Why? Have you got something else on?'

She shook her head.

'Good, because you start the brochure work on Monday. They wanted you sooner, but I told them you were busy this week. That's what I was trying to tell you earlier.'

'Part-time would be perfect,' Neil said. 'Now, Martin, anyone else you'd like to proposition before you leave?' He reached again for Jess's hand and gave him a very cross stare. 'Or else perhaps you'd like to leave and let the invited guests enjoy the party.'

Martin looked about to argue, but Ross put an arm round his shoulders and steered him to the door.

The lead singer tapped his mike. 'Ladies and gentlemen,' he announced. 'Please take your places on the dance floor.'

The band started playing.

'Tell me this isn't the "Macarena",' Harry said.

'Can't do that.' Sarah grinned, and they moved towards the middle of the floor.

Everyone started to follow them except Jess and Neil. Jess felt her chest tighten, as he pulled her towards him.

'Hi, gorgeous. So the photography business is going well,' he said, pushing his hands into his trouser pockets.

'You'll have to ask my partner and my secretary,' Jess said, 'but there seem to have been developments.'

The woman Jess had been talking to earlier grabbed Neil's arm. 'Come on,' she said. 'I know all the moves. I'll show you what to do.'

Neil put up token resistance, but the woman was determined. He'd just been dragged past Gary when Jess heard him say, 'Could you take over?'

Gary nodded and Neil handed over his dance partner.

'I know all the moves,' the woman said. 'I'll show you what to do.'

'Put your camera away Willersey.' Gary laughed. 'Or any deal is off.'

Jess grinned at the number of people struggling to remember the "Macarena" moves. She winced as one gentleman jumped and turned into someone else who was about three moves behind.

'Ninety degrees to the left,' she heard Sarah say.

Neil walked towards her bringing his arms straight out in front of him one at a time. Earlier, when she went round to his office, Jess had it all figured out: she would state her case, but seeing him walking, turning his right palm over, then his left and the three glasses of Prosecco she'd drunk had stripped her of all coherent thought.

By the time he reached her he had his hands on his shoulders and his arms crossed across his chest.

'Can I kiss you?' she asked.

He didn't answer. He didn't need to. The hand behind head move forgotten in one sweeping movement, he'd pressed Jess against his chest and cupped her face in his hands. He kissed her forehead, her cheeks and her neck. Her arms wound round his neck as his mouth found hers and she shuddered with pleasure.

'I'll take that as yes,' she whispered between kisses.

'I've missed you, Jess Willersey,' he said, dropping another kiss on her nose. 'The last two weeks have been the longest of my life. I didn't know it was possible to hurt so much. I wouldn't have blamed you for giving up on me.'

She reached up and kissed him again.

‘You do realise we’re in the middle of the dance floor,’ he whispered into her ear, when they came up for air.

The band announced one last song before tea – “Lay All Your Love On Me”.

‘Any shapes you’d like to throw to this one?’

‘Definitely,’ she said. ‘And for future reference, Neil Jackson, I never gave up on you.’

‘Which is lucky.’ Neil smiled down at her. ‘Because if I had to go home and tell Dudley you had, I couldn’t guarantee he wouldn’t do something stupid.’

‘In that case, tell him his future happiness is guaranteed.’

They rocked together in time to the music.

His and mine both, Jess thought, safe and warm in Neil’s arms, knowing there was no place on earth she’d rather be. And suddenly her future seemed bright, very bright indeed.

Thank You

Thank you, dear reader, for choosing to read *Recipe for Mr Perfect*. I hope you enjoyed it as much as I enjoyed writing it.

It was amazing to hear from so many of you how much you enjoyed *Recipe for Mr Right*. Thank you all for your messages and reviews. It meant so much. I hope you find this one is just as "perfect" – did you see what I did there? If you've enjoyed *Recipe for Mr Perfect* or *Recipe for Mr Right*, please leave a review for the book on Goodreads or the website where you bought the book. You can also follow me on Twitter for news on my next books (details on my 'About the Author' page next). Looking forward to hearing from you.

Lots of love

Anni x

About the Author

Anni lives in Wiltshire with her husband, her sister, two dogs, a cat and a grey speckled hen. She has had a number of short stories published in various magazines and her work also appears in a number of anthologies. She has wanted to write for as long as she can remember. As a child, she produced reams of stories. Thankfully most of them have been lost over the years, although the 'Attack of the Killer Tomatoes' did resurface recently! And when not writing, she read voraciously. Work might have got in the way for a while, but writing was a love that never died and she loves it as much now as she did back then.

These days, she writes modern day romances with – spoiler alert – a happy ending and a healthy dollop of humour thrown in.

Away from writing, Anni can usually be found behind a camera, walking her dogs, enjoying her husband's curries or one of her sister's bakery treats.

For more information on Anni visit:
www.twitter.com/anniroseauthor
www.facebocom/anniroseauthor
www.anniroseauthor.co.uk

More Choc Lit
from
Anni Rose

Recipe for Mr Right
A sprinkle of luck and a dollop of fate ...

Ruby Brooks is a little sceptical when her horoscope say she's going to have a fabulous year especially when she loses a boyfriend and a job in quick succession. Plus, a rogue kitchen fitter has run off and taken everything, including the kitchen sink!
So, Ruby takes luck and fate into her own hands with an unusual resolution she'll enter ten competitions a day, whether they're for her dream Japanese holiday or a year's supply of dog food (she doesn't have a dog), and win her way to happiness.
But when a Valentine's Day prize from a local restaurant results in chef Adam Finder (and his dog, Brutus) appearing in her life, is that luck or fate? And will Ruby ultimately find out that true happiness doesn't need to be won?

Visit www.choc-lit.com for more details.

Introducing Choc Lit

We're an independent publisher creating a delicious selection of fiction.
Where heroes are like chocolate – irresistible!
Quality stories with a romance at the heart.

See our selection here:
www.choc-lit.com
We would love to hear how you enjoyed *Recipe for Mr Perfect.* Please leave a review on the retail site where you purchased this eBook or visit **www.choc-lit.com** and give your feedback.
Choc Lit novels are selected by genuine readers like yourself. We only publish stories our Tasting Panel want to see in print. Our reviews and awards speak for themselves.

Could you be a Star Selector and join our Tasting Panel?
Would you like to play a role in choosing which novels we decide to publish? Do you enjoy reading women's fiction? Then you could be perfect for our Tasting Panel.
Visit: **www.choc-lit.com/join-the-choc-lit-tasting-panel**

Keep in touch:
Sign up for our monthly newsletter Choc Lit Spread for all the latest news and offers:
www.spread.choc-lit.com.
Follow us on Twitter: @ChocLituk Facebook: Choc Lit
and Instagram: ChocLituk.

Printed in Great Britain
by Amazon

68085834R00184